Praise for Alyssa Maxwell and her
Lady and Lady's Maid Mysteries!

A Pinch of Poison

"Colorful information on the postwar period is combined
with plenty of suspects, all neatly wrapped up in
the style of a classic mystery."
—*Kirkus Reviews*

"A sweet, delightful mystery, which is sure to appeal to
historical fiction and mystery readers alike."
—*Foreword Reviews*

"Along with a bracing mystery, Maxwell explores compelling
themes. Although this is from a slightly earlier time period, it's
a good match with Rhys Bowen's Her Royal Spyness series."
—*Booklist*

Murder Most Malicious

"Entertaining . . . some of the characters and scenes
are highly reminiscent of TV's *Downton Abbey,*
but Maxwell makes Phoebe and Eva distinctive
personalities in their own right."
—*Publishers Weekly*

"Maxwell provides a neat little mystery and a heavily atmos-
pheric look at life in a great house after the trials of the war."
—*Kirkus Reviews*

"Details of the lives of the nobility and their servants, and the
aftermath of the war, are woven throughout the story, and the
forward-thinking Phoebe is a charming main character."
—*Booklist*

"The story is so good, you don't want it to end."
—*Suspense Magazine*

"*Downton Abbey* fans will enjoy Maxwell's evocative
descriptions of a particular society as it transitions
from the Edwardian Age to modern times."
—*Library Journal*

Books by Alyssa Maxwell

Gilded Newport Mysteries

MURDER AT THE BREAKERS

MURDER AT MARBLE HOUSE

MURDER AT BEECHWOOD

MURDER AT ROUGH POINT

MURDER AT CHATEAU SUR MER

Lady and Lady's Maid Mysteries

MURDER MOST MALICIOUS

A PINCH OF POISON

A DEVIOUS DEATH

Published by Kensington Publishing Corporation

A PINCH
OF POISON

ALYSSA
MAXWELL

KENSINGTON BOOKS
http://www.kensingtonbooks.com

KENSINGTON BOOKS are published by

Kensington Publishing Corp.
119 West 40th Street
New York, NY 10018

All Kensington titles, imprints, and distributed lines are available at special quantity discounts for bulk purchases for sales promotion, premiums, fund-raising, educational, or institutional use. Special book excerpts or customized printings can also be created to fit specific needs. For details, write or phone the office of the Kensington Sales Manager: Attn. Sales Department. Kensington Publishing Corp, 119 West 40th Street, New York, NY 10018. Phone: 1-800-221-2647.

Kensington and the K logo Reg. U.S. Pat. & TM Off.

First Kensington Hardcover Edition: January 2017

eISBN-13: 978-1-61773-835-7
eISBN-10: 1-61773-835-2

ISBN-13: 978-1-61773-836-4
ISBN-10: 1-61773-836-0
First Kensington Trade Edition: December 2017

10 9 8 7 6 5 4 3 2 1

Printed in the United States of America

*To my husband, Paul. He's my Owen and Miles rolled
into one, and then some.
And to Joanne Murray, for a great idea!*

Acknowledgments

Many, many thanks to my fabulous editor, John Scognamiglio, who has believed in me and provided me with the opportunity to challenge myself creatively and to truly grow as an author.

And my deepest gratitude to the entire Kensington team for all their efforts in launching this series. I could not have asked for more.

CHAPTER 1

April 1919

"Ladies, although the war is over, it is not yet time for England to rest. Quite the contrary." Phoebe Renshaw, granddaughter of the Earl of Wroxly, looked up from her notes and braved a glance at her audience, ranged at tables in what had once been the ballroom of Haverleigh House, on the outskirts of the village of Little Barlow. When an intelligent brown-eyed gaze connected with hers, her spine straightened and her chin lifted as they typically did beneath her grandmother's scrutiny. Grams, a tall, slender figure in severe head-to-toe black, sat at the front and center table and nodded encouragement up at her. She smiled slightly for good measure, sending a bracing surge of pride through Phoebe. Funny that she still sought Grams's approval even at the ripe old age of twenty.

Sitting beside Grams, Phoebe's eldest sister, Julia, sighed and used her fork to push leftover bits of Cornish hen and mushroom-stuffed tomatoes around her plate. She was looking particularly splendid today in a sporty, flowing jersey ensemble in creamy beige with black trim, something from the latest collection of a newish designer named Chanel.

Only Julia could look so lovely while behaving so thoughtlessly. Before Phoebe could look away, Julia flicked a glance up at her, little more than a flutter of her eyelashes, but in that moment, her eyebrow quirked in a familiar way, as if to say, *Really, Phoebe, how much longer do you intend to bore us?*

Her confidence slipped. *Was* she boring her audience? And if so, why did Julia need to point it out to her? More to the point, why wasn't Julia up here with her? How lovely that would have been—the two elder Renshaw sisters, working together to better the lot of others. But no, since Papa's death in the war three years ago, Julia pretended to care about nothing, except the pleasure she apparently took in calling attention to Phoebe's faults. If Grams went into mourning three years ago and never quite emerged—rather like Queen Victoria had at the death of Prince Albert—Julia had turned off the better part of her emotions. Although why she turned her most acerbic sentiments on Phoebe remained something of a mystery, for Julia remained cordial toward their younger sister and simply chose to ignore their brother.

Phoebe knew better than to let Julia undermine her resolve.

Don't be a goose. You have a vital message to deliver. Remember the words you rehearsed, do not let your voice waver, and for goodness' sake, don't stutter!

"M-many of those we consider lucky to have arrived home from the war are in fact struggling daily to support their families, indeed, struggling to survive." Much to her surprise, she enunciated clearly after that initial stumble. "Our veterans, especially those wounded in the service of our country, deserve better. Those whom we hail as heroes need our assistance now more than ever, and so I thank the

Haverleigh School for Young Ladies for hosting us today, and for the students' efforts in collecting clothing, personal necessities, and household items to be dispersed among veterans and their families residing in the Cotswolds."

She moistened her lips and aimed an acknowledging nod and accompanying smile at headmistress Henrietta Finch, who sat at Grams's other side. She did not know the woman well, for while Phoebe had attended Haverleigh during most of the war years, Miss Finch had only stepped into the position a year ago. "Miss Finch, we owe you a debt of gratitude for embracing this cause and allowing the school to participate."

The woman, stout, square-jawed, and always flushed as if she had just run a brisk mile, tipped her head modestly in return. The assistant headmistress, younger and trimmer than her superior, pressed a hand to her bosom and also nodded, but far less modestly, in Phoebe's opinion. True, Miss Verity Sedgewick had insisted on overseeing each step of the preparations for today's luncheon, but she had been in the way more often than not.

Phoebe continued. "I thank all of you, our gracious guests here today—mothers, benefactors, members of the school's governing body—for your generous donations to the Relief and Comfort of Veterans and their Families, or the RCVF, if you will. Your pledges of continued support will ensure our success as we endeavor to assist our valiant young men—and women—to pick up the pieces of their lives and regain their dignity and self-sufficiency."

She stepped back from the podium. Polite applause spread through the room. It was enough to satisfy Phoebe, who wanted only to return to her seat and enjoy the array of desserts and glazed fruit that were to be served next. Speaking to large numbers of people was not her forte, but since the RCVF and this charity luncheon had been her idea, she'd had little choice.

Less than a month after the war ended last November she had realized she could not return to the idle life she had known before the war. No longer could she anticipate days filled with parties, picnics, hunts, and parlor games. The war years had taught her what it was to be useful, to give of one's time rather than endlessly taking, to solve problems and even, if one were clever enough, prevent them from arising. She hoped today's efforts, and future ones, would prevent families from going hungry and put clothes on their backs—minimal thanks for the great sacrifices suffered during the war.

Now all she had to do was step down off the speaker's platform without tripping. She was in the process of doing just that when a crash and a shout tore up the steps from the kitchen and along the service corridor, only partially muffled by the baize door behind her.

Several cries erupted and chairs scraped back as attendees leapt to their feet. Phoebe held up her hands. "Please, everyone, there's no need to panic. Just a small mishap, I'm sure. If you'll excuse me, I'll just go check on things. . . ."

With a startled expression, Miss Finch started to rise, but sank back into her seat when Grams placed a firm hand on her forearm. "My granddaughter can handle it."

With that endorsement, Phoebe hurried into the corridor. It registered in her mind that Miss Sedgewick had made no move to leave her chair. Apparently, her desire to help didn't extend to when help might actually be needed.

Belowstairs in the main kitchen, Phoebe quickly scanned for blood, burns, broken appendages. To her vast relief, the students and kitchen staff appeared sound enough, except for their sour expressions. A small crowd of young ladies in matching blue skirts and white shirtwaists hovered around the abundantly round figure of the school cook, Mrs. Honeychurch. The sounds of weeping drew Phoebe's attention to one girl in particular. Unruly spirals the color of newly polished copper spilled from a hasty updo, identifying a sixth form girl known for her shy, often nervous nature.

Oh, dear. What small disaster had occurred now?

It certainly wouldn't be the first. This morning's casualties had included not only a spilled quart of milk but a shattered pitcher as well, nearly a dozen broken eggs, a burned soda bread, and an oversight when it came to adding sugar to the lemonade. Unfortunately, several of the luncheon guests had been served before the mistake was discovered. That was, in fact, *how* it had been discovered.

It had also been Phoebe's idea to have the older students manage the luncheon preparations, and Miss Finch had given her wholehearted approval. "Most of these girls have little notion of what their servants endure each day simply in keeping their employers fed and happy," the woman had declared. "It's high time they learned."

Phoebe agreed. It had seemed like such *good* idea . . . in theory. The design for the invitations had been stylish, the menu plans inspired, the seating arrangements diplomatic, and the floral decorations cheerful yet refined. In these matters the girls exhibited high levels of proficiency, but of course that was to be expected of fashionable young ladies. When it came to the preparation and serving of food, however . . . suffice it to say, Phoebe felt obligated to personally see to the cleaning of Lady Stanhope's green China silk suit from the Redfern spring collection—as she had heard her ladyship specifically mention upon being splattered with orange-sherry glaze as the Cornish hens were served.

Phoebe was making her way over to the scene of this latest mishap when, from behind the center worktable, up popped Eva Huntford, lady's maid to Phoebe and her two sisters. She held a wire whisk brush in one hand and, in the other, a dustpan piled high with sticky, glazed berries and cut fruit that sadly sported a dingy coating of whatever other morsels had fallen to the floor during the course of the luncheon preparations. One of the kitchen maids appeared with a bucket and mop. The crowd of girls moved aside to let her through.

Phoebe didn't need an explanation to guess what happened, but as soon as the red-haired Lilyanne Mucklow spotted her, the girl's pale eyebrows, barely visible against her freckles, drew tightly together above her reddened nose. "I c-couldn't help it, Lady Phoebe! I tripped."

"Well, and what on earth did you trip over?" the cook asked, most unhelpfully. "There was nothing in your way."

Lilyanne's bright blue eyes shifted, lighting for an instant on another sixth form girl. Lady Zara Worthington's babyish features hardened to a scowl, prompting Lilyanne to quickly drop her gaze and shrug. "I didn't spill *all* of it."

"You spilled enough of it. There isn't enough to go around now, Lillian." Zara's violet-blue eyes narrowed accusingly. "The desserts we've worked so diligently to create will look positively uninspired without the fruit to garnish each plate."

"My name is *Lilyanne,* not Lillian." The girl wiped at her tears with the back of a freckled hand.

Another girl with plain features, lanky brown hair, and a sturdy frame intervened. "I glazed the fruit, so I don't know why *you* should complain so bitterly, Zara."

Zara Worthington's nostrils flared. "Jane Timmons, do not speak to me." She pushed her face closer to the other girl's. "Farm girls should know their place."

"Now, ladies, that will be quite enough," Mrs. Honeychurch said, but without the conviction of someone used to disciplining students.

The situation needed to be defused, and fast. With an attempt to make light of the accident, Phoebe patted Lilyanne's angular shoulder. "It doesn't matter how it happened, there's no use in crying over spilled fruit. We'll simply serve tea and dessert without it. But, Jane, we'll be sure to let Miss Finch know of your efforts in making the glaze. Now then, Mrs. Honeychurch, are the kettles warmed?"

"They are, my lady."

"Good. Girls, let the brewing begin."

As an orderly commotion resumed, Phoebe moved off to one side and motioned for Eva to join her. With lustrous dark hair pulled back in a tidy bun, striking green eyes, and a trim figure, Eva Huntford might easily have passed for one of the aristocratic ladies sitting in the dining hall. However, her serviceable black dress and sensible, low-heeled pumps identified her as the lady's maid she was. Phoebe longed to see Eva in something more elegant, but Eva wouldn't hear of it. The one time Phoebe had made the suggestion, Eva had rolled her eyes and laughed.

"Did you see what happened?" Phoebe asked her. She watched Zara Worthington as the girl bent in front of one of the ovens to remove a cake tin. Before she grasped the hot metal, Mrs. Honeychurch cried out Zara's name and shoved a pair of towels into her hands. Otherwise, the careless girl would have handled the pan barehanded and singed her fingers. Phoebe shook her head. "Did Zara intentionally trip Lilyanne?"

"I honestly didn't see, my lady."

"Is there some ongoing dispute between Zara and Lilyanne?"

"There is *always* some dispute between Zara and Lilyanne." It wasn't Eva but Amelia, Phoebe's nearly sixteen-year-old sister, who replied. Attempting to brush powdered sugar from the pleats of her uniform skirt, she sidled closer and whispered, "There are disputes between Zara and absolutely *everyone*, at one time or another."

Eva leaned over to assist Amelia in patting her skirt clean. "My lady, this is what aprons are for."

"Yes, sorry. I always forget."

Phoebe wanted to know more about Zara. "Is she often so disagreeable toward the other girls? I noticed she also spoke sharply to Jane Timmons for no apparent reason."

"Jane can take care of herself." Amelia absently tipped her head to one side as Eva repinned golden blond strands that had fallen loose.

"What about you?" Phoebe asked. "Is Zara unpleasant with you?"

"Sometimes, but I don't pay her much attention. As if I could care what that rattlebrain has to say. But Lilyanne does, unfortunately. She hasn't much confidence and doesn't stick up for herself."

"Do the other girls stick up for her?"

Phoebe's question sent a blush creeping up Amelia's already rosy cheeks. "Well . . . Lilyanne isn't the easiest girl to get to know. She spends most of her free time alone. Prefers her books to people. At least that's the impression I've gotten."

Phoebe treated her sister to a disapproving lift of an eyebrow. "Amelia, are you allowing the other girls to dictate whom you befriend and whom you do not?"

"I . . . em . . . I don't mean to."

"Lady Amelia," Mrs. Honeychurch called, "time to take your raspberry tart out of the icebox."

"Coming, Mrs. Honeychurch!" Looking relieved, Amelia scurried away. Eva called after her to walk and not run, lest another unfortunate incident occur. She turned back to Phoebe.

"You'd best get back to the dining hall, my lady."

"I think perhaps I'd better stay and help out here."

Eva shook her head. "If you don't go back, your grandmother is liable to come looking for you. Things are frenzied enough down here without the Countess of Wroxly poking her head in."

"Eva, you are right as always. Good luck. I'll have my

fingers crossed the remainder of the luncheon is smooth sailing."

Eva let go an uncharacteristic guffaw. "Now you're hoping for the moon, my lady."

"All right, ladies. Queue up with your desserts, please." Eva clapped her hands for attention. Slowly, the din of chatter subsided and the nearly twenty-odd girls lifted platters of blancmange, bread pudding, fruit tarts, petit fours, honey cakes, and other creamy, sticky, sweet concoctions. The rest carried full teapots draped in bright-colored cozies. Unmistakable pride glowed on each girl's face, and suddenly these past hours of frustrations, tempers, and tears seemed more than worth it.

Of course, that didn't stop Zara Worthington from imparting one last rebuff to a still teary-eyed Lilyanne. "I still cannot believe you ruined the glazed fruit."

"Never mind about that, Lady Zara," Eva said calmly, earning a haughty look from the girl, one that spoke of retribution if Eva didn't watch out. Eva ignored it and climbed the steps up to the corridor.

Assistant headmistress Verity Sedgewick peered in from the dining hall doorway. Like the gasses rolling across no man's land, a cloud of violet-scented perfume filled the corridor, prompting Eva to cough. She recognized the fragrance, for Lady Phoebe had received a bottle of it for her last birthday in February. It was Brise de Violettes, a new product and one of the few perfumes that succeeded in capturing the true essence of the flower. Lady Phoebe's came in a Baccarat crystal bottle and when she used it, she did so sparingly, unlike Miss Sedgewick. It struck Eva as odd that Miss Sedgewick could afford the same luxury on her school administrator's salary.

The young woman wore blue and white silk crepe that mimicked the girls' uniforms, yet with draping that hinted at the work of Paul Poiret—again, surprising for an assistant headmistress, but then again, Miss Sedgewick never missed an opportunity to remind people she hailed from a landed family in Hereford. Perhaps her relatives supplemented her income.

"Is everyone ready?" the woman called out as if the luncheon hinged upon her leadership, as if Eva couldn't manage to direct the girls into the dining hall.

"All ready, Miss Sedgewick," they responded in the practiced unison of schoolgirls, and formed a queue in front of her.

Lady Zara, her chestnut ringlets upswept and arranged to frame her face, shouldered her way to the front of the line. "I must be first. I'm to present Miss Finch with her Madeira cake as the rest of the desserts are being served. Look, Miss Sedgewick, didn't it turn out splendidly?"

Miss Sedgewick regarded the miniature cake, iced with a cinnamon and nutmeg glaze. "It certainly did, Lady Zara. Miss Finch shall be very pleased."

They held each other's gazes another moment, long enough for Eva to notice and wonder whether a silent communication passed between them. But perhaps Zara Worthington, as the daughter of an earl, felt a stronger bond with Miss Sedgewick, who was more her equal than any of the other staff.

Miss Sedgewick pivoted on her fashionable heel and preceded the girls into the dining hall—as if she had led them in their efforts from start to finish. Unhurriedly, she all but floated back to her seat and gave an authoritative nod for the girls to begin serving. Eva might as well have stayed downstairs in the kitchen. One by one they passed her, dispersing in an almost dancelike formation among the tables. Another minute or two, and Eva would retreat to her own cup of tea before helping Mrs. Honeychurch and the kitchen maids restore order to their domain.

Phoebe's gaze caught hers. Grinning broadly, she lifted her teacup in a toast and mouthed a silent *thank you*. As if Eva needed to be thanked—as if women in her position were typically acknowledged in any but an absent, offhand way. Her heart swelled with gratitude, and with pride, too, that her lady had grown into such a gracious young woman.

She watched Zara present Miss Finch with her special Madeira cake. After an exclamation of delight, the broad-faced, large-bosomed woman wasted no time in tucking in. One by one, the students set their various desserts on the tables and then moved to form a queue at the side of the room. When all had been served, light applause broke out among the assemblage. The girls curtsied and more than a few blushed with pleasure. At the rear of the room, an array of boxes and packages occupied a long table draped in colorful bunting. Collected under Lady Phoebe's directions, these were the personal and household items to be distributed among the needy families of the Great War's veterans. Each attendee at today's luncheon had made a generous monetary donation as well.

Eva smiled. Yes, Phoebe and the girls had much to be proud of. Today was a resounding success.

She was about to retrace her steps to the kitchen when a noise held her still. Despite the mingling conversations and the *oohs* and *ahs* as delicacies were sampled, a distinct choking sound reached Eva's ears. Concern became foreboding when the coughing escalated to forceful hacking. Heedless of whether she would be seen or not, she pushed the baize door wider. Miss Finch held a hand in front of her mouth and gripped the edge of the table with the other. Her shoulders shook violently.

"Good heavens, Miss Finch. Someone, pour her some lemonade." Without waiting for anyone to comply with her demand, the Countess of Wroxly snatched the pitcher from the center of the table. She poured a generous measure into a glass, but when she attempted to put it in the woman's hand, Miss Finch shoved it away. The glass fell, splashing lemonade onto the table linen before rolling and crashing to the floor. The other ladies at the table, most of them members of the school's governing body, leapt to their feet.

Eva abandoned all discretion. She entered the dining hall and hurried to the head table. Phoebe, her face etched with shock, attempted to reach for Miss Finch, but with flailing arms the woman stumbled backward. Ruddy color flooded her face, her several chins, her thick neck. Eva came to an abrupt halt. She no more knew how to intervene than the bug-eyed ladies surrounding her.

One idea presented itself amid the growing panic. "Lady Amelia," she called out, "run and fetch the nurse! Tell her Miss Finch is choking."

At a trot, Amelia began wending her way around the tables in her path. Lady Phoebe, meanwhile, seized Miss Finch's forearm to prevent her from falling over backward, while Miss Sedgewick did likewise on the woman's other side. The ladies seated farther back in the room finally realized something was terribly amiss at the head table. Tea and desserts abandoned, the assemblage came to their feet, their cacophony of voices echoing against the ceiling high above them.

"Quiet, everyone!" Lady Wroxly held up her thin hands. "Quiet, please. This isn't helping." She spoke next to the gaggle of ladies who had closed in around Miss Finch, each attempting, in shrill voices, to ascertain what was wrong. "Ladies, give her some air. Miss Finch, is there something caught in your throat? Nod once for yes."

Where was Lady Amelia and that nurse? The school's infirmary occupied the former music room at the back of the house, overlooking the gardens. It shouldn't have taken more than a few minutes at the most. Eva spotted Julia, or rather the back of her, as she fled the table and rushed from the dining hall. Eva barely had time to contemplate where Lady Julia might be going before a crash drew her back to the situation unfolding before her.

Miss Finch, though still held by Phoebe and Miss Sedgewick, had begun twitching and jerking. Her complexion turned garnet and her eyes bulged. To Eva's horror, she realized the woman was no longer hacking and sputtering, but heaving silently in a futile attempt to draw air into her lungs. With a great wrenching of both arms, she broke free of Lady Phoebe and Miss Sedgewick, pitched forward, doubled over, and dropped face-first onto the head table with all the deadweight of a sack stuffed with flour. Her plate rattled beneath her and her teacup went rolling.

CHAPTER 2

The ladies nearest the fallen woman screamed, their cries quickly taken up and echoed from table to table. The students, still lined up on the side of the room, began to weep, and a quick-thinking woman in a fox-head stole scurried over and herded them back into the corridor and down to the kitchen.

Eva rushed to the fallen woman's side. Phoebe reappeared at Miss Finch's other side, but before either could lay a hand on the headmistress, she slid grotesquely downward, taking the tablecloth and place settings with her as she collapsed to the floor. Dishes and glasses shattered around her; cutlery clattered; tea and cream and remnants of cake splashed and bounced. At first, no one moved, frozen in obvious disbelief. Then Eva sank beside her, hesitated, drew a fortifying breath, and slipped her fingers to the side of the woman's neck.

"Is she . . . ?" several voices hissed at once.

Eva looked up and found Lady Phoebe's anxious face. "I don't feel a pulse."

A chorus of shrieks raised a lament and invoked the Lord's mercy. Ladies huddled together with their arms around each other. Still others buried their faces in their hands, until footsteps from the main hall turned their horrified gazes in that direction, as if the assemblage believed Death, having fled too hastily, had decided to return to claim another soul.

Instead of a shrouded, formless creature, the school nurse appeared, clad in blue with a crisp white pinafore and matching kerchief. She strode briskly in, looking straight ahead and avoiding the stares converging on her. She carried a short length of rubber tubing and what appeared to be a hand-held pump very much like a concertina accordion. As the nurse grew closer, she attached the tube to a nozzle at one end of the pump, and Eva surmised this to be some kind of breathing apparatus. Amelia and Julia came in behind her, trotting every few steps to keep up. So that was where Julia had gone.

Lady Phoebe pushed to her feet. "Amelia, don't come any closer."

The youngest Renshaw sister paid no heed, but was forced to halt before reaching Miss Finch's inert form when Lady Wroxly adamantly stepped in front of her. "I'm feeling faint, dearest. Would you help me into the hall?"

"Oh, but Miss Finch—I want to know if she's all right." Uncertainty spread across Amelia's pretty features, but she linked arms with her grandmother and walked away. She apparently couldn't resist looking back several times before they reached the doorway and turned out of sight.

It was then Eva realized the nurse had yet to take action. The woman, about Eva's own age, had come to an abrupt halt and simply gawped down at her would-be patient. She clutched the apparatus so tightly, the rubber tubing compressed and the accordion threatened to collapse into uselessness. With her frizzled, strawlike hair and ashen complexion, she more resembled a patient than a healer. Why didn't she do something? What was she waiting for?

"Nurse, help her," Eva shouted. "Perhaps she can still be saved."

That broke through the woman's lethargy. She lurched forward, her feet crunching on china shards, and crouched beside Miss Finch. "Help me turn her." Eva complied, summoning the strength to shift the rotund woman. But once accomplished it became all too apparent that nothing could be done for the headmistress.

"Her face, it's already turning blue," Lady Philomena Albert whispered tremulously from a table away.

"Her fingernails, too," added her companion, who hung with both hands onto Lady Philomena's upper arm.

The nurse set down her breathing equipment and placed her fingertips against Miss Finch's neck, as Eva had done. After a moment, she gestured at the tubing and pump. "I'm afraid we won't be needing that."

The coroner scribbled a few more notes in his tablet while a pair of assistants grunted beneath their burden as they lifted the stretcher bearing the headmistress's body. They had covered her with a sheet, thank heavens. Eva still shuddered to think about poor Miss Finch staring up with sightless eyes from within her blue-tinged face. The speculation that had immediately spread among the students, staff, and luncheon guests alike had centered around three possibilities as the cause of death: stroke, heart attack, or, what Eva found most likely, choking. Miss Finch had been partial to almonds in her Madeira cake. Had one of them cost her her life?

The arrival of Chief Inspector Isaac Perkins and his assistant, Constable Brannock, a half hour later took everyone by surprise. A man in his middle years, Chief Inspector Perkins looked put out and irritable, no doubt from having his leisurely afternoon interrupted. He shuffled in, declaring the coroner a fussy old buzzard who didn't know one end of his business from the other. "Nonetheless," he added, "an inquest shall commence and I should appreciate everyone's cooperation."

"An inquest? What on earth for?" Miss Sedgewick had headed the man off in the entry hall and stood her ground. "Surely you're not suggesting . . ."

With a shocked expression, she forewent finishing her question. Neither did the chief inspector deign to explain himself. He'd merely stepped around her and commandeered one of the administrative offices. Presently, he was questioning the ladies who had been seated at and near the head table, including Julia, Phoebe, and the Countess of Wroxly. The rest of the guests had been sent home, and those with students attending the school had taken their daughters with them.

No sooner had Lady Phoebe joined Eva back in the dining hall than the inspector's assistant, Constable Brannock, asked to see them both together. The hairs at Eva's nape bristled. The luncheon had been Lady Phoebe's idea, and Eva had assisted in all the preparations. Were they suspected of something?

Constable Brannock must have noticed something in her expression, for he immediately put them at ease. "We worked well together last Christmas, didn't we? I thought it best we put our heads together again."

He didn't say a word about his employer, Inspector Perkins, with his pocked nose and rheumy eyes—sure signs of a man who enjoys his whiskey. He didn't have to. Last Christmas, an innocent man might have hanged if Constable Brannock hadn't taken matters into his own hands—and hadn't placed a certain amount of trust in Eva and Lady Phoebe.

"Tell me everything you remember," he said to them now. "Every detail, no matter how small it may seem."

They occupied Miss Finch's office, sitting opposite one another at the desk. He had removed his high-domed policeman's helmet, allowing waves of thick auburn hair to fall rakishly across his brow. In the window behind him, a vista of the school's garden and, farther away, the athletic fields and outbuildings, stretched into the distance among trees and hedges wearing the pale greens of spring. Eva thought the pastoral scene outside made a pleasing contrast to the harsh lines of his uniform as well as a colorful frame for his bright hair and keen blue eyes.

Eyes that missed nothing, she reminded herself. Though she had done nothing wrong, something about Miles Brannock always made her feel somehow . . . under a microscope.

"As I told the chief inspector," Lady Phoebe began, but Miles Brannock immediately interrupted.

"Forget what you said to Inspector Perkins. Pretend you've talked to no one prior to now. What was the first thing you noticed from the moment Miss Finch appeared to be in distress?"

Phoebe glanced over at Eva, and Eva nodded with a smile of encouragement. She, too, had been questioned by the inspector, but only briefly. Since she had been watching from a distance, Inspector Perkins had deemed her observations insignificant and summarily dismissed her. And as for Lady Phoebe, the man seemed to assume events had left her too distraught to be of much help as a witness.

"Well . . ." Lady Phoebe's brows knitted. "She seemed perfectly fine throughout most of the luncheon. Except . . ."

"Yes?" The constable's pencil hovered above his notepad.

"Her color wasn't good, but then it never is."

"Are you referring to the blue tint to her complexion?"

"No, sir. Miss Finch was ruddy—always ruddy. And she huffed and snuffled and . . ."

"Yes, my lady? And what?"

"I'm not painting a flattering picture," she murmured. "One shouldn't speak ill of the dead."

Constable Brannock laid down his pencil. "My lady, nothing you say can hurt Miss Finch now, but might help shed light on how she died."

Eva couldn't help herself from blurting her thoughts aloud. "We haven't been told anything, but can we not assume from your presence that foul play is suspected?"

The constable held Eva in his gaze for a long, uncomfortable moment. She had spoken out of turn. Were Lady Phoebe any other but a kind and tolerant mistress, she would have received a reprimand. For instance, had she been sitting beside Lady Julia in similar circumstances . . . well.

But she received no reprimand from either Lady Phoebe or the constable. Quite the contrary. His gaze softened—ironically making her more uncomfortable still—and he leaned with his elbows on the desk. "I can't tell you anything on the record. But off the record . . . because of the blue tinge to her skin and beneath her fingernails, the coroner suspects poison, and so do I."

Lady Phoebe's manicured hand flew to her lips. Eva's mouth dropped open as she processed this information.

"I assumed she choked on something," Eva said after a moment. "Or perhaps had a heart attack."

"As did I," Lady Phoebe said, "which is why I mentioned her color. As I started to tell you, she huffed when she walked and snuffed while she ate. I sat beside her, so I heard. I found it rather annoying, I'm ashamed to say, but it led me to believe she perhaps suffered from asthma, or as Eva said, a weak heart. Either of those conditions would explain her struggle to catch her breath. I've read that a full-on asthma attack can completely close the airways. *Never* did we suspect . . . my goodness . . ." Her gaze lighted on Eva. "Not another murder."

"I said no such thing, my lady," the constable said quickly and sharply. "So do not go spreading rumors."

It was on the tip of Eva's tongue to admonish the man to mind his manners when speaking to her young lady, but if she had learned anything about Miles Brannock since first meeting him back in December, it was that privilege and rank meant little to the Irishman, nor did he allow trifles like good manners to stand in the way of an investigation.

Lady Phoebe tilted her chin, signaling she hadn't liked the man's tone any more than Eva had. "Then, if I may be so bold as to ask, what *do* you suspect?"

"Considering this is a finishing school for young ladies and Miss Finch seems to have had no family and few acquaintances outside of her occupation, murder is highly doubtful. No, the chief inspector and I are considering accidental poisoning as the cause of death."

"You mean to say a poisonous ingredient somehow ended up in Miss Finch's lunch?" Phoebe asked.

A pang of guilt stabbed at Eva's heart, for she had been in charge of supervising the girls during the cooking and baking. "An ingredient such as . . . what?" She mentally called up images of the kitchen counters and worktables. What kinds of items had been present during the preparations? Flour, spices, broth, sugar, cooking wine . . . she couldn't remember any box, jar, or other container not specifically needed for the recipes. Could she have missed something?

Of course she could have. With all those girls and the many dishes they prepared, why, the kitchen had been pure chaos these past two days. But which dish, specifically . . . Her throat ran dry. "The Madeira cake. It was the last thing Miss Finch ate right before she began to struggle." And Eva remembered who had made the single-serving cake—Zara Worthington. She chewed her lip. Should she say anything?

Lady Phoebe nodded. "Yes, she ate every last crumb, and so quickly, I remember wanting to warn her not to choke. Oh, good heavens. If only I *had* said something. Perhaps she wouldn't have consumed the entire cake and might still be alive. Constable Brannock, what do you suppose could have gotten into it? Does the coroner know?"

"No, that will take time. Now, Lady Phoebe, if you would please go on with your account, I would be grateful."

Apparently, the constable's *please* satisfied Lady Phoebe, for she continued describing the events that led to Miss Finch's demise. But Eva felt anything *but* satisfied with his reassurances. In fact, she entertained serious doubts as to the validity of his claim. If accidental poisoning were truly suspected, why would the police bother questioning the luncheon attendees, none of whom had a hand in preparing the food? Beyond that, there had been that look on his face as he'd admonished Lady Phoebe not to spread rumors about Miss Finch's death. It was a look that reflected inner thoughts—dark ones. No, she was certain the police suspected someone.

Another image of Zara Worthington, this time sliding her Madeira cake from the oven, flashed in Eva's mind. Could the girl have had a reason for wanting Miss Finch out of the way?

Upon leaving Miss Finch's office, Phoebe found Grams, Julia, and Amelia waiting for her in the main hall, their spring coats belted, their handbags hooked over their forearms, and their handcrafted Pietro Yantorny pumps pointed toward the door.

Before they saw her, however, she let Eva slip quietly down the corridor to the rear of the house, where a set of back stairs led down to the kitchen and storerooms. Eva wished to have a look around, especially in the cupboards where the cleaning fluids and other such chemicals were kept, and to speak with Mrs. Honeychurch and her assistants. As soon as Eva disappeared around a corner, Phoebe approached her family members.

"Oh, good, Phoebe, here you are. We're all ready to leave." With her free hand, Grams patted her brow with a balled-up handkerchief, edged in black lace to match her endlessly black wardrobe. "What an ordeal of a day."

"I for one was ready to leave before the day began," Julia said with a sigh. "Quite before Miss Finch so rudely expired in front of everyone."

"Julia!" Grams's whispered reprimand echoed through the hall like a hissing dart. Julia pretended to remain unaffected by it, but Phoebe caught her momentary flinch.

"I don't see why I have to go home," Amelia complained with a sideways glance at Grams. "A lot of the other girls are staying. At home I'll just be sent up to my room and no one will tell me anything."

Grams ignored her and spoke to Phoebe. "Where is your coat and handbag?"

"I'm not leaving yet, Grams. And I hope you'll stay another few minutes. I'd like to ask you about something."

"Can't I stay behind with Phoebe?" Amelia eagerly put in, but was again ignored.

"Really, Phoebe? Playing inspector again?" If a sneer could be considered pretty, Julia's was, her perfect nose wrinkling and her Cupid's bow lips turning down at the corners in what many people—most of them men—would consider a charming pout. "Didn't you have enough of that game last Christmas?"

"An innocent man might have hanged," she reminded her sister, "were it not for my penchant for *games,* as you call them."

"Julia is right," Grams interrupted before Phoebe could make her next point. "This obsession of yours is dangerous, not to mention unladylike. Now, please collect your things. The carriage is waiting."

Again, Julia sighed, but this time her impatience wasn't aimed at Phoebe. Despite modern motorcars, Grams insisted on traveling short distances from home in her old but meticulously maintained brougham and matching pair of bays. Phoebe found it an endearing adherence to the old traditions—one of the more harmless ones. However, her elder sister saw it as a source of embarrassment to be seen clip-clopping through the village. She only endured it because experience had taught her that Maude Renshaw, Countess of Wroxly, always got her way.

Would she get her way now? The thought of cutting short her purpose here today brought on a sinking disappointment, until Phoebe remembered she was no longer a child and could, with diplomacy, ease out of Grams's clutches for an afternoon or so.

"Constable Brannock has asked for my help, you see—"

"To do what, exactly?" Grams interrupted again. "Didn't Miss Finch die of an apoplexy or heart attack?"

"Yes, Phoebe," Julia urged with mock sweetness, "*do* tell us what you know."

She could see that Grams wouldn't be budged unless she heard something that made sense to her maddeningly rational mind. Phoebe regarded her younger sister, who practically bounced on her toes, obviously keen to hear the news. "All right, but this must remain among us for now. It's doubtful Miss Finch died of natural causes. The coroner isn't certain yet, but the signs indicate some sort of poison. Accidental, of course," she hastened to add.

A little gasp slipped from Julia's mouth. Amelia's eyes widened as she pressed a hand to her mouth.

Grams remained cool, her gaze assessing. "And the constable wishes *you* to look into this? Really, Phoebe, as if any self-respecting man would send a slip of a girl to do his work."

"It's true, Grams. He wishes me to speak with the students, and perhaps a few of the mothers as well, not to mention the members of the governing body. The sight of the constable's uniform tends to put people on the defensive, especially the girls, who are shaken up as it is. He thought a more gentle approach would help loosen tongues."

"Loosen tongues? As in confessing to one's wrongdoings?" Grams pursed her lips. "If he believes this to be an accident, why would that be necessary?"

Grams certainly wasn't making this easy. "Because he still needs to trace the source of the poison, if that is indeed what killed Miss Finch. He needs to discover how it might have gotten into her food, where it came from, and where it is now. It must be taken away and disposed of. We don't want this to accidentally happen again, do we?"

Grams studied her a long moment, one in which Phoebe remembered Maude Renshaw's fair but firm manner in raising her and her siblings after Mama died years ago. In Grams's care, there had been no protesting bedtimes or study hours, no telling fibs, no shirking responsibility for one's deeds. *If only Grampapa were here.* Grampapa would have taken Phoebe's side. He almost always did.

But her grandmother's next words brought a wave of relief. "I suppose that does make sense. And of course the thought of genteel young ladies being questioned by the police makes one's skin positively crawl. I wouldn't be at all surprised if a good many parents called for the closing of the school were their daughters to be subjected to such an indignity."

"Exactly, Grams. And we must not let that happen. We are all of us Haverleigh women. The school must go on."

Grams heaved heavy sigh. "Yes, indeed it must."

Julia rolled her eyes while shaking her head, but Phoebe ignored her.

"Mind you," Grams said tersely, "you are not to over-step your bounds, young lady."

"I certainly won't, Grams."

"Oh, very well, then. Let's go." At Grams's clipped command, Julia set off walking toward the front door, but Grams called out her name to stop her. Julia turned around, looking puzzled and none too pleased. Grams pointed into the former receiving parlor, used now as a classroom. "This way, Julia. We will hear Phoebe's questions and answer to the best of our ability."

Amelia started toward the classroom, but Grams stopped her. "You wait here."

"But Grams—"

"Don't argue. Julia, come."

As Julia sauntered by her, Phoebe couldn't help flashing a triumphant smile. But she wished Amelia had been allowed to accompany them. As a student, her insight into the daily goings-on here could prove invaluable. Phoebe would have to speak with her at home later—discreetly.

"Unfortunately, Miss Finch was not universally well-liked," Grams said a few minutes later. Phoebe went utterly still, waiting. She had merely asked Grams about Miss Finch's policies when it came to overseeing her staff, but Grams seemed to want to discuss the woman's shortcomings as a headmistress. "I am afraid she shall not be greatly missed. Oh, initially, she seemed the ideal candidate. She had taught some fifteen years at a girls' school in York, and for another ten served as assistant headmistress and then chief administrator at a finishing school in Sheffield. But over the past year here at Haverleigh, she began introducing some rather radical ideas. It also came out that she had been an active member of the Women's Social and Political Union before and during the war."

Grams frowned in disapproval. "She may even have had dealings with that troublemaker, Marion Wallace-Dunlop."

Julia shuddered. "Hunger strikes and forced feedings. What *could* they have been thinking of?"

"They were thinking of political fairness for women," Phoebe told her. "But from what I understand, Miss Finch admitted to being a suffragist, but stopped short of joining up with the suffragettes."

The difference had rested in the persuasive tactics used to win the vote for women. The suffragists were no less determined to achieve their goals, but believed in civilized, legal means. The suffragettes, on the other hand, had organized marches that more often than not led to riots, arrests, and those beastly degradations Julia mentioned.

"Be that as it may," Grams said, "had we known more about her background, she would not have been hired. And of course, with our former headmistress perishing from the influenza last spring, and now so many people abandoning the countryside in favor of the cities—well, headmistresses don't exactly grow on trees, do they? Replacing Miss Finch was and will be trickier than one might expect."

"The suffragette movement aside," Phoebe said, "you mentioned Miss Finch introducing radical ideas. What were these?"

As a member of the school's governing body, Grams would have witnessed the discord firsthand. Her sliver-thin eyebrows lifted as she considered. "Some believed she was teaching unnecessary subjects, filling the girls' heads with useless information. The sciences, higher forms of mathematics such as a woman would never need in the running of a household. Subjects of that nature, while at the same time putting less emphasis on the social graces."

"I don't understand. Julia and I had instruction in the fundamentals of biology and chemistry, algebra, even a bit of physics." Yes, but not enough, she acknowledged, to allow her entry into one of England's universities. Not that she would have considered leaving Grams and Grampapa during the war years, especially after Papa died.

"As if any of *that* has ever come in handy," Julia muttered. She absently fingered a flaxen curl beneath the chic little veil of her hat.

"Be that as it may," Phoebe said, "why the sudden opposition to a varied curriculum?"

Grams glanced down the length of her nose at Phoebe. "Miss Finch took it too far. She encouraged the girls in her charge to aspire to unsuitable and unladylike occupations."

Something akin to an electrical charge ran up Phoebe's spine, leaving her momentarily unable to reply. When she once more gained command of her tongue, she remembered to govern her tone rather than blurting the words grappling for release. "Grams, during the war women took on all kinds of occupations, and successfully, too."

"The war is over, Phoebe, as I keep reminding you."

"But not all women are content to scamper back home with their heads down." She bit her lip. She hadn't meant to speak so candidly to Grams, and she could see by the severe look leveled on her that Grams didn't take it kindly.

"That is all well and good for young women of a certain class," she said sternly, "but as for the majority of the students at this school . . ." She didn't bother to complete the thought, but she didn't have to. Phoebe already knew Grams didn't like the idea of her own granddaughters taking on any but traditional roles in society. She wanted Phoebe and her sisters to be great ladies in the old sense, and Phoebe didn't have the heart to inform her such a thing didn't exist anymore, not as Grams knew it. And with so many men having perished in the war, a good many women would never find husbands.

But none of that had any bearing on the headmistress's death. She changed the subject. "Can you tell me who protested Miss Finch's curriculum the loudest?"

"Other than me, you mean?" The web of fine lines surrounding Grams's mouth deepened. "The head of the governing body, for one."

"You mean the Reverend Amstead?"

Grams nodded. "The very same. He's been quietly trying to raise support to have Miss Finch replaced."

"Replaced? That seems a bit extreme under the circumstances. It's one thing to disapprove of her educational philosophies, quite another to imply the woman was incompetent."

"To many people, Miss Finch's progressive ideas would be seen as incompetent—as a waste of time and money, since she had brought in new teachers the school wouldn't otherwise have needed."

Phoebe studied her grandmother, sad and disappointed that Grams might agree with such an assessment. "All right, so Mr. Amstead wanted Miss Finch gone. Who else?"

"Let's see . . . Then there are the Worthingtons."

"Zara's family."

"Yes. But they're presently out of the country, so they can't have done much complaining lately."

"Zara herself," Julia said with a shrug.

"How do you know that?" Phoebe asked.

"Amelia told me. She said Zara didn't appreciate being made to work so diligently, especially at subjects she never intends to think about again once she leaves school. Funny thing is, she still managed to receive some of the highest marks in the sixth form."

"Interesting . . ."

Julia burst out with a harsh laugh. "Oh, so now you believe Zara Worthington murdered Miss Finch?"

"Don't be daft, Julia. No one has said anything about murder. I only find it interesting."

Julia leaned her shoulder against their grandmother's and spoke in a stage whisper. "Are you fooled by this show of innocence, Grams? I think Phoebe is once again diving headfirst into the thick of it, just as she did last Christmas. Don't you think you should nip it in the bud immediately?"

Phoebe bristled. "Must you always make a joke of everything? Can you take nothing seriously? Not even a woman's untimely death?"

"That's enough, you two." Grams came to her feet with the briskness of a much younger woman. "Julia, come along. It's getting late and I need a good lie-down before dinner. Phoebe, we *will* see you at dinner, yes?"

It wasn't a question.

"Before that, I should hope," Julia said before Phoebe could answer. She stood and gave the front of her coat a tug to straighten it. "You do realize you monopolize Eva beyond all reason, don't you?"

"I'll be home long before dinner," Phoebe promised while at the same time ignoring Julia's observation. After they collected Amelia from her perch at the bottom of the staircase, Phoebe walked them to the front door. With a sigh of relief—one of many during the last quarter hour—she went in search of Eva, whom she found in the kitchen attempting to console a distraught Mrs. Honeychurch.

CHAPTER 3

"Mrs. Honeychurch, I need to ask you some questions. Would that be all right?" Eva regarded the stout woman who presided over Haverleigh's kitchen. They sat at the long table in what had once been the servants' hall of the manor house, back when Haverleigh was a private home. Not much had changed since then, as the hall was now used by the kitchen and cleaning staff for meals and as a gathering place during their unoccupied moments. The main difference was the lack of upper servants—butler, housekeeper, footmen, lady's maids—that one would find in an estate like Foxwood Hall.

Myra Honeychurch had prepared the meals here since before Eva herself had attended on scholarship, yet the boundary between servant and student had prevented them from knowing each other well. Not so now, for Eva's position as lady's maid put them on a par.

The woman's hands worried the edges of her apron as she leaned forward in anticipation of Eva's question. "Go ahead, Miss Huntford, ask." She sniffled. "This day isn't likely to turn any worse than it already is."

Eva wasn't sure about that. She drew a breath. "How

closely did Miss Finch supervise the comings and goings in the kitchen?"

Mrs. Honeychurch's red-rimmed eyes narrowed in puzzlement. "I didn't expect *that* question."

"What *did* you expect?"

The cook chewed her lip, considered, and ignored the question. "Miss Finch hardly supervised us belowstairs at all. She trusted me to run a tidy and efficient kitchen."

"And did you?" Eva asked bluntly.

"Of course I did. I always have."

"So then you might say you know every item that passes through the delivery door?"

"I catalog everything. You can take a look at my books if you like." The woman's tone took on a defensive note, not that Eva could blame her. Any self-respecting cook took a great deal of pride in her work. Yet, there was something Eva couldn't quite put her finger on.

"I'm quite sure the police will ask to see your books, Mrs. Honeychurch, as well as ask you a few questions of their own."

The woman's eyes widened a fraction, and—Eva couldn't be certain—seemed to shift to the doorway and back again.

Eva decided on another tack. "Then you and Miss Finch got on well, would you say?"

"I . . . What a question, Miss Huntford. Whatever do you mean?"

"Exactly that. Did you get on well, or not?"

Her lips jerked into a fleeting smile. "Yes, wondrously well. She was a good woman, the headmistress was. Better than most, I can tell you that."

"How so?"

Mrs. Honeychurch's gaze darted once more to the door before returning to Eva. "Well, she was a modest sort, never one to boast, but I knew how hard she worked, and how much she wanted for our girls here. A generous soul, she was." To Eva's consternation, the cook's features crumpled and she burst into tears. "Our dear Miss Finch, and in the end it really is *my* fault—all my fault!"

She collapsed against Eva's shoulder, her tears seeping through Eva's dress until the fabric clung and there were sure to be salty stains left on the broadcloth.

These, of course, were not the first tears to fall belowstairs. Earlier, the two kitchen maids had been thoroughly interrogated by Inspector Perkins, until one of them had broken down into sobs. The chief inspector had declared both girls simpletons—which Eva knew was not the case—but had drafted them into helping scour the pantries and cupboards for all possible sources of poison. They were presently placing their finds on the center worktable in the kitchen. Eva planned to interview them again—but much more gently than had the inspector. But first she had to calm an overwrought Mrs. Honeychurch.

"There, now, it will be all right," she murmured while patting the woman's hand. Yet, an uneasy sensation persisted. Mrs. Honeychurch was not being entirely aboveboard, and Eva needed to find out why. "You won't be blamed. Even if somehow a cleaning solution or some other substance made its way into—"

A wail drowned out the reassurance. "Don't you understand, Miss Huntford? This is *my* kitchen. *I* am responsible for everything that goes on here. It doesn't matter whose hand accidentally grabbed the wrong box, mistaking rat poison for flour, or Borax for sugar."

"I don't think anything like that happened, Mrs. Honeychurch, truly I don't." Yet Eva did, in fact, believe that very thing. Whether it occurred accidentally or intentionally remained to be discovered. Another idea occurred to her. Could Mrs. Honeychurch already know what killed Miss Finch, but was afraid to say?

"Poor Miss Finch," the woman went on while dabbing

at her eyes with her apron. "She put up a rugged front at times, she did, but that was to impress her authority on the girls. When they weren't about, Miss Finch was a lovely, caring soul. Lately, she hadn't been sleeping well—not well at all. She'd often come down late at night for a spot of chamomile tea or warm milk, and we'd sit up a while, j-just . . . chatting." The last word splintered on a sob.

Lady Phoebe stepped into the servants' hall and smiled gently down at Mrs. Honeychurch. "I'm sorry this is so distressing for you. You mustn't think you're to blame."

Eva had tried signaling with a frown and a little shake of her head, but Phoebe had failed to receive the message. The cook's tears came harder and faster. She broke away from Eva's comforting arms and ran from the room.

"Oh, dear, I didn't mean to upset her more than she already was."

Eva sighed. "You didn't, my lady. She was already terribly upset." She studied her mistress a moment, noting Phoebe's high color and her slight effort to catch her breath, as if she had run down from the ground floor. "What is it? Have you learned something new?"

Phoebe took the seat vacated by Mrs. Honeychurch. "As a matter of fact, yes. Grams just told me Miss Finch was not liked or approved of by everyone connected with the school. Some parents and members of the governing board wanted her replaced. Including Grams herself." She told Eva what she had learned.

"You're getting ahead of yourself, my lady. Miles Brannock insisted there isn't yet any reason to believe a poisoning would have been anything but accidental."

"I saw the way you looked at Constable Brannock when he made that assertion. No use denying it, Eva. You aren't convinced either."

Eva sighed. "As a matter of fact, Mrs. Honeychurch was acting rather strangely just now, and it couldn't be chalked up merely to grief. She seemed . . . anxious. I almost got the feeling she was hiding something. It even occurred to me she might know how Miss Finch died. I don't like to think it and I hope I'm wrong. Oh, but still," she hastily added, "I'm not saying I believe Mrs. Honeychurch did anything intentionally, but she might know more than she's admitting."

"Interesting, but think, Eva. Many of the desserts shared similar ingredients. Logic tells us if a foreign substance ended up in, say, the sugar, others would have been affected. But no, everyone else was perfectly fine. There have been no reports of illnesses of any sort. And I believe we can all agree that it was the Madeira cake that did Miss Finch in. Didn't Zara Worthington bake it?"

Eva thought back to Zara pushing her way to the front of the line and boasting to Miss Sedgewick about how splendid her cake turned out. "Yes, but surely you can't be accusing the Earl of Benton's daughter of intentionally murdering the headmistress. Besides, we don't know what kind of poison it was. Some are more slow-acting than others. Arsenic, for instance, would have taken days or weeks to kill Miss Finch. It could have been in her morning coffee, or even in her face powder, or anything she used on a regular basis—whether intentionally or not— and had nothing to do with the Madeira cake."

Phoebe tilted her head and considered. "I've read about arsenic being used as a murder weapon, with the victim gradually weakening as if from an illness. History is full of such cases."

"And Miss Finch was looking rather peaky even before the luncheon began," Eva pointed out.

With the stubbornness Eva knew all too well, Lady Phoebe shook her head. "The headmistress might have sometimes struggled for breath and tended toward a florid complexion, but I found her to be full of energy and enthusiasm. A slow poisoning would have robbed her of that vigor. As far as I can tell, she carried on with the same vitality from the day she started at Haverleigh right up until the moment she choked at the table."

"I'll admit, my lady, that does seem to be the case. But we mustn't be hasty and jump to conclusions."

"I propose we offer our services to the police in helping search the kitchen and pantries for suspicious ingredients." Phoebe rose from her chair.

Eva came to her feet as well and smoothed the wrinkles from the front of her dress. "Do you think the chief inspector will allow it?"

"I see no reason why he shouldn't. We'll help make shorter work of the search."

As Phoebe guessed, Inspector Perkins raised no objection to them helping out in the kitchen. In fact, he preferred Phoebe's and Eva's assistance over that of the kitchen maids, whom he still considered dull-witted, not to mention possibly responsible for Miss Finch's death. And Mrs. Honeychurch was of no use to anyone at present. Eva and Lady Phoebe therefore spent the next hour helping the kitchen maids pore over the luncheon recipes and gather the ingredients used in each dish.

They made notations about where each ingredient was stored, and what else was stored nearby. They collected all the cleaning solutions and—this made Eva shudder—the rodent and insect poisons, and set them on a counter separate from the rest.

Finally, Eva regarded sacks of flour and sugar, jars of molasses, honey, and jams, cooking oils, dried and fresh fruit, and both powdered and fresh herbs and spices. "What precisely was used in the Madeira cake?" she mused aloud.

"It's a simple recipe." Phoebe began pointing. "Flour, powdered sugar, butter, eggs, baking powder, and vanilla extract."

"Miss Finch liked almonds as well as nutmeg in hers, don't forget," Eva said. "And the glaze contained brown sugar, cinnamon, a tiny bit of cream, and more nutmeg."

"So how do we determine whether any of these ingredients are tainted?"

"You do not, my lady." Miles Brannock entered the pantry and stepped between them. "The inspector and I will take it from here. Thank you for separating out the ingredients that need to be analyzed."

His tone carried clear dismissal, and Eva thought he was right to do so. "You're welcome, Constable. My lady, perhaps we should leave now and let the officers complete the job."

Her young lady showed no signs of budging. "How will the analysis be conducted?"

"Samples will be sent to a police laboratory in Gloucester," the constable replied with a faint note of impatience.

"And will we be apprised of the results?"

Miles Brannock shifted his gaze to Eva, his fleeting expression begging the question, *Is she always this inquisitive?* Eva smiled and nodded, and Constable Brannock regarded Lady Phoebe. "If I agree to keep you informed, will you leave the finer points of the investigation to the authorities?"

"You engaged our services, after all, Constable. You do still wish us to speak with the students and staff, don't you?" she asked rather than answer his question.

He inclined his head. "If you would be so kind."

"I think I'll go and talk with Zara Worthington now, while the day is still fresh in her memory. Eva, I'll leave the staff to you. See if you can find out how well Miss Finch was liked among her employees."

"That is not what I asked you to do, my lady," the constable called to her as she made her way through the main kitchen. "I merely need their accounts of events leading up to the headmistress's death."

After tossing a smile over her shoulder, Lady Phoebe continued into the corridor and up the steps to the main floor. The kitchen maids, meanwhile, busied themselves with preparing dinner for the students who remained. Fresh supplies of meat, produce, and baked goods had arrived from the village and surrounding farms, as nothing previously found in the larders could be trusted. Inspector Perkins departed for parts unknown. Eva suddenly felt very much alone with Miles Brannock, who regarded her with a grin that left her decidedly uncomfortable.

"We haven't talked in a good long while, Miss Huntford."

"No, Constable. My duties keep me well occupied, as do yours, I am sure."

"You've ignored my invitations to join me for dinner several times now."

"I most certainly have not ignored you, Constable. I sent my regrets each time. As I said, my duties to the three Renshaw sisters keep me busy." She began needlessly straightening rows of containers on the work counter before her.

"Two Renshaw sisters," the policeman said. "Lady Amelia is here at school from Monday to Friday."

Insolent man. Eva gave a toss of her head, Lady Julia– style. She didn't appreciate being interrogated about her personal life. "Her sisters' needs are many."

"Even the most diligent lady's maid must be given some time off."

She stopped minutely adjusting the positions of boxes and jars and looked up to find him studying her. There was little about him of which she approved. He spoke out of turn, treated his betters with barely concealed disdain, and insisted on scrutinizing her in the most ungentlemanly way. She didn't doubt he possessed a wildness at his core for all his being an officer of the law. And yet . . .

Quite against her better judgment, she found him compelling. She had a position to maintain, young ladies to tend to. Though they might consider themselves all grown up, ladies Julia, Phoebe, and Amelia needed her, and she had neither the time nor the inclination to divide her attentions between them and a man—any man. Someday perhaps. Not now.

She angled her chin at him. "I visit my parents in my time off. They're aging, and my sister Alice lives too far to make the trip more than once or twice a year. And my brother . . ." She ducked her head and averted her gaze. Why had she brought up Danny? Danny, who perished in the war, whose death might have been avoided but for the egregious error—no, criminal negligence—of a commanding officer.

She didn't wish to discuss that with Miles Brannock, an Irishman who showed no sign of having served in the war that took so many British lives.

Please, don't let him ask . . .

But Miles Brannock did not ask about Danny, or anything else. He merely smiled in his cheeky, disconcerting way and said, "One of these days, Eva Huntford, you'll run out of excuses."

She decided to ignore the comment. "Tell me what you really believe killed Miss Finch. The truth."

Once again she became caught in his probing gaze. His lips tilted to one side before relaxing and parting. "Agree to have dinner with me, and I'll tell you."

"You are infuriating, Constable. Not to mention relentless."

"That I am, Miss Huntford."

"All right, then. If you insist, we'll have dinner . . .
sometime soon. Now what is it you believe?"

A sentiment sparked in his eyes, quickly doused when
he blinked. Before he spoke, he glanced through the doorway at the kitchen maids and drew Eva off to one side, out
of their hearing. "All right, this is what I think. Cyanide."

Eva gasped. "Are you sure?"

"Nothing is certain until the coroner makes his report,
but the blue tint of her skin and beneath her fingernails are
telling signs. And an odor of almonds seeped from the victim's open mouth when I viewed her in the morgue."

Eva recoiled. "How ghastly."

"It's part of my job. But tell me, did you notice such an
odor when you ran to the headmistress to help?"

She thought back on the confusing, frantic scene. "I'm
not sure . . . The desserts had been served, many of them
warm and giving off their fragrance along with the tea.
Almonds . . . it's possible, I suppose."

"Well, it doesn't matter, because if cyanide is to blame,
the coroner will find it."

"But how would anyone have gotten a hold of such a
thing? Arsenic I can understand. It's in rat poison."

"Some rat poisons also contain cyanide, as do insecti-
cides and some cleaning agents. I don't know for sure, but
I intend to find out."

Her suspicions concerning Mrs. Honeychurch rose up
again. Had a box of rat poison somehow become part of
the ingredients of Miss Finch's Madeira cake? What about
Zara Worthington? Could the mistake have been hers?
Even if it had been, Mrs. Honeychurch would ultimately
be responsible, as the woman herself had said.

Then again, Mrs. Honeychurch hadn't been the only
member of the staff to act strangely today. The nurse's hesitation in coming to Miss Finch's aid had been most un-
professional. Most *unnurselike*.

"The wheels in your mind are spinning, Miss Huntford, I can tell. Care to share?" The constable smiled—not his habitually impudent, often mocking smile, but a genuine one that brought warmth to his cool blue eyes and chiseled features.

"I'd like to speak with the nurse, if that's all right with you. I have a couple of questions that should be asked while the day is still fresh in her mind."

He placed a hand over her wrist to keep her from leaving. "Why the nurse? Was she down here during the preparations? Or involved in any other way?"

"No, not in the preparations. But it took Nurse Delacy rather long to arrive on the scene. I'd sent Lady Phoebe's sister to find her. The infirmary is on the ground floor, not far from the dining hall, yet it seemed to take forever. I could be wrong—nothing is completely clear about those moments, they were such a shock, but . . ."

"Yes? Do go on."

"Lady Julia left the room, and it was only then that the nurse arrived in the dining hall, accompanied by both sisters."

"As if it took the two of them to rouse her?"

"Yes, possibly. But perhaps she wasn't in the infirmary at the time, and Amelia had to search for her."

He sucked in his cheeks and considered. "Let's find out what delayed her. It might be nothing, or it could be important." Eva started to turn away again, but he hadn't taken his hand off her wrist. She questioned him with a lift of her eyebrow. "Perhaps we might discuss what you learn over dinner?"

It was her turn to smile. "Not tonight, Constable. My ladies suffered a shock today and will need me at home tonight."

"Then when?"

Her smile widened. Did she inject a trace of impudence

in it? A touch of mockery? Perhaps, but she had to admit it felt good to turn the tables on him. "Soon, Constable Brannock. Very soon."

An unnatural stillness claimed the sixth form hallway of the dormitory. The doors all stood closed, and although Phoebe could hear occasional murmurs from within, she detected no hint of the high spirits she remembered sharing with her classmates when they were left to their own devices. Of course, those moments had typically been few and far between, as her schooldays had adhered to a strict schedule of lessons, study time, and athletics.

She didn't wonder at the subdued atmosphere, after what the girls had witnessed earlier today. She did wonder, however, how much they had been told. Precious little, most likely, and certainly nothing about suspected poison. And as for the younger girls, most of their rooms were tucked away on the third floor, in what had once been the servants' quarters. As far as Phoebe knew, they had been told of Miss Finch's passing with little elaboration, and to keep them occupied, their lessons would continue, were even now commencing in the classrooms on the first and second floors of the wing that had been added to the original house. Thankfully, that wing kept them well away from the dining hall, and it was unlikely they had heard the disturbance at all. She only hoped the older girls kept the details to themselves.

How long would they all remain at Haverleigh? If the headmistress had been intentionally poisoned, there would be a mass exodus just as soon as parents could arrange to collect their daughters.

She came to a corner bedroom, the one she knew to be the largest of the rooms allocated to any student. She knocked, and upon hearing a "come in," opened the door and stepped inside. Zara Worthington stood before a full-length mirror and seemed to be admiring her chestnut curls. At least that was the impression she gave, leaning in close to the glass and fingering a ringlet beside her left cheek. That cheek dimpled as Zara glanced at Phoebe through the mirror. That the girl hadn't bothered to pull away and pretend not to be primping struck Phoebe as particularly shallow, considering the circumstances.

"May I help you, Lady Phoebe?" the girl said mildly. She made an adjustment to the wide silk band that swept her hair to the crown of her head while allowing loose spirals to dance around her face.

"Yes, I . . ." Phoebe hesitated, searching for the right words. She doubted the wisdom of blatantly questioning Zara about the Madeira cake, for that would only prompt the girl to become defensive. "I only wish to see that you're all right. That what happened today hasn't upset you too terribly."

"Oh, yes." Zara only now seemed cognizant of her inappropriate attention to her appearance. She dropped her hands to her sides and turned away from the mirror. "It was horrible. So distressing. Poor Miss Finch."

"I'm sure you'll miss her terribly."

The girl's short, rounded nose, almost certain to become downright stubby as she grew older, inched into the air. "I was her favorite. Did you know?" She went to perch on the arm of a little settee covered in tufted floral chintz. Phoebe let this statement dissipate on the slightly perfumed air, and with it a measure of Zara's haughty confidence. The girl flashed a nervous smile. "Miss Finch liked Amelia, too, of course."

Phoebe smiled a little and nodded. "Amelia was very fond of the headmistress. Very excited by the subjects Miss Finch added to the curriculum. I suppose you were, as well."

A shadow crossed Zara's face, and her lips twitched into

a pout. "I suppose. Though sometimes I wondered if it was all quite necessary."

"How so?" Phoebe strolled around the bed and sat facing Zara at the edge of the satin coverlet. "Don't you think having an education opens up choices in one's life?"

The girl shrugged. "If you're someone like Jane Timmons, or even Lilyanne Mucklow. Such girls have little chance of marrying well. They may need to find employment someday."

Zara spoke of the girls she had badgered in the kitchen. Jane, a local girl and the daughter of a sheep farmer, attended Haverleigh on a merit scholarship. Lilyanne was the daughter of an MP and inventor who had helped develop the engines that went into the Avro 504 aeroplanes during the war. That made him something of a hero, for it was said the allies could not have won the war without the Avro 504s.

"I see no reason why either girl won't use her education to her advantage *and* marry happily someday. You don't see the possibility of doing both?"

Zara's smile held both condescension and a certain slyness. "Lady Phoebe, you and I both know what our futures hold. Marriage to wealthy, influential men. Titled men. We'll take our places in society, and any work we do will be very much like what you did here today. Organizing charity events, sponsoring philanthropic projects, and the like."

"I haven't made any such decisions about my life," Phoebe said. "Are you certain you don't want something more?"

Zara's expression became genuinely puzzled. "How can there be anything more than presiding over a great household and upholding the traditions of our society? That is what women of our station do. We have a responsibility to set an example and to maintain our valued institutions."

Zara's reply didn't surprise Phoebe, considering what

she had learned about the girl's parents from Grams. They, like many others of their class, believed their daughter's place was in the manor house. She wondered, had they made plans to withdraw Zara from Haverleigh due to Miss Finch's modern ideas?

"Not everyone values those institutions as they once did," she told the girl gently. "The war changed so very much. And many of the wealthy young men who might have become influential leaders are no longer with us. Doesn't that make it vitally important that all members of our society, men and women, should be able to participate in the future of our nation?"

Zara came to her feet. "Good heavens, Lady Phoebe, are you a Bolshevik?"

Phoebe couldn't help chuckling. "No, Zara, rest assured, I am for king, country, and St. George. But never mind. No one can say you aren't a very accomplished young lady. Your efforts for today's luncheon were beyond exemplary." The girl dimpled prettily at the praise. "Your ideas for the invitations were lovely. And your Madeira cake . . . I know you made Miss Finch proud."

Had Phoebe gone too far in bringing up the cake? Had it occurred to Zara that Miss Finch died immediately after ingesting the miniature confection? If it had, she showed no indication now.

"Did she enjoy it? I do hope she did. I would find it of great comfort to believe dear Miss Finch's last moments were spent relishing the cake I made with my own two hands."

"Then no one helped you? Not Mrs. Honeychurch or any of the other girls?" Phoebe glanced around the well-appointed room to lend a casual air to her question. Meanwhile, she held her breath.

"Indeed not. The very idea. The cake was my own creation, following Miss Finch's favorite recipe. Do you think me incapable of following a recipe, Lady Phoebe?"

The vehemence of Zara's protest hardly seemed in proportion to the circumstances. It wasn't as if Phoebe had accused her of cheating on an exam, or of having another student prepare her homework for her. But perhaps today's luncheon symbolized the very activities Zara found important, around which she would someday plan her life—the organization of society events. She wondered, though, if these were the skills on which Zara placed value, how could she have been the favorite student of a woman who wanted more for her students? Had Zara been a proficient scholar despite her apparent aversion to academics, according to Amelia?

It was possible. As Phoebe had learned over the years, intelligence could be hiding behind the dullest of facades. All the more disappointing then, if Zara never reached her potential.

"Zara, did you look at each ingredient very carefully before adding it to the cake mixture?"

The girl's brow furrowed. Furtiveness lurked in the corners of her eyes. "Of course. What are you implying?"

Phoebe considered carefully before answering. If a mistake had been made, if indeed Zara had included rat poison or some other substance instead of sugar or nutmeg, the child would have to live the rest of her life with that burden. Even the suggestion could have a crippling effect on her future endeavors. It wouldn't do to place that burden on Zara without irrefutable evidence to support it.

"Nothing, Zara. Never mind." Phoebe stood, about to take her leave, when another question occurred to her. "Do you happen to remember seeing anyone hanging about the kitchen in the last two days who perhaps shouldn't have been there?"

Zara regarded her blankly. "How should I know who belongs in the kitchen? This was my first time down there. I suppose I enjoyed baking my cake, but I don't intend to make a habit of it." Zara rose from her perch in a sure message of dismissal. Yes, she would make a formidable mistress of the manor someday.

Still, Phoebe lingered, studying the girl. Phoebe had attended school with a dozen or so Zara Worthingtons—girls intent on following in their mother's footsteps. Well brought up and well taken care of, girls like Zara were pretty and vivacious in their youth. But Zara's future showed all too plainly in lips that pouted too easily, eyebrows that lifted too readily in judgment, hands that too often fidgeted—as Zara's now fidgeted with the pintucks down the center of her shirtwaist—rather than finding worthwhile occupation. Girls like Zara rarely made truly happy women. Phoebe had seen the evidence of it too many times to count, in friends of her parents and grandparents. And not all women were as lucky as Grams and Mama had been, marrying for love.

She had one more question for her. "Why do you dislike Lilyanne Mucklow and Jane Timmons?"

Zara blinked. It was obviously not a question she had been expecting, but it seemed to Phoebe a matter of course in thinking about unhappy people. Wasn't denigrating someone weaker than oneself also a sign of unhappiness?

"You were unkind to both of them earlier," she persisted.

"Was I? Well, as for Lilyanne, the careless thing did spill the fruit. Surely you don't think she should have been praised for that."

"An ounce of forbearance might have suited you better, don't you think?"

Zara turned away and went to her dressing table. Leaning with her hands braced on the marble top, she regarded herself in the mirror, then shifted her gaze to Phoebe again. "Lilyanne can't keep up with the rest of us, and I have neither the time nor the patience for anyone who can't keep up."

"I see. And Jane?"

"Jane is as common as the weeds in an untended flower bed, yet she thinks she's better than everyone else. She deserves to be put in her place, to remind her of the life she'll return to once she leaves school." Zara pulled the silk headband from her hair. As chestnut spirals tumbled down her back, she shook her head and combed her fingers luxuriously through their length, all the while staring with narrowed eyes at Phoebe through the mirror.

CHAPTER 4

As Eva entered the infirmary, she could almost imagine the lovely music room it had once been. A corner room overlooking the gardens, its arched windows extended some twelve feet high and flooded the interior with light, while hardwood floors, a coffered ceiling, and dark-stained wainscoting softened the glare. Beyond that, all traces of the room's former function had been stripped away. Now, a row of utilitarian, iron-framed beds, presently empty, occupied one wall of the room, along with an examining table flanked by curtained screens. Opposite them, glass-fronted cabinets held an array of vials, jars, bottles, cotton gauzes, and metal instruments whose spotless surfaces glinted brightly in the daylight.

Nurse Olivia Delacy sat at a desk in a corner off to the right of the door. A notebook lay open before her, a pot of ink at her elbow. Hunching, she dipped her pen and leaned lower to make an annotation. She obviously hadn't noticed Eva come in.

Details about the woman Eva had missed previously now caught her notice. Beneath her tidy nurse's kerchief, hair the color of overripe wheat appeared about as dry and brittle, the bangs a frazzled fringe lying stiffly across her forehead. An angular figure spoke of long hours on her feet with too little time for regular meals, and her hands, chapped and red, testified to habitually being plunged into strong soap, probably the solutions used to sterilize equipment and sickrooms.

Eva cleared her throat. "Excuse me, Nurse?"

The woman flinched upright. Her pen went flying, hitting the floor beyond the desk with a splatter of ink. Her hands flew to her bosom, which heaved erratically.

"I'm so sorry," Eva blurted. "I didn't meant to startle you. How clumsy of me."

Nurse Delacy lifted her face in Eva's direction, startling Eva in turn with the blatant fright lodged in the frozen features, the glazed eyes. For several seconds neither of them moved, and Eva found something in that jarring expression that turned her consternation to alarm and then cold, gaunt dread.

"N-Nurse?" she stammered. "Are you quite all right?"

The woman didn't immediately reply, but gradually panic loosened its grip on her features. Eva's apprehension faded as quickly as it had arisen, and for an instant she questioned her own sanity.

The nurse's hands slid down to rest in her lap. An incongruous chuckle broke from tautly stretched lips. "I . . . was so caught up in my work. Goodness." She paused for a breath, pushed her rolling wooden chair slightly away from the desk, and once more pressed a hand to her breastbone. "You must think me quite a goose."

Eva stepped closer then stopped, hovering halfway between the desk and the door. "If I'm disturbing you, I'll come back another time. I didn't mean to interrupt, or to cause you such a fright."

At that last word, Nurse Delacy's tongue darted across her upper lip. "No, it's quite all right. I was just . . ." She glanced down at her notebook, which Eva now saw contained lines and columns, with names, dates, and commentary written in a rigid, painstaking penmanship. "I was recording the time and details of Miss Finch's passing," she explained in a lower voice. "For the school records. We keep precise records here, you see."

"Yes, I understand." The same could be said about Foxwood Hall. Not a provision was used that wasn't accounted for, not a minute of the daily schedule left to happenstance, but instead clearly mapped out well in advance. "And I understand how your employer's death has shocked and saddened you."

"Please, sit." Nurse Delacy gestured toward a small, armless chair. Eva pulled it away from the wall and sat facing the nurse, who folded her hands on the desktop in a show of composure. "What may I do for you, Miss . . ."

"That's right. We were never properly introduced. I'm Eva Huntford. I'm lady's maid to the three Renshaw sisters. You must know Amelia."

"Indeed I do. A lovely young lady. But all three sisters? My goodness, you certainly have your work cut out for you, don't you, Miss Huntford?"

"No more than you, I'm sure, with all these students to look after."

"Oh, this?" She made a general sweep at the air, as if to encompass the entirety of the school. "This is nothing compared to"—she paused and swallowed—"to working in a . . . uh . . . in a hospital. Of course, now that Miss Finch is gone . . ." She trailed off with a shrug.

At those words, Eva seized the opportunity to ease into the very topic she had come here to discuss. "Surely you don't fear being dismissed because of what happened today."

"In these past couple of hours, I've been wondering if I

could have—should have—saved her. If I'd done something differently." She shook her head. "I don't know."

Until Eva had spoken with Miles Brannock, she might have agreed with the woman. If Miss Finch had been choking or suffering an attack of some kind, Nurse Delacy might indeed have been able to help her if she had arrived in the dining hall sooner. But if the headmistress had died of poison, especially a fast-acting poison such as cyanide, Nurse Delacy could not have changed the outcome.

"Perhaps you're being too hard on yourself." Eva might have added more, but she was too intent on gauging the nurse's every twitch and hesitation.

"In my profession," she said in an undertone, "one always wonders."

"I'm sure you came as soon as Lady Amelia found you earlier."

The nurse's gaze darted to meet Eva's, then fell quickly away.

"I suppose she couldn't find you immediately," Eva prodded, "or you would have been there sooner."

Sharp lines formed across the dry skin of the nurse's brow. "Are you insinuating I didn't come quickly enough? Then you do believe Miss Finch's death was my fault."

"I didn't say that. And I don't believe it made a difference to the outcome one way or another. I only meant . . . well, I watched the woman struggle for air until the moment she died. It happened so quickly, yet seemed like forever, if you can understand what I mean."

"Oh, yes, Miss Huntford. I understand all too well." A shudder sent a ripple down the woman's starched uniform. Eva waited for her to elaborate, but she remained silent. Eva could have kicked herself, for obviously her inept attempt to discover what delayed the woman's arrival in the dining hall had put Nurse Delacy on her guard.

As in the past, Eva questioned whether she was cut out for intrigue. Yet her instincts told her she had learned more here than appearances suggested. In the dining hall earlier, she had had to shout at Nurse Delacy to prompt her to action, for the woman had seemed to freeze up at the sight of the inert Miss Finch. Couple that with her mannerisms these past few minutes, and Eva concluded the nurse either had something to hide, or was of such a nervous disposition as to potentially render her incapable of performing her job. And that concerned Eva, whether or not the nurse had anything to do with Miss Finch's death.

Dinner seemed interminable that evening. The courses crept by at a snail's pace, especially since Phoebe's appetite had failed to accompany her to the table. How much longer before she might retreat upstairs and finally question her sister? At long last, Grams signaled to Giles and said, "We'll take our coffee in the library."

"Very good, my lady."

When the butler Phoebe had known all her life faltered and merely frowned in puzzlement as to how to proceed, Vernon, the head footman, sidled up behind his shoulder and murmured in his ear, "I'll send below for coffee, sir, while you help the countess up from her chair."

Had everyone else at the table overheard? They all appeared absorbed in placing their napkins just so beside their plates. Poor Giles had been showing sure signs of aging in recent months. The family had reached a silent agreement not to notice, while Vernon had taken on the task of issuing gentle reminders whenever they were needed. This way, an inevitable unpleasantness—that of Giles having to retire—could be forestalled as long as possible.

But Phoebe was still not free, for in the library Grampapa suggested a game of chess. With her brother, Fox, away at Eton, the role of chess opponent fell to Phoebe. Julia hadn't the patience for the game, and Amelia lacked the cunning to sacrifice "poor, innocent pawns" for the greater good.

Amelia, apparently, had been equally as eager to speak with Phoebe, for when Phoebe finally ascended the stairs, arrived at her sister's door, and prepared to knock, Amelia opened it, reached out, seized Phoebe's wrist, and pulled her inside. Amelia quickly closed the door behind them. "I thought you'd never come up. Eva and I have been waiting an age."

"You only came up yourself a few minutes ago." Phoebe shook her head with a wry laugh.

Eva stood before Amelia's dollhouse, a beloved item she refused to give up or have relegated to the nursery with all the other forgotten toys. The house was a miniature of Foxwood Hall, complete with turret, mullioned windows, and furniture that mirrored many of the pieces to be found in the real house, including Amelia's painted Italian bedroom set. Eva placed a tiny rose-brocade settee back into the Rosalind Sitting Room, identical to the real one down the hall, and came toward them with her hands folded primly at her waist.

"It's rather late," she said. "Perhaps we should talk in the morning."

Amelia scoffed. "It is not late. Besides, it's not as though I must wake early for lessons tomorrow. Grams has no intention of allowing me back at school until all questions about Miss Finch have been resolved. Oh, Phoebe, do you really believe she was murdered? That *is* what you told Grams and Julia earlier, isn't it?"

"No, I most certainly did not, and that is exactly why Grams made you wait outside the classroom. You're letting your imagination run away with you."

Clearly chastised, Amelia compressed her lips and offered up one of her innocent, *who me* expressions. Phoebe decided to take pity on the child, for as she had just pointed out, Amelia had let her imagination run wild. An ounce of truth would help rein those notions back to a manageable degree.

"All right," she said, taking her sister's hand, "let's sit. You'll be thrilled to know you can be of help."

Amelia's eyes brightened and she drew in an audible breath of excitement. "Come, Eva. You sit, too."

"Why don't the two of you make yourselves comfortable on the settee, and I'll stand behind you and take down your hair?"

This time it was Phoebe and Amelia trading smiles. Amelia knew as well as Phoebe that Eva always sought to maintain the boundaries between them. Phoebe had come to realize her lady's maid duties were Eva's anchor, her way of establishing where she belonged in the scheme of the world, and she took those duties as seriously as a soldier takes his orders from the chain of command.

Thus situated, with Eva searching for hairpins, Phoebe bade Amelia to explain what she knew about the goings-on at the Haverleigh School for Young Ladies.

"What don't I know," the girl said with a puffed-up sense of importance Phoebe immediately forgave. "First, I can tell you Miss Sedgewick and Miss Finch never did get on well. They put up appearances, but any of the students, especially the older ones, could tell you they wasted little love on each other."

"And why is that?" Phoebe turned her head slightly so Eva could find more hairpins.

"Isn't it obvious? Miss Sedgewick is genteel, and Miss Finch was not. In fact, some of the girls suspected she might have hailed from even lower than the middle class. It does happen, that somehow a girl manages an education—

Sunday school, a scholarship—" Her mouth formed an O, and Amelia twisted around to look up at Eva. "I'm so sorry. I didn't mean—"

"No offense taken, my lady," Eva said lightly. "I am a farmer's daughter who, as you said, managed an education in just that way. I'm grateful for it, and grateful to be here serving you and your sisters." She smiled as she spoke, and if secretly Eva Huntford did feel anything resembling resentment toward her lot in life, Phoebe detected not one hint of it—not in her expression, her words, or her cheerful attendance to her daily tasks. Eva ran her fingers through Phoebe's hair, unraveling it and fanning it out over Phoebe's shoulders. Then Eva did the same with Amelia's darker golden locks.

"Go back to what you were saying, Amellie." When they spoke privately like this, Phoebe often reverted to Amelia's babyhood nickname, a name Amelia herself had coined in her inability to achieve the correct pronunciation. "How do you know Miss Sedgewick held Miss Finch in low regard?"

"Actually, I think the disdain went both ways. But Miss Sedgewick often looked at Miss Finch in that way—you know, that way women particularly have."

Phoebe shook her head. "No, I don't know."

"Like Miss Finch wasn't worth her notice, and as if she caught Miss Finch trespassing in her private garden."

At this, Phoebe chuckled. "And what exactly does that look like?"

Eva came around the sofa to face them, and Amelia said, "You know, Eva, don't you?"

"I do, my lady. As if Miss Sedgewick caught a whiff of something sour."

"That's it." Amelia turned to Phoebe. "You see, Eva understands."

A little pang clutched at Phoebe's heart. "Have people shown you that look, Eva?"

"It doesn't matter, my lady." Before Phoebe could protest, Eva went briskly on. "So Miss Sedgewick didn't particularly esteem Miss Finch, which in turn caused Miss Finch to return the sentiments, at least discreetly. How did the students feel about the headmistress?"

Amelia held out her hand and waggled it a bit. "Some liked her, others didn't. She makes—that is, she *made*—us work much harder than Miss Osbourne ever did. You don't know how easy you had it, Phoebe. Miss Finch was demanding and accepted no excuses."

"Granted no quarter," Eva said with a grin.

"None," Amelia confirmed.

"I do know that Zara Worthington's parents didn't approve of Miss Finch's curriculum, and neither did Zara," Phoebe said.

"No, but she always does well." Amelia scrunched her brow. "I never *can* quite understand it. Zara never seems to study, is never working on assignments when the rest of us are, and during lessons she always has the most bored expressions." She shook her head and shrugged. "She must be some kind of genius."

Phoebe doubted that. But Amelia's comments piqued her curiosity. Perhaps Zara's school records bore looking into.

"I have a question I'd like to ask you, my lady," Eva said to Amelia. "It's about Nurse Delacy. I noticed you and she didn't return immediately to the dining hall, and when you did return, Julia was with you."

"The oddest thing, it was as if Nurse couldn't understand me. I might have been speaking another language entirely. She merely stood there in the middle of the infirmary, staring back at me with a blank expression. I pleaded and urged, but she didn't move. Then Julia came and Nurse snapped out of it."

"That's very odd indeed." Phoebe traded a look with Eva. "You mentioned she seemed nervous when you spoke to her this afternoon."

"More than nervous, my lady," Eva replied. "Downright frightened."

A knock sounded at the door. Before Amelia could call "Come in," the door opened and Grams crossed the threshold. A crescent-thin eyebrow rose in assessment. "So, a lengthy dinner, chess, and reading aloud isn't enough to tire you out and send you all to bed, eh?"

Amelia came to her feet. "Phoebe and I were just talking while Eva took down our hair, Grams."

"I should go and see if Lady Julia needs me," Eva murmured, and started toward the door.

"Stay right where you are, Eva. You three are as thick as thieves." Grams closed the door behind her with a soft click. She approached the sofa, and Eva ran to bring a side chair closer. Grams lowered herself into it and clasped her hands in her lap. "Now then, tell me everything you know."

CHAPTER 5

"My lady," Eva said the next morning as she laid out Phoebe's clothes, "there is something I didn't tell you last night. Something I learned from Constable Brannock."

Phoebe slipped from between the covers and swung her feet into the slippers Eva had just placed closer to the bed. "And what is that?"

Eva selected a plaid, waist-length jacket to go with the matching narrow skirt she had just draped across the foot of the bed. "Constable Brannock believes he knows what kind of poison killed Miss Finch, and if he is correct, it's less likely her death could have been an accident."

"You're only telling me this now? Why did you wait? Oh, never mind." Lady Phoebe gave a dismissive wave of her hand. "Had you told me this news yesterday I'd have had to tell Grams last night or be forced to lie to her."

Eva nodded in agreement, then went into the dressing room to retrieve a pair of leather and canvas lace-up boots. When Lady Wroxly had demanded her granddaughters tell her everything they knew, she had not pressed Eva in the same way, but seemed content with Eva's murmured accordance with what ladies Phoebe and Amelia told her. The sisters conveyed merely what they knew to be true, that the cause of death appeared to be an accidental poisoning, but the police were taking no chances and were exploring every avenue. If Lady Phoebe had chosen to leave out her own suspicions, Eva could hardly fault her for that.

When she returned with the boots, Phoebe asked, "So tell me. What kind of poison does the constable think was at work?"

Eva took the liberty of sitting on the bed beside her young mistress, cradling the meticulously cleaned boots in her lap. "Cyanide, my lady."

"My goodness. Is he certain?"

"Those blue tinges, especially beneath the fingernails, are apparently a telling sign."

"But how would such a thing as cyanide make its way to a girls' school here in the country?"

"He said some rat poisons and cleaning chemicals contain the poison. Now more than ever, the constable will want to know if anyone bore a grudge against Miss Finch."

"Then help me get dressed. We need to return to the school as soon as possible, not only to continue with our questions, but to help make arrangements for the remaining students to leave Haverleigh. They can't stay now, not with a shadow of murder hanging about the place."

"No, indeed, my lady."

After attending to Phoebe, Eva made short work of readying Lady Amelia for her day, not difficult since she would not be attending school and would be spending at least the morning hours at home. Lady Julia was another matter.

"I'd like to look my best today, Eva," the eldest Renshaw announced as Eva helped her into her satin wrapper.

Eva's heart sank, but she merely smiled and said, "Are you going somewhere special today, my lady?"

"I'm meeting a friend in the village and then we're off to Cheltenham for lunch and a bit of shopping."

"How lovely, my lady." Eva thought it unusual for Julia to have planned to meet in the village rather than here at home, and that in turn made her wonder who this friend might be. Did Julia not wish her grandparents to know with whom she planned to spend the day?

She didn't ask. Only a few months ago she had attempted to advise Lady Julia about her personal life, and had been swiftly cut off at the knees. Today she dressed Julia's hair as her ladyship wished and helped her into a stylish Worth suit of burnt-orange wool trimmed with beaver at the collar and cuffs. Lovely for spring, yet warm enough to ward off any lingering winter chill. Julia dismissed her, and Eva breathed a sigh of relief.

By midmorning, she and Lady Phoebe arrived at Haver-leigh. Upon entering the building, Eva swallowed against the faint queasiness that always assailed her whenever she traveled by motorcar. She doubted she'd ever get used to it, but no use complaining, as automobiles were here to stay.

Muffled voices drifted from behind closed doors, yet even so, the place held an unnatural stillness for a school day. "I don't suppose they're holding regular classes after what happened," Eva whispered.

Phoebe gestured to a nearby classroom. "Nor are they leaving the girls to their own devices. It sounds as if the French mistress is talking to the students rather than con-ducting a lesson."

"They must be discussing what happened. I'm sure the girls are terribly upset and bewildered."

Phoebe nodded and moved on, leading the way down the hall to the administrative offices. She knocked on the door marked MISS VERITY SEDGEWICK, ASSISTANT HEADMISTRESS, but it was from the room next door that a voice called out to them.

"If you're looking for me, I'm in here."

The door that bore the placard MISS HENRIETTA FINCH, HEADMISTRESS stood ajar, and Phoebe opened it wider and led the way inside. Miss Sedgewick, a woman perhaps two or three years older than Eva, sat behind the paneled oak desk, ledgers open before her, a pen in her hand. She was an attractive woman, with glossy raven hair and eyes rimmed with sable lashes, and skin so pale as to be nearly translucent, but for a pleasing blush of color in her cheeks. Eva sometimes wondered whether her striking looks were entirely natural, or helped along with a skillful use of the cosmetics slowly becoming popular with even respectable women.

"Good morning, Miss Sedgewick," Phoebe said in greeting. "I hope we're not interrupting you."

The woman placed her fountain pen in its holder beside a matching inkwell. "Not at all. What might I do for you, Lady Phoebe? I noticed Lady Amelia did not come back to school today, or have you brought her with you?"

"No, my grandmother has chosen to keep her at home presently."

"I'm most sorry to hear that. Is the poor dear terribly distraught over yesterday's tragic event?"

Were her sympathies a smidgen overplayed? Her sweetness rather cloying? Eva watched Miss Sedgewick closely as Phoebe replied to her question.

"My sister is aggrieved over what happened, of course, but my grandmother's decision to keep her home is a precaution. One that might be best exercised with all the girls."

"Why do you say that?" Miss Sedgewick tilted her head and arched her bold brows. "All possible contaminants have been removed from the pantries and iceboxes. Why, just this morning, another delivery of fresh foodstuffs arrived, so there can be no more accidents. My students are quite safe, I assure you."

My students, she said. Eva stole a sideways glance at Phoebe. Had she noticed the slip? For a slip it had to have been. There had not yet been time for the school's governing body to determine who would replace Miss Finch.

"Can you be so certain, and is it worth the risk?" Phoebe persisted.

Miss Sedgewick's lovely dark eyes turned to Eva. A manicured hand, smooth and white, pointed toward the wall. "Miss Huntford, do move that chair closer so your mistress may sit."

It was not the order that rankled, for indeed it was just the sort of thing a lady's maid was accustomed to doing. Yet, a note in Miss Sedgewick's tone had seemed intent on reminding Eva of her place.

Well and good did Eva know her place. She didn't need anyone to remind her.

She brought the chair closer and held it while Phoebe settled into it. Then Eva backed up several steps and simply stood. As soon as the other two resumed talking, however, her pique faded and a sense of foolishness came over her. Had Miss Sedgewick really spoken with anything other than a desire to see Lady Phoebe made comfortable?

She had to admit Phoebe and Amelia had spoiled her, treating her at times more like a friend than a servant. She could not and should not expect the same from others.

"Indeed, Lady Phoebe," Miss Sedgewick was saying, "a number of the students were whisked home yesterday by their mamas—understandable, perhaps, but in my opinion unnecessary. I believe they'll soon see reason and return their daughters to school. In the meantime, I am easing the remaining girls back into their lessons. Carrying on is the best policy for them. Creating a panic through a mass exodus will do no one any good."

Phoebe glanced over her shoulder at Eva, her expression conveying a private message: what now? Eva gave a slight shrug and an even smaller shake of her head. There was nothing to be done, then, until the police reached a more definitive conclusion about Miss Finch's death. While caution seemed the most reasonable course, especially where children were concerned, Miss Sedgewick seemed immovable on the subject of sending the students home. The assistant headmistress had, however, made one quite reasonable observation, which was that creating a panic would do no one any good. And Eva felt sure introducing the word *cyanide* to the conversation would send ripples of fear and panic throughout the school.

No, they must wait for the police to make their official statement.

Phoebe came to her feet, as did the assistant headmistress. Phoebe extended her hand and Miss Sedgewick shook it lightly. "Thank you, Miss Sedgewick. We won't keep you any longer. If there is anything we at Foxwood Hall can do to assist you, you need only ask."

"Thank you, my lady. That is most generous of you." She came around the desk. "I'll see you out."

"No need. Eva and I don't wish to keep you from your work. Besides, we thought we'd linger and speak with the older girls, see how they're holding up after yesterday."

Miss Sedgewick's cordial smile slipped. "They're doing quite well, my lady. It would be rather irregular—"

"Yes, but you see, as a member of the governing body, my grandmother asked me to check on them."

"Did she?"

Phoebe raised her eyebrows and nodded.

"I see. Well, then, in that case. I believe half the sixth form girls are having their French lesson and the other half are"—she glanced at the locket watch pinned to her blouse—"at Etiquette and Elocution." With a sigh the woman returned to her chair.

"We'll wait until their lessons have ended."

In the corridor, Phoebe drew Eva away from the doorway. "Perhaps as I talk to some of the girls, you might take Jane Timmons aside. She and Zara Worthington don't get along, but Jane is quite able to stand up for herself. Something tells me the girl is an observant one. And I thought you might be the better choice to speak with her."

"I'd be happy to, my lady. Jane and I have a common bond in being the daughters of local farmers. Perhaps she'll feel comfortable confiding in me."

The rumble of a heavy vehicle pulling up the drive and a blaring honk-honking drew them to the sidelights on either side of the front door. Not one but two approaching vehicles spit gravel from beneath their tires.

"More deliveries for the kitchen?" Eva mused out loud.

"Why, Eva, that's Owen Seabright. What on earth is he doing here?"

Before Eva could venture a guess, Phoebe hurried outside and down the steps to the drive. Eva followed and remained beside her while Phoebe waited for a lorry and, leading the way, a sporty motorcar to pull up. At the speed at which the latter was traveling, Eve didn't feel entirely confident she would not have to push her mistress out of harm's way.

The motor car, its top down, was a three-wheeled Morgan Runabout with two wheels in front and one in back. Such lightweight cyclecars had been known to leave competitors behind in a cloud of exhaust in many a national race prior to the war.

Ugh. Riding in Lady Phoebe's Vauxhall was bad enough. The thought of a vehicle capable of such high speeds made Eva's knees wobble. Apparently, she wasn't the only one wobbling as the car came to a stop. Phoebe made a funny little sound, half-muffled cry and half squeak, as the Runabout skidded to a stop.

Phoebe watched in disbelief as Owen Seabright—Major Lord Owen Seabright—braked the Runabout and stood up on its floorboards. Turning to her, he reached up and dragged his herringbone cap from his head, exposing thick black hair that was appealingly tousled. What a cavalier figure he cut standing above her with his arms outstretched, his grin broad and carefree, and his shoulders straining his unbelted trench coat that undulated with every ripple of the breeze.

She waited for the blush that seemed always to creep into her cheeks at the very sight of this man, this war hero who commanded the respect and admiration of others despite his being shy of thirty by two, perhaps three years. The Seabrights were old friends of the Renshaws, his grandfather having been a great friend of Grampapa. He had spent last Christmas at Foxwood Hall, and she had hardly been able to glance in his direction without a mortifying and telling heat claiming her face. Yet, when she had been so certain he considered her merely a child, he had taken her in his arms and kissed her.

And then he had left Foxwood Hall, and she had not seen or heard from him since.

Now she realized two things. One, that perhaps the spring breeze, tinged with morning coolness, had saved her from that dreadful blush. And two, she stood with her hands pressed to her lips in a show of feminine delicacy. That wouldn't do. She dropped her arms to her sides, then crossed them in front of her, and raised her chin.

"Owen, what a pleasant surprise," she said more calmly than she felt. Behind him, the lorry squealed to a stop with a belch of black, smelly oil. "High time you decided to grace us with your presence."

With that, she pivoted on her heel, climbed the steps, and went back inside. A moment later, Eva's tread echoed behind her.

"My lady, what was that about?"

"I haven't the faintest idea. The man quite disappeared after Christmas, didn't he? One can only assume he found our little hamlet a crashing bore to be avoided at all costs." She kept walking—to where, she didn't know. She had no destination in mind, except to put distance between herself and Owen Seabright, at least until she regained her composure. Honestly, showing up out of the blue without a word of warning. What was he thinking?

"Why are you angry?" Eva's shoes pattered faster as she caught up with Phoebe's brisk pace. "My lady, don't you find anything at all coincidental that he brought a lorry with him?"

Phoebe stopped and turned so suddenly, Eva ploughed into her. They caught each other's forearms for balance, and then Phoebe frowned. "What do you mean?"

"The lorry, my lady. The donation collection. Perhaps he's brought more supplies."

"Yes, the lorry. I hadn't thought of that." A wave of chagrin mingled with her annoyance. "He took me so by surprise. Why didn't he write, or telephone or . . . something?"

"I couldn't say, my lady."

She blew out a breath. "I suppose I'd better go apologize."

At that moment, however, a bell chimed, and doors opened, both upstairs and down. Uniformed students streamed out in orderly lines, but as soon as they began to merge in the open hallway all sense of order became swept away in a rushing tide of comings and goings. Girls ascended the stairs as others came down. The switch between lessons, Phoebe surmised. She craned to see above heads to the front door, which now stood open upon a bright burst of sunlight, cool air, and a tousled gleam of darkness towering above the students.

Phoebe began wending her way to him, like swimming against a relentless current, until little by little the crowded hallway became less so. Finally, the classroom doors closed once more and only the muffled voices of the teachers could be heard.

That left Phoebe facing Owen with only a couple of comfortable yards between them. "It's good to see you again," she said contritely.

"Could have fooled me." His words accused but his grin forgave. "I'm sorry. I should have heralded my imminent arrival in some socially acceptable way."

She decided the safest course was to let the matter drop. "Why *have* you come?"

"Your donation drive, of course. Your grandfather told me all about it when we spoke last week."

A little ember sparked and burned just beneath her breastbone. He had spoken to Grampapa? Telephoned the house and not asked to speak with her? She resisted the urge to let her bottom lip slide between her teeth. Instead, she found a smile and a gracious word. "How very kind of you. What have you brought?"

He laughed lightly. "Need you ask? Woolens from my mills, of course. Bolts of fabric, but also clothing and blankets." He sobered and leaned in a bit closer. "Can they be of use to you?"

"No, not to me. But to the many families struggling since the war ended, yes, they'll be of great use."

"Then come and see." He took her hand and headed for the door. "By the way, there's still room in the lorry, so if you like, we can load up what you've collected here and you can tell me where you'd like the deliveries made."

Phoebe halted; a half a step later he stopped and turned

to her with a quizzical look. "Owen, thank you. This is very kind of you."

He smiled, spreading warmth inside her. "We'll talk, Phoebe. I know you're peeved with me. You have a right."

She was already shaking her head, saying no, but he placed a finger across her lips. "No use denying it." His gaze strayed to Eva, still hovering behind them. Phoebe smiled and nodded to her, a signal that everything was all right. For she knew her own behavior influenced Eva's. If Phoebe was angry with someone, Eva was likely to be sympathetically angry as well. She was forever supporting Phoebe, physically, emotionally, and in whatever whim happened to seize Phoebe at any particular time.

"Eva," she said, "perhaps you'll let Miss Sedgewick know we'll be moving the donations out of the dining hall. I believe the school has a new handyman. Please inquire if he's available to help."

"Yes, my lady." Eva bobbed a curtsey and turned around to go.

The lorry, Phoebe discovered, was more than half filled with boxes, but the remaining space appeared adequate for the supplies waiting inside. It looked to be an army surplus vehicle recommissioned for civilian use, with SEABRIGHT TEXTILES emblazoned in blue and gold lettering above the windshield and along the side of the bed. Beneath the lettering, a round seal peeked out proudly from a green background. *My goodness, the eagle and star— isn't that part of the Seabright coat of arms?* She couldn't help chuckling as she pointed. "Your family must positively squirm when they see this."

"They do their best not to see it. In fact, they do their best not to see me. It can't be easy for them, having a son dirtying his hands in trade."

Owen hailed from an old landed family, and if Phoebe thought Grams was hopelessly entrenched in the old world with its strict etiquette and hard and fast rules, Owen's parents made her look positively avant-garde. But that hadn't stopped him from taking an inheritance from his maternal grandfather and turning it into a lucrative endeavor, not to mention a useful one.

"How many people do you employ now?"

"Between the scouring plant, the looms, sewing machines, storage and shipping, several hundred."

"You don't say." Phoebe hadn't expected quite that number. "Men and women?"

"Yes, men and women both."

"And you treat them fairly and pay them well?"

His lips curled in a smile that split upon a burst of laughter. "I've missed you, Phoebe."

"Then why did you stay away so long, and with barely a peep out of you?" As soon as she'd spoken, she wished she hadn't.

"You *have* been angry with me."

She studied him from beneath her brows, and then shook her head. "Never mind. Come, I'll show you what we've collected so far." But inside, when they reached the threshold of the dining hall, she came to a jarring halt, feeling as though the breath had been knocked out of her. She hadn't entered the room since the police had cleared it yesterday, and the memory—the cries and shrieks and the horrible thud of Miss Finch hitting the table—rose up like a barricade to block her entrance.

"Phoebe, what is it?"

"That's right. You wouldn't have heard yet. Owen, something terrible happened here yesterday."

"I'd thought you and your mistress had left, Miss Huntford." Miss Sedgewick scrutinized Eva's length, down and then up again, assessing every inch along the way. Eva surmised she was supposed to feel self-conscious of her plain black dress, gray overcoat, and serviceable low-heeled shoes, but she only wished to deliver her message and be gone. "Have you forgotten something?"

"No, indeed, Miss Sedgewick. There is a delivery outside of more supplies for the donation drive, and rather than add them to what we have here, we are going to move the items collected by the students out to the lorry. Would the handyman be available to help?"

Miss Sedgewick came to her feet, her attractive features tightening. "No one informed me of this arrival. Who is this mystery benefactor? I certainly don't intend loading up the fruits of our efforts into the lorry of a total stranger."

"The benefactor is Lord Owen Seabright, and he has only just arrived. He owns Seabright Textiles, you see, and he is no stranger to Lady Phoebe and her family."

"Humph." She pursed her lips and seemed to consider, her brows gathering. Finally, she tossed down her pen. "I'll go and greet him, and discuss what is to be done."

Eva said nothing, but wondered what on earth made the woman believe she was suddenly in charge of the project initiated by Lady Phoebe. Then she remembered the second part of her quest. "Is the handyman available?"

"I wouldn't know. You'll have to find him and ask him yourself."

"Is there no telephone line to his quarters?" There hadn't been when she had attended Haverleigh on scholarship, but that had been ten years ago.

"No, Miss Huntford, there is not. You'll find him in and around the work sheds or greenhouse. His name is Elliot Ivers, and to tell you the truth, he's a bit of an idiot. Now, if you'll excuse me, I mustn't keep my guest waiting another moment."

Miss Sedgewick, dressed in a sea blue silk suit with an elongating skirt edged in satin, came around the desk and strode past Eva, summarily dismissing her. Her perfume, however, lingered, making Eva's nose itch as it had yesterday.

She wondered again how Miss Sedgewick managed to dress so far above her income. What other indulgences did the assistant headmistress enjoy, and how did she come by them?

Setting her curiosity aside, she made her way down the corridor, passing other classrooms that had once been a morning room, a ladies' sitting room, a conservatory, and, of course, the music room, now Nurse Delacy's infirmary. She thought about checking in on the woman, to see if her nervous disposition persisted, but first she needed to find the handyman.

She knew her way around well enough, and in fact as a student had worked in the school greenhouse, among other jobs, as a way to defer costs not covered by her scholarship. As at Foxwood Hall, a high wall of hedges concealed the greenhouse and work sheds from view. Bordering the rear-facing terrace, a small flower garden was just awakening from its winter slumber with a pretty mosaic of snow-drops, camellias, and the sunny tips of daffodils pushing through the soil. Beyond the garden, Haverleigh's grounds consisted of tennis and badminton courts, a cricket field, a lawn bowls green, a croquet course, and, in the distance, the pond where the girls rowed in summer and skated in winter.

Eva smiled as memories assailed her. Not that she hadn't been challenged by girls like Zara Worthington. As a village girl attending on scholarship, she had been considered by some of her peers—and even some teachers—a charity supplicant, there by the grace of her betters. Which was true, she supposed. She shrugged now as she often had then. No matter what anyone said about her, she knew an opportunity when she saw one and wasn't fool enough to turn her back to it because someone called her a name or wouldn't allow her to sit at their luncheon table.

But, love her parents though she did, coming to Haverleigh had transported her to a completely different—and completely wonderful—world than she had known on the farm. While the wealthy girls had lamented the plainness of their uniforms, Eva had privately reveled in the near-perfect fit, the quality of the fabric, and the fact that no one else had owned the garments before her. And going out-of-doors no longer meant tending to livestock and plucking eggs from beneath hens, but coming out to these grounds to engage in friendly competition and games of skill.

She might have become a teacher, but her education had been cut short after Dad's accident—a broken wrist that mercifully healed well. But it had taken months to set properly and Eva had been needed back at home. Home she had gone with never a word of complaint in her parents' hearing, for they could not have borne the guilt of her disappointment, especially when her scholarship had been retracted and given to another girl. Well. She had learned enough at school to rise from farm girl to cook's assistant to her present position at Foxwood Hall.

At the towering privet hedge, she came to a gate tucked into the foliage. From somewhere on the other side someone whistled a tune. She went through, trying to remember the name Miss Sedgewick had spoken. Mr. Evers? Mr. Inness? She spotted him at the open door of a shed, a wrench in one hand and a mallet in the other.

"Mr. . . . em . . ."

He closed the shed door and turned his back to Eva as he ambled along the path leading to the greenhouse. He was a lanky man with a long, loose stride. She hurried to catch up to him. "Mr. . . . Evans, is it? If I might speak with you a moment. . . ."

Clad in a plaid flannel shirt and corduroy work trousers,

he continued on as if he hadn't heard her. Was he hard of hearing? Eva was running now, and only caught up to him because he stopped to search his pocket for a ring of keys, and then find the correct one to unlock the greenhouse door. Eva came up behind him.

"Excuse me, I wonder if you might lend me a hand."

He whirled around to face her, his expression filled with such alarm, Eva thought immediately of Nurse Delacy. She waited for him to say something—to smile and laugh away the obvious start she had given him. But he didn't. He said nothing and didn't make a move.

Up close she saw that he was much younger than expected, more boy than man, or was it the result of his startled expression?

She chuckled awkwardly. "I'm terribly sorry to have startled you. There's something in the house we'd like your help with. Miss Sedgewick told me where I'd find you," she added when his features failed to relax. He couldn't quite be as old as Phoebe, she decided, nor had he quite achieved a grown man's physique. His dark hair, though cropped short, looked as if he hadn't run a comb through it upon waking that morning, and now that Eva took a better look at him, his wrinkled clothes suggested he might have slept in them.

"Miss Sedgewick," he repeated, his voice devoid of inflection.

"Yes, that's right." Eva tried to smile reassuringly. "She sent me out to find you."

"No." He recoiled and attempted to back away, but hit the greenhouse door hard enough to rattle the panes. "I didn't mean to . . . didn't . . ."

It was Eva's turn to grow alarmed, yet in his demeanor she found something so familiar, it tugged at her heart. Fear, a sense of being utterly lost—she saw it in his unfocused eyes just as she had seen it the day they'd received the news that Lord Wroxly's son had perished in the war. Each of her young ladies had been rendered inconsolable. Even Julia—especially Julia. She had cried in Eva's arms and clutched at her shoulders until they had throbbed from the pressure of a relentless grip. After crying herself out, Lady Julia had pulled away, wiped her eyes, and sworn never to speak of her father's death again. To Eva's knowledge, she had made good on that promise.

But this boy showed none of Julia's strength or resolve. Her better sense urged her to retreat down the path, put as much distance between her and this obviously unbalanced young man as she could. Yet, she couldn't persuade herself to move.

"Please, is there something I can do for you? Someone I can send for?" Did he know of Miss Finch's death? Perhaps she had shown him kindness, and now he feared for his employment. That certainly made sense. She thought better of mentioning the headmistress now, as he might become even more distraught. Instead she said, "Why don't you come inside with me? Perhaps the cook might make you a cup of tea, and then you can help us with the packages we're loading." When he didn't move, she reached out and touched his elbow.

He snatched his arm away, cried out some unintelligible words, and darted past her. He had disappeared from sight before Eva could sufficiently recover from her astonishment to turn around and see where he went.

CHAPTER 6

Owen blanched as Phoebe described the events of the previous day. More than once his gaze strayed through the doorway into the dining hall, to the very table where Miss Finch had breathed her final, choking breath.

When she finished, he reached for her hand and held it in both of his. "Dear Lord, Phoebe, this is too much. You shouldn't have to live through such a thing ever again. But at least this isn't quite the same as what happened at Christmas. That was murder, and this—"

"Could be murder as well. We don't yet know. The police believe—or at least Constable Brannock believes—she was poisoned with cyanide. He's waiting for the coroner's official report."

"A good thing Brannock's still on the job. He certainly proved his worth at Christmas." He released an audible breath. "Well, I should think you'll stay out of this one." His gaze narrowed. "But you won't, will you?"

She smiled down at their joined hands and partially rejoiced that the embarrassing blushes that typically plagued her in Owen's presence seemed to have permanently subsided. "Actually, the constable asked Eva and me to see what we could find out from the staff and students. It's easier for us to talk to them than for him, as I'm sure you can understand."

"Speak with whom?" a voice behind them asked.

As if being caught doing something elicit, Phoebe slipped her hand from Owen's. She lamented the loss of his strong fingers around hers for a second or two, before Miss Sedgewick swept toward them, her raised eyebrows indicating she did, indeed, just catch them at something. Or was that merely Phoebe's imagination?

The woman's rolling, feline stride made her flowing skirt undulate in gentle waves. She extended her hand several paces away, acting very much the hostess welcoming a guest. A cloud of perfume enveloped Phoebe.

"Miss Sedgewick," she said after clearing her throat, "this is Lord Owen Seabright. He has brought more donations from his own mills, and he has offered to help us transport everything to the Red Cross distribution centers."

"My deepest condolences on the loss of your headmistress." Owen grasped her hand and bowed slightly over it before releasing her.

"Yes, thank you." Miss Sedgewick's sorrowful look lasted all of an instant before she gazed up at him with a beaming countenance. "My lord, your assistance with the donations is most generous. On behalf of the entire school, I cannot thank you enough."

"You're very welcome, but it's Lady Phoebe you should thank. This was all her idea, from what I understand."

"Oh?" Miss Sedgewick smiled a bit too prettily for Phoebe's liking. "Well, it was, after all, a joint effort. Without the school—"

"That's true," Phoebe interrupted her. "Without Miss Finch's gracious cooperation, we would not have achieved nearly so much. And of course there was the hard work of the students. They truly rose to the occasion. I'm very proud of them all."

Miss Sedgewick's smile, frozen in place, lost a measure of its enthusiasm. She turned her attention back to Owen in a manner obviously meant to exclude Phoebe. "I do hope you'll stay and be my guest for tea. Would you care for a tour of our little school? We're very proud of what we accomplish with our young ladies."

"I'm sure you are," Owen replied with another deferential bob of his head, "but I'm afraid I'll have to decline both, for now. We need to load these boxes. I believe we're waiting for your handyman, if he's available."

"Now that's odd. I sent Lady Phoebe's maid out for him some minutes ago. She should have returned by now." Her lips curled at the corners. "Lady Phoebe, is your maid in the habit of becoming lost?"

"No, she is not," Phoebe all but snapped. A brisk clicking of heels sounded in the main hall.

Miss Sedgewick chuckled. "Why, that must be her now, and from the sounds of it, she is alone. If you'll excuse me, I suppose I'll have to go and find Elliot myself."

Before Miss Sedgewick could leave, Eva came through the doorway, lines of anxiety etched in her face. She and Miss Sedgewick assessed each other from head to toe, and then Miss Sedgewick once more excused herself and swept away.

Phoebe gestured for Eva to join her and Owen. "What's wrong?"

Her maid came to a breathless halt. "I can't say with any certainty, my lady, but I just tried to engage the handyman's services, and he reacted in the queerest way." She described the encounter.

"This is the second person to behave this way since yesterday." For Owen's benefit, Phoebe explained, "Yesterday, Eva tried to speak with the school nurse, and the woman reacted in a similar manner. Isn't that right, Eva?"

"Indeed, my lady." Eva's expression conveyed bewilderment. "Perhaps it's me."

"It is most certainly not you," Phoebe assured her. "But something very odd is going on at this school. Do you think the nurse and the handyman could have been afraid of Miss Finch?"

"I suppose, but it was when I mentioned Miss Sedgewick to the handyman that his nervousness turned to fear and he babbled about not having done—well, whatever it was. He never made anything clear."

"You say he seemed disoriented and childlike?" Owen asked.

"He did, my lord."

"Dangerous?"

"No, I wouldn't say dangerous. I had no sense of that. Merely fearful. Before I went looking for him Miss Sedgewick told me he was something of an idiot—to use her word."

"Perhaps the poor man was wounded in the war, and left permanently addled." Phoebe turned to Owen. "Is that possible?"

"Certainly. I've seen it before. Almost anything can set off an episode—thunder, sudden noises, surprises . . . Many soldiers continuously relive the horrors of the battlefield, even believe bombs are dropping or they're about to be caught in machine gun fire."

"How horrible. I did take him by surprise," Eva said with dismay. "Had I known of his condition, I certainly would have approached him differently."

Phoebe patted her hand. "I'm sure you would have. It wasn't your fault. Miss Sedgewick should have been more specific. But if the man is a war veteran, perhaps something can be done for him. Perhaps a doctor can help him. This *is* what the RCVF is all about—helping those who served our country. But some needs are beyond the comfort of blankets and warm clothing. I think this bears looking into."

"Yes, it does. We'll need to find out more." Owen went to the table and hefted a crate. "In the meantime, since our handyman appears to be missing in action, I'll carry these out, while my lorry driver loads and arranges."

"I'll help." Eva lifted one of the smaller parcels, still a sizable load. Phoebe picked up another. Miss Sedgewick returned, this time with a slender youth whose shoulders barely filled his work shirt. He stood with his head bent, eyes on the floor.

"I found him," Miss Sedgewick said, "right where I said he'd be, Miss Huntford. Funny you didn't see him." Her tone implied it wasn't at all funny, but an oversight that caused her considerable inconvenience. "My dear Lady Phoebe, you mustn't carry that, you'll strain yourself. And you, Lord Owen—we can't have you injuring your back." She darted an order over her shoulder. "Don't stand there sulking at your shoes, boy. Go and take those cartons this instant."

The youth stepped forward but halted, his gaze shifting from Phoebe to Owen to Eva and back. He obviously didn't know whom to relieve first of his or her burden. "Never mind, this is nothing," Phoebe said, despite the slight ache already spreading across her shoulders. "Not heavy at all."

"Nor is this." Owen stepped past the young man. "And we'll finish much more quickly if we all lend a hand." With his chin he gestured toward the table holding the donations. The handyman—Elliot, Phoebe believed Miss Sedgewick had called him—straightened his shoulders and hoisted the largest of the crates, one Phoebe would have thought needed the strength of two men. Yet he accomplished the feat as if the container held nothing more substantial than goose down. With a sure stride he left the dining hall.

Now it was Miss Sedgewick who appeared uncertain as to what to do next. She hesitantly walked to the table, eyeing the various bundles. Owen followed Elliot into the main hall, and Eva went out next, clearly ignoring the assistant headmistress.

"Perhaps, Miss Sedgewick, you might open the front door for us," Phoebe suggested.

"Oh . . . yes, of course." The woman trotted out after the others, and with a mocking grin and a shake of her head, Phoebe trailed after her.

With the truck loaded and ready to be off, Eva left Lady Phoebe and Lord Owen to say their good-byes. She felt no qualms about doing so. In fact, quite the contrary. If something were to grow between them, as Eva felt fairly certain it would, she would feel safe in the knowledge that her lady could not do better. Events at Christmas had more than proved that. But Lady Phoebe wasn't ready, not for something lasting. She had more maturing to do, more confidence to gain, more knowledge of the world to acquire. But someday, the several years' difference in age between her and Lord Owen, which now seemed so formidable to Phoebe, would shrink away to nothing, and Phoebe would know herself to be his equal. Then, and only then, would a commitment between them be possible.

As Phoebe asked her to do, she returned to Miss Finch's office. Upon being beckoned with an offhand "come" in response to her knock, she entered and said, "Miss Sedgewick, I'd like to ask you about the handyman."

The woman, her nose once more practically buried in school documents, looked up with a scowl. "I'm frightfully busy, Miss Huntford. Miss Finch, I'm afraid, did not leave the most accurate of accounts, and I am burdened with the task of making sense of them."

Were there discrepancies? Had Miss Finch been skimming off the school finances? And if so, had someone discovered her thievery and decided to be rid of her? That would seem to implicate a member of the governing body, for who else would have access to the accounting records? Except for Miss Sedgewick, of course. Eva would have liked to question the assistant headmistress, or better yet, look over her shoulder at the records. But had Miss Finch truly kept untidy accounts, or did Miss Sedgewick merely want the governing body to believe so? Eva felt inclined to believe the latter. Then Miss Sedgewick could take credit for restoring order and garner their praise.

"I won't keep you long," Eva said. "Do you know what's wrong with the handyman? Did he fight in the war?"

Miss Sedgewick sighed. "What difference does it make? He is as he is. Honestly, I don't know why Miss Finch hired him. True, the previous handyman retired, but there are others to be found in the world, aren't there? This one simply showed up one day, and Miss Finch informed me he would be employed here from now on. I suppose she felt sorry for him or some such nonsense. If you ask me, he should be given the sack immediately."

"Does he not perform his job to your satisfaction? Just now we found him to follow directions to the letter, and my goodness, his strength. What else could anyone want in a handyman?"

"He's not right, I tell you," the other woman murmured. She tapped the end of her pen on the desktop for emphasis. "Not right in the head."

"Which should earn him our compassion, not our disdain, Miss Sedgewick."

"Meaning exactly what, Miss Huntford?"

Eva had already gone too far. Why stop now? "Meaning, I think you're being very unkind."

"How dare you? Do you know whom you are addressing? That you, a maid, should be so impertinent. I'm no farm girl, Miss Huntford. If not for my father's lack of a son, which led to some distant cousin inheriting my family's wealth, I should be at this moment living in a great country house in Hereford. Perhaps you've heard of it? Bennington Downs."

Eva kept her chin level and calmly replied, "No, I haven't heard of it."

"No? Of course not. Why should you have?" She allowed her gaze to dip, as she had done previously, taking in every nuance of Eva's serviceable attire. A pity she didn't realize her scrutiny didn't discompose Eva in the least. One of them felt satisfaction with her lot in life, and it clearly wasn't Miss Sedgewick. Her origins would explain her penchant for expensive clothing, although not her means of coming by them. And yet she wore precious little jewelry, and what she did wear—the little pearl drop earrings, the locket attached to a gold chain—were commonplace enough. The clothing and the jewelry simply didn't match, and Eva wondered why.

"My concern is merely for Mr. Ivers," she said. "If he is a war veteran, perhaps Lady Phoebe can arrange for him to be helped."

"Yes, lovely. Are we quite finished?" Miss Sedgewick flicked her wrist in dismissal. "As I said, I'm frightfully busy."

"For now." Eva hesitated, weighing the wisdom of uttering one last comment. In the end, she couldn't help herself. "Don't worry, Miss Sedgewick. I'm sure the governing body will find a competent headmistress before too long. And then your burdens will be lifted."

She caught the merest edge of fury sharpening Miss Sedgewick's features before pivoting on her heel and leaving the office.

Phoebe quickly discovered the difficulty in attempting to speak with the students individually. There were simply too many of them. She needed a way to winnow them down to the few most intimately tied to Miss Finch. In the common room used by the sixth form girls, she hosted afternoon tea, though she had asked Mrs. Honeychurch to provide sandwiches rather than cakes. The latter, she feared, would summon ghastly images of the day before and unduly upset the girls. They crowded onto every surface that might be used to sit upon, including pillows on the floor. They were not quite twenty in number now, however, for some had left yesterday with their mothers. Gently, Phoebe encouraged them to speak of their favorite subjects, favorite teachers, their plans after graduation. As yesterday in the kitchen, she found herself focusing on the same three students.

Today saw them considerably subdued, their squabbles, for the moment, forgotten. Zara Worthington treated Jane Timmons to only the slightest curl of her lip when they found themselves seated close together. Lilyanne sat apart from the rest, but this struck Phoebe as a matter of habit rather than any present sullenness, for the girl seemed content to sip her tea and pluck sandwiches as the trays were passed around. Yet, unless Phoebe was imagining things, an undercurrent ran between all three, subtly connecting them. Whenever one shared her experiences at Haverleigh, the others paid close heed. Not so the other girls, whose attention wandered once someone else spoke.

"She frightened me a little, sometimes," Lilyanne Mucklow admitted in a particularly unguarded moment, in reply to Phoebe's suggestion that they share memories of Miss Finch. "She was so . . ." Her brow creased as she searched for the right word. "So *large*." When some of the girls giggled, Lilyanne blushed deeply and shook her head. "I don't mean physically. I mean her way of speaking and moving and her insistence that we learn to do the same. I found it terribly off-putting and, well, discomfiting." Her fair cheeks burned. "But I suppose I shouldn't say such things. Not now."

There were a few nods of agreement, although whether they were agreeing with Lilyanne's assessment of Miss Finch, or agreeing that she shouldn't speak critically of the woman, was not clear to Phoebe. Most of the girls merely reached for another sandwich.

"She wanted us to be able to assert ourselves," Jane Timmons clarified in her husky voice. Phoebe heard a faint note of impatience, as if perhaps Jane and Lilyanne had discussed this before. "She wanted us to not only have knowledge, but be able to use it. The days of retiring young ladies are over, and Miss Finch wished to prepare us for the modern world."

" 'Modern world.' " Zara Worthington scoffed. "What does that mean, precisely? I never felt Miss Finch ever made it particularly clear. What are all these opportunities now open to women? No one can really say, can they? It's not as though people are at all eager to put their health in the hands of lady doctors, or allow a female to oversee their finances. If you ask me, nothing much has changed at all. You either marry well and live a happy life, or you struggle as people have *always* struggled. *How* they struggle may have changed a bit, but the fact of it has not and there's an end to it."

Nods of assent followed this declaration, much to

Phoebe's dismay. She had hoped these young girls possessed more of an adventurous spirit.

"Our new headmistress, whomever she will be," ventured another student, "might not share Miss Finch's views. Doesn't that mean school will go back to the way it used to be, with dance and French and music and the rest, but without all those other subjects Miss Finch insisted we learn?"

"I for one will not miss algebra or chemistry," said a pretty, plump girl with lovely golden hair that reminded Phoebe of Amelia's.

Remembering what Eva had told her earlier—that she believed Miss Sedgewick badly wanted the position of headmistress—Phoebe decided to test out the notion on the girls.

"Perhaps Miss Sedgewick will take over for Miss Finch. Surely she will continue with Miss Finch's curriculum."

"Hardly," Zara said with a laugh.

"Are you saying they disagreed on that point?"

Several girls traded glances and nodded.

Phoebe hoped she wasn't pushing her luck with her next question, for she didn't want the girls to realize the purpose behind her queries. "Was it a point of contention between them?"

When no one volunteered a reply, but rather slid their gazes away, Phoebe prompted, "It's perfectly natural for colleagues to disagree. In fact, it's often desired. It creates a rather healthy balance."

Murmurs of agreement mingled with deeper sounds of dissent. Phoebe didn't pursue the matter any further, at least not that aspect of it. "At any rate, Miss Sedgewick could very well be your next headmistress. Unless, of course, she doesn't wish to be." Though a statement, she let her voice rise as if asking a question.

Jane, who sat near Phoebe, spoke so quietly, most of the others could not have heard her—but Phoebe most certainly did. "Miss Finch will be rolling in her grave if Miss Sedgewick takes over."

Zara apparently heard as well, for she gasped and then compressed her lips without commenting. Phoebe held Jane's gaze a long moment. The girl obviously felt no qualms about what she'd said, for she showed no hint of taking it back. Defiance danced in her hazel eyes, and the confidence of her own convictions brought an entirely new dynamic to her unremarkable features, one that assured Phoebe that, though a farm girl she might be, Jane Timmons would venture far beyond those fields and pastures once she left school.

Yes, Jane embodied just the sort of girl who would benefit from Miss Finch's educational philosophies. Yet many people, including parents, would disapprove, of both society girls abandoning their traditional roles, and of ordinary girls taking it into their heads to rise above their stations.

From beyond the common room, the schedule bell chimed. The girls put their teacups and plates aside and came to their feet. "It's time for our group music lesson," Zara announced. In addition to individual lessons, the sixth form girls formed an orchestra three days a week. Such had been the case in Phoebe's day as well, although her musical talents were negligible at best, much to Grams's dismay.

As the girls streamed out, Lilyanne made her way over. "Lady Phoebe, when will Amelia be returning to school?"

"It's just Phoebe, Lilyanne, and I hope soon. Shall I tell her you said hello?"

"Yes, all right. Tell her I . . . miss her." The girl gave an almost apologetic smile before turning abruptly and striding away.

Phoebe couldn't help feeling sorry for her. To be so shy and ill at ease certainly set one at a disadvantage generally, but never more so than at boarding school, where such traits landed one solidly at the bottom of the pecking order. She sighed, watching the girl trail after her peers. Just as Phoebe felt certain Jane Timmons would be a leader in whatever she undertook in life, she felt equally certain Lilyanne would become a shadow at the edge of the crowd. Unless, of course, someone took her in hand and showed her how to trust in her own abilities.

As the patter of the girls' footsteps receded, the two kitchen maids appeared with large trays and promptly began gathering up the remnants of tea. Eva appeared next, looking pale.

"My lady, Chief Inspector Perkins, Constable Brannock, and Mr. Amstead have all arrived."

The Reverend Mr. Amstead was the head of the school's governing body as well as the school's spiritual advisor. His presence here meant something significant had happened. Phoebe placed a stack of plates on a tray as a swarm of butterflies took flight in her stomach. "They have news?"

"Yes. Come quickly." As they started down the stairs, Eva told her, "Constable Brannock found me after I'd spoken with the French mistress, who, by the way, seemed quite believably content with her position here and had no issues with Miss Finch. Neither did several of the teachers I've spoken with. But the constable said the coroner has submitted his report. They're in Miss Finch's office."

"Miss Sedgewick certainly didn't waste any time in claiming her new territory. Let's hurry." She continued down almost at a run, then skidded around the corner of the staircase in her hurry to hear the news firsthand. Miss Sedgewick's door stood closed, but Phoebe didn't wait for a reply to her knock before entering.

All gazes swiveled in her direction. Judging by the inward slash of her eyebrows, Miss Sedgewick clearly disapproved of this intrusion. Chief Inspector Perkins, looking disheveled in an ill fitting Norfolk jacket and matching trousers, gruffly cleared his throat. "I'll thank you ladies to wait outside. We have business to discuss."

Phoebe drew herself up and looked him straight in the eye. "Inspector, I am here on behalf of my grandmother, who, as you well know, is a senior member of the governing body. She will want a firsthand account of whatever it is you've come here to say."

"Humph. Very well." His lips pinched, he turned to face Miss Sedgewick.

Mr. Amstead studied Phoebe a moment longer, as if weighing her ability to comprehend important matters, and perhaps entertaining a doubt or two. They did not know each other well, for the vicar presided over the Anglican congregation in the neighboring town of Kenswick, while Phoebe and her family attended the smaller church here in Little Barlow.

Mr. Amstead was a middle-aged man, perhaps in his forties, with peppered hair and a hunch that was not the result of old age, but rather of spending the better part of his time with his books. As Grams had told her, the vicar had been widowed several years ago, and found solace in his theological studies rather than seeking the company of a new wife.

Chief Inspector Perkins cleared his throat and drew in his paunch as much as he was able. "Miss Sedgewick, it is time to close the school and send your students home."

"Close the school?" The assistant headmistress pushed to her feet. "You can't mean that. Mr. Amstead, surely you don't agree. Miss Finch's death is tragic indeed, but—"

"Now, Miss Sedgewick," the vicar said in a placating

tone, "hysterics won't help matters. Please listen to what the chief inspector has to say."

"I assure you I am not hysterical, sir. I merely—"

Mr. Amstead laced his hands together and raised them as if in prayer. "Miss Sedgewick, please."

"But . . ." She sank back into her chair.

"You see," Inspector Perkins said more gently than Phoebe would have given him credit for, "it now looks as if the poisoning might not have been accidental. The coroner has confirmed cyanide as the cause of death. And that opens up the possibility that someone intentionally murdered poor Miss Finch."

"Oh, but . . ." Miss Sedgewick's voice trembled. For the first time since Phoebe had met her, she appeared at a loss. "Who would do such a beastly thing? And why?"

"That is what we intend to find out, ma'am. In the meantime, the safest course would be to send the girls home."

"But what will happen to the school?" Miss Sedgewick silently appealed to each man in turn, as if one of them must hold the answer. "This could mean the end of Haverleigh. Once word of this gets out, we'll be ruined."

"Not necessarily, Miss Sedgewick." Mr. Amstead's tone of condescension could not be missed. "Once the culprit has been discovered and apprehended, we may continue as always. I am not necessarily in agreement with the inspector on the need to evacuate the students, but his views take precedence here. I am sure this is only a temporary precaution. Isn't that correct, Inspector?"

"Most certainly," he agreed, though in Phoebe's opinion he didn't sound as if he held much conviction. He sounded more like a man in a hurry to be off. "Miss Sedgewick, please begin notifying parents immediately. This very afternoon."

"All right, if you insist." Miss Sedgewick shook her

head with a look of concern. "But I happen to know a few of our parents are abroad at the moment, or come from rather far off. What shall be done about those girls?"

"They're welcome at Foxwood Hall," Phoebe spoke up. "And I've no doubt other local families would be happy to help out as well."

"I'm sure that would be satisfactory. Thank you, Lady Phoebe." The young woman opened a drawer, slid out a notebook, and began leafing through it. "What a horrid turn of events. Poor Miss Finch!" She glanced up from the open book with a mournful frown. "We had our little differences, you know, but she was a mentor to me, and a dear friend."

Her sorrow raised a lump in Phoebe's throat. Her acknowledgment that disparities had existed between her and Miss Finch rang true with what Jane Timmons had said, but also revealed a softer side to the assistant headmistress. She had been easy to dislike, especially after the way she treated Eva, but perhaps they had been too quick to judge.

"The staff, however, should remain," the reverend said. The others regarded him in surprise, Phoebe included. Eva and Constable Brannock, listening but silent these many minutes, traded incredulous glances.

"Will that not put them at risk?" Phoebe asked.

"Perhaps," the man said with a lift of a tufted eyebrow, "but it will also send the message to parents and our benefactors that the school has every intention of reopening once the investigation is complete and the guilty party is behind bars. And there is no reason to believe anyone but Miss Finch should be targeted. Isn't that correct, Inspector?"

"Yes . . . er . . . generally speaking, there is no reason to believe anyone else will fall victim. Most murders are crimes of passion. The well-thought-out murder spree is a rare event indeed."

Tell that to the victims of Jack the Ripper, Phoebe thought.

"There you are then." The vicar held out his hands and smiled. "Wouldn't you agree this is the best course, Miss Sedgewick?"

"I . . . whatever you say, sir."

CHAPTER 7

Once the first telephone calls were placed, parents began arriving almost immediately. Chauffeur-driven mamas in fur-trimmed coats came sweeping through the corridors to scoop up their daughters and whisk them to safety. Eva offered to help with the packing and the distributing of last-minute assignments, but Miles Brannock had another idea.

"Eva, will you come and lend me a hand?" He spoke without stopping on his way up the main staircase. He didn't pause to see if she would follow. She hesitated. What could he want? She hoped it wasn't an excuse to be alone with her. She watched his retreating back, tall and straight inside his uniform coat, and realized he would not allow personal concerns to interfere with police business. The very idea was absurd, and a sense of foolishness gripped her as she started the climb.

He led her beyond the second-floor classrooms and opened a door upon a bedroom large enough to have once belonged to the lady of the house. There all similarities ended, for the furniture here, though more than adequate, was of plain pine and durable fabrics. The constable momentarily took Eva aback with the boldness of his stride as he entered the room. Whenever she entered one of her ladies' bedrooms at Foxwood, it was with a respectfully soft step that acknowledged her place in their household. However, she soon realized the occupant of this particular bedroom would not be returning.

"This is Miss Finch's room."

"Aye." The constable stopped to scan the furnishings. "I've never had to search through a woman's things before. That's why I asked for your help. As a lady's maid, you're far more accustomed than I as to where a woman might stash her secrets."

That brought a disconcerting wave of heat to her face. She turned away. "What are we looking for?"

"Anything out of the ordinary, or something that might allow us a glimpse into the headmistress's life."

"A diary, perhaps?"

"Or correspondence." He approached the writing desk and glanced back at her over his shoulder. "Would you take the wardrobe? And the bureau, if you wouldn't mind."

As he bent over the desk to open the first of several drawers, Eva smiled at the notion that this often irreverent man would shy away from rummaging through a woman's personal effects. Her smile quickly faded as she remembered Lady Phoebe doing just that last winter, although it had been a man's belongings she had riffled through. Her dear Lady Phoebe, touching a man's unmentionables . . . and very nearly being caught!

She drew in a breath and squared her shoulders. The wardrobe let out a whine as she opened the double doors, as if to protest the intrusion. A waft of scent assaulted her nose. Not Miss Sedgewick's expensive Brise de Violettes, but something obviously less expensive, judging by the cloying sweetness that nearly made Eva sneeze. A variety of items hung before her, from shirtwaists to skirts to walking ensembles to dinner gowns. Though a respectable enough wardrobe, simplicity defined the whole, which Eva judged by the quality to be store-bought, machine-made, and not personally tailored. She slid each garment along the cross-bar to separate it from the rest, and slipped her fingers into pockets and folds. Next she crouched and examined the floor of the closet and found only an assortment of house shoes and slippers. She almost backed away and closed the doors, but noticed the upper shelf just above her head.

"There might be something up here, but I can't see."

The constable slid a desk drawer closed and crossed to her. "I'll look."

He did so easily, without having to crane his neck much at all, and Eva became very much aware of his greater height and the bulk of his uniform-clad shoulder beside her own. She noticed, too, a slight trace of hair tonic lingering about him, and as she breathed it in, a funny sensation gathered in the center of her stomach. Inhaling again, she compressed her lips and let her eyes fall closed. . . .

"Eva?"

With a start she opened her eyes.

"Are you all right? You looked as though you might faint."

"No, I . . ." Oh, dear. She what? Quickly, she turned to face the room. "I was just thinking of where to search next."

"The bureau," he said, a slight grin forming on his lips, one on which she dared not focus.

"Yes. Of course." She moved away from him, and immediately regained her equilibrium. Or almost immediately. In truth, she somewhat blindly opened the bureau's topmost drawer and plunged her hands into piles of folded fabrics.

She felt the heat of Miles Brannock's scrutiny on her another moment before he went to the small bedside cabinet. Eva gradually focused on her task. The drawer contained handkerchiefs, scarves, and stockings. She even pulled up an edge of the satin drawer liner, but nothing appeared to her searching gaze. One after another she searched through underthings, petticoats, nightgowns, and more. If Miss Finch had anything to hide, she certainly hadn't put it in the obvious places.

"Would you mind very much checking through her jewelry box?"

At the constable's request, she pushed the last drawer closed and pressed to her feet. On the dressing table sat a rather plain wooden box with a bit of marquetry along the edges, and a silver clasp that opened easily at the flick of her fingertip. Still standing, she bent lower to examine the contents before realizing she might take the liberty of perching on the cushioned bench. Just as barging into the room had felt untoward, so did making herself at home at the dressing table of another woman, and a woman who had been her superior in every way.

Lady Phoebe would scold her for that kind of thinking, but shedding such notions came much easier to an earl's granddaughter than to such as she—grateful for her position and unwilling to jeopardize her future.

"Do you see anything unusual?"

Once again, Eva started at Miles Brannock's nearness as he leaned over her shoulder.

"Em . . . let's see." There wasn't much. A few strands of beads, a few bracelets and hair combs, some earrings. "None of this appears very valuable."

"Is there anything a man might have given her? Anything that strikes you as romantic?"

She couldn't help angling a glance up at him through the mirror and releasing a chuckle. Simply hearing the word *romantic* from this man's lips seemed as absurd as it was unexpected. She wondered, what did Miles Brannock find romantic?

She swallowed and returned her attention to the jewelry box, removing several items and laying them out across the tabletop. "Crystals, jet, enamel, brass—there really is nothing here of great value or that speaks of a male admirer." And then the implications of his query struck her. "Are you suggesting a suitor might have murdered her?"

"Suitor, beau—it's more common than you would care to think."

"Well, as I said, there is nothing here that indicates there had been a man in her life. Poor Miss Finch," she couldn't help adding.

"Indeed. But where else to look?"

Eva replaced the jewelry and closed the box. She then glanced through the dressing table drawers but found only hair pins, creams, powders, and pots of rouge. The woman's brush and comb set lay before her. She ran her fingers over the smooth wooden handles and thought how odd, and how utterly sad, that their mistress would never again lift them from the table and set about the nightly routine of brushing out the day's coif.

She swiveled around on the bench, turning her back to the abandoned tools of a woman's daily toilette. Where else might Miss Finch hide something of importance, if indeed she possessed anything to be shielded from prying eyes? Beneath the mattress?

"Miss Finch seems to have been a woman without secrets," she mused aloud.

"Everyone has secrets," the constable corrected her. "And sometimes the best hiding place is in plain sight, right under everyone's noses."

"Eva, there you are." Lady Phoebe stood in the open doorway. "I've been looking for you."

Eva surged to her feet. "I'm so sorry, my lady. I—"

"It's my fault, Lady Phoebe," the constable said from across the room. He didn't look particularly contrite. "I asked Miss Huntford to lend a hand in looking through the victim's possessions."

"Yes, so I see." Lady Phoebe crossed the threshold. "It's no matter, Eva. But it seems Zara, Jane, and Lilyanne are all to come home with us, since their parents cannot come for them at present. They're packed and ready to go."

"Zara, Jane, and Lilyanne?" Eva repeated, incredulous.

"Yes, you see Zara's parents are abroad, Lilyanne's father is a widower and an MP, presently tied up with a Parliamentary committee, and it seems Jane Timmons's younger siblings are all down with head colds."

"Goodness, my lady, we shall have our work cut out for us, shan't we?"

Lady Phoebe's only reply was a wry lift of her eyebrows.

"Eva, what on earth is going on? Who are these girls who just stampeded past my door?" Lady Julia stood at the open door of her bedroom, one hand on the knob and the other propped on her hip. She wore her dressing gown, and a single braid dipped over one shoulder to dangle in a rope of gold halfway to her waist.

Eva burned to question Lady Julia in return, for she hadn't yet arrived home last night when Eva helped ready the others for bed. It was none of her business, of course, but her protective instincts buzzed. She worried for Lady Julia. No matter what Phoebe claimed about changing times, well-bred young ladies didn't stay out until all hours, especially after merely going shopping with a friend. Or *had* Julia gone shopping, and did she return home last night, or early this morning?

Sometimes Julia seemed bent on being another Lady Diana Manners, who shocked society before the war by going about unchaperoned with a wild set and turning up in all manner of unsavory places. Eva didn't know how or why her parents, the Duke and Duchess of Rutland, had put up with such behavior, but Lady Wroxly surely would not.

Eva couldn't help herself. "I trust you enjoyed your shopping excursion into Cheltenham yesterday, my lady?" If her tone hinted at something other than an innocent shopping trip, Lady Julia should realize that if Eva noticed her inappropriate actions, others would as well.

"Yes, I did, thank you, Eva." Julia's gaze burned into her. "Now would you please inform me as to why our tranquil home is suddenly overflowing with teenaged girls? Was that Zara Worthington I saw leading the pack?"

"It was, my lady. She and two other girls from the school will be staying with us until their parents can make arrangements for them to return home."

Julia leaned against the lintel and wrapped both arms around herself. "You can't mean they've closed the school?"

"They have indeed, my lady." She caught Lady Julia up on what the police had concluded thus far.

"Cyanide." Lady Julia shook her blond head and hugged herself tighter as if warding off a chill. Then her nose wrinkled. "How long will they be here?"

"I really couldn't say, my lady. Would you like me to ready you for the day?"

"I suppose you've been charged with looking after all of us?"

Eva inclined her head, not trusting herself to answer verbally lest she give the impression the arrangement was not to her liking.

Lady Julia smiled sympathetically. "Poor Eva. Well, I for one shall make myself as scarce as possible and not add to your burdens."

"It's no burden, my lady." Eva certainly didn't want

Lady Julia engaging in any reckless behavior—like staying out most or all of the night—on her account. "I truly don't mind. Besides, the girls seem very cooperative and willing to help each other with as many tasks as they can manage. Ladies Phoebe and Amelia even helped the others arrange their hair."

"Even Zara?"

Eva couldn't help laughing at her skeptical tone. "Lady Zara did require a bit more handiwork than the others."

"Well, please help me arrange mine and then I'll be happy to do for myself."

"My lady, really, it's my job, after all."

Lady Julia had turned into the room, but now stopped and said over her shoulder, "Eva, how often am I this considerate?" Before Eva could venture an answer, she went on. "If I were you, I'd seize what is sure to prove an exceedingly rare opportunity."

Not long after setting Lady Julia to rights, Eva received a summons to report to the Petite Salon, a lovely little parlor on the ground floor overlooking the corner gardens. She arrived to find Lady Amelia and their three guests seated around the table often used for informal meals in the absence of company. There were no place settings in front of the girls, however, but textbooks, pens, and paper. Lady Wroxly and Lady Phoebe occupied the camelback settee near the bay window, their heads bowed over the assignment instructions handed out to the students before they left Haverleigh. Lady Wroxly wore her habitual black silk, as she had since her son died in the war, her only concession to a later stage of mourning being that the fabric possessed a sheen rather than the dull crepe of full mourning.

"I should think we can handle this rather nicely, as long as we keep to a strict schedule," the countess said in her precise diction. "French immediately after breakfast, fol-

lowed by mathematics. I believe we shall amend the curriculum a bit to reflect the type of figuring required by a
wife in the running of her household."

Lady Phoebe stiffened. Her jaw pulsed, no doubt with
words she struggled to hold back. Considering how Lady
Phoebe approved of Miss Finch's curriculum, she must
burn to protest her grandmother's interference.

"And then there is history," Lady Wroxly continued.
"After luncheon comes literature—I see their reading has
already been assigned—and science." Her head came up.
"I believe your grandfather will be most happy to lead them
in their science studies. Plants, butterflies, a bit of stargaz-
ing." Lady Phoebe's forehead wrinkled in obvious perplex-
ity but she remained silent as her grandmother went on.
"Perhaps he'd enjoy taking on the history lessons as well.
Following tea, they may make use of the music room to
practice their instruments and the library for quiet study.
After dinner—"

A groan rose from the table. Her ladyship wasted no
time in ferreting out its source. "Zara, are you suffering
from indigestion?"

"No, Lady Wroxly."

"Then perhaps you detect a flaw in the scheduling of
your studies?"

The girl's full lips turned down in a pout. "No, Lady
Wroxly."

"Good. Then let's commence, shall we?" Her ladyship
came to her feet, something she did without assistance and
that brought her to the considerable height of nearly six
feet. Lady Wroxly carried herself straight and tall, with
nary a hunch as so many women of stature were wont to
do. Her black skirts, floor length in the old style, swept the
Aubusson rug as she came around the table. She picked up
a cloth-bound volume and opened it to where a ribbon
marked the place. "Now then, I shall oversee your French

lesson, after which Eva and my granddaughter will take over with mathematics. *Maintenant, ouvrez vos livres et commençons. Jeanne, veuillez lire et traduire le premier paragraphe de la page cinquante-sept?"*

Eva joined Lady Phoebe on the settee. As the girls opened their French textbooks and Jane Timmons began reading, in a passable accent, the paragraph Lady Wroxly had indicated, an uncomfortable sensation came over Eva. She had once wished to be a teacher, true, but she had cut her studies short and felt no more qualified to lead a lesson than the girls themselves. Why, Zara Worthington and Jane Timmons had each completed more schooling than Eva, who never made it past the lower sixth form.

Would the girls perceive her deficiencies and refuse to take her seriously? At present they were paying close attention to the countess. Even Zara Worthington seemed intent on making a good impression. But of course, her parents would be well acquainted with Lady Wroxly, and Zara could never hope to misbehave for her ladyship and get away with it.

Amelia said Zara excelled academically, but no one could discover how she did it since they never saw her studying. Perhaps that mystery would be revealed in the next several days, or however long this situation lasted.

After correcting Jane's syntax one or twice, Lady Wroxly said, *"Lilyanne, veuillez prendre plus de Jeanne?"*

It was Lilyanne's turn to read and translate. A wave of crimson swept from her neck to her hairline, clashing garishly with her cinnamon-colored spirals only partially tamed by pins and hair combs. Beside her, Zara lowered her face over her book and snorted—not loud, but loud enough to be heard by all. Lilyanne's complexion turned brighter still and beads of perspiration dotted her brow.

Lady Wroxly snapped her own book closed. *"Zara, nous n'avons pas tolérer l'impolitesse en cette maison."*

Eva had learned enough French to translate: We do not tolerate rudeness in this house.

Zara flinched upright, the bloom in her own cheeks deepening. She raised dark eyebrows in a show of innocence. "Yes, Lady Wroxly. Forgive me."

"*En français,*" the countess sternly insisted.

"*Oui, Madame. Pardonne-moi.*"

With a lift of her eyebrow, her ladyship turned back to Lilyanne, whose fiery discomfiture showed no sign of relenting. "*Procéder.*"

Displaying none of Jane's confidence, Lilyanne began a faltering recitation, stumbling every few words. Her poor performance brought a decided pinch to Lady Wroxly's lips, but the woman rose to the occasion by not allowing her patience to fail her. Instead, she quietly hinted at the pronunciations each time they eluded poor Lilyanne's tongue.

Eva's palms became moist on the girl's behalf, and on her own behalf as well, for once again she considered her inadequacies as a teacher and wondered how on earth she would pretend she had anything significant to convey to these girls. A whisper broke into her insecurities.

"Is something wrong? You're not feeling ill, are you?"

Eva merely shook her head, but Lady Phoebe responded with clear disbelief in the tilt of her chin.

"I don't believe I'm up to this, my lady," Eva confessed in a whisper.

"Nonsense. Besides, you're mostly here for moral support for me. You'll help me keep them in line," Phoebe said with a quiet chuckle. "And we are taking their mathematics lesson beyond household concerns, providing I can persuade Grams to amuse herself elsewhere."

A throat-clearing interrupted their murmurs, and Eva glanced up to discover Lady Wroxly raining disapproval down on them both. Lady Phoebe leaned away and Eva folded her hands in her lap and cast her gaze contritely on the floor. Goodness, when the countess looked at her like that, she might as well still be a schoolgirl herself. She listened attentively until it was time to begin the math lesson.

"I think that went splendidly," Phoebe declared nearly an hour later as she and Eva crossed the Great Hall together. Minutes ago, Grampapa relieved them of their schoolroom duties by enthusiastically stepping in with a rousing lesson on the Restoration. He even came equipped with books from Foxwood's library, several maps, and a letter written by Edward Hyde, first Earl of Clarendon, who was instrumental in restoring the monarchy.

"It went much better than I'd feared," Eva conceded.

"I don't know what you were worried about. They're teenaged girls. We have nothing to prove to them, other than they must do as we say." Phoebe smiled at the thought of Zara Worthington's failed attempt to explain the difference between algebraic expressions and transcendental numbers. "Did you notice how Zara struggled?"

"I did, my lady. It's puzzling, given her academic merits at school."

"My thoughts exactly."

"Perhaps the distress of Miss Finch's death and the upheaval of leaving school has had its effects on her."

"Perhaps." Yet Phoebe's curiosity over the discrepancy in Zara's performance persisted. Though decidedly none of her business, she felt the urge to do a little poking about in school records. "You know, Eva, there could be something significant about Zara's good marks."

Eva came to a halt, her expression shrewd. "Do you mean her marks might be fabricated?"

"It's possible, isn't it? Especially considering who her parents are. The Earl and Countess of Benton are among the school's most generous benefactors. In fact, such has been the case for several generations now."

Through the dining room doorway, footmen Vernon and Douglas could be seen setting up for luncheon. Phoebe drew Eva aside, out of their view. "Do you suppose Miss Finch had been inflating Zara's marks to keep her parents happy?"

Eva compressed her lips and darted a glance at the dining room. She leaned closer to Phoebe. "I've another theory, my lady. Have you noticed Miss Sedgewick's clothing? I would swear she wore a Poiret the other day at the luncheon, and if her perfume isn't the same Brise de Violettes you received for your last birthday, I'm not worth my weight in old pewter as a lady's maid."

Phoebe considered. She *had* noticed Miss Sedgewick's costly fashions, and thought perhaps they had come to her secondhand from a relative, or that her father's heir treated her generously when it came to her wardrobe. But . . . "Do you think Miss Sedgewick has been adjusting Zara's marks, and Miss Finch found out and . . ."

"I'm only making observations, my lady." Eva drew a breath and let it out slowly. "But I might not be the most objective person to make such judgments. To be honest, I don't like the woman. And she does not care for me."

"As long as we're being honest, I don't particularly care for her either. But you can be certain I intend to get to the bottom of Zara's academic performance. By the end of the day we should have an even better idea of where she excels and where she shows deficiencies. She did do well in French, but my guess is she has spent a lot of time in France with her parents. Oh, and now that I think about it, I believe she had a French governess. Amelia might know. I'll ask her at the first opportunity."

"Whether Miss Sedgewick has been changing Zara's marks or not, I am convinced she has coveted the headmistress's position for some time, my lady."

"Yes, but is either a motive for murder?"

With that thought, Phoebe freed Eva to attend to her chores belowstairs. She hated to admit it but Julia had been right when she accused Phoebe of monopolizing most of Eva's time. That wasn't fair to her sisters, nor to Eva herself. There were shoes to clean, jewelry to polish, and clothing to press, not to mention the minor alterations Eva often made to their garments. Thank goodness more staff had been hired in the months since the war ended, so that Eva no longer needed to help out with other tasks belowstairs.

There were still nowhere near as many servants on the estate as before the war, but even Grams and Grampapa conceded that the world had changed dramatically. House parties were smaller, meals rather less elaborate, and the old dictates about which rooms may be used at particular times of the day had been relaxed considerably. Before, the Petite Salon would never have been used for dinner nor the library for coffee afterward, and rarely had the same room been used for more than one purpose throughout the day. Yet, they still dressed for dinner. Grams insisted, for it was what "civilized people do." And poor Eva now had twice as many ladies to see to each morning and evening.

Grams in her wisdom had assigned their visitors bed-rooms in the family wing, rather than the guest wing on the other side of the gallery. That was why, hours later, a chorus of voices floated up and down the corridor outside Phoebe's room, accompanied now and again by the tramping of footsteps that made her wonder if young ladies or a battalion of foot soldiers had accompanied her home from Haverleigh. Meanwhile, her fears for Eva—and Eva's sanity—appeared to be coming true as that stalwart soul hurried back and forth between rooms.

Phoebe was just sliding a final pin to the simple bun she had fashioned herself when a shout and a cry sent her leaping up from her dressing table. Holding her evening dress so the hem wouldn't catch beneath her heel, she followed the sounds of acrimony into the room that had once been her parents'. Jane Timmons and Lilyanne Mucklow were sharing this room, and Phoebe was surprised upon entering to find Zara Worthington standing at one end of a fringed, velvet shawl while at the other stood Lilyanne. The garment was stretched out between them as each gripped a corner and tugged. Lilyanne's face flamed. Zara's bright blue eyes all but fired bullets at the other girl.

Off to one side, a much calmer Jane said, "You'll tear it in half, and then neither of you will have it."

"It's mine," Zara snapped. "Mother brought it home from her last trip to Venice. This little sneak stole it from my room."

"It is *not* yours." Lilyanne's voice was choked with sobs, and a tear rolled down the girl's ruddy cheek.

Phoebe grasped the shawl halfway between the two girls. "Both of you let go at once. You're acting like children, and if my grandmother should hear you, she'll—" Phoebe broke off, but she needed no further persuasion than mention of Grams. Both girls released their corner and the shawl drooped on either side of Phoebe's half-closed fist. "There now. What is this all about?"

"She stole it."

"It's mine."

The two girls spoke at once, so that Phoebe shook her head and raised both hands to her ears. "It will soon be *my* shawl if you cannot explain in a civilized manner." She chuckled inwardly. When had she started to sound so like a teacher? This morning's lesson had left its mark upon her as much as on the girls.

Perhaps more so. Right now they certainly weren't acting like educated young women.

"Lilyanne," she said, "tell me your version of what happened."

The girl's freckled arm came up, an accusing finger

pointing at Zara. "She came barging in here and pulled my shawl right off my shoulders."

"That's because it's mine!"

Amelia came into the room with Eva close behind her, both looking bemused. Amelia's hair was half up and half trailing over one shoulder, waiting to be pinned in place. "What's going on in here?"

Without answering her, Phoebe held up the shawl and appealed to Eva. "Do you remember unpacking just such a shawl for Lady Zara?"

"Why, yes, I do, my lady."

"Would you please go and get it?"

Eva left and returned several moments later with a nearly identical garment draped across her forearms. "Is this it?"

They beheld a velvet shawl in tones of russet, deep blue, and subdued gold, in many respects quite similar to Lilyanne's. On closer inspection, however, Zara's bore a leaf pattern, while Lilyanne's sported florals.

"Zara? Is that one yours?"

The girl's pout emphasized the slope of a decidedly weak chin. "I suppose it is."

"Then don't you owe Lilyanne an apology?"

Zara's lips flattened. "I'm sorry. It was an easy mistake, given how similar yours is to mine." She ended with a barcly audible *humph,* as if the similarities were somehow Lilyanne's fault.

"Hardly what I would call a gracious apology, but thank you, Zara." Phoebe handed the shawl she held to its proper owner. "Are you all right, dear?"

Looking at the floor, Lilyanne nodded.

"Then I propose we all finish readying ourselves for dinner." Phoebe went to her sister and affectionately tugged at the loose section of hair. "We can't have you showing up in the dining room half undone, now can we?"

Some twenty minutes later, Phoebe pulled up the rear as she herded the girls along the corridor. Julia, looking lovely as usual in a dress of black lace draped over green silk, fell into step beside her.

"High time you ventured out of your room," Phoebe teased. "You missed all the fun."

"A calculated move on my part. I heard quite enough through my door, thank you."

"That may be, but I should think you might take a turn entertaining our guests after dinner and before bedtime. Eva and I, as well as Grams and Grampapa, have had more than enough of them for one day."

"Sorry, I won't be here. I'm going out after dinner."

As Julia spoke, Grams's bedroom door opened. Grams halted on the threshold and raised a crescent eyebrow. "Indeed, you are *not* going out, Julia. You are needed here tonight."

"Oh, Grams, not tonight." Julia sighed, long and loud. "I promise I'll take them on a tour of the gardens tomorrow. Or help them with their French. Or whatever you wish me to do."

"This has nothing to do with the girls." Grams smiled archly, raising a little frisson of anticipation at Phoebe's nape. "We're expecting another guest for dinner tonight. In fact, I'm quite sure he's already here, having a chat with your grandfather. Having the girls here is a bit of an inconvenience, considering, but it can't be helped."

Julia assumed a wary expression. "What other guest?"

"Wallace Bagot has returned from India, and he's very keen to see you." Grams stepped closer and added in a whisper, "He's inherited his estate, you know."

Julia groaned. "Good heavens, Grams, not Wally Bagot."

Grams merely smiled and breezed past them. Phoebe started to follow, but stopped when she noticed Julia hadn't moved. "Well? Aren't you coming? Wally is keen to see you, after all," some imp inside her made her add, along with a nonchalant "I suppose this changes your plans for later."

The disappointment on Julia's face made Phoebe wish she'd held her tongue, while at the same time piquing her curiosity as to whom Julia had planned to meet. She didn't dare ask, especially when Julia honed in on her with such disdain, Phoebe nearly flinched.

"I'm sorry," Phoebe said contritely. "I can see you're disappointed. If you like, I could try to distract Wally away so you can make your exit."

Julia sniggered. "As if you could. You really are intolerable. You do realize that, don't you?" With that, Julia brushed by her, her elbow jostling Phoebe's as she went.

CHAPTER 8

"My lady, do you know about Lilyanne's knee?" The next morning, Eva brushed the braid out of Lady Phoebe's hair and prepared to coil it in a simple twist, as she typically wore it. "It seems she had an accident on the tennis court. Another player swung her racket right into her knee, opening a gash that required stitches."

"I'd no idea. When was this?"

"About a week before the luncheon. I noticed the wound as I helped her on with her stockings this morning. You'll never guess who the offending player was."

Lady Phoebe, who had been gazing at Eva through the dressing table mirror, turned full around to face her. "Not Zara, surely?" Eva nodded, and Phoebe sighed. "We had better keep close watch on those girls. We can't have one of our charges suffering open wounds during their stay here. How ever would we explain to their parents?"

"Zara claims it was entirely an accident. They were playing doubles. If you ask me, my lady, their tennis instructor should have known better than to pair the two of them."

"Who is the instructor? Is it one of the teachers?"

"Miss Everett, the household studies teacher. But that's not all. When I asked Lilyanne about it, she said Nurse Delacy acted strangely that day. 'Un-nurselike.' And when I asked her what *that* meant, she said upon first examining the wound, the nurse suddenly excused herself and hurried away. She left Lilyanne sitting in the infirmary all alone, holding a compress to her bleeding knee."

"Good heavens. Then what happened?"

"Some ten minutes passed, and then the nurse returned and tended her patient. She offered no explanation, nothing. Just simply returned, cleaned the wound, and stitched it up. Meanwhile Miss Finch had gotten word of the accident from Miss Everett, and arrived at the infirmary a few minutes before Nurse Delacy returned. According to Lilyanne, the headmistress was most displeased. I believe the word she used was *livid*."

"Did she tell you how Miss Finch addressed the matter? Was Nurse Delacy reprimanded?"

"Lilyanne didn't say, but I daresay no official action was taken against the nurse with Lilyanne present."

"No, of course not." Lady Phoebe, obviously mulling over this information, turned back around to face the mirror, and Eva continued winding her red-gold hair into a tidy coif and pinned it into place. "This is all very odd indeed. First you report that the woman is as skittish as a grouse in hunting season, and now it seems she balks over the job she was hired to do. Where did she work prior to coming to Haverleigh?"

"She never said, not in my hearing. She only referred to her position at Haverleigh as being less taxing than working in a hospital."

"I believe it's time we discovered a bit more about Nurse Delacy. Let's plan on returning to Haverleigh right after the mathematics lesson this morning."

"Very good, my lady."

Phoebe sat silently a few moments longer while Eva retrieved her jewelry cask and set it on the dressing table. Phoebe reached in and selected a coral and gold necklace. "If you ask me, the one person connected to the school who would know most about poisons and their effects would be Nurse Delacy. And her nervous behavior certainly casts suspicion on her."

"But what motive, my lady? Especially when compared with Miss Sedgewick, who wants the headmistress's position."

"Wanting someone's position is one thing, but being willing to kill for it is quite another." Still holding her necklace, Lady Phoebe rose and paced the width of her bedroom, coming to stand by the wide windows overlooking the rolling front grounds. Eva gathered up her discarded robe and nightgown from the bed, and then crossed the room to help Lady Phoebe on with her necklace. Outside, a light fog misted the morning sunlight angling through the trees, creating a watercolorlike effect that appeared deceptively tranquil. Violence, as both she and Lady Phoebe had learned, might lurk in the most peaceful of scenes.

Lady Phoebe turned to face her. "If cyanide was used, as Constable Brannock believes, how would someone like Miss Sedgewick come by such a thing?"

"If we knew that, my lady, everything would be much clearer."

"But what do we know about Olivia Delacy? Where is she from? What did she do before coming to Haverleigh?"

Eva didn't answer, as she knew the questions were rhetorical. The moment they concluded their lesson with the girls, Lady Phoebe bade Eva to hurry to retrieve her coat and meet Phoebe outside on the drive.

"Do let's be off." Lady Phoebe leaned across the passenger seat to open the door for Eva. "Before Grams wants to know where we're going."

But before Eva had settled herself and closed the car door, Lady Julia came bustling out of the house. Eva guessed by Lady Phoebe's tensed hands on the steering wheel that she was considering pretending she hadn't seen her sister and driving off, but Lady Julia was too quick to open the passenger door.

"Eva, would you squeeze over, please," the eldest Renshaw said rather than asked.

"Julia, we're on our way to—"

"I don't care where you're going, Phoebe, you can drop me in the village."

"There isn't room for three," Lady Phoebe protested.

That didn't deter Julia, who ducked in preparation of climbing in. Eva slid over, freeing up little more than a few inches of leather seat. Julia slid in next to her, and Eva attempted to make herself smaller still.

"Julia, is this necessary?" Phoebe tapped her hands impatiently against the steering wheel. "Why not call down to the carriage house and have Fulton collect you in one of the other motorcars? Or better still, learn to drive."

"Driving is a vulgar thing for a woman to do," Julia quipped.

"Oh? Then I'd gladly spare you the ignominy of witnessing one of my more vulgar displays."

Eva didn't miss the anxious gaze Julia darted at the house. "Just drive," she said tersely. "Or I'll complain to Grams that you're monopolizing Eva again and upsetting the routine of her daily chores."

More than anything, Eva wished to ask both sisters to leave her out of their squabble, but she kept silent. Speaking would have required she draw a full breath, and even shallow breathing was difficult enough as it was. But the family's strict policy of never discussing private matters before the servants had never extended to her as far as the Renshaw girls were concerned. Over these past few years she had been privy to more altercations, accusations, and yes, apologies, than she could count.

Phoebe put the motorcar in gear and pressed the accelerator. The Vauxhall lurched forward. "Just where are you going that you didn't wish Grams and Grampapa to know? For that is the only reason you would lower yourself to jump in with Eva and me."

"None of your business. Just drop me near the hat shop."

Lady Phoebe grinned but kept her gaze on the road. "A clandestine meeting with the milliner. How very intriguing."

"Meanwhile, you are butting into police business again." Julia, too, stared straight ahead through the windscreen. "Aren't we a pair? I'll keep your secret if you keep mine."

"Quite frankly, I don't know what your secret is." Lady Phoebe shrugged. "But I do remember Grams saying Wally Bagot would be by for luncheon."

Lady Julia made no reply, but her anger seethed in palpable waves from her person. They drove in silence until they entered the village through the medieval gates and continued down High Street, passing rows of shops constructed of Cotswolds' distinctive, creamy stone, until they reached the little milliner's shop on the corner across from the post office.

Lady Julia opened the door and slipped out. Closing the door behind her, she braced her hands on it and leaned in. "Remember, not a word. If anyone asks, you've no idea where I've gone."

Lady Phoebe merely smiled and pressed the accelerator. Eva suddenly had reason to wish Julia back in the vehicle with them. Her presence had somehow resulted in Lady Phoebe driving slower than usual, but now she sped up, prompting Eva to grip the door handle and grit her teeth as the village streaked by.

They passed the square and were about to leave the village behind them when a Silver Ghost, with its long bonnet, sleek running boards, and gleaming chrome fittings, whooshed by them. Phoebe braked so suddenly, Eva thrust both hands against the dash to prevent being propelled forward and striking her head against the windscreen. She regained her equilibrium to discover Lady Phoebe clutching the wheel and craning over her shoulder to watch the other vehicle rumble away down High Street. The color had drained from her face.

"My lady, what happened? Are you quite all right?"

She spoke in a raw, breathless rush. "That was Henry Leighton."

Alarm shot through Eva, until common sense explained what they had seen. "No, my lady, surely that was Lord Theodore Leighton, or more properly, Lord Allerton, as he is called now. He is merely driving his brother's car."

Her mistress's fingers relaxed their grip on the steering wheel, and she slowly straightened in her seat. "Of course, what a goose I am." Her eyes narrowed. "Yes . . . Theo Leighton. It makes sense now."

"What does, my lady?"

Lady Phoebe laughed lightly. "Julia came into the village to meet up with the new Lord Allerton, and she doesn't want my grandparents catching on. Poor Wally Bagot. I wonder how long it's been going on . . ." She brought the Vauxhall back into gear and resumed their drive, a little smile playing about her lips.

Eva, too, silently considered how long Lady Julia had been clandestinely seeing the new Marquess of Allerton. She thought of two nights ago, when Lady Julia had been out exceedingly late, or perhaps exceedingly early the following morning. Had she been with Lord Allerton? But why the sneaking around? Would not a marquess be considered an ideal husband for the eldest Renshaw granddaughter? But then she remembered. The new marquess inherited the title and the holdings, but little in the way of a fortune. His elder brother had squandered away most of it.

Months ago, when speaking playfully of Lady Julia's ideal husband, she had said he must be rich, among other attributes. Then why this interest in Theodore Leighton?

"Oh, hullo there, Miss Sedgewick." Phoebe poked her head into Miss Finch's office, where she knew she would find the assistant headmistress. "How are you today?"

The woman looked up from her work with a frown. "Er . . . Lady Phoebe. You're back." She hesitated a fraction of a moment before adding, "Again."

"Yes, I'm back. I wanted you to know how well the girls seem to be doing with us up at Foxwood."

"Girls?" The woman seemed to draw a blank. Today she wore a smart suit with military-style tailoring and silk moire lapels in a contrasting shade of rose. As Eva had pointed out, costly attire for an assistant headmistress.

"Yes, you know. Zara Worthington, Jane Timmons, and Lilyanne Mucklow. They're keeping well up on their studies, thanks to my grandmother's strict scheduling of their time. Although"—she watched the woman carefully as she spoke—"Zara is having a bit of difficulty. Does she typically struggle with her lessons?"

"Zara?" She sat up straighter and set down her pen. "She is one of our best students. Always high marks."

"Really? Perhaps it's the upset, and being away from familiar surroundings."

"Yes, that would be it, Lady Phoebe."

"I wonder if you might let me have a look at her marks—just to give me an idea of where she excels and where she might need a bit of extra tutoring." Her gaze drifted to the bank of wooden filing cabinets against one wall.

Miss Sedgewick followed her gaze and drew back almost defensively in her chair. "I'm afraid I cannot. Student records are quite confidential, for parents' eyes only. I'm sorry."

"I understand. I simply would hate for Zara to fall behind and have those high marks falter when she returns to school."

"We won't let that happen," Miss Sedgewick said quickly. Too quickly? Too emphatically? Perhaps. She eyed Phoebe expectantly, her impatience evident in the kink forming above one eyebrow. "Is there anything else I can do for you?"

Phoebe treated this as an invitation to sit. That knot in Miss Sedgewick's brow tightened. Phoebe spoke in a murmur. "I wished to speak with you about Nurse Delacy."

"Nurse Delacy?" She folded her arms on her desk and leaned forward. "Has she done something?"

"No, it's not that—not precisely." She decided to leave Eva's name, though not her observations, out of the conversation. "It's just that I've noticed she's a bit of a nervous sort. Would you agree?"

"Why, now that you mention it, yes. I've always thought so. I even mentioned it to Miss Finch, but she waved my concerns away. She seemed confident in Olivia Delacy's nursing skills."

"Do you know where she worked prior to coming to Haverleigh?"

"I haven't the faintest idea. I asked Miss Finch, but all she said was she had worked in hospitals for several years before coming to us." She craned forward like a baby bird straining to pluck a worm from its mother's beak. "It's all rather mysterious, if you ask me, my lady. And then there's Elliot."

"The handyman."

"Yes. He, too, came to us from nobody knows where. Except for Miss Finch."

"Did you ever simply ask Elliot where he is from?"

"My lady, you saw him. He's worse than a child. He won't speak to me at all, and says precious little to anyone else. And then there was that fright he gave me the other week."

"Fright? He seemed completely docile to me."

"Well, he . . . he tried to give me a flower."

Phoebe tried unsuccessfully not to smile. "Sounds positively devious."

"You don't understand." Her nostrils flared with wounded dignity. "He tried to force it on me. He wouldn't take no for an answer. He practically had me up against a tree, and when I told him to leave me alone, he simply wouldn't."

"Did you try taking the flower? It sounds to me like an overture of friendship."

"Lady Phoebe, I don't mean to be rude, but you obviously lack experience when it comes to dealing with mental deficiency. He may seem docile, but one never knows what will set him off. I fear he is a danger to the students, but Miss Finch simply wouldn't listen to reason."

Phoebe's experience with Elliot shed doubt on Miss Sedgewick's assessment, yet a tiny doubt niggled. Perhaps she and Eva should pay a visit to Elliot before they left Haverleigh. If anyone could speak with him, it was Eva. While loading the donations onto the truck brought by Owen Seabright, she and Elliot had established a kind of rapport, if one could call it that. It's true he had barely uttered a word, but he had smiled readily for Eva and had eagerly taken her directions in loading the packages.

But talk of the handyman had opened an opportunity for Phoebe's true purpose in visiting the assistant headmistress. "So Elliot is one of the school's more recent hires. Isn't Nurse Delacy also new to her position?" She assumed what she hoped was merely a curious, offhand expression. "Does she hail from the Cotswolds originally?"

"I believe she has once or twice referred to Aldingham,

and that her parents live there still. Not far from here, as the crow flies. But I'm afraid I know as little about her home life as I do about her former position." She pursed her lips, for a moment resembling nothing so much as an aging spinster. In an instant the illusion vanished, leaving a woman most observers would term a beauty, or nearly so. "Should I permanently take over the headmistress position, there will be no further secrets kept here at Haverleigh."

"That would certainly be your prerogative, wouldn't it? Should the position become yours, that is."

The woman's mouth tightened again, etching tiny lines that revealed her to be older than she'd perhaps like people to think. "Lady Phoebe, is there some reason you're inquiring about Nurse Delacy?" She turned her head slightly, angling her gaze. "Do you suspect her of . . . something?"

The word *murder* hung in the air between them. Phoebe had her suspicions, but she refused to react with as much as a blink. "Miss Sedgewick, I am merely concerned about the future of Haverleigh, as is the Countess of Wroxly. In future, I fully intend to become more involved than ever." She had no qualms about invoking the authority of Grams's title and her position in the school's governing body. The mention produced the desired effect on Miss Sedgewick, who almost forcibly relaxed her shoulders and smoothed the frown lines from her forehead.

"How, uh, very kind of you, my lady."

"Yes, well, the Haverleigh School means the world to me, as it does to the entire Renshaw family." She stood, bringing Miss Sedgewick to her feet as well. They shook hands across the desk, and then Phoebe turned to go. She had gotten what she came for—the name of Olivia Delacy's hometown. She hadn't lied. The future of Haverleigh concerned her greatly, and whether or not the nurse had a hand in the headmistress's demise, her delay in coming to Miss Finch's aid could speak of future troubles for the school. Granted, given the nature of the headmistress's death, there hadn't been anything anyone—doctor or nurse—could have done to change the outcome. But what if a student suffered a grievous injury or illness, and Nurse Delacy dragged her feet or was nowhere to be found at a critical moment?

What if that emergency involved Amelia?

Phoebe's concerns were enough to warrant digging into the woman's background. It appeared a drive to Aldingham was in order.

Eva and Phoebe let themselves out the French windows of the conservatory, whose function had changed little since Haverleigh had been a private home. Gone were the wrought-iron and wicker furnishings that made this an indoor garden and a haven on rainy days, but plants still grew in abundance here—palms and ferns, small fruit trees, and vibrant assortments of flowers. The girls were instructed in horticulture here, as well as in the more practical arts of flower arranging and floral decorating. Eva couldn't help smiling wryly at the thought of Jane Timmons eagerly turning her attention to the former, while Zara Worthington would only perceive the value of the latter.

"I'll be close by should you need me," Lady Phoebe said to her before Eva continued on alone.

Phoebe had filled her in on everything Miss Sedgewick said about the handyman, and now Eva longed to hear Elliot's side of the story. Could she coax the words from him? She and Lady Phoebe had decided Eva had the best chance of winning Elliot's trust if she went alone. While she didn't believe he would snap and harm her as Miss Sedgewick suggested, she did believe he flustered easily and that it wouldn't take much to render him silent.

She shielded her eyes from the noon sun as she picked

her way along the path to the gate in the privet hedge. Although the last time she had trod this path there had been no one out on the athletic fields, she had not felt the same sense of abandonment as she did today. Even with Lady Phoebe not far behind her, the utter silence resonated through the trees and grazed the stones of the house with velvet-clad fingers. She sensed the utter emptiness of Haverleigh down to the very pit of her stomach and in the core of her heart—a significant portion of which had been shaped by this place. For the first time since Miss Finch's death she perceived how very much would be lost should Haverleigh be forced to close its doors permanently.

A clang-clanging disturbed the quiet, and Eva spied Elliot through the open doorway of one of the larger maintenance sheds close to the building's kitchen wing. This housed, among other apparatus, a coal-fed generator used to power the lights and water heaters belowstairs when the general electricity failed, as it sometimes did during inclement weather. Beyond the structure, the kitchen garden stretched, where tiny green shoots poked their way through the soil.

She scraped along the graveled walkway and cleared her throat before speaking, hoping to avoid startling the young man. "Hullo there, Elliot. Making repairs?"

The mallet he'd been using to adjust a valve stopped in midair above his head as he turned. It struck Eva that having the skill to repair electrical contraptions took more than an ability to follow directions. There was no one issuing instructions now. Elliot was working independently, and surely it took an intelligent mind to do so. She suspected the handyman was not the mental deficient Miss Sedgewick believed him to be.

"Repairs," he repeated after intently studying her a moment.

"Yes, you're fixing the generator so Mrs. Honeychurch can run a smooth kitchen, yes?"

"Smooth, yes."

"I'm sorry to interrupt your work. Shall I go?" She took a chance in asking, but remaining when he might not wish her there wouldn't help her cause.

He shook his head and placed his mallet on a flat surface of the generator. "Load packages?"

She smiled. "Not today, Elliot. In fact, I came by to thank you for your help the other day and to see how you're getting on." She knew she couldn't take the direct approach and ask him outright about the incident Miss Sedgewick had referred to. "You do excellent work. It seems like quite a lot for one individual. Do you also maintain the greenhouses and the gardens?"

"Gardeners come. I help. I like the flowers."

"I see. The gardens will surely be spectacular in another couple of weeks."

He grinned and looked down at his feet. Even in the dim lighting of the shed, the tips of his ears glowed rosy with pleasure. Eva's heart warmed to him even more, while her disbelief in Miss Sedgewick's claims flourished. She took another chance.

"Flowers make such lovely gifts, don't you think?"

His grin waned. Now as he stared at the floor, a wary expression clouded his features. His shoulders sagged and he clutched at something inside his collar. Light glinted, and Eva guessed he wore some sort of necklace. "Not good to give a flower."

Her heartstrings tightened with sympathy and with guilt, too, at having obviously raised an unpleasant memory. "But it is good, Elliot. I assure you, anyone would be delighted to receive a flower from the Haverleigh gardens. I certainly would be."

He was shaking his head, his gaze still pinned on the flagstones at his feet, his fingers tightening on what she now clearly saw was a metal chain around his neck. A section of links reflected the sunlight, but the adjoining section appeared dull and tarnished. "Didn't mean to."

She eased closer to him. "Elliot, were you rebuked when trying to hand someone a flower?"

"She's pretty, and the flower was pretty." He shuddered and retreated a step or two until his back came up against the generator's main housing.

"Do you mean Miss Sedgewick?" Eva asked as gently as she would a small child.

He didn't reply. Didn't nod or shake his head or move at all. Eva felt an overwhelming urge to throttle Miss Sedgewick.

"Don't want to go," he finally whispered.

"Go where?" He didn't answer, but his meaning suddenly dawned on her. Miss Sedgewick must have threatened to sack him. All that had saved him, presumably, had been Miss Finch's authority. Now, with Miss Finch gone, Miss Sedgewick made it clear she would dismiss Elliot the moment she filled the headmistress position—*if* she did. Eva longed to reassure Elliot about his employment. The words leapt to her tongue but she allowed them to go no farther, for she could guarantee him nothing. The governing body might view Miss Sedgewick as the most qualified and convenient replacement for Miss Finch.

And then Elliot would have to go. She shook her head at the irony. With so many men lost to the war, and the legions of others who had since abandoned the countryside in favor of factory work in the cities, this gentle soul—who wanted nothing more than to tend flowers and tinker with whatever needed fixing—was to be denied work because of one woman's lack of empathy and generosity.

Ah, but Eva wasn't lady's maid to the daughters of the

House of Renshaw for nothing. Lady Phoebe, through her grandparents' influence, had worked miracles before. Eva had no doubt she would work one again.

Holding her breath and hoping she wouldn't frighten Elliot, she reached out and pressed her hand to his forearm. "Don't you worry about a thing. And if anything else upsets you, you be sure to let me know about it."

CHAPTER 9

As Phoebe turned the Vauxhall toward Aldingham, the question of who wanted Miss Finch out of the way seemed as winding and elusive as the road that disappeared and reappeared beneath the oaks and wide ash trees growing along the rolling hills. So far, she could see no clear picture of events, but only snippets of possible motives and opportunities.

"What we know so far is that Miss Sedgewick wants to be headmistress," she said to Eva, who sat clutching the door handle with one hand and the edge of the seat with the other. "Nurse Delacy was in danger of losing her position due to her odd reaction to Lilyanne's injury, and has since shown an aversion to doing her job with any measure of proficiency."

"Zara Worthington's academic performance also raises questions," Eva added through gritted teeth.

Phoebe accelerated up a hill and eased the vehicle around a bend, bringing the low stone border wall to within inches of the motorcar's side panel. She bit back a grin as beside her, Eva stiffened against the back of the seat and pressed her feet more firmly against the floorboards. "Goodness,

Eva, I'm a better motorist than that. You might try trusting me."

"I trust you, my lady. What I don't trust is hurtling down narrow lanes at speeds that were never meant for humans."

"Then you'd better hope I never take up flying."

Eva tossed her a panicked look, prompting Phoebe to let go a round of laughter.

"At any rate," she said, "Zara's marks would seem to point back to Miss Sedgewick, if indeed she had been doctoring them to keep the girl's parents happy."

"Then again, my lady, what if Miss Finch had been adjusting Lady Zara's marks, but recently had a change of heart?"

Phoebe waited for her to elaborate, but Eva returned to studying the road ahead as if she could clear it of all hazards by the sheer force of her will. "Are you suggesting that Zara might have wished ill on Miss Finch?" A rocky patch of road prompted her to tighten her hands on the steering wheel while the vehicle tottered and bounced. "It's difficult to envision a child committing murder. . . ."

Eva didn't drag her gaze from the road. "She's not much younger than you, my lady. And she did bake Miss Finch's Madeira cake."

"Yes, you're right. We can overlook no one." Before them, the trees parted like curtains to reveal the distant shops and homes of a village scattered across a wide valley, surrounded by a checkerboard of fields and pastures. A river intersected one end of the village, spanned at several points by pretty stone bridges. "That would be Aldingham up ahead."

"Thank goodness," Eva murmured. The road took a winding route into the valley and brought them to a thoroughfare similar to that of Little Barlow, lined by quaint, gable-roofed structures of warm-hued, Cotswold stone. Pedestrians bearing parcels traveled the sidewalks, going in and out of shop doors and stopping to chat on corners. "So now what, my lady? We haven't got an address. Do we just start asking questions of strangers on the street?"

Phoebe slowed the motorcar. "I'm not sure. This seemed like such a good idea—" In midsentence she jolted the Vauxhall to an abrupt stop, sending both herself and Eva lurching toward the dash.

Eva stopped her forward momentum with one hand while thrusting an arm across Phoebe to keep her in her seat. "My lady, I do wish you wouldn't do that!"

"Sorry." But as Eva set herself to rights, Phoebe pointed up at a sign hanging beside the arched portico of a stone and stucco cottage. "Look, Eva. It says DR. CHARLES DELACY." She eased the motorcar to the side of the road and switched off the engine. "I believe we've found the right place. Come along. Let me do the talking first—I'll get us in the door—and then you subtly take over. I don't wish to intimidate them into an overzealous state of courtesy. Such is often the burden of my station, unfortunately."

Some ten minutes later Phoebe and Eva were ensconced in the Delacys' parlor directly behind the doctor's surgery. Mrs. Delacy, who managed her husband's appointments and accounts, had done a double take when Phoebe introduced herself, and immediately invited them in for tea, which she said she had just been preparing. The doctor's schedule being clear for the next hour or so, the good man had mirrored his wife's astonishment before echoing her invitation and insisting they make themselves at home.

Phoebe took in faded floral wallpaper, dark upholsteries, and side tables crowded with framed photographs, vases, and figurines. A petite woman with kindly blue eyes and small, efficient hands, Mrs. Delacy poured tea and handed round the cups. Beneath her lashes she darted a glance at her husband before asking, "To what do we owe this honor, Lady Phoebe?"

"Miss Huntford and I were traveling in the area, and I happened to remember that your daughter mentioned being from Aldingham." Not entirely a lie, Phoebe reasoned, for all her modifying of the facts. She hadn't introduced Eva as her lady's maid, but merely as *Miss Huntford*. The Delacys could interpret it as they wished. Eva's serviceable attire might reveal her position, or they might believe her to be somehow associated with one of Phoebe's philanthropic projects. In fact, with her next words she encouraged that notion. "As perhaps you might guess, I am gradually following in my grandmother's footsteps in matters concerning the Haverleigh School, and taking on a number of her responsibilities as time goes on."

Dr. Delacy, a stocky individual with a head of shockingly white hair, pensively stirred his tea. "You must be a great source of pride to the Earl and Countess of Wroxly, my lady."

"Thank you. As your daughter must be to the both of you," she said, having been served up the opportunity so neatly. She didn't waste another moment. "I don't suppose you've heard from her since the unfortunate occurrence with Miss Finch." She had noticed the lack of telephone wires strung through the village and presumed the Delacys communicated by letter and personal visits.

Mrs. Delacy looked up sharply. "Unfortunate occurrence?"

"But surely you know? Miss Finch, the headmistress, is no longer with us."

Once again, the Delacys traded looks. "Do you mean to say she has been dismissed?" the doctor asked.

"Oh, dear. I'm so sorry to be the one to tell you, but Miss Finch has passed away," Phoebe gently explained.

"But how?" Mrs. Delacy pressed a hand to her breastbone. "And when?"

With a slight nod, Phoebe signaled to Eva to take over.

"Two days ago. The police have identified the cause of her death to be poison." Eva paused for dramatic effect. "Cyanide."

Mrs. Delacy's teacup rattled in its saucer, while her face turned nearly as white as the bone china. Beside her, the doctor seemed to have stopped breathing.

"We didn't know," his wife said at length in a small voice. "Neither of us has had a chance to read the papers, what with so many patients in and out lately. I'm surprised Olivia didn't come round to tell us."

"Perhaps your daughter didn't wish to upset you with such ill news." Eva leaned slightly forward in her chair. "The incident was terribly upsetting for her, for you see, she was unable to help poor Miss Finch. The headmistress had quite expired before your daughter could arrive on the scene."

"Miss Finch hired Olivia," the doctor said almost absently. Then, more pointedly, he added, "One can't help but wonder what this means for Olivia's position. Will she be retained, do you think?"

"Good heavens, that's right." Mrs. Delacy once more pressed a hand to her breastbone in a gesture that seemed meant to prevent her very being from shattering. "What will she do?"

"She's very lucky that you live so close by." Eva set her cup and saucer on the table beside her.

"Olivia, move back in with us?"

Phoebe admired how deftly Eva ignored Mrs. Delacy's blurted question. "I expect she inherited her medical skills from you, Dr. Delacy. Has she ever assisted you in your surgery?"

Before he could answer, his wife slid to the edge of her seat as if about to leap to her feet and run from the room. "Olivia, work here? No. She's made her own way, *in* her own way, and we're proud of her. *Very* proud." She broke off and drew a tremulous breath. Her eyes glittered in the room's old-fashioned gas lighting. Her husband reached over and patted her hand.

"There, there, my dear. It's quite all right. Of course we're proud of Olivia." He turned to Phoebe and Eva, though Phoebe had the impression his words were directed mainly at her. "You must think us rather odd indeed. Please understand, our daughter served in France, and the war years were very difficult for all of us. We—"

"We never knew from one day to the next whether we would receive one of those dreadful telegrams," his wife interrupted. "Olivia worked right behind the front lines at a casualty clearing station, and often rode with the ambulance trucks to collect the fallen soldiers. The things my poor girl has seen . . ."

"Don't, my dear." Dr. Delacy shook his head and smiled sadly. "Don't distress yourself. I'm sure Lady Phoebe and Miss Huntford quite understand."

Phoebe nodded emphatically. "You daughter's service was most heroic, and England thanks her for it."

But as if she hadn't spoken, Mrs. Delacy murmured, "How *can* they understand? The war takes its toll, it changes people and . . ." A scowl from her husband silenced her. With a shaky hand she raised her teacup to her lips, all but hiding her face behind it.

Phoebe drained her own tea. Though no longer hot, it nonetheless burned all the way down her gullet. Or was it the guilt of having dredged up painful matters and rendering these people distraught? She came to her feet. "We've imposed on you long enough. It was never our desire to upset you. Quite the contrary. We only wished to make your acquaintance. Is there any message you'd like us to convey to your daughter?"

"Ask her to write when she can." Mrs. Delacy gestured at one of several, overburdened side tables. "We haven't a telephone, you see, though the district promises we shall be connected very soon." She gave half a laugh. "They've been saying that for years now."

"I'll, er, see you out." Dr. Delacy opened the door into the narrow hallway that spanned the house from front to back. At the front door, he paused. "Please don't judge us too harshly. I also spent part of the war in France, though I was not there as long as my daughter. No one who served returned home exactly as they had been. From the highest general to the lowliest private digging trenches, we were all affected in one way or another."

Phoebe searched his face, lined with weariness and disillusionment. What, exactly, was he trying to tell her? Was he making generalizations, or speaking specifically of his daughter? She didn't have the heart to question him further. "I do understand the sacrifices made by England's war heroes. My own father, and Miss Huntford's brother, never returned."

"You both have my sincerest condolences. But in some instances, those who did not return are more fortunate than some of those who did."

With that, Dr. Delacy bade them good day, and in heavy silence Phoebe and Eva made their way back to the Vauxhall.

Upon arriving back in the environs of Little Barlow, Lady Phoebe surprised Eva by accelerating past the gates of Foxwood Hall. She had thought their adventures were over for the day. Apparently, she had thought wrong. Briefly, she considered the sewing, ironing, and jewelry cleaning that awaited her. At least she was no longer required to help with the other household chores as she had been during the Christmas holidays, when they had been shortstaffed. She also pondered the scowls sure to crease Lady Julia's brow when Eva finally did return to work, though those scowls might be aimed more at Lady Phoebe than at Eva herself.

And yet, if Lady Phoebe had offered to drop her home first, she would have put up a protest and demanded—as much as a lady's maid *can* demand—where her lady intended going and what she intended doing once she arrived. *Impetuous* was a word that best described Phoebe Renshaw at times, and Eva would never forgive herself if something happened to her young lady that she might have prevented.

She ventured a guess as to their destination. "The school?"

"I want to talk with Nurse Delacy myself. I'd like to observe her reaction when we tell her we visited her parents."

"Do you think it's wise to admit where we went today?"

"She'll find out anyway the next time she visits home. Our questions left the Delacys visibly shaken. Much went unsaid."

"Olivia Delacy might have little or nothing to add. There is no reason she should be compelled to admit anything to us."

Lady Phoebe changed gears as they crested a hill and started the descent. "True, but as with her parents, her demeanor might speak volumes."

Once through the village, they continued at a speed that sent wind whipping at Eva's hair and yanking tendrils painfully from her bun. She thanked goodness when the school came into view, then craned forward in her seat to make out two police vehicles, among several others, parked near the main entrance.

"What can that be about?"

"I don't know, but I intend to find out." Lady Phoebe negotiated the last turn in the drive and rolled to a stop beside a faded but sturdy-looking Morris Oxford two-seater. "Isn't this Mr. Amstead's car?"

"I couldn't say, my lady."

Inside, the sound of weeping echoed from down the corridor. In reply to Phoebe's puzzled glance, Eva said, "I believe that is coming from the headmistress's office."

Phoebe's eyes widened. "Do you suppose they've decided to give the position to someone other than Miss Sedgewick?"

She didn't wait for Eva to answer, but led the way along the hall. A small crowd that included Mr. Amstead filled the headmistress's office. Chief Inspector Perkins, his belly straining his suit coat, stood just inside the door, glaring at a spot beyond Eva's field of vision, but which she determined to be the source of the weeping. Constable Brannock's bright red hair stood out among the more ordinary browns, blonds, and grays of the others occupying the office. He held a small pad open on his palm and jotted down notes. Miss Sedgewick stood poised behind her chair at the desk, her chin tilted and her lips pursed. The others comprised two gentlemen, one elderly and one middle-aged, neither of whom Eva recognized, and two women who must be their wives, and whom she remembered glimpsing at the RCVF charity luncheon.

Suddenly, the scene became all too familiar as a small voice, clogged with sobs, choked out, "I didn't do anything wrong, I swear I didn't. It wasn't me."

The words hurtled Eva back to the troubles and misunderstandings that plagued Foxwood Hall last Christmas. A footman accused, a maid forced to give evidence against him. She shook the memory away in order to concentrate on what was happening here, before her eyes.

"As we all know, cyanide is an ingredient of some insect and rat poisons. Did you or did you not spray rodent repellent around the kitchen and pantries the very day before the luncheon?" Inspector Perkins looked down his pocked nose at his fingernails, as if bored with the proceedings.

"I did, but I was careful. I'm always very careful. I dusted the floor and crevices only. Nothing else. It could not have gotten onto the pots and pans, nor the dishes. I swear."

"We have been all through the kitchen and pantries," the inspector continued relentlessly, "and no other source of cyanide has been found."

Lady Phoebe cast Eva a look of astonishment and made her way into the office. "What is going on here?"

No one answered. Miles Brannock looked up from his note taking, spotted Eva through the doorway, and strode out into the hall. "What are you doing here?" he whispered.

"We came to—never mind," she whispered back. "We never expected this. Is this kitchen girl being arrested?"

The maid, her hair tucked up in an old-fashioned mob cap that sat askew on her head, stood backed against the office wall. The more elderly of the two wives moved to Lady Phoebe's side. "Inspector Perkins has determined Miss Finch's death to be an accident, caused by this daft girl's incompetency."

The weeping increased in volume.

"Is this true?" Eva asked the constable low enough to prevent the others from hearing. "How can he be certain? Zara Worthington made the cake. How do we know she didn't accidentally add the toxic ingredient?"

"If she did," he whispered back, "do you think the inspector is going to accuse her? The daughter of an earl?" His jaw tightened and he hissed air through his teeth.

"You don't believe the maid did it, though."

He gave a tiny shrug, and Eva concluded there hadn't been a thorough enough investigation to determine with any certainty what happened. But the chief inspector's shortcomings no longer surprised her.

Inside, Phoebe demanded answers. "How often is the kitchen sprayed for rodents?"

"Every few weeks, my lady," Miss Sedgewick supplied, "or more as needed." She darted glances at the two well-dressed couples, undoubtedly members of the Haverleigh governing body. "Mostly it is a precaution. We maintain the strictest standards of cleanliness and order in this school."

"Then why did this girl—" Phoebe paused and addressed the kitchen maid herself. "Your name is Bernice, I believe?" When the girl nodded, Phoebe continued. "Bernice, why did you spray for rodents the day before the luncheon? Had you seen a rat on the premises?"

"No, my lady." Bernice sucked in a trembling breath. "It was on my list of things to do."

"Was that list written by Mrs. Honeychurch?"

"No, my lady. By . . ." Her gaze wandered to the desk, and the woman standing behind it. Miss Sedgewick gasped.

"That list is the same every month. It is up to the kitchen staff to modify their schedule of chores to accommodate special events in any given month."

Phoebe turned to the woman. "Did you remind the kitchen staff of this?"

Miss Sedgewick visibly bristled. "Of course not. Why should I concern myself with what goes on from day to day in the kitchen? That is Mrs. Honeychurch's domain, and I am quite content to leave such matters to her. If she was too busy before the luncheon, then this"—her lips turned down as if a sour taste had entered her mouth—"individual should have had the intelligence to forestall spraying the kitchen or at least ask first."

"I am sure you are right, Miss Sedgewick," the elderly

gentleman said. "The governing body is eager to have this matter settled and return the students to school as quickly and quietly as possible."

Lady Phoebe snapped her hands to her hips in a way that would have surely drawn censure from her grandmother. "And Bernice?"

The inspector hefted a tangled eyebrow. "With all due respect, my lady, this is hardly a matter for you to concern yourself with. Why don't you run along and allow—"

"Inspector Perkins," she interrupted so boldly, Eva inwardly flinched, "I am here as a representative of my grandmother, Lady Wroxly. I have every right to inquire into the proceedings so I can make an accurate report when I see her later today."

Eva chewed her lip and wondered how often Lady Phoebe could summon her grandmother's influence before someone finally called her bluff.

"Yes, well . . . I suppose." The inspector's hand wandered to his coat pocket, but fell away quickly. Eva didn't doubt he had instinctively been reaching for his hip flask, but thought better of it. Even so, he made no attempt to hide his disgruntlement at being dictated to by a twenty-year-old woman.

"Do you mean to arrest Bernice?" Lady Phoebe asked.

"Of course not," one of the gentlemen replied. "Didn't you hear the inspector? Miss Finch's death has been ruled an accident. The girl is to be sacked, the students are to return, and we shall all put this unpleasant business behind us."

"And not a moment too soon," Miss Sedgewick said with all the aplomb of a hostess who has just been informed by her butler that dinner was about to be served. She jabbed a finger at Bernice. "You are to pack your things and be gone from the premises within the hour."

Lady Phoebe blocked the maid's path to the door. "But if Miss Finch's death was an accident, why sack Bernice?"

"We cannot have such a careless oaf endangering our students," the younger of the two wives said. She reached up with a gloved hand to make an unnecessary adjustment to the brim of her hat. "I would be happy to answer any questions your grandmother might have, Lady Phoebe. Have her telephone me, if she wishes. Good day."

She and her husband took their leave, and the rest followed. Eva and Constable Brannock moved away from the doorway to allow them passage into the hall. Miss Sedgewick herded young Bernice out of the office and toward the back of the house, to the service staircase, with terse commands of "Move along now. Hurry up. Don't dawdle."

Lady Phoebe and Mr. Amstead filed out last, right after the inspector. The vicar bore a troubled expression, which deepened when Lady Phoebe stopped him with a blunt question.

"Sir, you are the current head of the governing body. Are you in agreement with what just happened here?"

He seemed to weigh his answer carefully before he spoke. "This is a complicated matter, my lady. I believe this may be best for the school."

"That a girl is dismissed from her employment while a woman's murderer goes unpunished?"

"The inspector has found no evidence to warrant an arrest, my lady. You must understand, the resources of our small district are limited. As are those of the school, should we lose our most generous benefactors. No, I must agree with the others that the sooner this matter is resolved, the better for everyone."

"Swept under the rug, you mean."

Eva gasped at Lady Phoebe's brashness. Would the vicar take offense? Would word of this reach Lord and Lady Wroxly's ears? But the man showed no sign of exasperation as he hunched a bit lower and spoke quietly.

"Between the two of us, Lady Phoebe, I've no doubt we shall find a position for Bernice before the passing of much time. I'll even write a letter of reference myself. She should not suffer for what was, in the inspector's judgment, an accident. Somewhere other than a school, I should think." His eyes gave a little twinkle of humor, and Eva was relieved to see Phoebe's lips turn up in a smile.

"Thank you, sir."

"Shall I walk you out, my lady?"

"No, I'll not be leaving just yet. I'd like to deliver the good news to Bernice, if that's all right."

"Of course, my lady. Please give my best regards to Lord and Lady Wroxly."

Lady Phoebe stood watching the vicar as he proceeded down the corridor and let himself out. Then she whirled about to face Eva and the constable. "An accident, my foot. It's Christmas all over again, and something must be done before it's too late. We three need to talk privately."

CHAPTER 10

"Nurse Delacy's own parents were unnerved to speak of her," Phoebe explained to Constable Brannock a few minutes later in the garden behind the conservatory. She looked to Eva for consensus, and received it in the form of a nod. "They told us their daughter served at a casualty clearing station right behind the front lines, and even helped the medics in the ambulances."

The constable swore under his breath—at least, Phoebe believed the word he murmured with a strong Irish cadence to be an oath. "If that is the case, our nurse could be a deeply troubled individual."

"You're talking about shell shock, aren't you?"

"I am, my lady."

"And can such an individual suddenly snap?" she asked.

"We know from experience they can," Eva reminded her. "Christmas taught us that, if nothing else."

"Yes, and no," Phoebe replied after a moment's consideration. "I believe the person you're referring to would have snapped even if there had never been a war." By unspoken agreement, she and Eva never discussed that person by name, for it dredged up too many unsavory memories along with a heavy measure of guilt.

Eva nodded and gave a little shrug. "Yes, true, but Nurse Delacy has certainly shown signs of the war having affected her mind."

The constable shoved his hands into the pockets of his woolen uniform coat. "Such as what? What have you two learned that you have yet to share with me?"

"You can wipe that suspicious look from your face, Constable," Phoebe said tartly. "This is something we only just learned from one of our young guests at Foxwood Hall. It appears Lilyanne Mucklow was injured on the tennis court. She received a gash on the knee from a racket, and when the nurse saw the wound she simply turned away and strode off. Left Lilyanne holding a compress to her bleeding knee. According to Dr. Delacy, his daughter served for years in the war, yet she is unable to deal with a sporting injury? That doesn't make sense."

The constable's eyes closed, and he stood for a moment as the breeze lifted the ends of his bright, wavy hair. His eyes slowly opened. "Yes, it does. You cannot imagine what Nurse Delacy has seen."

"Can *you* imagine it, Constable?" Eva, perhaps unconsciously, stepped closer to him, her expression searching and almost eager.

Phoebe shivered at the shadow that crossed his face. He said, sharply, "No, Miss Huntford. I cannot."

Phoebe didn't at first understand why Eva looked crestfallen, until she remembered that months ago, when they had first made Constable Brannock's acquaintance, Eva hadn't trusted him. Not least of the reasons was that she believed he had shirked his duty during the war. When so many other men had served their country, Eva hadn't liked that a fit man had remained at home, while her own brother had died. Phoebe didn't think it would help to point out that if Miles Brannock had gone to war, he might have died as well.

She decided to bring them back to present concerns. "Do you believe the distress of the war might have affected Nurse Delacy's judgment, and prompted her to do something regrettable?"

"It's very possible," he said.

"More possible than Bernice having poisoned a cake pan with rat poison?"

"Aye, my lady. I have trouble believing that, unless our Bernice had a reason to want Miss Finch dead. I've questioned the girl, and I didn't detect anything ingenuous in her answers. But there is the matter of the handyman and the fright he caused Miss Sedgewick."

Eva, left brooding these past few moments, roused herself. "You know about that? Did Miss Sedgewick tell you?"

"She did. She told you as well?"

Phoebe nodded. "She's made it clear she'd like to see Elliot dismissed."

"I spoke to Elliot earlier today," Eva added. "I don't believe he did anything but offer a flower to Miss Sedgewick. The dear boy doesn't have a malicious bone in his body that I can detect. It was Miss Sedgewick's imagination run amok, if you ask me."

Constable Brannock eyed her levelly. "If you'll forgive my saying so, you've been wrong before, Miss Huntford."

Eva blanched, and Phoebe inwardly shrank in sympathy. It was true, Eva *had* misjudged someone in the past. They all had, but Eva had taken it most to heart.

"Thank you for pointing that out, Constable," she said calmly, but with an edge of ice. Constable Brannock offered an apologetic look, and Eva recovered her composure enough to speak again. "When I spoke to Elliot, he did something rather telling. I reminded him about the in-cident with Miss Sedgewick, and he became fretful and grasped a chain, or a necklace, he wears beneath his shirt. The gesture seemed meant to ward off ill feelings, and I concluded it must be something particularly meaningful for him to seek comfort from it."

The constable tilted his chin in interest. "Could you see what it was?"

"No, as I said, he wore it beneath his shirt, but when I spoke of the flower he attempted to give Miss Sedgewick, he immediately reached into his collar for it. It looked to be silver, I believe."

The constable shifted his domed helmet from one hand to the other. "Why silver, particularly? It seems unlikely he would own anything of value."

Eva thought a moment, her nose slightly scrunched as she obviously tried to remember. "It looked tarnished, un-evenly so. That's why I thought it was silver."

"That would be odd, actually," Phoebe said. "Silver that sits loose in a drawer tends to tarnish rather quickly. But when worn next to the skin, it retains its luster indefi-nitely."

"I'd like to learn more about this piece of jewelry."

Eva raised an eyebrow at the constable. "Do you think it's significant?"

"At this point, everything is significant," he replied. "Nurse Delacy's war experience, Bernice's kitchen chores, even a handyman's necklace. Everything that doesn't make perfect sense at this school is a circumstance to be ques-tioned."

Phoebe drew a breath in preparation of diving into deeper waters, perhaps the deepest yet, for she was about to cross a line by involving one of their highest ranking students. But as the constable said, all unusual circumstances were to be questioned. "We've discovered something else that doesn't make sense—Zara Worthington's high marks. From what we've seen with our own eyes, the girl has little aptitude for academics, yet she is considered one of the school's top students."

"I'll give you that's strange, but I'm not seeing the point, my lady."

"Don't you see," Eva said with a huff of impatience, "it's likely someone has been altering her marks, possibly to keep her influential parents satisfied."

"Yes, and if someone decided to stop falsifying Zara's records, it might have raised fierce resentments." Phoebe waited for the constable to show signs of understanding.

He did not. "I imagine that might cause a bit of a to-do, but murder—over a schoolgirl's marks? Hardly likely."

Phoebe crossed her arms. "Haven't you noticed that Miss Sedgewick dresses as though she has a fortune at her disposal?"

"Does she now?"

"Yes, she does," Eva affirmed. "Her clothes are expensive, and they are not leftovers from previous seasons as might be the case if they were hand-me-downs from wealthier relatives."

"And you are sure of this because . . ." Constable Brannock's skepticism showed in his expression.

"Because I am a lady's maid," Eva said pointedly, "and it is my job to know such things."

Phoebe nodded vigorously. "It is, and she does, Constable."

"All right, the woman spends a tidy sum on clothing. I understand she hails from a landed family in . . ." He gestured at the air.

"Hereford," Eva supplied.

He inclined his head. "Perhaps her relatives have endowed her with a generous allowance."

"Then why does she work at a school?" Phoebe shook her

head. "In my opinion she is a woman who would be much happier out in society than tucked away at a girls' school. No, the two occurrences—Zara's marks and Miss Sedgewick's clothing—seem too much of a coincidence to me."

He narrowed his eyes in sudden comprehension. "Are you suggesting the girl's parents have been paying Miss Sedgewick to alter their daughter's marks?"

"It's highly possible." Phoebe gave him a moment to consider, before adding, "And it's also possible that Miss Finch discovered the deceit, and was murdered to prevent a lucrative situation from ending."

He was shaking his head before she'd finished speaking. "Miss Sedgewick, a murderess? Doing harmless favors for profit I can see, but poisoning her superior? A well-bred lady dirtying her hands with the likes of cyanide? I'm sorry, my lady, I cannot fathom it."

"She would have had the opportunity, as she made quite a nuisance of herself in the kitchen prior to the luncheon." Phoebe looked at Eva. "Isn't that so?"

"Miss Sedgewick was underfoot more often than not. Except, of course, for when she might truly have been needed." Eva smiled without mirth.

"If nothing else, the records should be examined for falsifications." Phoebe crossed her arms in front of her. "As you yourself said, Constable, what doesn't make perfect sense must be questioned."

"Is it fair to be tossing my own words back at me, my lady?"

Phoebe smiled. "At least take a look in Zara's files, please."

"I can't, my lady."

"What do you mean, you can't?" she demanded.

Eva spoke at the same time. "Can't, or won't, Constable?"

"Both of you calm down. I can't. Inspector Perkins has closed the investigation, and legally I can't be traipsing into Miss Sedgewick's office and pulling open file drawers. I'd lose my job."

"Miss Finch's office," Eva murmured.

Constable Brannock took their measure with a long, cool stare. He pushed out a breath. "I can't do it, but what I can do is lure Miss Sedgewick away from the office long enough for a couple of stubborn young women to do a bit of snooping."

"You'll understand, Miss Sedgewick, that Chief Inspector Perkins wishes to ensure the well-being of the students before he can give his permission for classes to resume. Until all stipulations are met, Haverleigh is still considered something of a crime scene."

Eva and Lady Phoebe stood pressed against the stairwell wall, waiting for Constable Brannock to lead Miss Sedgewick to the service stairs at the back of the house, well out of the way of her office. Their voices echoed along the corridor. Eva craned forward and peeked around the banister. She could just make them out as they exited the headmistress's office.

"A crime scene?" Miss Sedgewick slipped her hand into the crook of the constable's elbow, an act that had Eva suddenly wishing ill on the woman—not a grave ill, but an awkward stumble, an ink smudge on her nose, anything to undermine her poised, perfectly groomed facade. "But I thought the inspector said Miss Finch's death was an accident."

"True, but an accident that could easily have been prevented. The correct term is *involuntary manslaughter*. And it's only to save the school the ignominy of a public trial that could call into question the staff's competence that we are using the term *accident* and dismissing all possible legal action. Unless you are in disagreement with that?"

"Goodness, no, Constable." Miss Sedgewick raised her free hand to her temple as if feeling a faint coming on. "A scandal of that sort would do nothing to bring back our dear Miss Finch, but could very well shut us down forever. No, I thank Inspector Perkins for his astute judgment in the matter."

"Then the sooner you and I inspect the kitchen to make sure all potential poisons are now cleaned out of ordinary cupboards and put under lock and key, the sooner the students may return." Constable Brannock led Miss Sedgewick around a corner, taking them out of sight.

Even so, Eva stood watching for several more moments, saying over her shoulder to Lady Phoebe, "Let's just be sure they won't suddenly return for some reason."

"The constable won't let that happen." Lady Phoebe hopped down from the bottom step. "And from the sounds of Miss Sedgewick's admiring simper, I very much doubt she's in any hurry to relinquish the attentions of Constable Brannock. Still, we had better do this quickly."

Eva lingered on the step as Lady Phoebe scurried along the hall to the headmistress's office. Her stomach seemed to have dropped to her feet, thrust there by Lady Phoebe's observation concerning Miss Sedgewick and the constable's attentions. Eva knew very well she shouldn't care. She had no right to care, for she had certainly staked no claim on Miles Brannock, for all his persistence in trying to further their acquaintance. She had practically pushed him away—and for good reason. Her ladies needed her, and everyone knew a married lady's maid posed all manner of inconveniences to her employers. Not that he'd asked her to marry him, or hinted that he might. But either a man's attentions led to marriage, or they led a woman to her ruin. At this stage of her life neither alternative seemed particularly appealing.

Except . . . Constable Brannock *did* have a certain appeal, she must admit, at least privately, in her heart of hearts. And seeing the likes of Verity Sedgewick on his arm—well, a giant ache grew in the vacant spot her stomach had occupied until about a minute ago.

"Eva," Lady Phoebe hissed from the open doorway of the office, "are you coming?"

Eva crossed to her at a trot. "Sorry, my lady. I was just thinking . . . I do hope the constable doesn't get in trouble for lying."

"He's not lying, particularly. I'm sure parents will want assurances that such a dreadful thing will never happen again, and the constable is doing just that. Inspector Perkins will no doubt take credit for having instructed him to do so. Now, then . . ." She trailed off as she surveyed the room and the tall, wooden file cabinets that filled one wall. She went to the closest and read the letters printed on the front. "*A* through *E*. Worthington will be in the last cabinet."

Eva went to the last one, gripped the handle of the middle drawer, and pulled, to no avail. "It's locked."

Lady Phoebe groaned. "I hadn't thought of that. I suppose we'll have to search the desk for the key, but Miss Sedgewick might have it on her."

"Well, let's just see . . ." Reaching behind her, Eva slid a hairpin from her bun. Then she crouched in front of the drawer and carefully inserted the pin into the lock. She twisted one way, then another, slid the pin out slightly, twisted again, and heard a click. She slid open the middle drawer, and began thumbing through the files. "Here it is, my lady, Worthington." She pulled out the thick cardboard folder and handed it over.

"How did you do that?"

Eva smiled. "My brother Danny taught me a long time ago."

Their gazes met and held in shared sadness and sympathy for what each of them had lost in the war. Then Lady Phoebe spread open the folder on the desktop. In it were three years' worth of assessments on Zara's progress, spanning the time since she enrolled to the present. Phoebe emitted a *hmmm* as she pored over both handwritten and typed pages as well as lists of subjects and marks.

Eva watched as her lady separated a large envelope from the stack of reports and opened it. "Look at this. Another set of reports." She gasped. Her eyebrows surging toward her hairline, she abruptly lifted her chin. "It isn't Miss Sedgewick who has been altering Zara's marks, it was Miss Finch. See here."

Eva leaned across the desk to view these other reports. Lady Phoebe's forefinger jabbed at a printed column, and then slowly traced a path down the page. Lady Zara's marks in the subjects she enjoyed—etiquette, deportment, music, dance—were high and straightforward. But in academics, each of the marks entered by her instructors had been inked out, changed, and initialed with *HF.*

"Henrietta Finch," Eva murmured.

"Indeed." Lady Phoebe shook her head. "This certainly changes things, doesn't it? I wonder why Miss Finch would feel compelled to falsify Zara's marks. What benefit to her? And why keep a record of the fact? She just as easily could have disposed of the original marks."

It was Eva's turn to shake her head in mystification. "It made sense that Miss Sedgewick would have entered into an agreement with Lady Zara's parents, in order to maintain her own expensive tastes."

"We were obviously wrong about Miss Sedgewick. I suppose she has generous relatives after all. Perhaps her clothes *are* secondhand, worn once and discarded. But Miss Finch certainly didn't dress above her means, did she? Or exhibit any behavior that could be considered extravagant."

"Perhaps she saved the money for her eventual retirement."

"Perhaps. A favor now for a comfortable life later." Lady Phoebe sifted through a few more records.

"A favor," Eva repeated. "My lady, perhaps Miss Finch didn't do this for money, but for some other sort of favor."

"What else could an earl do for a headmistress? Miss Finch never married, and thus had no children whose futures she needed to secure. And as far as I know, her own parents were deceased, so it wasn't for them that she compromised her integrity as a school official."

Eva compressed her lips, hesitant to voice the notion that sprang to mind. But if they were to find justice for Miss Finch, even unpleasantness needed mentioning. "Just because Miss Finch never married, my lady, doesn't mean she never had a child."

Had she expected her mistress to gasp or blush or raise a hand to her breastbone in shock? Lady Phoebe merely studied her and then nodded, proving to be more worldly than most people would have suspected. "If she had, he or she would be grown by now, or nearly so. Perhaps Miss Finch hoped for a good position somewhere for a son or daughter—surely an earl could arrange that. My goodness, Eva, if Miss Finch does have an offspring somewhere, he or she must be told about her death. Just think how horrible it would be if your mother passed away, and you didn't learn of it until months or years later?"

Lady Phoebe said this offhandedly, yet a pang struck Eva at the thought of Phoebe and her sisters being told of their own mother's passing years ago. Eva hadn't been in the Renshaws' employ then, but that didn't prevent her from imagining the pain of such a revelation. She *had* been on hand, however, when the news came about Phoebe's father. As excruciating as that had been, at least the Renshaw siblings had had the security of knowing their grandparents would continue to care for them. Would a child of Miss Finch have the same assurance?

Likely not, for such a child would have been kept a heavily guarded secret to preserve Miss Finch's reputation as well as her employment prospects. If such a person existed, he would more than likely find himself very much alone now in the world.

"It's also possible, my lady," Eva felt pressed to point out, "that Lord and Lady Benton did not offer a favor to Miss Finch in exchange for tampering with their daughter's marks. They might have demanded it based on something they learned about Miss Finch, whether she had a child or some other secret from her past."

"Yes, and in either case, we can't simply ask Lord and Lady Benton about this, for to do so would be to accuse them, and they would immediately take the defensive."

"Then how do we set about discovering whether Miss Finch had a child, or what other secret she might have been hiding?"

"Wait one moment . . ." Lady Phoebe had been shuffling through Lady Zara's records again, and something apparently caught her eye. She separated a page from the others and perused it more closely. "Miss Finch must have had a change of heart. There's a letter here, unsent by all appearances. '*My Lord and Lady Benton,*'" she read, "'*this is to inform you of your daughter's academic probation. Lady Zara is no longer meeting minimum standard requirements as set forth in the Haverleigh Certificate of Education . . .*'" Lady Phoebe glanced up. "This is most puzzling. Whatever made Miss Finch change those marks in the first place seems to have suddenly lost its importance, or at least its persuasive powers. Miss Finch changed her mind only two weeks ago, Eva. Lord and Lady Benton were already abroad by then, so what prompted the headmistress to write this letter?"

"A quarrel of some kind between Miss Finch and Lady Zara?"

"I don't know," Lady Phoebe murmured, "but this would certainly qualify as something that doesn't make perfect sense."

CHAPTER 11

Sleep eluded Phoebe that night. Her struggles to find a comfortable position merely resulted in her legs twisting in the bedclothes, making her more uncomfortable than before. Did Zara Worthington's altered marks have anything to do with Miss Finch's death? Zara had opportunity. She might have slipped any amount of rat poison into Miss Finch's Madeira cake.

Or could she? Wouldn't someone have noticed her reaching for an obvious poison? Would a young lady like Zara even know about rodenticides? And if she had slipped some into the cake recipe, wouldn't Miss Finch have tasted something amiss? The woman had attacked her dessert with much more than polite acquiescence. She had positively hummed with pleasure as she consumed its entirety.

Giving up on sleep, she sat up and set her feet on the floor, intent on taking up the book she had started last night. Cries from beyond her bedroom door had her snatching up her dressing gown and running into the hallway instead. What now?

She stood a moment, trying to gauge where the sound originated. Her parents' bedroom. Just as she reached the door, Amelia came out of her room and spotted Phoebe. "I thought I heard . . ."

Weeping drew them both into their parents' former bedroom, where they came upon Jane Timmons sitting up in bed and leaning over to shake Lilyanne's shoulder. "Wake up. You're having a bad dream."

"It was me, my fault . . . Miss Finch . . ."

Jane, her straight hair falling out of the plait that plunged down her back, turned her plain features toward Phoebe and Amelia. Phoebe switched on the overhead light. Lilyanne tossed in the bed, twisting the covers even more than Phoebe had twisted hers. Her mottled cheeks glittered with tears, and her bright russet curls stuck out every which way, as if Lilyanne had been tugging at them.

The girl suddenly went silent and opened her eyes with a startled "Oh!"

"You were having a nightmare and crying out in your sleep," Jane said none too gently. "See? Even ladies Phoebe and Amelia heard you." For all the words might have seemed abrupt, Jane nonetheless reached out to smooth Lilyanne's hair back from her perspiring brow. "It's all right now. No harm done."

Except . . . Phoebe had heard what Lilyanne said. *It was me, my fault . . . Miss Finch.* Judging from Amelia's shocked expression, she had heard as well. Despite Jane's reassurances, Lilyanne's tears continued to flow, and her gaze, gleaming with remorse, arced across the room to lock with Phoebe's. Phoebe went to the bed and sat at the edge opposite Jane.

She straightened the bedclothes and arranged them over Lilyanne's legs. "Would you like to talk about it?"

Her eyes large and luminous, she nodded. She chewed her lower lip until it whitened between her teeth, then glowed red when she released it. "It was me," she said in a whisper.

Phoebe barely breathed. "What was you, Lilyanne?"

She was aware of Amelia going to the other side of the bed and climbing up to sit beside Jane. Both girls kept silent, but Phoebe felt the riveting weight of their curiosity.

"Miss Finch." Lilyanne swept a hand through her hair, her fingers tangling in the curls. She tugged them through with a sigh. Tears slid down her cheeks. "The cake. I prepared it. Not Zara. It was me. It was so busy in the kitchen, no one really knew who did what. So I gathered the ingredients and mixed them together. Zara only poured the batter into the pan."

She left off, and Phoebe asked, "Why you? Zara was supposed to have baked that cake and she took the credit for it."

"She threatened me if I didn't help her. She said I'd be sorry if I didn't do as she said."

"From what I understand," Phoebe said gently, "Zara makes your life miserable at every turn. What would have changed?"

Lilyanne choked back a sob. "I thought maybe this time she would relent and be nicer."

"Has that ever happened before?"

"No."

Phoebe nudged Lilyanne's chin higher with the backs of her fingers. "Did you ever tell Miss Finch about how Zara treats you?"

Amelia supplied the answer. "Miss Finch had a strict policy about telling tales. She always wanted us to work out our own problems."

Jane nodded. "That's true. Miss Finch always said life isn't fair, and the sooner we learn to live with that, the better."

Lilyanne's mouth curled downward, and bitterness entered her voice. "I did tell Miss Finch about Zara once, and she didn't give a fig."

"It's not that she didn't care." Jane patted Lilyanne's

knee. "She wanted us to learn to be strong and stand up for ourselves. And I believe she was absolutely correct."

Phoebe wanted to hush the girl, as her opinion didn't seem to lighten Lilyanne's mood.

"Perhaps," she said, "but I know Miss Finch didn't care for me in the least."

"I'm sure that wasn't the case," Phoebe was quick to assure her, but Lilyanne adamantly shook her red ringlets.

"It's true. She thought I was weak, and she was right. Zara could cheat and bully all she wished, and Miss Finch turned a blind eye or worse, praised her for being the top student. Because Zara is strong, just like Miss Finch wanted. That mattered more to her than anything else. But now she's dead, and it's my doing, and what's more, I'm not all too sorry to see her gone. I wish I were, but I'm not." She dropped her head into her hands and began weeping again. "And for that, I shall surely burn in hell."

Phoebe's insides went still. Even her heart felt suspended in her bosom, and all her senses seemed poised on a precipice. Crying out in a dream was one thing, but Lilyanne was awake now. Did she just make a confession? Or were these merely the rantings of a distraught girl who felt alone and misunderstood by everyone around her? She touched the girl's shoulder. "I'm sure it wasn't your fault, Lilyanne. You said you gathered the ingredients yourself?"

"I did."

"And did you gather anything not on the recipe list?"

Lilyanne's wayward spirals spilled forward as she shook her head.

"And when you mixed them, did you see a container of rat poison or anything else nearby that could poison the cake?"

"N-not that I can remember."

"Then how can it be your fault?"

"But I was the last person preparing the batter right before Zara poured it and placed the pan in the oven. I also mixed the glaze, although Zara spread it over the top. Who else could be responsible?"

The next question Phoebe wished to ask was whether Lilyanne watched Zara place the cake in the oven. Could Zara have sprinkled in an extra ingredient on the sly? But she daren't plant that notion into any of the girls' heads, or they'd likely be at each other's throats with accusations.

She didn't like saying it, but in the interest of putting Lilyanne's mind at rest—at least long enough for them all to get some sleep—she explained, "The police believe the kitchen maid, Bernice, might have sprayed rat poison near the pots and pans. Accidentally, of course. So you see, it wouldn't have been your fault."

Lilyanne's head came up. "Truly?" A little spark of hope ignited in her blue eyes, even as an ember of guilt burned in the center of Phoebe's chest.

"Truly." She helped the girl lie back down and raised the blankets to her chin. Then she looked over at Amelia and Jane, still sitting together on the other side of the bed. "All right, you two. The crisis is over. I hope I don't have to tell you both that there is no need to mention this to anyone in the morning."

Jane shrugged and crawled under the bedclothes beside Lilyanne. Amelia followed Phoebe to the door. After exchanging good nights, Phoebe and Amelia stepped into the hall and closed the door behind them.

"I certainly never expected a scene like that in the middle of the night." Phoebe let out a weary breath. "I'm beginning to think nothing at that school is as it should be." She took Amelia's hand. "Any chance you'll go right back to sleep?"

"After that?" Amelia shook her head. "I could use some warm milk with cinnamon."

"Good. I can't sleep either. Let's sneak downstairs. I need some information, and right now you're the only person I trust to supply it."

Eva attempted to school her features as she stared out the Vauxhall's windscreen, but it proved an arduous task. So much so, she quite failed at maintaining a neutral expression, and Lady Phoebe noticed as much.

"Really, Eva, you needn't worry about my killing us here on the estate road. The way is level and clear, and I'm barely pressing the accelerator."

Lady Phoebe spoke the truth. The estate road that linked Foxworth Hall with its stables and beyond could not have presented a more amicable prospect for a motorist. Flat and smooth, the paved road wound gently beneath a canopy of budding elms and oaks, and was flanked by grassy swales and flower beds carefully placed to look like the haphazard design of nature.

But that was not the case when Eva and Lady Phoebe traveled this road by truck last Christmas, and it was that memory that made her long to return to the familiar embrace of the house.

"It's not your driving, my lady. It's what occurred at our destination last time we were there."

Phoebe's eyebrows gathered. She took one hand off the steering wheel and reached over to pat Eva's shoulder. "I know, and I'm sorry. I just couldn't think of anywhere else to meet Constable Brannock without being seen or overheard. If we are going to assist him in finding Miss Finch's killer, we must do so secretly, or we'll put his job at risk."

Eva nodded. The stone and slate carriage house and stables filled her view beyond the windscreen, but rather than enter the wide, cobbled courtyard, Phoebe veered to the right and kept going about another half mile down the road. Here, the small vehicle began to rattle and pitch as the road beneath them became cracked and rutted. Several winters' worth of ice and snow had taken its toll, and Lord Wroxly had seen no reason to keep up repairs on this unused stretch of roadway.

The Vauxhall came to a stop beside what Eva recognized to be Miles Brannock's motorcar. He would have entered the estate from the service driveway, so as not to be seen from the house. But where was he? Eva saw no sign of him either along the road or the budding trees and foliage on either side.

Lady Phoebe set the brake. "This is strange. His motorcar is here . . ." She peered into the shady dimness of a woodland path that forked away from the road. "Perhaps he walked over to the gamekeeper's cottage."

A wave of dread gripped Eva. The last time she had been in this exact spot, it had been snowy, dark, and she and Lady Phoebe had been forced to trek to the cottage, abandoned since before the war. The place was set far enough away from the house and the stables that no one could have heard their cries for help. . . .

Lady Phoebe seemed to read her thoughts, for she gave her hand a squeeze. "It's all right. You mustn't dwell on what almost happened here last time."

Eva didn't bother explaining that the fear of almost losing her dearest girl would never entirely leave her. She merely opened the car door, climbed out, and fell into step behind Lady Phoebe. Rather than dwell on the past or questioning why her mistress felt this need to search for the constable rather than wait for him by the motorcars, she concentrated on keeping her footing over rocks, tree roots, and tangles of weeds. Soon enough, the gamekeeper's cottage, made of stone and slate like the stables, came into view in its small clearing. An air of abandonment, of dusty stillness, hung about the place, magnifying the sounds of the surrounding forest. Sunlight fell in shafts through the overhanging trees, dancing each time the wind blew.

She jumped when Lady Phoebe called out, "Constable, are you here?"

It was all Eva could do not to shush her, as if she might awaken last winter's ghosts. Ridiculous, but she couldn't deny the sense of relief that washed through her when Miles Brannock stepped around a corner of the cottage and tipped his helmet to them.

"Terribly sorry, my lady. Miss Huntford," he added with another bob of his head, "I arrived early and thought I'd make sure things here had been taken care of properly."

Eva understood what he meant. Her gaze traveled to a low mound near the storage room door. As soon as the weather permitted, Lord Wroxly had indeed properly taken care of things here, to ensure there could be no repeats of last winter's events.

Lady Phoebe didn't waste a moment on pleasantries, but got right to the point. "Thank you for meeting us where we could speak privately. I know it seems irregular, but if my grandparents—" She broke off at the snapping of twigs from behind the cottage. Memories sent chills of fear racing down Eva's back and she very nearly grabbed Lady Phoebe's hand and began running. In the next instant, Lord Owen Seabright came around the same corner the constable had.

"What are you doing here?" Lady Phoebe demanded, echoing Eva's own thoughts, except a good deal more defensively. Sometimes the way Lady Phoebe reacted to Lord Owen reminded Eva of her own reactions to the constable. As if his proximity threw her slightly off kilter, and she couldn't quite breathe properly.

"Glad to see me again, are you?" Lord Owen, looking

rather dapper in well-tailored Norfolk tweeds, flashed a lopsided grin.

"Lord Owen paid me a visit this morning," the constable said in explanation. "He's done some checking."

"Checking on what?" Phoebe asked, but the constable held up a hand.

"You first, my lady. You said you learned a few things yesterday."

"Yes, I did. First of all, Zara Worthington didn't bake the Madeira cake for Miss Finch. Lilyanne Mucklow did."

Constable Brannock frowned. "Why would they lie?"

"Because Zara was *supposed* to have done it, but she bullied Lilyanne into doing the work for her. Zara only popped the cake into the oven and later poured the glaze over it—the glaze that Lilyanne also made."

"But again, why would Lady Zara continue to lie in light of Miss Finch's death?" Lord Owen came to stand beside the constable.

"Because, my lord," Eva supplied, "then Lady Zara would have to admit she lied in the first place. Better to keep silent, I should think, and wait to see if she is accused of anything. If not, she need never expose her deceit."

"Indeed. But that isn't all." Lady Phoebe glanced at Eva. As soon as their lessons with the girls ended this morning, they had debated whether or not to inform the constable about Lilyanne's revelation following her nightmare. Eva nodded at her now, for she believed if they were to discover what happened to Miss Finch, they should hide nothing from Miles Brannock. Phoebe swallowed. "I'm sure this was just the outpouring of a lonely, insecure young girl, but Lilyanne said she wasn't sorry about Miss Finch's death, because she felt certain Miss Finch didn't like her and in fact treated her poorly."

"Frightened her, actually," Eva added.

"Motive and opportunity," the constable murmured.

"I can't believe that of Lilyanne. Zara, perhaps, though even that is hard to envision. But Lilyanne?" Eva shook her head.

Lady Phoebe took up her argument. "Lilyanne is a typical teenaged girl, if a particularly shy one, Constable. At that age, most of us believe there is some adult in our life who is set against us. We only told you of this because Eva and I agreed we should keep nothing from you. If we are to find justice for Miss Finch, we must form a clear picture of events—all of them. If Lilyanne bore ill sentiments toward Miss Finch, surely others did as well."

Lord Owen placed his hand on the constable's shoulder. "When you think about it, Brannock, having the Mucklow girl mix the cake could have been a ruse to take suspicion away from the actual culprit."

The constable considered. "This Zara, you say she's a bully?"

Lady Phoebe described some of the incidents Amelia had told her about. Then Eva recounted Miss Finch's philosophy concerning the girls standing up for themselves and not intervening in their squabbles.

"And when you lured Miss Sedgewick out of the main office," she said, "we discovered that it was Miss Finch, and not Miss Sedgewick, who had been changing Zara's marks."

"Interesting." Constable Brannock removed his helmet and pushed his curling mop of hair off his brow.

"That's not all that's interesting," Lady Phoebe said. "Apparently, Miss Finch decided not to perform any more favors for Zara. We found a drafted letter in Zara's records informing her parents that she was now on academic probation."

The constable let out a low groan. "I truly don't wish to be suspecting young ladies of murder. I truly don't. Is there anything else?"

"Isn't that enough?" Phoebe held out her hands.

"Actually, there is something else." Amelia had confided in Eva about Jane Timmons only that morning, before lessons began. Jane had been last to arrive in the Petite Salon and seemed rather breathless as she took her place at the table. Amelia had leaned to whisper in Eva's ear, and now Eva repeated the gist of it for the constable. "It seems Jane Timmons has a habit of sometimes arriving late to her lessons, especially the early morning ones."

At this, Miles Brannock and Lord Owen traded mystified expressions. Lord Owen said, "A late sleeper? Brannock, you'd better arrest that girl straight away."

Eva's cheeks heated as the two men chuckled, but their teasing didn't deter her. "Jane is not a late sleeper. And like her, I attended Haverleigh on scholarship. I assure you, I would never have broken even the smallest rule for fear of expulsion. As it was, I had to leave school before graduation anyway, but my time there was of greater value to me than I can ever express. We have continued the girls' lessons at the Hall, and Jane has proven herself to be an exceptional scholar. I cannot believe an intelligent girl in her position would be so careless of school rules without some very pressing reason."

The men's grins faded. Phoebe flashed a satisfied smile. "Amelia told me about Jane's tardiness last night, Eva, but I'd completely forgotten. I'm glad she also thought to mention it to you." She turned to the constable. "It could be important, couldn't it?"

His lips taking on an ironic slant, he exchanged another look with Lord Owen. "If the current trend continues, I'll soon have reason to be suspecting the entire student body." He sobered quickly enough. "She bears watching, this Jane Timmons."

"We'll keep a close eye on her," Eva assured him. "But you said you'd learned something as well?"

With a hand gesture, Constable Brannock deferred to Lord Owen, who cleared his throat. "It's about the handyman. I've tried to trace the youth's origins, but Elliot Ivers seems to have been conjured out of thin air."

Lady Phoebe's frown mirrored Eva's own mystification. "Then he didn't fight in the war?"

"Not as far as I can tell. There are no records of him having ever been in uniform. No records of him existing at all."

Phoebe's eyes narrowed to pensive slits. "Do you suppose he's using an assumed name?"

"The thought did occur to me," Lord Owen conceded.

"As it did to me," Constable Brannock said. "Yet the idea of an assumed name seems a rather complex one for a chap like Ivers."

"Very true." Lady Phoebe nudged at the pebbles on the ground with the pointed toe of her boot. "Eva, I suppose we should have searched for his employment papers when we had access to Miss Finch's files."

"There might not be any employment papers, my lady," Eva replied. "It's quite possible Miss Finch found him somewhere, took pity on him, and simply hired him on."

"That does make sense, especially since Miss Sedgewick seems to have no information about him. Still, Miss Finch had to be paying him, and to do that she would have to keep an accounting of the outgoing funds."

Eva shook her head. "Not if his wages consisted of room and board and the occasional quid from petty cash."

"Well, if that's everything for now," the constable said, "I'd best be getting back before Inspector Perkins starts wondering what I've gotten up to. My lord, are you ready to go?"

Lord Owen answered the constable with a suggestion of his own. "Phoebe, if it's all the same to you, I'll come up to the house and pay my respects to your grandparents."

"Eva and I came in the Vauxhall. I'm afraid there isn't room."

Eva heard the disappointment in Lady Phoebe's voice and came up with an immediate solution. "I don't mind walking back, my lady. Truly," she was quick to add before Phoebe could protest.

"Never mind," the constable said. "I'd be happy to give Miss Huntford a ride along the service road."

"I wouldn't wish to impose. The walk will be good for me and it's a lovely day." While that had been true up until now, the weather decided to betray Eva with a burst of wind that sent clouds scuttling to block the sun.

"Nonsense." This from Lady Phoebe. Her tone brooked no debate. "Eva, go with the constable. I'll see you at home."

By the time Phoebe drew the Vauxhall up beside the front door, a light rain had begun to fall. "It's a good thing the constable gave Eva a ride," she said to Owen. She drew her collar up and tugged her hat brim down. "Shall we make a run for it?"

The front door had already opened and Mr. Giles stood waiting for them. A footman strode out and opened the motorcar door for Phoebe. Owen let himself out the other side, and as they entered the house, the footman slid behind the steering wheel and set out for the carriage house, used to house the family's variety of vehicles, from Grams's carriage to Grampapa's Rolls-Royce.

Mr. Giles had barely collected Phoebe's and Owen's hats and overcoats when Julia came sprinting down the wide staircase with a scowl plastered across her face.

"High time you got back. I trust you brought Eva with you, or have you—" Her expression altered in an instant. "Owen, I didn't see you there."

"Hello, Julia." Owen crossed the hall with his hand extended. It grated on Phoebe no end that when Julia placed her own hand in his, Owen didn't merely shake it but brought it to his lips. Julia simpered like a debutante. "It's wonderful to see you again."

"And you, Owen, though I really must scold you." Julia's hand remained resting on his though he'd already loosened his hold.

Mr. Giles put the coats in the cloakroom and slipped discreetly away.

"What has kept you away so long? I'd all but given up hope that we would ever see you again." Julia fluttered her eyelashes and smiled as only Julia could—like the sun bursting through clouds to banish the rain. Phoebe suppressed a groan.

"I've been dirtying my hands in business again," he said, smiling broadly, "but you don't want to hear about that."

"Goodness, no, you're quite right. But it *is* good to see you looking so well. So robust. Managing those nasty mills of yours obviously agrees with you, though one cannot help but wonder why." She wrinkled the perfect slope of her nose.

Owen laughed as though Julia had just made the funniest observation. "Such places are certainly not made for the likes of you." He took both her hands and held her arms out. "You're looking splendid as always."

Her smile faded. "I would be, if our lady's maid were ever anywhere to be found when she's needed." She fingered the golden twist she had obviously fashioned for herself that morning, then dropped her hand and apparently dismissed the subject. "My grandfather is in the library. I know he'd love to see you. Grams is still in the Petite Salon with our young charges from the school."

"Are you coming?" He held out his hand to her again.

"You go on in. I'll be right behind you. I just need a word with my sister first." The way Julia's mouth hardened when she said *my sister* provided Phoebe with ample warning of what was coming. The moment Owen disappeared across the hall and into the library, Julia bore down on her. Phoebe's stomach tightened as she prepared to do battle.

CHAPTER 12

"What do you suppose you're about," Julia said sharply, "monopolizing Eva's time the way you've been doing? Bad enough Grams has her teaching those silly chits, but there's nothing I can do about that. There is plenty I can do about you. I'm fed up with it. Grams is going to hear about this the moment lessons are over for the day."

Phoebe let out a weary sigh. "Julia, can't you for once see past your own petty concerns? Eva and I have been—" She didn't finish. She couldn't come right out and tell Julia that she and Eva were helping with a murder investigation—especially when that investigation had been called off by the chief inspector. "We have been busy with the RCVF, and now the school itself, which has suffered a terrible tragedy, or had you forgotten?"

"I remember quite well, thank you. And if you wish to involve yourself in every do-gooder cause you can think of, it's fine with me. But Eva was hired to perform a specific job in this house, and you are preventing her from doing it. Perhaps you enjoy looking like a commonplace frump—obviously you do—but I believe in upholding the integrity of our family. It is not enough to be of a noble house, one must look and act the part if we are to maintain our positions in society."

A commonplace frump. Phoebe heard little after that phrase, for Julia's unkind assessment sent the blood rushing in her ears. She couldn't help stealing a glance down at herself. She could boast neither Julia's height nor her graceful slenderness, nor had she been blessed with Julia's deep blue eyes and bright golden hair. No, an intrusion of green turned Phoebe's eyes a decidedly ordinary hazel, and just enough red had infiltrated her hair to prevent her from being a fashionable blonde. Those things she could do nothing about. But she *had* dressed hurriedly this morning and without Eva's help, choosing a simple tea-length skirt, lace-up boots, and a cream shirtwaist. After morning lessons she had tossed on her spring coat and rushed out the door to collect Eva around back at the service entrance for their meeting with Constable Brannock.

She hadn't expected Owen Seabright to be at that meeting as well. If she had, would she have taken more care with her morning preparations? She wished she could toss her head and deny the very notion of being so vain. If the truth were told, even upon discovering Owen at the cottage, she hadn't given her appearance a second thought. But thanks to Julia, she now saw herself quite clearly in Owen's eyes.

Frump. A little ball of misery gathered at the core of her being. Through that awful roaring in her ears, words penetrated—ugly, hurtful words that held enough truth to render Phoebe unable to deny them. Julia was still talking, and though much of what she said passed through Phoebe unheard, enough found their mark with stinging accuracy.

Why did Julia loathe her so? What had Phoebe ever done to deserve such disdain? She could think of nothing to excuse her sister's behavior.

"Perhaps you're right," she heard herself saying. "Perhaps I have none of your poise or style, nor can I ever hope to gain the admiration of everyone around me the way you do." She couldn't let Julia see the extent of her distress. Her sister was nothing if not astute, and she would likely guess the reason why.

Owen.

She pulled herself up straighter, blinked her eyes clear, and pressed her face closer to Julia's. She didn't know where her next words originated, or that they had even existed inside her, but they tumbled forth, strong and distinct. "But for all that, Julia, I still prefer to be myself, rather than be you or like you. I'd rather die an old maid who has done some good in the world, than be someone who chose merely to uphold the integrity of her social position."

Pivoting, she blindly made her way across the hall and to the library. She might have preferred the privacy of her bedroom, but retreating upstairs would have meant Julia had won this round. Phoebe would rather endure the scrutiny of a thousand curious gazes than allow Julia the satisfaction of knowing she had undermined her confidence.

On the library threshold, she pulled up abruptly. Not two, but three men presently occupied the grouping of chairs by the hearth. Grampapa had his feet up on his favorite leather hassock, reminding her of his recent complaint of swollen ankles. Dearest Grampapa seemed to have arrived at an age when a man no longer enjoyed robust good health, and that worried her greatly, especially since he typically proclaimed, "We mustn't bother Dr. Reynolds with anything so trivial."

Owen perched in an armchair, his body coiled as if ready to spring into action if needed. He noticed Phoebe, smiled, and stood. The third man, Mr. Amstead, sat in the wing chair with one leg crossed. He uncrossed them and also came to his feet.

Before she could enter or greet the vicar properly, a voice behind her said, "Phoebe, you're home. Good." Grams placed a hand on her shoulder and nudged her into the room. "I believe you'll be interested in what the vicar has come to discuss."

Grams crossed in front of her to take possession of the other armchair across the small Pembroke table from Owen's. "Now then, Mr. Amstead, what is this about Miss Sedgewick not informing parents that the school will reopen?"

Still shaken from her confrontation with Julia, Phoebe remained standing, hovering over the little group. This news came as a surprise, for she had believed Miss Sedgewick eager to have the students return and restore a sense of normalcy to Haverleigh. Odd, but she found herself siding with the assistant headmistress. She wasn't satisfied with the conclusion the chief inspector had reached and didn't think it would be prudent to return the girls to school too soon.

Mr. Amstead and Owen resumed their seats, and the elder man said, "Lady Wroxly, Miss Sedgewick is expressing concerns about reopening the school before a permanent headmistress has been named."

"That's not at all what she said the other day." Grams's brow furrowed. "She's always seemed like an agreeable young lady. Why is she suddenly being difficult?"

"I don't believe Miss Sedgewick means to be difficult, Lady Wroxly," the vicar returned. "With the school having been thrown into such disarray, she wishes to avoid any further uncertainties with the potential to disrupt the girls' lives again."

Such as a second murder? Phoebe schooled her features not to give away her thoughts. "It is an odd change of heart," she observed instead. "Only the other day Miss

Sedgewick seemed eager to reopen the school." Grams nodded in agreement.

"That's true, Lady Phoebe," the vicar replied, "but perhaps the incident with the kitchen maid distracted her from her true sentiments."

With a little grunt, Grampapa shifted his feet to a more comfortable position on the hassock. "Do you agree with her, Vicar, that the school shouldn't be reopened?"

"Generally speaking, no, my lord." The man steepled his hands beneath his chin. "I understand her hesitancy, but I feel keeping the school closed and the students scattered will be more disruptive than bringing them back before the headmistress position is resolved."

"Not that we don't enjoy having the young ladies with us," Grampapa said with a fond twinkle in his eye. "Ah, I enjoy seeing their eager, youthful faces. They are welcome for as long as needed."

"The governing body hasn't yet had time to post an advertisement for the position." Grams paused as Vernon, the head footman, entered with the tea tray. Grams gestured for him to set it down on the sofa table, then she herself leaned forward to begin pouring. "And once that is done, it will take time to sort through the applicants. It could take weeks. Surely Miss Sedgewick doesn't propose keeping the school closed these next several weeks?" She glanced up at the vicar. "One lump or two?"

"Do you suppose her hesitancy has to do with her wanting the position?" Phoebe mused aloud. She couldn't be sure if Grams's disapproving look was aimed at her, or at Miss Sedgewick's possible machinations. Grampapa, however, appeared to give the notion serious consideration.

He said, "If that were the case, wouldn't it better suit her purpose to reopen the school and show the governing body how adept she is at running things?"

"Not if she hopes to compel the governing board to make a speedy decision in her favor," Owen said. He accepted a teacup from Grams's outstretched hand.

Phoebe nodded her agreement and marveled that he had spoken her exact thoughts aloud. "Keeping the school closed would encourage parents to put pressure on the governing board to find the swiftest and most convenient solution. In short, Miss Sedgewick."

"Well, if that's her game, I highly doubt it will work." Grams sat back in her chair and pensively stirred her tea. "The governing body will not be manipulated. Besides, several of us have discussed the matter. She is rather too young for such a position. It would be highly irregular."

"She might prove a more satisfactory headmistress than Miss Finch." The vicar sighed. "I do not mean to speak ill of the deceased, but there were many who disapproved of her, well, shall we call them *progressive* ideas. Filling the students' heads with stuff and nonsense they'll never need in life. So impractical, not to mention the unnecessary cost. If you ask me, Miss Sedgewick, though young, may be the more sensible of the two."

Phoebe couldn't help herself. "Mr. Amstead, excuse me for speaking out, but times are quickly changing and women's education must change accordingly. Miss Finch understood this and—"

"*Eh hem.* Phoebe, that will be enough."

"I'm sorry, Grams, but—"

"My dear." Grampapa's soft voice did what Grams's stern warning failed to accomplish. Any further argument stuck in Phoebe's throat. Grampapa nodded at her, his mouth pinched but his eyes kindly . . . ever patient. He held his hand out to her and she went to stand beside his chair.

She sensed Owen's gaze upon her, and a waft of heat enveloped her face. But when she braved a glance in his direction, he showed her a small smile and—if she weren't mistaken—a nod of admiration. Of agreement. She raised her chin, confident in her opinion even if her grandparents believed she'd spoken out of turn.

Grams continued as if their little interlude hadn't happened. "While I agree some of Miss Finch's ideas bordered on outlandish, I think what the school needs is a happy medium, someone who can please everyone." She gazed up at Phoebe, all trace of censure gone. "Wouldn't you agree?"

Phoebe knew she had been forgiven, and told a small lie to stay in Grams's good graces. "I believe that is sensible."

"Perhaps a married woman would suit," the vicar said. "Such a headmistress would better understand the values we wish to instill in our young ladies. For it does occur to me that a woman who has lived all her life outside the state of matrimony can have little idea of the virtues and rewards of being a wife."

Grams's mouth turned down at the corners. "A married woman who works? I should hardly think so. What kind of wife leaves her family to their own resources?"

Another protest lodged in Phoebe's throat. Could a woman not be a devoted wife and mother and still pursue a career of her own? Must she choose between one or the other with never a compromise in sight?

She swallowed and said nothing.

"Ah, yes, very true, my lady. A widow, then," Mr. Amstead suggested.

Grams tilted her head and considered a moment. "A widow may do nicely. As long as we are agreed that Miss Sedgewick, though a viable candidate for headmistress at some future date, is not yet ready for the role. Why, she might wish to marry someday. She's far too attractive to be considered wholly on the shelf."

"Agreed then, my lady. But how do you propose we

handle the situation? For it is quite apparent that she would like the job." Mr. Amstead raised his cup, but set it back in its saucer without drinking. "It's a rather sticky situation, if you ask me. We don't wish to upset Miss Sedgewick, for we might end up losing her as well. And wouldn't we be in a pickle then?"

Grams tilted her chin. "Mr. Amstead, you are the head of the governing body. What do you propose we do?"

The man shifted as if his chair had suddenly become uncomfortable. He tugged at his collar. It was clear he would rather defer to Grams's authority. Was he uncomfortable in his role on the governing body? Perhaps afraid of offending one of Haverleigh's more illustrious patrons? Grams waited for his reply, one eyebrow arcing in expectation.

"She must be spoken to," he said. "I shall do so this very afternoon, my lady."

Grams considered. "No, tomorrow morning will be soon enough. I shall come as well, and any others of the governing body who are available."

The vicar's relief was palpable.

"Would you like me to go with you, Grams?" Phoebe offered.

Her grandmother studied her with one of those assessing gazes that once made Phoebe squirm—which still had the power to do so, upon occasion. "You may come along if you wish," she said at length. "But it seems you've been tossing my name about rather liberally of late. If my name is to retain its power, I shall have to make an actual appearance every now and again, shan't I?"

Phoebe nodded and fought not to squirm.

"I've a good mind to keep driving until you agree to have dinner with me."

Eva watched Foxwood Hall fill the windscreen as they drew closer. Would he pass the house and keep going? Injecting mirth she didn't feel into her voice, she asked, "Do you intend to kidnap me, Constable?"

"Miles."

She opened her mouth to protest, but he spoke again. "We're alone, and needn't stand on ceremony." He slowed the vehicle. "It's not as if I'm planning to take you to a nightclub in Piccadilly. All I'm asking is a friendly supper at the Amberley Arms in Cheltenham. It's quite respectable, I assure you, and I'll have you back at a decent hour."

She drew a deep breath to steel herself. "Miles, I'm flattered. Truly. But perhaps you don't understand how much I am needed at Foxwood these days. Not only do I have my usual three ladies to look after, but three more besides now that the school is closed."

"All the more reason to get that school open again."

"Yes, well. There is nothing I can do about that." She wondered, would she free up time to spend with him if she could? She stole a peek at him from beneath her lashes. An Irishman through and through, he possessed enough charm and cheekiness to worm his way into the heart of any woman. Why her? Why not someone without obligations holding her to one place?

"I think you use those young ladies of yours as an excuse."

His observation startled her. Was he right?

"I think the idea of becoming close to anyone—especially me—frightens you."

She studied him again. Intently. And skewed her lips as she shook her head. "You are insufferably impertinent."

" 'Tis my privilege as an Irishman."

"For now at least, I must return to work," she said. They arrived at the fork where the road split, one way continuing to the service entrance of the house, the other to the village road. "You can drop me here, thank you."

They came to a stop and as she fumbled with the latch,

he reached across her. His sleeve brushed her middle and she flinched, imagining a flesh to flesh spark though they each wore layers of clothing.

He reached the latch and opened her door. At the same time, his sleeve rode up, revealing a wristwatch with an unusually large dial with a faint glow and prominent numbers. The piece disappeared into his sleeve again as he drew his arm away and placed his hand back on the steering wheel.

"Is that an aviator's watch?" she asked.

His jaw tightened. "It is."

The terse answer rendered her momentarily speechless. "You're a pilot?"

"No. Not anymore."

She yearned to ask him more, and yet didn't dare, for every line and plane of his face forbade it. Had she been wrong about him? Initially, she had believed he hadn't fought in the Great War. Or had he been a pilot before the war and an accident—a crash—rendered him incapable of fighting? But then, how could he be a policeman?

No, she returned to her previous assumption. He hadn't fought in the war. He was simply too whole, too healthy, too self-assured.

Lord Owen was self-assured, and though he had taken a bullet to the shoulder, on the surface he seemed perfectly fit. She glanced over again at Miles. She simply didn't know. Whatever his past, he seemed unwilling to discuss it with her. And that made her wary.

"Good day, then," he said. Though he tried to sound casual, she heard the tension in his voice.

"Good day." She tried to smile. She climbed out, holding her skirts as she did so to prevent them riding up her shins. Before she shut the door behind her, he leaned across the seat to peer up at her.

"Just so you know, I won't be giving up." He grinned and waggled his eyebrows, and as he drove away, one hand waved at her from his open side window. Such a puzzling man.

Back at the house, she removed her coat and hat and headed for the valet's service room, where a mound of ironing awaited her, along with alterations to two of Amelia's day dresses and one of Julia's gowns. Yet, she hadn't time to plug the electric iron into the wire that hung from its ceiling socket before the housekeeper rounded the doorway in a swirl of black serge that swept the floor.

Mrs. Sanders had been at Foxwood nearly as long as Mr. Giles, and though most of the staff showed a healthy fear of her, Eva liked the woman. She maintained order with the precision of fine clockwork and treated everyone fairly, if sometimes sternly. Still, Eva understood the quietly murmured nickname of "Old Ironheart," not only reflecting the woman's iron fist in running the house and scheduling duties, but also her wiry hair and gray eyes.

"It's about time you got back," the woman said in lieu of a proper greeting.

Eva blinked. As an upper servant, her duties weren't overseen by the housekeeper, and she didn't typically speak to Eva in such a tone. "I'm sorry, Mrs. Sanders. Is there a problem?"

"I'll say there is. Lady Julia has rung for you several times this afternoon and sent a note down saying you are to go up to her the very moment you set foot back in the house."

Oh, dear. She set the still-cold iron on its trivet. "Thank you, Mrs. Sanders. I'll go up straightaway."

As she passed the woman on her way out, Mrs. Sanders placed a hand on her shoulder. "Good luck. I only hope you've got a good excuse."

"Me, too."

She ran up the back staircase in record time, her boots raising a staccato that echoed against the tiled walls. Once through the door into the family's bedroom wing, she slowed her steps on the fine wool runner. Softly, she tapped on Lady Julia's door.

"Yes, come in."

Eva swallowed and opened the door. "My lady, I'm so sorry to have kept you waiting."

"My heavens, *there* you are." Eva braced for a scolding but Lady Julia continued in an even tone. "It's quite all right, Eva, I don't blame you."

Her relief was short-lived. Julia stood in the doorway of her dressing room. Behind her, bright colors spilled from open drawers. The armoire doors gaped as well, the usually well-ordered contents pushed willy-nilly as if ransacked by thieves. Eva bit back a sigh of dismay. Worth, Erté, Redfern, Poiret—all crushed one against another. A tedious afternoon of ironing and steaming precious fabrics stretched before her.

"This is Phoebe's fault." Lady Julia went on in the same calm tone that belied the spark in her eye. "She seems to believe you work exclusively for her and I intend to speak to my grandparents about it. But in the meantime . . ." She gestured for Eva to come in and shut the door, which she did without a word before moving into the dressing room.

She hadn't overestimated the mayhem Lady Julia had wreaked, and now she didn't underestimate the time and effort it would take to put things to rights.

In the middle of the havoc, the golden-haired Lady Julia stood as composed as an angel. "We're expecting company for dinner tonight. I need you to help me find the perfect dress and jewelry, and then work your very best magic on my hair. Perhaps a bit of powder and rouge, too. I want to look especially beautiful tonight. Nothing ordinary will do. I wish to astonish."

That little speech rendered Eva momentarily mute. Then she lowered her eyebrows and nodded. "There is a young man you wish to impress." The new Lord Allerton perhaps? "He must be very special, my lady."

"Special? You don't understand at all. It's Wallace Bagot coming for another try, and this time I intend showing him I'm so far out of his realm he could never hope to snare me. The very idea." She tossed her head and laughed. "Come, Eva. Let's turn me into a jewel so sharply faceted poor Wally Bagot will slice his fingers clean off if he dares try to touch me."

CHAPTER 13

Phoebe left Eva at home the next day when she and Grams set out for Haverleigh. She would have done so even if Julia hadn't cornered her again last night after poor Wally Bagot left Foxwood in a dither. Phoebe had known the moment Julia entered the library before dinner what her game was. She had rarely seen her elder sister looking so beautiful or so aloof. Like a china doll of such intricate design, it promises to shatter at the slightest tough.

Wally Bagot wouldn't likely be back anytime soon.

Julia must have been feeling especially triumphant, because later, when Phoebe encountered her upstairs, she issued demands like a monarch who had never been told *no*. Phoebe allowed her to rant but listened very little, and when Julia finally felt silent with that haughty slant to her lips, Phoebe had told her in the simplest terms possible that she'd had no intention of asking Eva to accompany her away from home today.

Dearest Eva. Because of Phoebe her tasks had piled up, but she never uttered a word of complaint.

"You're quiet this morning." Grams's observation snapped her out of her musings. The carriage jostled along the cobbles of Little Barlow's High Street. Phoebe glanced out her window and spied Myron Henderson sweeping the walkway in front of his haberdashery. His movements were stiff and labored, and he leaned on the broom as much as he used it to sweep away dust and fallen leaves. Mr. Henderson had lost his leg from the knee down in the war, and wore a prosthetic fashioned of heavy wood and steel. The contraption kept him upright but made walking a precarious endeavor. He was yet another soul who never complained, but went about his daily business with a grace Phoebe could only hope to someday achieve.

"Contemplating my shortcomings," she replied.

For a moment Grams said nothing. Was she, too, preoccupied with her granddaughter's deficiencies? "You remind me of me, when I was your age," she said at length.

Phoebe lifted her chin. "What—" She broke off, having been about to ask an impertinent question if ever there was one. But what *could* have changed the Countess of Wroxly from a spirited young woman to the staunch traditionalist sitting beside her today? Surely not Grampapa. Phoebe couldn't imagine dearest Grampapa ever leveling a single word of criticism at Grams. He was far too kind and amiable for that.

Grams smiled vaguely. Her eyes took on a faraway look. "I was once in the habit of speaking when I shouldn't and believing things I knew little about. I even had the audacity to correct my elders a time or two."

A wave of disappointment swept over Phoebe. She wished Grams could understand her and the hopes she held for the future. She looked down at her hands, and was surprised when one of Grams's covered her own. "It's all right, my dear. We all grow up. I did. And now I've grown old. Some of my patience has been lost along with my youth and I often forget that with time and experience, you'll come to an understanding of the world just as I did." She paused and gave Phoebe's hands a squeeze. "I do not mean to thwart you . . . *too* much."

If a tiger had sprouted wings and took off flying, Phoebe could not have been more flabbergasted. Grams had never said such a thing to her before, never implied that her word could be taken as anything less than law. She was obviously referring to yesterday's conversation in the library, when she had cut Phoebe's opinions off at the root. Grams had never apologized for such a circumstance before, and Phoebe didn't know quite how to respond. Grams saved her from having to.

"Never mind. Suffice it to say that despite a certain hardheadedness that admittedly runs in our family, you are growing up rather nicely and I'm proud of you, even if you do sometimes want for a smidgeon of prudence." She sighed. "I suppose such things are not in quite the same demand as previously. Only . . ." She took Phoebe's hand firmly in her own pale one, the fingers long and slender, the skin grown delicate and papery with age. "Do not forget who your people are, and those who came before you."

Phoebe swallowed. This was not merely Grams apologizing for being short with her yesterday, this was Grams revealing her deepest vulnerability—her fear of a rapidly changing world where she and others like her felt less and less in control. The Countess of Wroxly desperately clung to the old traditions because they made sense to her and made her feel safe, and because, as Grams had said, she had grown old. She no longer had the capacity to change, or to change to the degree the modern world required. Phoebe must not forget that. Grams had protected her growing up, and now it was Phoebe's turn to protect her grandmother as much as she could.

"I won't forget, Grams," she promised, more solemnly than her grandmother could know. "I never would."

"Good." Then, as if they had only been discussing dinner

or the weather, Grams released her hand and ducked to see out the window. "We're here, and I see by the motorcars that several of the others are here as well."

Inside, they met with Mr. Amstead and several other members of the Haverleigh governing body. Miss Sedgewick, clearly taken aback at the number of individuals milling outside her office, led the way to the dining hall where, as she stated, they would have ample room to discuss whatever had brought them to the school today. At the threshold, however, she and everyone else came to an awkward halt. Even Phoebe stared into the room with something akin to apprehension. The tables were bare and the floor swept clean of all signs of Miss Finch's untimely passing, yet the walls seemed to echo with her choking gasps and the crash of falling china.

"Goodness," Lady Philomena Albert murmured. She raised a hand to finger the fox collar draped around the shoulders of her beige silk overcoat. "I haven't set foot in here since . . . well, you know. Perhaps we should meet elsewhere. Veronica, what do you think?"

Lady Stanhope, the woman to whom Lady Philomena addressed her question, traced the wide doorway with her gaze as if sizing up a threat. "I think it will be all right, Philomena."

She didn't sound very certain. When no one moved, Grams pushed past Mr. Amstead and crossed the threshold. She turned about to face the others. "We're here to discuss the reopening of the school. That means our students shall be using this room again. How can we send them in if we ourselves are afraid to enter?"

She obviously didn't expect an answer, but stalked in her floor-sweeping black silk to a table at the very center of the room. Phoebe didn't hesitate to follow. The clatter of footsteps proceeded in her wake. When everyone had taken their seats, Grams prodded the vicar.

"Reverend? Perhaps you'd care to begin. I'm sure Miss Sedgewick is curious about why we wished to meet with her today."

"Oh, I, uh . . . Yes, well." He cleared his throat, and Phoebe wondered if he had this much trouble starting his Sunday sermons. He removed a handkerchief from his coat pocket and dabbed his brow. Phoebe's patience began to slip away. Besides ladies Philomena and Stanhope, three others from the governing body trained expectant gazes on him. "We are concerned about the amount of time the school has been closed," he said, "and how much longer it will remain closed. You have expressed a wish to wait until a new headmistress is chosen."

"Why, yes, that is correct." Miss Sedgewick sat stiffly upright, her shoulders back and her chin level. Her spine remained several inches away from the back of her chair. "As I have said, bringing in a new headmistress is likely to cause upheaval in the school's routine. The students have gotten used to Miss Finch's ways, such as they were. A new headmistress will bring with her new methods of doing things."

The gibe about Miss Finch wasn't lost on Phoebe. She narrowed her eyes on the woman as she continued.

"Why bring the girls back now? Wouldn't it be best for the governing body to make its decision, and only then resume studies according to whatever guidelines the new headmistress cares to establish?"

"There is sense in that," Lady Stanhope said.

Lady Philomena scoffed. "Not if it means *not* reopening the school before the summer holidays. Think how far behind the girls would be then." A murmur rose as the ladies began speaking at once, each with a differing opinion.

The vicar held up his hands. "Miss Sedgewick, is there another reason for your hesitation in reopening the school?"

Her dark eyebrows twitched. Beyond that, she revealed little of her thoughts. "One cannot be too careful with young ladies."

"Yes, that is true." Lady Stanhope sent a placating smile at Miss Sedgewick. It seemed clear to Phoebe with whom the woman sided. "My own Pricilla is a most sensitive girl. She has had several nightmares since I brought her home, and she has developed the distressing habit of staring down at her food until I can persuade her she need not fear its being tainted. So yes, I agree we mustn't act hastily. We have engaged a tutor for her in the meantime. I see no reason why the other students should not have tutors."

Phoebe bit back a retort. Not every student's family could afford a tutor. Jane Timmons would go without lessons were she not a guest at Foxwood Hall. But she saw no reason in arguing *that* point. Though she wholeheartedly disagreed with Miss Sedgewick's reasons for keeping the school closed, she did in fact side with the woman on the main point. Until all aspects of Miss Finch's death were resolved, it made no sense to risk the students' welfare by bringing them back to Haverleigh.

Dared she express that opinion? She felt fairly certain Grams had brought her along so she might observe firsthand the workings of the governing body, and *not* so she could weigh in herself. These women, and the vicar, too, would think her hopelessly impertinent. Perhaps she should wait, then, and see what conclusion they reached. . . .

The ringing of a telephone echoed from the corridor, and moments later the French mistress entered the dining room. "Miss Sedgewick, a call for you. It's a student's mother and she says it's urgent."

Miss Sedgewick let out a long-suffering sigh and pushed back her chair. "It is *always* urgent. If you will excuse me, I shall return just as soon as I can."

Mr. Amstead came to his feet as well. He reached into his breast pocket and drew out a briar and tortoiseshell pipe. "I think I'll step out for a few moments, ladies."

They waved him on and continued their debate. Lady Philomena remained adamant that the girls must return to their lessons. Lady Stanhope, on the other hand, staunchly defended Miss Sedgewick's view that a new headmistress must first be found. Was she in favor of Miss Sedgewick taking on the role?

Phoebe perused the woman's attire and for the first time noticed the similarity in size between her and Miss Sedgewick. Could Lady Stanhope be supplying Miss Sedgewick with clothing? It would explain how an assistant headmistress came by such costly items, but certainly raised a new question of *why*.

Phoebe ran through what she knew about Lady Stanhope, wife of Sir Raymond Stanhope, a wealthy baronet and banker from London. Their daughter, Pricilla, was younger than Amelia, one of the secondary school girls of respectable academic aptitude but certainly no prodigy. Phoebe suddenly remembered hearing rumors when Pricilla first entered Haverleigh that her father had married beneath him. Well, that could mean any number of things, from Lady Stanhope having been in his employ to her having hailed from the middle class. In her experience, where a rush to judgment marked the norm, it was rare that "marrying beneath one's station" meant anything truly sordid. And looking at Lady Stanhope with her perfect coif and impeccable tailoring, it was near to impossible to imagine her in what could be called sordid circumstances. She certainly didn't strike Phoebe as a former chorus girl, and it was a rare parlor maid indeed who could attain Lady Stanhope's level of refinement.

But perhaps Phoebe should find out more. . . .

"Someone help me—get him off of me!" The shout rocketed through the open windows overlooking the front of the house.

Grams glanced in that direction with a start. "What in heaven's name?" She rose to her feet, prompting the others to theirs as well.

Phoebe hurried over to the window. What she saw forced a gasp from her lips. "The handyman is attacking Mr. Amstead. Quickly, we must help him."

With more speed than Phoebe would have given her credit for, Grams intercepted her before she reached the main hall. "You can't go out there. You might be hurt."

"Then who will help the vicar? There is no one here but the staff and us." With that, Phoebe pushed past Grams and in another moment reached the front steps. "Mr. Ivers! Elliot! Release the vicar at once. At *once*, I tell you!"

But Elliot seemed not to hear her. He gripped the vicar's wrist in one hand, and with his other hand swung a long-handled garden spade in a wide arc. The metal end connected with Mr. Amstead's head with a resounding gong, and a shove sent the poor man tumbling over backward. Elliot stood over him then, holding the spade high in the air. Would he swing again?

Grams cried out Phoebe's name as she ran down to the driveway, only vaguely aware of the voices of the other ladies gathered on the steps. Grams shouted a "No!", but Phoebe reached Elliot and gripped his raised arm in both hands.

"Elliot, you must stop this. You've hurt the vicar."

He struggled against her while the spade swung in the air over her head. A sweep of black streaked past the edge of her vision, and she heard Grams's voice. "You will cease this unruly behavior this instant, young man. Now, hand me that garden tool."

Elliot didn't calmly hand over the spade, but his momentary distraction provided Phoebe an instant or two to realize what needed to be done. "Elliot, Miss Huntford would be frightfully displeased with you right now. Please, give me the spade. That would make Miss Huntford very happy."

"Miss Huntford?" Elliot glanced around as if Eva might appear from behind one of the nearby shade trees.

"Yes, I should very much like to tell her how cooperative you've been today, as you were when you helped us load the packages onto the donation truck."

"I helped."

"Yes, you did. Now . . ." She trailed off as she applied pressure to his arm, gently coaxing it downward until she could remove the spade from his fist. The fight had drained from his limbs and his fingers opened easily. "There now, that's better."

On the ground, Mr. Amstead groaned and reached up to rub the crown of his head. Phoebe realized it was the first sound he uttered since he'd fallen. He must have passed out. She turned to address the ladies huddled together on the steps. "Run and get Nurse Delacy. And call Dr. Reynolds." A woman, one of the staff judging by her sensible day dress, hurried back inside.

Grams knelt on the ground beside the vicar and fanned him with a gloved hand. "Mr. Amstead? Ward, can you hear me? Are you sensible?" She peered up at Phoebe. "I don't see any blood."

Miss Sedgewick came running down the steps and sank onto the drive at the vicar's other side. Phoebe turned her attention back to Elliot, standing docilely with his head bowed. Whatever had prompted the attack seemed to have spent itself, and she felt quite safe with him now. Even at the height of his aggression, she had not thought to be afraid he might turn his violence on her.

"Why did you do that?" she asked him gently. His answer took her aback.

"Fire."

Mystified, she shook her head. "There is no fire here." But then she remembered. "Mr. Amstead came out to smoke his pipe." Quickly, she surveyed the ground. At first she saw no trace of the piece, but upon further examination, she found it lodged in the box hedge beneath one of the windows. Not far from it lay an open box of matches, most of them scattered over the grass.

"You saw the flame the vicar used to light his pipe," she said, and he nodded.

"Flames . . . took everything away. Took *him*." He slammed his eyes tight and shuddered.

A cold draught settled over Phoebe's heart. "Who, Elliot?" she whispered. "Did someone die in the flames?"

He gave a stubborn shake of his head. *No.*

She didn't believe him, and guessed his silent denial conveyed a deep-seated fear rather than the truth. Gripped by a certainty that something terrible had once happened to him—perhaps the very thing that had left him so childlike—she drew breath to prod again. Just then a vehicle turned from the main road onto the drive.

Miles Brannock opened his door before he'd quite brought the motorcar to a stop, and in another instant he was out and striding toward her. His face was grim, his features stony. Apprehension spread through Phoebe and she looked to see if Elliot exhibited any signs of fear or an intent to run away. But he only watched the constable with a blank expression.

"What happened? I was told on the telephone that he"— Constable Brannock gestured with his chin at Elliot—"went on a rampage and attacked Mr. Amstead."

"I wouldn't exactly call it a rampage—" She stopped. In fact, that was exactly what Elliot's attack had been. He'd flown into a rage, very nearly uncontrollable. And Phoebe wondered, if Elliot and Eva hadn't forged a bond, what might have happened today? How would she have stopped the young man from further injuring or even killing the vicar?

"Did he hurt anyone else?"

At the constable's question she shook her head. "No, all his ire seemed directed at Mr. Amstead. As soon as I mentioned Eva—Miss Huntford—he calmed down."

Grams and Miss Sedgewick helped the vicar to sit up. Constable Brannock addressed him. "Sir, do you know why you were attacked? Can you tell me what happened immediately before it happened?"

"I don't know . . . I came out to smoke my pipe. We were having a meeting, you see, and Miss Sedgewick was called away to the telephone." He ran his fingers through his hair and then glanced at them, as if checking for blood. "I came outside and struck a match, and as soon as I held it to my pipe, this young fellow came barreling out from I know not where. He knocked the matches and pipe from my hands, and then . . . well, then he hit me . . . I think. Everything went black, and I woke up on the ground. Head hurts like the *dickens*."

"You're going to be all right, Mr. Amstead." Grams turned to Miss Sedgewick. "We need to bring him inside. Can you support him while we help him stand?"

Nurse Delacy scurried out of the building and down the steps. "I'll take this side, Lady Wroxly," she said, and lifted the vicar's arm around her shoulders. Together, she and Miss Sedgewick walked him inside.

Two more motorcars came puttering up the drive, raising clouds of dust. Grams shielded her eyes from the sun with her hand. "Here is our chief inspector."

"Yes, and Dr. Reynolds." A jangling drew Phoebe's attention back to the constable as he clamped a pair of handcuffs on Elliot's wrists. Elliot grimaced, but said nothing. "What are you doing?"

"Arresting him for assault, my lady." The constable took hold of Elliot's arm.

"But you can't. He's like a child. He didn't mean to harm Mr. Amstead."

"Is that our perpetrator?" the chief inspector's voice boomed out. He started toward them with a lumbering stride. He looked Elliot up and down as if sizing up a nag to be put out to pasture. "Well, Brannock, take him in."

"I'm sorry, my lady. I have no choice." The constable nudged Elliot to begin walking.

Eva had just finished readying Lady Julia for her day when Lady Phoebe telephoned to tell her what happened at the school, and to let her know the constable required her assistance. Dismay gripped her as she settled her younger charges in the Petite Salon with a passage of *Le Bossu de Notre-Dame* to translate. Lady Phoebe was due home within the half hour and would continue the girls' French lesson then.

Miles Brannock's motorcar awaited Eva just outside the service entrance gates. When he saw her, he quickly jumped out and hurried around to open her door for her. "Thank you for agreeing to come."

He maneuvered the car down the drive and onto the village road.

"I'll do anything I can to help Elliot. Surely there must be a misunderstanding."

He shook his head. A rabbit darted across the road and he braked to avoid it. "Lady Phoebe intervened. Elliot attacked the man with a garden spade."

"This doesn't sound at all like Elliot. He's always been completely docile and accommodating."

"For you."

"Well, yes. That *is* my experience of him." She frowned

at the windscreen. The sunny morning dimmed, and the trees suddenly appeared gaunt and cheerless despite their spring buds. "I don't suppose he said anything in his defense."

"Nothing. That's why I—that is, *we*—need you. Lady Phoebe said it was when she mentioned your name to Elliot that he stopped his assault and gave up the spade."

"Was the vicar terribly hurt?"

"It doesn't appear so, though he might be suffering from a concussion. Dr. Reynolds saw him and he's been taken to hospital in Cheltenham."

"My word. Poor Mr. Amstead. Poor Elliot." A thought had her half turning in her seat to better regard the constable. "Could the vicar have said something to provoke Elliot? Even without meaning to? People can sometimes say the most awful things to servants with never a thought to how hurtful they're being. They don't always . . . well, *understand* that servants have the same sensibilities as everyone else."

Chagrined at having said too much, she looked away. The truth was, some aristocrats didn't consider servants to be quite human, and Eva had more than once suffered the indignity of being talked about as if she didn't exist. Never from the Renshaws, but from guests, or at the other great houses where she had traveled with her mistresses. It was part of her job to endure it, part of her life, something she had long ago accepted. She didn't want or need anyone's sympathies, and she certainly didn't wish to see anything approaching pity in Constable Brannock's eyes.

He didn't so much as look over at her, but one hand left the steering wheel to lightly graze her sleeve. "Yes."

That was all, except for another glimpse of that watch of his. As if he caught the downward line of her gaze, he gave a flick of his wrist that brought his sleeve down, and resumed his hold on the wheel.

Why did he wear it, if he didn't wish it to be seen?

They arrived at Little Barlow's tiny police station, no more than a storefront with a holding room in back. Chief Inspector Perkins used Little Barlow as his headquarters because he lived here, but he served several other villages in the district as well, each with their own constable, and reported to the main constabulary in Gloucester.

Constable Brannock—she still stumbled over thinking of him as Miles, much less addressing him as such—led her through the front office and into a cramped hall that separated the office from the holding cell. Here she confronted a formidable wooden door with a small barred window set just above her eye level. She rose up on tiptoe and glimpsed a crown of nut-brown, disheveled hair. She needed no other distinguishing traits to recognize Elliot.

"May I go in and speak to him? I can't see persuading him to talk through a door."

In answer, the constable inserted a key into the lock. "I'll be right here if you need me."

With his hands draping his knees, Elliot hunched at the edge of an inhospitable-looking bunk. The room contained little else. A narrow barred window placed high up admitted enough light to see by. She avoided looking at a battered metal chamber pot in the corner.

He peered up warily through a shock of hair that had fallen over his brow. Their gazes locked, and he remained stock-still, as if to be sure she was real and not an apparition. Then he straightened and did something that twisted her heart. He smiled.

"Miss Huntford."

"Hullo, Elliot. I thought you might care for some company." Before she could go on, the door squeaked open wider and the constable placed a wooden chair in the room. She mouthed a thank you as he backed out, and dragged the chair closer to Elliot. She took her time settling onto it and arranging her skirts. "I understand there was a bit of unpleasantness at the school earlier. Would you like to tell me what happened?"

He resumed contemplating the floor.

"I'd like to help you, if I can. But I cannot do that if you won't talk to me. I thought we were becoming friends, Elliot."

He nodded solemnly.

"Then you can trust me." She sat very still, her hands folded in her lap, her feet pressed flat on the floor. She wished to appear as unthreatening and composed as possible. "Earlier today, were you angry at the vicar?"

A frown creased Elliot's brow. His lips moved but no sound came out.

Eva leaned slightly forward. "I only wish to understand. You were such a help with the donation packages. I wish to help you in return."

"There was fire," he whispered so low, she had to strain to hear.

On the way here, the constable had explained about the vicar and his pipe. "You mean when Mr. Amstead struck a match to light his pipe?"

"No fire." He shook his head, his forehead furrowing tighter still. He fingered the collar of his work shirt.

"But fire can be helpful, sometimes. Why, just the other day you were adjusting the kitchen generator. The coal fire generates electricity."

He shrugged. "Some fires are good. Some are bad. The fire that . . ."

"That what, Elliot?"

"Took him away."

Now she was getting somewhere. "Who went away? Was it someone you cared about very much?"

He nodded. "Father."

His eyes misted, and ache grew in her chest. "Did your father die in a fire?"

He nodded again. His fingertips disappeared inside his collar, and she remembered the chain he wore. Though she couldn't see it, when his fingers curled she knew he must be gripping it. It might very well have belonged to his father.

She believed she was beginning to understand. A coal fire in the generator might not seem dangerous to him, but a fire literally held in someone's hand might remind him of his father's death. "When was this, Elliot?"

He shrugged.

"Can you tell me where, then?"

"Mustn't."

"Mustn't what? Tell me about it?"

"Mustn't ever speak of it." He blinked, clearing away the moisture that had gathered in his eyes. He glanced up at her, and a curtain seemed to fall across his features, effectively shutting her off from what lay behind.

She sat back and tried not to let her frustration show. He almost seemed to be reciting his answers by rote, such as they were, as if . . . as if he'd been schooled in his responses. It occurred to her she had taken a too direct approach, that she had gone about this all wrong.

"Tell me, Elliot, are you originally from the Cotswolds? From a village nearby?" When he cast her a puzzled look, she groped for a way to clarify, and hit upon one. "Did the town or village where you grew up look much like Little Barlow? Were the shops and houses built of the same sort of stone?"

"Golden?"

"Yes, exactly. The golden Cotswold stone."

He nodded.

"And was your home surrounded by our rolling countryside?"

Another nod.

"I've traveled around a bit. Perhaps I've been there. What was the name?" She asked as if he had already told her but she had forgotten. Deceptive, yes, but she needed to break through his reticence.

He hesitated so long, she despaired of him ever answering, until he murmured, "James."

It was her turn to form a puzzled frown. "James? Is that the name of a town?" She hardly thought so. "Your father, or perhaps a relative?"

His lips flattened and he seemed to draw into himself, his shoulders angling sharply inward. He had closed up again, and this time she decided she had pressed him long enough and to no avail. She slowly came to her feet. "Elliot, is there anything I can bring for you?" Without waiting for his answer, she noted the thin blanket folded at the foot of his cot and the lack of a pillow. She didn't know if Elliot could read, but even if he didn't she thought perhaps some magazines might help him pass the time. There were some back issues of the *Strand* in the servants' hall at home. She didn't think they'd be missed.

"I'll come again soon," she promised. When he once more cast his gaze to the floor, she crouched in front of him and covered his none-too-clean hand with her own. "You won't be forgotten here, Elliot. Never fear."

Constable Brannock relocked the cell door and walked with her back into the main office.

"I suppose you heard everything," she said.

"Most of it. It would appear his father's death might have triggered what happened earlier."

"Will that help him? Poor dear, he might have believed he was helping the vicar, not hurting him."

"That all depends." They stopped by the larger of two desks, and the constable deposited the cell door key into a drawer and then locked that with another key on a ring he'd taken from his coat pocket. "If it comes out that he has done something like this before, the court might decide he should be locked away."

"How frightful! We can't let that happen. If only we could find out more about him. But it seems he doesn't trust me any more than he does anyone else. If only—" She broke off with a gasp.

"What is it?"

"When I asked him where he grew up, he said James. It just occurred to me what he meant. My goodness, of course."

"Of course *what,* Eva?"

"Where is the one place in any town or village where someone like Elliot might feel at home? Might feel welcome and safe? And thus be most familiar with?"

"You're speaking in riddles now."

"Miles, the parish. St. James could be the name of the church in the town where Elliot grew up."

CHAPTER 14

"I'm going up to London to visit the Davenports and I'm taking Eva with me. There is nothing you can do about it, Phoebe."

Looking up from the map spread open on her escritoire, Phoebe regarded Julia standing in her bedroom doorway. She wore a skirt that narrowed stylishly a few inches above her ankles overlaid with a drop-waist tunic. A light coat would complete the travel outfit, but Julia hardly appeared the carefree traveler. She positively fumed. Her nostrils flared and her eyes sparked. Phoebe sighed and shrugged. "I doubt Grams will let you. Eva's needed here to help with the girls."

Julia stalked into the room and shut the door behind her—nearly a slam. "You have been treating Eva like your personal servant and I am bloody tired of it."

Phoebe flinched at the word that shot out of Julia's prettily bowed lips. "My goodness, you *are* incensed. Well, I'll have you know I had nothing to do with Eva leaving this morning. Constable Brannock wished her to talk to the handyman from the school. There was a frightful to-do there earlier, and the poor chap has been arrested. Mr. Amstead is in hospital."

"What has any of that to do with me? Why must you be so tiresome and *why* can't you keep your nose out of everyone's business?"

Phoebe went back to studying her map. It was a travel guide of the Cotswolds that showed scenic routes and pointed out sites of interest, including churches and chapels. Eva had shared her revelation about Elliot with her. She found three churches called St. James—a Church of England in Westford, a Catholic church in Farmingworth, and a Methodist chapel in a tiny village called Chadham.

Though it might sidetrack her a bit from discovering the truth of Miss Finch's death, she couldn't simply ignore the plight of a young man who couldn't speak in his own defense. She had hoped she and Eva might explore together, find Elliot Ivers's home, and learn more about him—perhaps something that would garner the court's sympathy. But though she loathed admitting it, Julia was right about Eva. Phoebe had been taking her away from her regular duties, but it wasn't so much Julia's perceived hardships that preyed on Phoebe's conscience, but the knowledge that Eva was still required to complete her chores each day—all of them, no matter how few hours were left as evening drew upon them.

A knock at the door interrupted her thoughts and whatever further complaints Julia had been leveling at her, which she had thoroughly ignored. Amelia came in with Lilyanne behind her.

"Julia, there you are," the youngest Renshaw sister said brightly. "It's come to my attention that Jane and Lilyanne have never been to Bath. *Can* you imagine? So we'd like to go this afternoon, but Grams said we had to ask you to come with us. Will you? Please? Do say yes."

Julia's brow crinkled. "Sorry, I've plans to go up to London today. Ask Phoebe. She has nothing better to do."

"Excuse me, did I just hear you say you were going up to London?" Amelia and Lilyanne stepped aside as Grams swept in behind them. She didn't wait for Julia's answer. "You are not going to London, Julia. I need you here."

"But Grams—"

Grams turned her attention on the younger girls. "You two run along and ring for Eva to help you and the others get ready. I'll be there presently and we'll plan your visit to Bath." All smiles now, Amelia and Lilyanne practically bounced out of the room, and Phoebe noticed with a burst of pleasure that they were holding hands.

"Now then, Julia." Grams's voice dipped low. "You have done precious little so far to assist with our visitors. As of today that will change. A trip to Bath will provide an educational experience for them as well as an enjoyable outing, and I will rely on you to see that they make the most of their time there. Eva shall accompany you."

"But Grams . . ." Julia trailed off, and Phoebe could just hear the question her sister longed to ask. *Why don't you go with them, Grams?* But even Julia wouldn't dare risk such impertinence with their grandmother. Instead she pleaded, "My plans are made. Althea Davenport and her family are expecting me. There are theater tickets and dinner plans, a luncheon tomorrow . . ."

Grams said, not unkindly, "You should have inquired with me first."

"I didn't know I had to," Julia mumbled.

"What was that?"

"Nothing, Grams. What am I to do about the Davenports?"

"My dear, that's what telephones are for, no?"

Julia took on a decidedly tragic mien. Rather much,

Phoebe thought, for dashed hopes concerning the Davenports, especially when she hardly ever mentioned Althea's name these days. Phoebe determined it best to forego all signs of gloating, and resumed studying her map. She had lost Eva as her travel companion, yes, but she had gained the luxury of an entire, guilt-free afternoon, where she needn't worry about lessons or mediating arguments between their young guests.

She set out in the Vauxhall shortly before Julia and the girls were to drive away in Grampapa's Rolls-Royce. With her map tucked in her handbag, Phoebe first headed to the village.

When she arrived at the police station, she found Chief Inspector Perkins occupying the larger of two desks in the front office. His feet were propped on the desktop and he leaned back in his swivel chair with a newspaper opened in front of his face. He peered over it as she stepped inside. She saw no evidence of Constable Brannock anywhere.

"Ah, Lady Phoebe." He hastily refolded the paper and set it aside. "What might I do for you today?" He eyed the parcel she carried.

"I have some magazines and things for Elliot, if that's all right."

"Yes, yes, of course. I'll have to have a look first."

She laid the bundle on the desk and tugged one end of the twine to untie it. Plain brown paper fell away to reveal the magazines, a blanket and pillow, and some separately wrapped cheese and baked goods. "I assure you there are no files or crowbars, Inspector. May I take them back? Miss Huntford wished to be here but had business elsewhere today. I should like to let Elliot know she is thinking about him."

"Wasting her thoughts on an imbecile with violent tendencies?" The man's sigh sent a whiskey-tinged waft in

Phoebe's face. She recoiled and only just stopped herself from fanning the air with her hand. He unlocked a drawer and brought out a key.

It was all she could do to remain civil. "Thank you, Inspector. I shan't keep you long." She rewrapped the bundle as the man pushed out of his chair. She followed him into the back corridor and waited silently as he unlocked the cell door.

"You've got a visitor," the inspector said gruffly. "Sit up. There's a good lad. No sulking. It's her young ladyship from Foxwood Hall come to do you an enormous kindness, so you'll be treating her with respect or I'll—"

"There is no need for threats, Inspector." Phoebe stepped around him and entered the cramped, stuffy room. "Good morning, Elliot. I've brought you some things to make you more comfortable." She held out the bundle.

He sat at the corner of his cot against the wall, his knees drawn up and encircled by his arms. He peeked sideways at her through a fringe of hair, and then tucked his chin lower.

Inspector Perkins jabbed a finger in his direction. "What did I tell you?"

"Inspector, please. If you'll just wait outside, I won't be but a moment."

The man's eyebrow slanted in disapproval, but he stepped back into the tiny corridor that barely accommodated his girth.

Phoebe approached the cot and set the parcel down. "These are actually from Miss Huntford. She wished to come herself, but couldn't get away this morning. I'm sure she'll visit you just as soon as she may. Would you like to see what she sent?"

Without waiting for an answer, she again peeled away the corners of the wrapping. For an interminably long moment Elliot didn't so much as blink. Just as she was about to back out of the room, he turned his head. She smiled at him, hardly daring to hope for a reciprocal gesture.

"There's a blanket and food and a few other things," she said eagerly, but quietly. She didn't wish to frighten him. A glance over her shoulder brought the inspector into view. He leaned against the doorway of the front room, his shoulders hunched and hands in his coat pockets. An off-key little tune emanated from his pursed lips.

She turned back to Elliot. "Once I leave here, I'll be embarking on a bit of an excursion. I've errands to run, you see, but I've never been to some of these places. Perhaps you've heard of them? Farmingworth? Do you happen to know where that is?"

Elliot looked at her blankly. He reached out, and with one finger stroked the brown wool blanket peeking out from the bundle.

"Hmm. I must also pass through Westford. Have you ever been there?"

He uncurled his arms and legs and swung to the edge of the bed where he could sit up properly. With both hands he delved into the pile she had brought him. He found the food and carefully unwrapped it.

"Our cook included some of her famous Eccles cake and a date and walnut loaf. I know you'll enjoy them." She looked over her shoulder again. The inspector continued whistling his tune and now studied his fingernails. "Tell me, Elliot, do you know of a village called Chadham?"

About to break off a bit of the date and walnut loaf, he went utterly still. Phoebe's breath—indeed the very blood in her veins—froze. Had she struck upon something? The moment ended all too ambiguously as Elliot returned to sampling the loaf with a small bite.

Had he truly reacted? Phoebe wasn't quite sure. But perhaps.

"Good-bye for now, Elliot. I'll . . . em . . . give Miss Hunt-ford your regards. I'm sure she'll be by soon to see you."

"Miss Huntford."

"Yes." Oh, why couldn't he have spoken when she men-tioned the villages? She sighed and made her way out.

The inspector nodded at her as she passed him, and went to lock the cell door. Phoebe walked through to the front room to discover Constable Brannock had returned.

She spoke quickly, before the inspector returned. "I can't be certain, but he might have reacted to the name of a village I mentioned. I'm going to take a drive there and see what, if anything, I can find out."

Something in the constable's expression put her on the alert, but before he could reply, Inspector Perkins returned. "Is there anything else, Lady Phoebe?"

Such a tiresome man. "No, that's all for now, Inspector. Good day to you both."

Outside, the engine of a familiar, three-wheeled Run-about puttered directly behind her Vauxhall. With her handbag swinging from her elbow, she dug in her heels and propped her hands on her hips.

"So this is why Constable Brannock looked at me the way he did. He knew you were outside waiting for me."

The handsome, ebony-haired man grinning broadly at her from behind the steering wheel laughed. "He did in-deed, Phoebe. I ran into Brannock this morning and he told me about what Miss Huntford learned from Elliot yesterday. I assume you're going exploring. Get in."

"What do you mean, you ran into Constable Brannock? How? What are you still doing in Little Barlow?"

"I've taken rooms at the Calcot Hotel." He waggled a finger at her. "You're dabbling in trouble again."

"Yes, well. I don't need a babysitter."

"Yes, you do."

"Owen—"

"I'm joking. Do get in." He reached over and opened the passenger door for her. "Unless you'd rather go motoring up and down the Cotswolds alone. Doesn't sound like much fun, though, does it?"

"What do you mean, you can't find her?" Eva had come upstairs to help the girls on with their outerwear, only to be confronted with Lady Amelia's unexpected announcement that Jane was nowhere to be found. "Lady Wroxly told me you all wished to go to Bath today."

"We did—that is, we do. We discussed it last night, and Jane was as eager as Lilyanne to go, since she has never been. But she was up before any of us, and we haven't seen her since."

"Surely she's downstairs somewhere. Did you check?"

Lilyanne nodded, and Amelia said, "That was our first guess. But she's not in the morning room, the library, or anywhere else we could think of. We checked the billiard room and Rosalind Sitting Room, too."

Eva considered the most likely places a young lady would wish to visit on the estate. "And she's not outside in the gardens?"

"If she were, we'd be able to see her from my bedroom windows, wouldn't we?" Lady Amelia frowned and nipped at her bottom lip. "Where on earth could she be?"

Dressed in bright spring colors, Julia emerged into Amelia's bedroom from the dimness of the hallway. She wore her coat and carried her new toque hat with flowers decorating the band. "Where could *who* be? Aren't you all ready to leave yet?"

Lady Amelia continued chewing her lip and exchanged an ominous look with Lilyanne. Eva folded her hands at her waist and drew a fortifying breath. "It appears we'll be delayed a few minutes in leaving, my lady. Jane appears to have gone off somewhere, though I'm sure we'll find her directly."

Lady Julia, her jaw stiffening, released a weary sigh, pivoted on her heel, and stalked from the room. "I'll be downstairs in the library—waiting. Come get me the very *instant* the child is found and ready to go."

"She certainly doesn't seem at all concerned about Jane, does she?" Lady Amelia observed, and Lilyanne agreed with a solemn shake of her head.

"I'm quite sure there is nothing to be concerned about," Eva reassured her, though a small doubt niggled. A certain memory struck her then, of another girl who went temporarily missing. Last winter, Eva had discovered the parlor maid handing out food to needy local children near one of the hothouses out past the kitchen garden. Perhaps Jane had gone out through the service courtyard and wandered in the same direction. Hedges and well-placed trees blocked the view of that area of the grounds, and Amelia might not have seen Jane from her windows.

"I have an idea," she said, and proceeded to help the girls on with their coats. "Where is Lady Zara, by the way?"

"Waiting in her room," Amelia said with a roll of her eyes. "She's behaving quite like Julia about the whole matter. Says she couldn't care less about seeing Bath again, that it's just a pile of rubble these days, and she would much rather stay at Foxwood. But Grams said she must come along." She bent lower as Eva pinned her hat in place, and then Eva did the same for Lilyanne.

"Then please go and get her and all of you wait in the library with Julia," Eva said.

"Don't you want us to help look?" Amelia sought consensus from Lilyanne. "We could spread out, each of us take an area."

"I don't mind helping, Miss Huntford," the redhead said shyly.

"As much as I appreciate that, girls, I believe it would be better for you to stay together in the house. Otherwise it could take half the morning to gather all of you together again."

After seeing the girls into the library, Eva hurried below-stairs, grabbed one of the ready cloaks hanging on a row of pegs by the courtyard door, and hurried outside.

For April, a brisk wind circled the courtyard walls. Eva held the cloak closed and stepped through the gate onto the path. She skirted the kitchen garden, waving to Nina, the newest kitchen maid. Then she strode up and down the aisles between the greenhouses. Pervading stillness but for the birds and swaying trees told her no one was about.

An uneasy sensation came over her. According to Lady Amelia, Jane often made a habit of arriving tardy to lessons, while offering up little or no excuse. Was this a continuation of that behavior? Was she merely exploring Foxwood, or had she slipped away on some errand she didn't wish anyone to know about? Eva turned back and made her way slowly toward the hedge that marked the separation between the service grounds and the gardens. Footsteps crunched behind her. She turned to see Jane Timmons coming through the trees on the far side of the kitchen garden. The girl saw her and stopped in midstep, her expression registering surprise. Then she continued around the garden's perimeter.

"Good morning, Miss Huntford."

"Jane, where have you been? I've been looking for you."

"Oh, I'm sorry." She smiled and brushed strands of fine brown hair away from her face. She wore a simple gray skirt, serviceable ankle boots, and a military-styled trench coat over a shirtwaist. "Just out for a walk."

"Without telling anyone? Lady Amelia had no idea where you'd gone. We were growing worried."

"Well, I'm back now. Has Amelia arranged for us all to go to Bath?"

"Jane, I must ask you where you were."

For an instant the girl looked at a loss. Then her confidence fell back into place. "As I said, I was walking. There's nothing quite like a morning ramble, is there?"

Eva hesitated. If she brought up Jane's habitual and unexplained tardiness at school, Jane might realize the disclosure had come from Amelia. Eva didn't wish to create ill feelings among the girls. But from now on she would keep a closer eye on Jane Timmons. "While you are at Foxwood Hall, we are responsible for you, Jane. Please don't leave again without telling someone."

"All right, I won't. Shall we go now? I'm excited to see Bath, and we don't want to waste the rest of the morning." Jane set off walking, leaving Eva with admonitions fading on her lips and little choice but to follow.

CHAPTER 15

Phoebe soon understood why the Morgan Runabout typically outraced so many other motorcars. She also began to understand why Eva often clutched the seat as they motored about in the Vauxhall. Not that the Vauxhall ever achieved speeds such as those now sending the countryside streaking past.

"Even if you hadn't needed me today . . ." Owen trailed off as he slowed for a small gaggle of geese ambling across the road. Phoebe was about to protest that she hadn't *needed* him, not really, when he continued. "I'd have telephoned you anyway. I've discovered a thing or two about your Nurse Delacy."

"You made inquiries into her war service?"

"I most certainly did. The woman bears watching, and frankly I'm astounded that she would have been hired on at a girls' school. Or anywhere she would come in contact with helpless patients."

Phoebe instinctively reached up to hold her hat as the Runabout hit a bump. "What *did* you discover? I was under the impression she served valiantly all through the war. Her parents said she was stationed right behind the front and often went to collect the fallen soldiers in the ambulances."

"She did. And her nursing skills proved exemplary. She helped save many a life."

"Then what was the problem?"

"Can you bear a chilling story?"

"Owen, please tell me what you've learned."

"Very well. Last autumn, right before the war ended, it seems a soldier was admitted to Nurse Delacy's triage station. Severe burns, and both legs gone. He should have died, and probably would have, but he didn't—not of his injuries."

"I don't understand."

His face grim, Owen stared out the windscreen. "Reports are that he begged for death, the pain was so great." He stopped again and darted a glance at Phoebe. She nodded and beckoned for him to continue. "Olivia Delacy was the nurse supervising the night shift. In the morning, the soldier was dead."

"That's hardly condemning."

"As I said, his injuries weren't what killed him. The doctor determined he died of asphyxiation. As if someone held a pillow over his face until he expired."

"Oh, dear lord."

"No charges were made, but Nurse Delacy was immediately sent home."

Feeling vaguely queasy, Phoebe hugged her middle with her left forearm and pressed her right hand to her lips. "She killed him to end his misery."

"There is no conclusive evidence she did, but it's possible."

"Highly possible, I'd say, or why was she abruptly sent home? She must have snapped."

Owen only inclined his head and focused on the road.

"And if indeed she snapped once and killed that soldier, how do we know she hasn't snapped again since? Or won't snap tomorrow?"

"I'm afraid we don't."

"Then . . . do you think she could be responsible for Miss Finch?" In Phoebe's mind, it was a rhetorical question. She had already added Olivia Delacy's name to her list of suspects.

"There is one glaring difference that speaks in her favor," said Owen. "The soldier was a broken man who would never be whole again. Miss Finch, on the other hand, was a healthy woman in her prime, no?"

"I suppose one might say that. She certainly had many years of her career left ahead of her."

"Then what reason might the nurse have had to do the woman in?"

A possibility sprang to Phoebe's mind. "Perhaps Miss Finch discovered what Nurse Delacy did—or might have done—in France and as a precaution planned to sack her."

The discussion ended when they reached Farmingworth. They found St. James Catholic Church and spoke to the monsignor. An elderly man, he remembered nothing about a boy named Elliot Ivers, nor anyone with Elliot's condition. They returned to the road and continued on toward Chadham—the village to which Elliot had given that minute reaction, and the place Phoebe considered their true destination.

They crested a hill, then started down a steep slope ending in a narrow curve walled on both sides by hedgerows. Owen pressed the accelerator. Of their own accord Phoebe's feet jammed against the floorboards and her hands braced against the dash.

The Runabout immediately slowed and Owen glanced over at her. "Why didn't you ask me to slow down?"

"Oh, I . . ." She scrunched her features. "I don't know, really."

He laughed. "I thought you might enjoy the feel of flying."

"This motorcar certainly seems like it might take flight at any moment. It's just that I've never ridden in anything so fleet. It does take getting used to."

"Think you could?"

She regarded the dash and the gear stick. "This vehicle looks to predate the war. You've owned it a rather long time, no?"

"I have."

"Then you must be fairly proficient at driving it."

"Passing fair."

She relaxed back against the seat and tugged her hat lower on her brow. "Have at it, then."

He gunned the engine, but not, she noticed, until they had rounded the next bend and an open stretch of road presented itself before them.

The wind tugged at her hair and slapped at her cheek. Her heart raced along with the vehicle. "I've been curious about something and have wished to ask." She raised her voice to be heard. "I hope you won't think me impertinent."

"Ask away."

She studied him a moment. Though his disclosure about Olivia Delacy never strayed far from her thoughts, her curiosity about Owen Seabright—about the kind of man he was—could not be stifled.

He was so very different from most other men she knew, so very . . . what was the word? *Unaffected*. Not that he didn't wear his confidence like an expertly tailored suit. But of all the young men she had ever met, he alone seemed to derive his sense of self from his accomplishments—his mills, his service in the war—rather than his family's pedigree. How *had* he escaped the usual trappings of privilege? She made up her mind to ask her question. "When your brother died, why did you not take on his title as your father's heir? You don't even seem entirely comfortable with people addressing you as Lord Owen."

He had been the Honorable *Mr.* Seabright, until last spring when his brother, Edgar, died along with so many others during the influenza epidemic.

His hands tightened on the steering wheel. "I'm not."

His terse reply sent regret sweeping through her. She should not have brought it up, should not have ruined their lovely morning drive. "Never mind. You *do* think me impertinent."

He shook his head. "I don't. It's just a difficult subject to talk about. I had been perfectly happy as Father's younger son. I had my own plans and my own means of achieving them. And in so doing, I learned the fewer boundaries between myself and those who work for me, the better. Titles are just more walls between people."

"But as their employer, you *are* above them."

"True. But I refuse to turn a blind eye to conditions in my mills, or demand more than my workers are capable of giving. I've learned that mutual respect makes for smoother operations and superior goods."

"And you think a title interferes with that."

"I know it does. A title makes others afraid to approach a man. I want my workers to be able to converse with my foremen, and my foremen to converse with me. That's the only way to run a business, Phoebe. The only way to keep one's finger on all aspects of one's industry."

"How bourgeois," she teased.

He laughed again. "Indeed. Such notions are hardly in keeping with fusty old titles."

They drove on through farmland and small villages, stopping sometimes for sheep or cows crossing the road. While they talked of other things, she couldn't help wondering, in a corner of her mind, what would happen when Owen finally inherited his father's estate with all of its honors. Would he walk away from it—let the title revert back to the crown? Such a notion shocked her . . . and at the same time thrilled her with its newness, its daring. A man who wasn't afraid to rely on his wits and abilities only. She smiled, though she wondered if she would have the courage to do the same. Poor Grams would be appalled.

They passed a clay-lined dew pond surrounded by a small herd of black Dexter cows enjoying a midmorning drink. Beyond the fields rolling away to the east, a spire poked up from the tops of some trees. Phoebe pointed out her window. "There, that must be St. James of Chadham, among those beech trees."

They proceeded to a fork and a signpost that pointed the way. What had appeared close from the main road turned out to be much farther along the twisting lane. They passed a handful of cottages set well back from the road. Farm plots stretched out behind them, bordered by tapering, dry-stone walling. Each modest homestead appeared in need of new shingles or thatch, and cried out for fresh paint on doors and shutters.

Chadham proper, bordered by hills on one side and a rushing stream on the other, boasted a few shops situated around a shady square. There were a few people about, all of whom turned a curious eye to the intruding vehicle and the two strangers who occupied it. Owen parked the Runabout in front of the rectory, which couldn't be larger than a couple of rooms, perhaps three.

The man who answered Phoebe's knock stooped to avoid hitting his head on the lintel. He had kindly gray eyes, though slightly sunken, as if he'd been ill or hadn't been sleeping well. Phoebe guessed his age to be fifty or there-abouts. His thin lips pulled back in a smile. "Yes? May I help you?"

"Excuse me, sir, but are you the rector of St. James?"

"Yes, I am Pastor Davis."

"My name is Phoebe Renshaw and this is Major Owen Seabright," she said, deciding his former rank, rather than his title, might inspire a bit of trust. "We'd like to inquire about someone who might have been a member of your congregation a while back."

"When would this have been?"

She traded a quick glance with Owen. "We don't know, exactly. This individual is rather in a bit of trouble, you see, and we're attempting to find out more about him. Specifically, whether he has any family."

The man opened the door wider and stepped aside. "Please, do come in."

He bade them make themselves at home in his tiny par-lor. Threadbare patches in the furniture attested to the room's contents having seen the better part of the last cen-tury as well as the present one, and Pastor Davis seemed relieved when they turned down his offer of refreshments.

"His name is Elliot Ivers," Phoebe said after describing the handyman, "and he is presently sitting in jail in Little Barlow accused of attacking another man. The victim is also a vicar—perhaps you know him. The Reverend Ward Amstead?"

The minister shook his head. "No, I'm afraid I haven't had the pleasure. But this Elliot, er . . ."

"Ivers," Phoebe clarified.

"Yes. You say he indicated he might be from Chadham, but he didn't actually tell you as much?"

"That's correct, sir. You see, Elliot doesn't speak much. He's rather simple. Oh, not his abilities—he is quite a skilled workman and follows directions just as well as you please. He's employed by the Haverleigh School for Young Ladies."

"If he works for this school, as you say, doesn't someone there know his history?"

"I thought news travels fast these days," Owen said. "But obviously you've not heard. There was an untimely death in Little Barlow several days ago. The individual who hired Elliot, and who might have known more about him, is deceased."

"Good heavens. Are you supposing this Elliot—"

"No," Phoebe said quickly. "Not at all, sir. The matters aren't related." She glanced at Owen again. "At least we don't think they are."

The pastor patted his knees and blew out a breath. "Well, I'm afraid I cannot help you. I've never heard of Elliot Ivers, and don't know of anyone fitting his description. Of course, I've only been here three years now. We Methodist ministers move about every few years."

"Could you perhaps take a peek in the church records?" Phoebe asked. "It's terribly important."

"That would take time. But I will do. Mowbury lies not far from here, and I sometimes ride there on my bicycle. Have you a telephone at your disposal?" Phoebe eagerly nodded. "Leave me the exchange and number. If I find anything in our records, I'll ride in and telephone you from the post office there. Will that suit?"

"Yes, very nicely, sir, thank you." Phoebe rose, signaling the two men to do the same. Pastor Davis saw them out.

Eva and her charges arrived back at Foxwood Hall late in the afternoon. The girls had shown an eagerness to see all that Bath provided of interest, from the old assembly rooms to the Roman baths and everything in between. Even Lady Zara joined in the spirit of the day, assigning herself the task of tour guide to show off her familiarity with the city. Lady Julia, meanwhile, slipped away more than once—into a shop here, a bakery there—promising to meet them at their next destination but more often than not arriving as Eva and the girls were leaving.

At least she hadn't lost sight of any of the girls. Jane Timmons's early morning jaunt had put Eva on her guard. She made certain there were never more than a handful of paces between her and each of the girls.

She was bone tired as she dragged herself up the back staircase to the bedrooms to collect shoes that must be cleaned and polished and overcoats that needed brushing before she retired later that night. Immediately after depositing the outerwear in the valet service room, she must come back up and ready everyone for dinner. She hoped there were no guests this evening requiring her to shower extra attention on Lady Julia.

With several coats draped over her arms and a basket full of shoes, she knocked at Lady Zara's door last. No answer came. Odd. The girl hadn't been in any of the others' rooms. She knocked again. Nothing.

Setting down her basket, she quietly opened the door. "Lady Zara, are you here?"

The room lay in shadow. None of the lamps had been switched on. A tremulous breath fluttered in the far corner. As Eva's eyes adjusted to the darkness, a figure—hunched, her knees drawn up—took shape in a chair.

Yet another crisis? There seemed to be no shortage among these girls. They'd had such a lovely day, too, or so Eva had thought. She hadn't heard a single unkind word from anyone—not even Zara, though neither had she gone out of her way to be particularly friendly to Jane or Lilyanne.

"Lady Zara?" Eva closed the door behind her and set down her burden of coats and shoes. She crossed to Lady Zara and crouched before her. "My lady? What's wrong?"

Lady Zara didn't look up, but seemed to shrink farther

into the chair. A sheet of paper drooped from her fingers. A letter? The girls had probably checked the post upon their return.

Eva tried again. "Not bad news from home, I hope?"

A sob slipped from Lady Zara's lips. And then another, and finally a torrent that broke like a summer storm. The paper drifted to the floor at Eva's feet.

"My poor dear girl. Is someone at home ill?" This could well be what had kept the Earl and Countess of Benton from returning to England to collect their daughter.

Her face in her knees, Lady Zara choked out, "Worse than that."

Eva's heart twisted. Someone close to Lady Zara must have died. A grandparent? Parent? She reached up and stroked a spiraling lock of chestnut hair that had fallen loose. "I'm so very sorry, my lady. This is something I understand. Lady Amelia will understand, too—"

The girl's head snapped up. "You mustn't tell Amelia anything."

"But why ever not? You needn't suffer alone when—"

"No! It's too humiliating. You must swear silence." Her voice fierce, Zara raked the curls back from her swollen, tearstained face. "Swear it, Miss Huntford."

"I don't understand. This is nothing to be ashamed of." She attempted to touch the girl's shoulder, but Lady Zara flinched out of reach.

"Discovering yourself on the brink of destitution is nothing to be ashamed of?"

A moment stretched as Eva tried to understand. She glanced down at the letter, lying faceup on the floor, but it was too dark to read. She could make out only the coat of arms embossed in red foil at the top of the page, and a curling, swooping signature at the bottom. "Destitution? You mean no one has died?"

"Died? No, but I wish I would." The last word dissolved into a wailing lament.

"My lady, you mustn't say such things. Surely this is only a temporary setback for your family." Was it? Eva had no idea but she had snatched at the first words that entered her mind.

"It isn't temporary, you dullard. The houses will be sold, and all our lovely things. The money is gone to income and death taxes and bad investments and . . . and I shall have to leave school and there will be no dowry and no coming out and no husband for me, ever! How I hate Papa for doing this to me!"

At a loss, Eva sat back on her heels. In truth, that last outburst had dampened her sympathies a smidgeon, especially when Lady Zara's parents probably had more resources at their disposal than they let on. Perhaps they would not be able to continue in the extravagant style to which they had become accustomed, but neither would they be walking a path to the workhouse. The state of being *poor* had an entirely different meaning for those of the upper classes, and it involved few of the harsh realities of true poverty.

At a knock at the door, Lady Zara fell silent and her eyes became gleaming circles in the dimness. "Who is that? Send them away."

At a second knock, Eva rose and went to open the door.

Lady Amelia stood outside, with Jane and Lilyanne behind her. "We thought we heard someone yelling. Is Zara all right?"

"She's fine, my lady," Eva said.

Lady Amelia craned her neck to see around Eva. "Why is the room dark? Zara, what's wrong?"

"Go away!"

The three girls conferred by trading silent looks, and

reached a unanimous decision. "Excuse us, Eva." Eva had no choice but to step aside as Amelia led the other two into the room and switched on a lamp.

"We're not going away, Zara. If something is wrong, we wish to help."

Lady Zara sprang up from the chair and threw herself facedown on the bed. "You don't understand," she sobbed.

"You're quite right, we don't." Jane strode to the side of the bed. "How about for once you don't push the rest of us away and instead try trusting us? It might result in you having three new friends. Perhaps," she added in the merest of whispers.

"Why are you doing this?" Lady Zara sobbed into the pillows. "Why won't you just leave me alone?"

"Because it would be horrid of us to simply walk out and ignore you," Amelia explained gently. She sat on the edge of the bed and leaned to stroke Lady Zara's back.

Slowly, Lady Zara rolled over and pushed upright. More hair had fallen loose—great, heavy, twining locks. She draped it back off her shoulders and away from her face. She searched the room until her gaze lighted on Lilyanne. She pointed at her. "You'll certainly have a good laugh once you hear."

Lilyanne blushed to the roots of her flaming hair, but her eyes held steady as she shook her head. "I won't, Zara. I'm not like that." Eva heard the implied sentiment— Lilyanne was not like Zara herself. "I can see that whatever has happened is quite serious, and only a beast would laugh at another's ill fortune."

Eva experienced a surge of pride in the girl's generosity—all things considered. She was proud of all three girls for showing Lady Zara more kindness than she had ever shown any of them. Would Zara waste the opportunity? It was entirely up to her to rise to the occasion or not, and Eva was preparing to back out of the room and leave them to it when Lady Zara suddenly thrust a finger in her direction.

"Miss Huntford, go ahead, *you* tell them. They'll find out eventually anyway. And I can hardly bear to speak the words again."

The others turned their attention on Eva, and she explained what little she knew. When she was done, Jane assumed a mystified expression. "Is that all?"

"All? Don't you understand? It's *everything*." Lady Zara moaned.

Jane shook her head. "No, it isn't. So you won't be wildly rich any longer. This is why Miss Finch wanted us to learn as much as we can at school—so that we have skills and knowledge and can depend on ourselves in life."

"Didn't you hear?" Zara snapped. "I shall have to *leave* school. My parents can no longer afford it." She broke into sobs again, fell prone on the bed, and curled onto her side.

Jane climbed up beside her. "My family can't afford my tuition either, but I have a scholarship. Perhaps you'll also be awarded a scholarship."

"I'm not smart like you."

"Nonsense," Jane replied. "You simply aren't in the habit of trying much, are you? I suppose you didn't have to, with Miss Finch helping you along the way she was."

Lady Zara picked her head up off the mattress. "You knew about that?"

Eva, too, snapped to attention at Jane's disclosure. She hadn't thought anyone else but she and Phoebe knew about Miss Finch's altering of Zara's marks. She wondered how Jane become privy to that information.

Meanwhile, Jane shrugged. "I guessed," she said, rather evasively. "It seemed the only logical explanation."

Eva continued to wonder about that, but Lilyanne's next words startled her from her thoughts.

"We can help you with your studies."

Lady Zara twisted around to view Lilyanne. Her puffy eyes narrowed and her brows gathered. "Why would you do that?"

As Jane had done, Lilyanne shrugged. Her lips tilted in a small, shy smile.

Lady Zara scowled. "Oh, but what would I do afterward? *Work?*" The word dripped with distaste. "Shall I be like Miss Sedgewick, well-bred but forced to earn a living? Or like—" Her gaze drifted to Eva. Yes, she supposed to a girl like Zara Worthington, born to ease and advantage, Eva's life might seem insufferable. But that didn't stop Eva from holding her chin level and meeting Zara's gaze head-on.

"Yes, you can work," Jane said decisively. "You'll find something you're good at and enjoy, and earn your own money and be your own mistress. I don't see anything tragic in that."

Lady Amelia had been quiet thus far, hanging back and looking slightly uncertain. Eva understood why. Of the girls, she alone now inhabited the realm of the upper classes. How to fashion a persuasive argument in defense of employment when she herself would face no such decision unless she did so purely by choice?

Yet, Eva would not have her young lady believing she need apologize for her privileged life. She caught her eye, smiled, and nodded, for it had been Amelia who had brought the other two here to investigate the sounds of distress coming from the room; Amelia who always had the well-being of others forefront in her mind. Eva quietly crossed the room to her.

"You were right to insist on coming in, my lady," she whispered. She gestured at Lady Zara. "I believe she'll be all right, now that she has friends to count on."

Amelia tossed her arms around her in a brief embrace. "Thank you, Eva."

"If that will be all, I'll go now and tend to the outerwear before I return to help you all dress for dinner." Before Eva closed the door behind her, she glanced in one more time to see all four girls sitting on the bed, and Lady Zara wiping her tears away on the handkerchief Lady Amelia handed her.

CHAPTER 16

After dinner that evening, Phoebe told Eva what Owen had learned about Nurse Delacy. Eva surprised her with how calmly she digested the news.

"I have to say, my lady, I'm not altogether shocked that she might have taken some drastic action during the war. The woman is frightened and skittish and she's certainly hiding something. The question is, does she have something else to hide?"

"Such as Miss Finch's death?" Phoebe stood up from her dressing table and hugged her wrapper around her. "One would assume Miss Finch inquired into the nurse's previous employment before hiring her, and that she didn't discover the incident with the dying soldier."

"But would she? Nurse Delacy was never charged with anything, merely sent home." Eva gathered up the hairpins she had removed from Phoebe's hair. "Then again, perhaps Miss Finch found out later. Someone who knew of the nurse's deed might have alerted Miss Finch to the truth. Even the suggestion that the nurse might have taken a life would make Miss Finch wary of her."

"Quite possible. If Owen could find out, someone else

could, too. Possibly even someone who was there at the same triage station. A patient, a doctor. Who knows? What I do know is it seems Haverleigh is a haven of secrets. Nurse Delacy, Zara, Lilyanne, Jane, Miss Sedgewick, Elliot, even Mrs. Honeychurch—all of them seem eager to protect some mystery or other."

"Don't forget Miss Finch herself, my lady. Adjusting Zara's marks, and then changing her mind."

Phoebe paced, her arms hugging her middle. "Yes, Miss Finch herself . . ."

Two days later, Mr. Giles alerted Phoebe to a telephone call. She went into her grandfather's study and closed the door. She lifted the candlestick base from the desk and placed the receiver to her ear. "This is Phoebe Renshaw."

"Good afternoon, Lady Phoebe. It's Pastor Davis. I have some news for you. Have you the time now?"

Her pulse picked up speed. "Yes, Pastor, please go on."

She heard a shuffling sound, as if the man shifted position and moved the receiver from one ear to the other. Then he said, "Well, I haven't had time yet to peruse all the church records, but what I did pore through revealed no mention of your Elliot Ivers."

"Oh, I see." He considered this news? Phoebe stifled a sigh. "Well, thank you, Pastor—"

"There's more, my lady. I came into Mowbury this morning—I'm there now—and happened upon the deacon of their church here. I've discovered the most extraordinary thing. While the church that stands in Mowbury now is called St. Katherine's, it wasn't always so. There was a much older church in town, but it burned down a few years before the war, along with the rectory and the sexton's cottage."

"Was the name of this church St. James?" she asked eagerly.

"Indeed it was, my lady. It was some years before a new church was erected, and the parish decided to rededicate the sanctuary. Start over, as it were. You see, the fire was quite a traumatic event. The vicar died, and his housekeeper and her son barely escaped with their lives."

"Good heavens." She mulled this over a moment. The housekeeper and her son. . . . Could they have been Elliot and—Phoebe whisked a hand to her lips—Miss Finch? Could Miss Finch have been Elliot's mother?

She was jumping ahead too fast and made a physical effort to stay her excitement. "Pastor, did you learn the names of any of these people? The vicar? The housekeeper?"

"The vicar was Father Jessup Burland."

Father. Some Anglican clergymen, especially within the more formal Anglo-Catholic tradition, preferred that term over Mr. or Pastor. Elliot had indicated to Eva that his father had died in a fire. Could he have been referring to Father Burland? "And the housekeeper?"

"Her name was Mrs. Edith Fairgate. But here is the truly dreadful thing, my lady. Her son, who was only five or six years old at the time, is believed to have started the fire. Quite by accident, of course, but the mother was so remorseful, she took her boy and moved away. No one knows where they went or what became of them. Do you suppose the son and the young man you're trying to help are one and the same?"

"It's possible, Pastor, but it sounds as though we've run into a dead end." If she could only discover how Miss Finch came to hire Elliot. If she was not his mother, had she known him previously? Could she be a relative? She thought back on what she knew about Miss Finch. According to Grams, she had taught for many years at a school in York, then served as an assistant headmistress at a school in Sheffield. She wondered, did they know for a fact that

Miss Finch had taught as long as she claimed? References could be forged. She fairly buzzed with speculation.

But in the next instant, she cut her thoughts off short. Miss Finch could not be Elliot Ivers's mother. The Haverleigh governing body would not have been satisfied with mere letters of recommendation. They would have made careful inquiries and been thorough in their scrutiny of any headmistress they hired.

Then who was Elliot Ivers, and where had he spent the past dozen years?

"I'm sorry I can't be more help, my lady," the pastor said. "Oh, I just remembered. There was also a curate, but he was away at the time of the fire and also left Mowbury immediately after. I couldn't get his name, but if I manage to learn it, would you like me to telephone again? He may be able to supply you with more information."

"I would, Pastor, thank you. You've been a great help." An idea came to her. "Tell me, do you have war veterans and widows among your parishioners?"

"We most certainly do, my lady. A good dozen of our families continue to suffer in the aftermath of the war."

"I've established a local charity for the Relief and Comfort of Veterans and their Families. The RCVF. I shall add St. James Methodist Church to our list of drop-off points."

"How very generous of you, my lady. Thank you."

After she rang off, Phoebe hurried outside to the greenhouses, where Eva was assisting Grampapa with the afternoon biology lesson. Phoebe looked on, counting off the minutes and bouncing on the balls of her feet. Finally, Grampapa declared the lesson a grand success.

"You clever girls make an old man proud," he told the girls heartily. "Go on with you, then. Have a bit of free time before Lady Wroxly gathers you for your next lesson."

The girls drifted away with rather less enthusiasm than

their teacher. Phoebe accepted Grampapa's arm and walked with him back to the house. She found herself embroiled in a game of chess before she was finally able to escape to her room and ring for Eva.

"I believe I've learned something about Elliot," she burst out the moment Eva closed the bedroom door. She related Pastor Davis's telephone call. "The fire occurred about a dozen years ago. Elliot would have been a small child, and it's possible his mother took on an assumed name after they disappeared, because no one could ever discover what happened to them. I'm guessing Elliot Ivers isn't his name at all."

Eva held up her hands. "Perhaps we should slow down just a bit, my lady. There is no real proof that this boy and Elliot Ivers are the same person."

"But he could be, Eva. What exactly did Elliot say to you when you visited him in his cell?"

"He said his father died in a fire."

"Did he? Try to remember his exact words."

Eva's forehead pinched with concentration. Then her eyebrows rose. "Yes, I remember now. When I asked him if he had lost someone in a fire, he said, 'father.' Not 'my father,' but just 'father.'"

"I thought as much. And he told you he was from James. Surely that must be St. James Church—not merely the church he attended, but where he actually lived, in the sexton's cottage."

"My lady, you could be right about this."

"I believe I am, Eva. What's more, I believe there has to be a link between Elliot and Miss Finch. At first I thought perhaps she was his mother, but his mother was the vicar's housekeeper. I can't see how such a woman could have risen to the position of headmistress, or how the school's governing body could have failed to verify Miss Finch's teaching references. Still, it's not entirely impossible. I should like to speak with Mr. Amstead. I truly believe the lighting of his pipe somehow triggered the memory of the fire, and in Elliot's mind he acted to protect Mr. Amstead, not attack him."

After a hesitation, Eva said, "If Elliot is the same boy and he did set that fire years ago, how many people will believe he acted out of consideration for the vicar, and not malice?"

"He was just a small child at the time of the fire. It wouldn't have been his fault. A terrible accident, nothing more."

"I can believe that," Eva said in an ominous tone, "but others may not. Tell me, my lady, how many *accidents* is one young man allowed before he is declared a danger and locked away for good?"

Early the next morning, Eva once again found herself zooming along High Street through the village and up to the school. Earlier, she had risen at her usual time to discover Lady Phoebe already dressed and waiting for her on the ground-floor landing of the back stairs.

"My sisters and the others won't need you for two hours at least," she had said. "So no one can protest your accompanying me on an errand this morning." She had sent Eva back upstairs for her coat, and off they went.

Lady Phoebe changed gears as they left the village behind them. The engine revved and the Vauxhall rushed forward on a burst of speed. "I tell you, Eva, if there is anything more to be learned about Elliot Ivers, we will find it at the school."

Eva held the brim of her felt hat against the wind pouring through the open sides of the motorcar. "Miss Sedgewick didn't seem to know anything about him. Only that Miss

Finch hired him and refused to let him go. I don't trust much about the assistant headmistress, but I believed her about that. And now Miss Finch isn't here to tell us anything."

"Perhaps Constable Brannock missed something when he searched her bedroom."

"Perhaps." Eva didn't think so. Just in the short amount of time she had helped the constable search, they had gone through most of the room and found nothing of interest.

Funny, Eva might have said as much to Lady Phoebe, but the very thought of discussing being alone in the same room—a *bedroom*—with Constable Brannock turned her mouth dry and her tongue to lead. Luckily, Phoebe went on talking.

"Don't you see, Eva, that if Elliot and Miss Finch are somehow related, she might have left something to him. A fund or an annuity that could be used to secure his future and see that he's cared for."

"I daresay I hope you're right, my lady." The engine revved as they climbed a hill, but Eva's musings kept her too busy to grip the seat or clench her teeth. Someone somewhere must know where Elliot came from. Surely Miss Finch couldn't have been the only person in the world who knew of his origins.

When they arrived at the school, she once again felt an overwhelming sense of stillness and abandonment, reminiscent of the ruins of castles and abbeys she had toured with her young ladies. The mist that rose from the lawns to cloak the grounds and buildings in muted tones of silver didn't help. A school needed activity, voices, those moments of joyous, controlled chaos before students settled in for their lessons. A school needed life, but Miss Finch's death seemed to have drained the life right out of Haverleigh. Would the school ever fully recover?

Inside, they didn't go many steps before Miss Sedgewick confronted them from her office doorway. "Back again, are you? I fail to see the purpose of yet another visit, Lady Phoebe. And please don't tell me your grandmother sent you. I'm afraid that excuse is wearing rather thin." Her arching eyebrows might as well have been directed at a naughty schoolgirl. Eva wondered where the woman found the impudence to speak to the Earl of Wroxly's grand-daughter that way.

"I am here today of my own accord, Miss Sedgewick." Lady Phoebe showed not the slightest discomfiture. "I'm here on behalf of Elliot, who is in need of our assistance."

Eva took in Miss Sedgewick's attire. She wore a pleated skirt embellished with covered buttons, a shirtwaist dripping with lace at the collar and cuffs, and a belted jacket with three-quarter sleeves and buttons that matched those on the skirt. House of Worth, if Eva weren't mistaken. She narrowed her eyes, uncaring if the assistant headmistress thought her insolent.

"What on earth can anyone do for a brigand like Elliot Ivers?" Miss Sedgewick snapped. "He should be locked away permanently."

"That's very unkind of you," Lady Phoebe said calmly. "Very ungenerous. He seems quite alone in the world. Are we to let him languish in a cell because of something that might not be his fault?"

"*Humph*. I suppose that spade jumped into his hand and insisted he attack the vicar." Miss Sedgewick sniggered meanly. "What can you imagine you'll find here that can possibly help him? I told you he showed up one day and Miss Finch hired him. That is all there is to the story."

"And you know *nothing* about why Miss Finch hired him?"

"The goodness of her heart, one supposes."

Lady Phoebe gazed at the woman a long moment, and Eva hid a smile when Miss Sedgewick began to fidget. Then Lady Phoebe crossed to the stairs. "If you'll excuse us."

Miss Sedgewick hurried along the corridor to head them off. "Where do you think you're going?"

"To Miss Finch's bedroom, of course."

The assistant headmistress hopped up onto the first step and attempted to block their way. "Lady Phoebe, I cannot allow that."

"I'm afraid that unless you pick me up and carry me out, there isn't much you can do to stop me."

Miss Sedgewick seemed to weigh this option, and Eva couldn't stay silent. "Don't you dare," she murmured.

"I'll call your grandmother," the woman threatened.

Lady Phoebe shrugged and stepped around her.

"I'll call the police. I'm sorry, my lady, I don't wish to, but you *are* trespassing."

"I understand, Miss Sedgewick. But I'm afraid Chief Inspector Perkins won't be roused from his chair for such a crime as this, and in all likelihood Constable Brannock will be interested in anything we should happen to find."

Lady Phoebe continued up the stairs. Eva couldn't resist the tiniest of smirks as she passed Miss Sedgewick. The woman responded with a glare every bit as poisonous as the Madeira cake that killed Miss Finch.

"My goodness, that was unpleasant," Lady Phoebe said as they reached the landing. "Which room was it again?"

Eva led the way along the corridor past the classrooms. "This one, my lady. I do hope it isn't locked. We didn't think to ask for the key—not that Miss Sedgewick would have handed it over."

"I'm not worried." Lady Phoebe grinned. "I already know what magic you can work with a hairpin."

The door was not locked, but opened easily when Eva

tried the knob. A gasp sounded, alerting them they were not alone in the room. A plump figure in pale blue leaned over the writing table, one hand inside a gaping drawer, the other curled around the edge of her starched apron as though she might draw it around her for protection.

"Mrs. Honeychurch," Lady Phoebe exclaimed. "What are you doing here?"

"I . . . I . . . that is . . ." She snatched her hand from inside the drawer and straightened.

"Eva, please close the door." Lady Phoebe crossed to the writing table. "You're searching for something."

"N-no, my lady."

"Of course you are. The only question is what."

Mrs. Honeychurch wrung her broad hands together and sent a silent plea to Eva. Eva went to stand beside Lady Phoebe. "Do you know something about Miss Finch you haven't told us?"

"No, nothing. There's nothing. It's just that . . . well, Miss Finch's personal effects will need to be cleared out for the next headmistress, won't they? And as no one seemed interested in doing so, I-I thought I'd just get started. You understand . . ."

Lady Phoebe caught Eva's eye and nodded, then angled her chin. Eva understood, for it was a signal they had used before. Just as Eva had taken over questioning Nurse Delacy's parents, she would do so now, for the cook would feel more comfortable talking with a lady's maid than with an earl's granddaughter.

She took Mrs. Honeychurch's hand. "Let's sit down and discuss this. We're your friends, Mrs. Honeychurch, and we're Miss Finch's friends as well. All we want is to learn the truth about what happened to her, and if you know anything that could help her find justice, you mustn't keep it to yourself."

She led the cook to the settee by the fireplace.

"I'm sorry, Miss Huntford, but I don't know anything about Miss Finch's death. I swear I don't."

"No, perhaps not about her death, but her past." Eva broke off with a gasp as a memory flashed. Only days ago, she had sat and consoled a despondent Mrs. Honeychurch over the loss of the headmistress. The very same headmistress who would sip chamomile tea and chat with her in the servants' hall late at night. "Mrs. Honeychurch, I believe you *do* know something about Miss Finch you haven't told us. Whatever it is, you must come clean. Has it anything to do with Elliot?"

"Oh!" Mrs. Honeychurch cried out as if Eva had stuck her with a pin.

"You needn't fear to confide in us, Mrs. Honeychurch. Is Elliot the reason you sneaked into this room this morning? Were you looking for something that links him to Miss Finch?"

The woman shivered from head to toe as if caught in an arctic blast. "I swore I'd never tell. I gave my most solemn oath."

"To whom? Miss Finch?" *Or her murderer?* Eva, too, shivered at the thought.

"I swore to Henrietta I'd take her secret to my grave." The cook tented chapped hands against her chin. "She trusted me, you see. She hoped if anything ever happened to her, I might be able to convince the new headmistress to keep Elliot on. Or even . . . look after him myself, if it came to that. But—but no one must ever know . . ."

"Know what, Mrs. Honeychurch?" Eva demanded. "What aren't you telling us?"

Mrs. Honeychurch shook her head repeatedly. "It's too dangerous. I c-cannot say."

Slowly, Lady Phoebe came around the settee to sit in

one of the armchairs opposite. She made barely a sound, and once sitting, she didn't move again, but kept her gaze pinned on Mrs. Honeychurch, who seemed not to notice her at all. Eva patted the woman's hand until she regained a modicum of control and calmed herself.

"Miss Finch is gone now," Eva said gently, "and there is no one to act on Elliot's behalf—no one except you, Mrs. Honeychurch. Besides, Miss Finch's death releases you from your oath."

"Except that it doesn't," the woman replied, shaking her head again. "Henrietta said I must *never* talk about Elliot's past. Oh, poor Elliot, suffering in that horrid jail cell. . . ."

"Yes, Mrs. Honeychurch, exactly." Eva placed her hand on Mrs. Honeychurch's, hoping the physical contact would help inspire her trust. "Understanding his past might aid us in helping him now."

"Yes, but . . ."

"Please, Mrs. Honeychurch. Elliot's future is in your hands."

"Lord help me." The cook nodded as if answering her own private question. Then she lifted her apron to wipe her eyes. "Miss Finch told me that if the wrong person discovered the truth, she and Elliot would be in grave danger. Then she told me *I'd* be in danger as well if I ever told anyone." She swallowed and dabbed at her eyes again. "And you see, the secret is out. It must be, or Miss Finch would still be alive. Someone, whoever it is, *knows,* and he'll be back. For Elliot. And for me, Miss Huntford."

"But I assure you, Mrs. Honeychurch, Lady Phoebe and I pose no danger to you. Don't you see, if the secret is already out, the best way to protect yourself and Elliot is to let other people know."

She allowed Mrs. Honeychurch all the time she needed to consider those words. At least a full minute passed, perhaps two. Then Mrs. Honeychurch slowly nodded. "Perhaps you're right. But please, Miss Huntford, you'll hold this in the strictest confidence?"

"As far as I am able. No one need ever know my information came from you."

The woman released a shuddering breath. "All right, then. Elliot was Miss Finch's nephew. Her sister's child. There is no other family left."

Eva glanced over at Phoebe, who compressed her lips and showed little sign of surprise. The cook's tears brimmed again, and while Eva certainly understood her emotional state, she needed the woman to focus. "What did Miss Finch tell you about Elliot's past? How did he come to be in danger?"

"I don't know. She was vague. She said the less I knew the better."

Not the answer Eva hoped for, but her mind raced nonetheless. There seemed little doubt left that Elliot was the child who set fire to St. James Church. But what happened to him afterward? Pastor Davis said he and his mother simply disappeared. Where did they go? How did Elliot come to be working at the school under his aunt's supervision? "Perhaps you can tell me this, Mrs. Honeychurch. When did Miss Finch first begin caring for Elliot?"

"When his mother died."

Eva already thought as much. "And do you know how, and when, his mother died?"

Another shake of the cook's head brought a wave of disappointment edged in frustration. "Henrietta didn't tell me either of those things, and it wasn't my place to pry, was it?"

"No, I expect not."

"But I did have a sense that Elliot hadn't been in Henrietta's care long. I can't say why, exactly. It was just a feeling I got. And another thing. I don't think the sisters got along most of their lives. Henrietta talked about her sister rather sadlike, as if she had more than a few regrets. But before she died, she told Henrietta whatever it is that could endanger all of them."

"I see." Eva mulled this over and concluded this secret would lead them straight to Miss Finch's murderer. "Is there anything else?"

The cook crumpled the corner of her apron between her hands. "Not that I can think of just now. Is there . . . well . . . any reason Miss Sedgewick must learn about my being here in Miss Finch's room?"

Miss Sedgewick, who had secrets of her own. Eva conjured a reassuring smile. "I don't believe she ever needs to know. I take it you were searching for any information that links Elliot to Miss Finch, and that you found nothing of interest?"

"That's right, Miss Huntford. I didn't want any such information falling into the wrong hands."

"Most of the room has already been searched, but Lady Phoebe and I will take another good look to be certain. Thank you, Mrs. Honeychurch, you've been a great help."

After the woman left, Lady Phoebe moved to the settee and sat beside Eva. "What do you make of all that?"

"I'm not quite sure, my lady. I wonder how a mother and son managed to disappear for years without anyone finding out where they were. Had Miss Finch known of their whereabouts all that time, or did her sister contact her more recently?"

"Which raises the question of whether the sister knew she was dying—perhaps of some ailment—as opposed to passing away suddenly." Lady Phoebe folded her hands in her lap and stared down at them. "Eva, you don't suppose Elliot might have had a hand in his mother's death, do you?"

"My lady, what a dreadful notion. But I'll admit it's a question that must be considered."

"It could have been another accident, like the fire." Lady Phoebe hesitated before adding in a murmur, "If indeed the fire *was* an accident."

An icy shiver traveled Eva's length. "One thing can't be denied. Death seems to follow Elliot like a shadow."

CHAPTER 17

Constable Brannock's disappointment was palpable when Phoebe met him in the village later that morning. She couldn't help an inner smile, however, when she considered the reason for the policeman's letdown. He had hoped Eva would come as well. Unfortunately, Phoebe hadn't dared keep Eva away from home longer than necessary and had brought her directly back to Foxwood Hall following their visit to the school.

Eva's parting words had haunted her all the way back into town. *Miss Finch's involvement in Elliot's life had to be what led to her murder.* She hadn't wanted to think it—hadn't liked acknowledging that an innocent woman died because of the sins of another. But whose sins? Both she and Eva believed Elliot knew, that he could solve this mystery today if only they could entice him to speak.

She and the constable walked along High Street together, passing shops and absently nodding their greetings to pedestrians. "Thank you for meeting with me, Constable."

"You said it has to do with Elliot."

"Yes, and Miss Finch, too. That is, Miss Finch's death."

The constable came to an abrupt halt outside the smithy's shop. From behind the building came the incessant clanking of a hammer on an anvil, a din that grated on Phoebe's nerves. "I think you had better explain, my lady."

They resumed walking while she related what she and Eva had learned from Mrs. Honeychurch. She included Eva's last supposition about Miss Finch. By the time she finished, Constable Brannock's brow had drawn taut.

"None of this bodes particularly well for Elliot, you understand. From what you say, his past is a violent one that led to Miss Finch's death." Phoebe started to protest, but he cut her off. "That is how a jury will see it, my lady."

"If Elliot is in any way responsible for the terrible things that happened in either the past or the present, I don't believe he did them with any intended malice. You know how he is, Constable. He's like a child. I don't believe he has a violent or unkind bone in his body."

"He upset Miss Sedgewick and sent her running to escape him not long ago."

Phoebe harrumphed. "That was more than likely Miss Sedgewick being difficult. All Elliot wished to do was hand her a flower. But that's precisely my point. He didn't mean to upset her. He simply doesn't understand the repercussions of his actions. I believe the same is true of his attack on Mr. Amstead."

"You believe Elliot tried to help the vicar by striking him with a garden tool?" The constable clasped his hands behind his back. His strides lengthened, and Phoebe quickened her pace to keep up. Was he about to dismiss her and her theories? She wouldn't let him.

"I believe the flame the vicar used to light his pipe brought back the terror of the fire he experienced as a child, and sent him into a panic."

"The fire he might have *started* as a child—if indeed Elliot is that same child."

"Can there be any doubt?"

"Yes, my lady, there can. Without Miss Finch to corroborate the facts, we are left guessing. And the police are never happy when forced to guess. Besides, whatever happened in Elliot's past doesn't change what he did in the present. He attacked the vicar and has been arrested for assault."

"What will happen to him if he's convicted?"

"He'll either spend time in jail, or . . ."

Phoebe didn't like the gloomy note as his voice trailed off. "Or what? Please don't spare me."

"Or considering his limitations, he might be committed to an asylum."

It was Phoebe's turn to grind to a halt, forcing several passersby to lurch sideways to keep from bumping into her. "That would be dreadful. Constable, please, we cannot let that happen. Perhaps I can persuade my grandfather to find a place for him at Foxwood Hall, where he'll be supervised and cared for."

"My lady, I'm afraid you're getting ahead of yourself. Before your grandfather can be persuaded of anything, Mr. Amstead must first be persuaded to drop the charges against Elliot."

After leaving the constable, Phoebe's next stop brought her to the Calcot Hotel, a Georgian-style guesthouse on the outskirts of the village. Set on a ridge, the hotel enjoyed expansive views of rolling fields and distant hills. She had one more errand to perform today, one inspired by Constable Brannock's words. But she decided against setting out alone. This errand called for reinforcements, someone who commanded the respect and admiration of other men.

"Shall we take the Runabout?" Owen Seabright shoved his arms into his trench coat sleeves as they exited a lobby decorated in deep greens and dark woodwork. He blinked in the glare of the midmorning sunlight.

"We'll go in my Vauxhall," Phoebe said, leading the way. She grinned at him over her shoulder. "I'll drive."

"As you will, my lady." His baritone chuckle smacked of intimacy.

Phoebe pretended she hadn't noticed. "Thank you for agreeing to come. You might do more to persuade the vicar than I can."

"Based on what you told me on the telephone, I'm not completely convinced the vicar should be persuaded." He opened her door for her before circling the bonnet and letting himself in the passenger side. "Especially if you intend on bringing Elliot to Foxwood Hall." He stretched out his legs as much as the space in front of him allowed. "I'd like some kind of assurance you won't be putting yourself and others in danger."

She wanted to say something clever in reply, something flippant to nip such notions in the bud and silence the mistrust directed at poor Elliot. But Owen's concern for her—and for her family—left her disconcerted and ridiculously tongue-tied. She instead concentrated—mightily—on easing the Vauxhall onto the main road.

They entered the village of Kenswick shortly before noon. Unlike Little Barlow, Kenswick's main road wiggled over hilly terrain, with clusters rather than long rows of attached shops and homes. And unlike Chadham, where they had met with Pastor Davis, Kenswick displayed signs of steady, if modest, prosperity in its tidy gardens, freshly painted trim, and decorative shop signs.

The Anglican church presided from a picturesque hollow at the edge of a wood, with a circular garden in front presenting an array of colorful, but still tightly furled buds. A graveyard stretched off to one side, with the rectory and garden in back. As Owen handed Phoebe out of the Vauxhall, she spied the lacy edges of an orchard just coming into bloom.

"Charming setting," Owen observed.

"Indeed, it's lovely. Mr. Amstead must enjoy living here. I do hope he's available to speak with us."

"He's expecting us, isn't he?"

She started walking. "Don't worry, I telephoned ahead. I left word with his sexton."

Their knock nevertheless went unanswered.

"That's odd," Phoebe said. "Shall we walk around back?"

They found the vicar in his walled garden. His coat off and his shirtsleeves rolled up to the elbows, he leaned over a clay pot. He appeared to be working the soil loose around the roots of a sapling. On either side of the garden, twisting branches supported canopies of dusky rose and paler pink blossoms. A delicate fragrance scented the forest-cooled air. Phoebe breathed in refreshing draughts.

Then she called out, "Hello, Vicar."

Mr. Amstead flinched and looked up, his hands stilling in the soil. "Lady Phoebe?" He grinned broadly. "Goodness, to what do I owe the pleasure? And Major Seabright, I believe?"

They entered the garden through a wooden gate. "You're looking much recovered, Mr. Amstead," Phoebe said, noting a lack of bandage where Elliot had struck the vicar on the head.

"Much improved, thank you. Forgive me for not shaking your hands." Mr. Amstead held up his soil-caked hands.

"We're sorry to interrupt your gardening," Phoebe said. "Didn't your sexton tell you I telephoned?"

"Did you telephone?" He shook excess dirt from his

fingers. "I don't know why Alfred insists on answering the telephone. He's terribly hard of hearing. I'm sure he had no idea what you said."

"Oh, dear."

Beside her, Owen laughed. "He wouldn't make much of a secretary, then."

"No, indeed," the vicar agreed. "What did he tell you, my lady?"

Chagrined, she replied, "He said, 'Mr. Amstead is at home today and would be pleased to meet with you at your convenience.'"

The vicar gave a whoop. "That does sound like Alfred. It's what he says whenever he answers the telephone, unless he knows I plan to be away from home. But come. I'll wash up and we'll have some tea."

Before they could take many steps, a man appeared outside the garden wall. He removed a rather beaten-up, wide-brimmed hat to reveal a head of flaxen hair and a smooth, youthful face. "I'll be off now, Mr. Amstead," he called. Holding his hat against his chest with both hands, he offered a quick, deferential bob in Phoebe's general direction.

The vicar waved. "Yes, fine, Harry. See you Sunday." He turned with a smile to Phoebe and Owen. "My deacon. A timid young man. I find it hard to imagine him leading a congregation someday. Well, shall we?"

He led the way into the rectory through a rear door. Owen lagged behind them, then hastened to catch up. As he did, he said, "You've got a lovely garden, Mr. Amstead. Are those peach trees?"

"Yes, and apricot. I make my own jams and jellies, something I learned from my darling grandmother. I'd be honored if you'd sample some with our tea."

The vicar disappeared down a hallway after inviting

Phoebe and Owen to make themselves at home in his parlor. He reappeared a few minutes later with clean hands
and wearing a change of clothing.

He bustled past them into the kitchen. "I'll just set the
kettle to boil. . . ."

Soon they were enjoying steaming cups of strong tea
and plates of toast with the promised jam. Phoebe tried
both varieties and found them excellent, as good as anything Mrs. Ellison made at home. "You've got quite a tal-
ent, Mr. Amstead." She noticed Owen staring down at his
toast and jam with a vaguely troubled expression. "Don't
you think so, Owen?"

He looked up as if startled from a reverie. "Yes. Yes, indeed. Very good."

The vicar accepted their compliments with a modest nod.
"Now tell me, what might I do for you, Lady Phoebe?"

She set her cup and saucer aside. "I wished to speak to
you about Elliot Ivers."

"Ah, yes. Poor young man."

"Then you do have some sympathy for him."

"I do, Lady Phoebe. Anyone can see he is not quite . . .
well . . . right."

Phoebe looked to Owen for encouragement. He nodded
once, indicating that she was doing well enough on her
own. They had agreed Owen would only intervene if the
vicar showed signs of balking. "I had a talk with Constable Brannock this morning, and he said if Elliot is convicted, he could be sent to an asylum."

The vicar chewed pensively at a corner of his toast.
"And you don't wish this to happen."

"No, I don't. I believe there are extenuating circumstances behind Elliot's actions. What's more, I don't believe he meant to harm you. Everything I've learned about
Elliot in the past couple of days leads me to believe a past

trauma sent him into a panic when he saw the flame from your match."

Mr. Amstead, too, deposited his cup and saucer on a side table. With a frown, he crossed one leg over the other. "And what might this trauma be?"

"You won't be surprised to hear it was a fire, when Elliot was a boy." She told him about the fire at St. James Church and the death of the vicar there, and about how Elliot and his mother disappeared afterward. He appeared to give Phoebe the whole of his attention, his complexion deepening, his lips compressing, and his shoulders hunching as he leaned forward in his chair.

"Miss Finch's nephew?" he murmured when Phoebe left off. He silently mulled over the revelations, and Phoebe didn't interrupt. Several long moments passed, and then he spoke again. "Are you certain—*quite* certain of all this?"

This time, Owen issued a small admonition with his dark eyes. *Be honest.* Phoebe cleared her throat. "I'm afraid I'm only certain of the relation between Elliot and Miss Finch. The rest I surmised based on evidence from speaking with Pastor Davis in Chadham. But it all fits, doesn't it?"

"Except for the years where there is no record of Elliot." Mr. Amstead sat back in his chair and uncrossed his legs. "Knowledge of those years would confirm or deny that Elliot was the child who survived the fire."

"Yes." Phoebe couldn't deny it. Her hopes for Elliot began to wane. If she couldn't prove the past trauma of the fire, how could she persuade the vicar to drop the assault charges? "I'm sorry we wasted your time, Mr. Amstead."

She started to rise, but the vicar gestured for her to remain sitting. "I didn't say you wasted my time, my dear. Whether or not Elliot was the boy who watched a church go up in flames, taking a beloved pastor with it, he is still deserving of our sympathy and our assistance. I shall speak to Inspector Perkins about dropping the charges. What's more, I'll suggest he release Elliot into my supervision. I believe I can help the young man." A playful gleam entered his eyes. "I'll be careful not to light my pipe anywhere near him."

Phoebe surged to her feet. "Thank you, Mr. Amstead. This is most kind of you. I cannot thank you enough."

They left shortly after. Owen was oddly quiet as they drove back through Kenswick. Phoebe was about to question him when he said, "Something about that seemed . . . I don't know . . ."

"Too easy? I'll admit there was a moment when I thought all hope for Elliot was lost."

"Perhaps. But it's as though from the moment we arrived, some memory has been trying to break through all the other noise in my head."

"What on earth do you mean?" With a laugh, Phoebe changed gears.

"I don't know. It started in the garden, actually. It's probably nothing."

"Maybe it was the scent of the peach and apricot blossoms. They say aromas are particularly keen when it comes to arousing deep-seated memories. Perhaps you're remembering a similar garden from long ago."

"That must be it." He crossed his arms and hunkered lower in the seat, and said little else during the trek back to Little Barlow.

That afternoon, Eva accompanied Lord Wroxly and the girls into the forest beyond the park for their daily science lesson. Today they searched for varieties of moss, and to assist them, Lord Wroxly carried a magnifying glass and a copy of *Elementary Botany* by Henry Edmonds. To Eva's mind, the book looked rather tattered and out of date, but she supposed not much could have changed about moss since its publication.

She hadn't traipsed amongst the pines since last Christmas. Like the gamekeeper's cottage, the forest evoked frightening memories. These she kept to herself and kept pace with the others, though she would have preferred retracing her steps to the house. The girls, at least, seemed in high spirits, but then they had come to appreciate Lord Wroxly's outdoorsy lessons when compared to their much more structured tutorials with Lady Wroxly. Eva believed the relinquishing of school uniforms also added to their cheerfulness, and she was glad to see Zara in a simple blouse and flounced skirt beneath her light coat, rather than in something Jane Timmons could never hope to wear.

Then again, judging from the news Zara had received from her parents, she might not be wearing clothes designed in Paris anymore, either.

"Gather round, ladies," Lord Wroxly said, opening his arms wide. During their walk across the gardens and park, Eva couldn't help noticing, in the sunlight, how much his lordship's hair had thinned in recent months, or how much more lined his skin had become. Lord Wroxly had ruled over Foxwood with what the staff often called his kindly velvet fist for nearly forty years. Sadness clutched her heart. She couldn't imagine this place without him.

He led the girls to a yew tree where he bent his rather formidable girth at the waist and held his magnifying glass close to a patch of fuzzy green at the base. "You, too, Eva. One is never too old to learn."

"Why must we learn about moss, Lord Wroxly?" Zara's question at one time would have been peevish, but today her voice carried only curiosity.

"Do you not realize, my dear, that in addition to moss being an important seed bed for other plants and a home for small organisms within the forest, some species of moss is used for fuel, and was even used during the war for medicinal purposes. Moss, once cleaned and dried, can be applied to wounds beneath bandages to prevent corruption. Many a soldier has moss to thank for his limbs, indeed for his very life."

"A quite practical application for science, then," Jane commented with a satisfied lift of her brow.

"Correct," Lord Wroxly said. "Now then, each of you will have a turn with the magnifier. I believe I've found some spores here. . . ."

While Eva appreciated Lord Wroxly's enthusiasm and the girls' good-natured attention to the lesson, her mind wandered. Lady Phoebe had managed a quick telephone call earlier, transferred belowstairs to Mrs. Sanders's office, to let Eva know about her conversation with Constable Brannock. She wondered how Lady Phoebe had fared with the reverend Mr. Amstead. Had she been able to appeal to his charitable side and convince him not to press charges against Elliot? If so, then what? Knowing Lady Phoebe, she would have no trouble persuading her grandfather to provide the young man with work and a home here at Foxwood.

Questions, however, continued to linger. Why so much secrecy about his past? Yes, the fire, but he had been a small child at the time. What dangers did Miss Finch perceive? If Eva had learned one thing during her years in service, it was that no secret could ever be thoroughly protected. Someone, somewhere, always discovered the truth. So who else might know of Elliot's identity?

A burst of laughter startled her from her speculation. She looked up just as Amelia held the magnifying glass to her eye, making it appear huge. The girls laughed, and next she held it up to her lips and pursed them tight. Zara reached for it, but Lord Wroxly redirected their attention back to the spongy growth on the north sides of the trees.

Zara. . . . A sensation welled up inside of Eva—a pressing urgency that she had missed, or perhaps disregarded, something important.

Zara . . . Miss Finch . . . Elliot.

Her breath hitched. Zara's marks. Miss Finch had changed them—not Miss Sedgewick as they had first suspected, but the headmistress herself. Why—*why* would she falsify official school records and thus risk her employment? Not for money. Not for luxuries. No, those would have been Miss Sedgewick's reasons.

To protect Elliot?

The remainder of the lesson went on interminably while Eva prayed Lady Phoebe would be home by the time Lord Wroxly led them out of the forest. When at last the lesson ended, it was all she could do not to run, as the girls did, up the sweep of lawn and through the gardens. After letting herself in through the service entrance, she asked several of the staff whether Lady Phoebe had returned home. Their shrugs fueled her agitation, until Mrs. Sanders approached with a disapproving frown and a stiff stride that rustled her housekeeper's skirts.

"What's wrong, Mrs. Sanders?" Had Lady Julia complained again about Eva's unavailability? Well, then she had better speak to her grandfather about it, for Lord Wroxly had asked her to accompany the girls outside.

"It's Lady Phoebe."

Eva's heart surged to her throat. Her knees threatened to give way. "What's happened?"

The housekeeper's scowl deepened. "She's in the valet's service room, waiting for you." With a shake of her head and a cluck of her tongue, Mrs. Sanders retreated down the corridor.

Eva let out a whoosh of relief. For a moment, she had thought perhaps her dear lady had been in an accident, that her motorcar had gone off the road and . . .

But no, it was merely Mrs. Sanders feeling out of sorts to have one of the family trespass on her territory. In Mrs. Sanders's view, the family shouldn't even know the way to the back staircase.

She hurried into the valet's service room, which she shared with Lady Wroxly's lady's maid and Lord Wroxly's valet for the cleaning and polishing of footwear, ironing, mending, and pretreating fine laundry. One entire wall of shelves held polishes, cleaning solutions, brushes, and buffing cloths. A small sink occupied one corner, an old potbellied stove stood opposite.

Lady Phoebe sat perched on a stool at the wide worktable. She smiled as soon as Eva entered the room. "Mr. Amstead has agreed not to press charges against Elliot. He'll speak to Inspector Perkins, and has even volunteered to find a place for him. I don't know, though. I'd like to see him here at Foxwood. There would be so much more to occupy him on the estate than at a church." She paused and scrutinized Eva. "Aren't you pleased?"

"I am, my lady."

"You don't look it." Her expression turned serious. "What's happened?"

"Nothing, my lady. Except that something occurred to me, and I've been most eager to discuss it with you. It's about Elliot."

"By all means, tell me."

Eva pulled up a stool beside her, and only briefly reflected that several months ago she would not have dared take such a liberty with any of her ladies. How things had changed between her and *this* lady. "This afternoon, I went with your grandfather and the girls out to the forest to observe moss."

"Moss? How very interesting." Lady Phoebe's tone suggested she thought just the opposite.

"Exactly, my lady. My mind wandered, and I began thinking about Elliot and Miss Finch and the secret she seemed so desperate to protect. And then suddenly it struck me." She leaned in closer and lowered her voice. "Lady Zara's marks. Why would Miss Finch have changed them? What I think, my lady, is that possibly Lady Zara somehow discovered the truth about Elliot."

Lady Phoebe gasped. "And Zara blackmailed her into changing her marks? Do you think she would do such a thing?"

"Lady Zara these past couple of days? Perhaps not. But the Lady Zara we met at school?" She didn't finish the thought, but let Lady Phoebe mull it over, which she did with little nods that grew more pronounced with each passing moment.

"Have we been wrong to trust her? Is this change for the better merely an act?"

"I don't wish to believe that, my lady."

"Nor do I. Nor do I wish to believe that any student would resort to something as underhanded as blackmail. But if she did, then both Miss Sedgewick and Miss Finch are exonerated of altering school records. Poor Miss Finch. Poor Elliot." Frowning, she slid off the stool. "Once again, we're left with suspicions and too little information. Eva, this reminds me of Christmas, when Lord Allerton's death seemed to center around Julia. Only this time, it's Elliot and now Lady Zara. Their names come up again and again—too often to be ignored."

Yes, that had occurred to Eva as well. Still, she voiced a caution. "Lady Julia turned out to be innocent of all blame, my lady."

"And I hold out the same hope for Lady Zara. But I don't intend to go on presuming things."

"What are you going to do, then?"

"I'm going to speak to Zara. Quite bluntly. Tonight."

CHAPTER 18

Phoebe waited until after well after dinner, when everyone else had retired for the night. As they had agreed beforehand, Eva knocked on her door and came in. "The girls are all in bed, my lady. I left Zara alone in her room, reading a book. Now is as good a time as any."

"Thank you. Wait here, please." Phoebe buttoned up her wrapper and tiptoed down the corridor. At Zara's door she knocked softly—she didn't wish to attract the notice of the other girls—and went in.

Zara glanced up from her book, surprise plain on her face. "Is anything wrong?"

Phoebe might have answered in the negative, but why reassure the girl when there indeed might be something terribly wrong. Silently, she crossed the room, aware of Zara's growing curiosity, and sat facing her at the edge of the bed.

Zara's brow furrowed. "Something *is* wrong."

"You tell me, Zara."

She closed her book, a guide to flower garden design, and set it aside. "I'm sure I don't know what you mean."

Phoebe hesitated, but only for dramatic effect. She wanted

Zara off balance as well as off guard. Then, bluntly, she said, "Why did Miss Finch change your marks?"

Zara's violet-blue eyes opened wide. "What? That's absurd. She wouldn't do any such thing, I'm sure."

"Wouldn't she, Zara? I saw the evidence of it myself, yet I said nothing until the likely reason for it occurred to me."

"What likely reason? You're accusing me of . . . of what?" The threat of a sob thickened Zara's protest.

"First tell me the truth. Did you persuade Miss Finch to change your grades?"

"No! Of course not. I . . ."

"You what, Zara? It's time to come clean about what happened and about what you know."

Her distraught features rearranged themselves into mystification. "What I know—about what?"

Either the girl excelled as an actress, or in this, at least, she was telling the truth. "All right, let's start again. I *know* Miss Finch changed your marks. There is no use denying it. The question is why."

"But I told you, I don't know . . ." Zara grabbed the pillow beside her and hugged it in front of her. The tears rolling down her cheeks seemed genuine enough. Phoebe hardened her features and waited in silence, forcing Zara to be the next to speak. She hadn't long to wait.

Zara swiped the back of her hand across her cheeks, but that didn't stem the tide of falling tears. "I *had* to. If my parents had known how badly I was doing, they'd have ordered me home from school and . . . and . . . oh, Phoebe, it would have been dreadful. They'd have taken away all my privileges and been positively beastly. I'd have been kept under lock and key with nowhere to go and no company. Even my parents wouldn't have been there. They wouldn't have cut their travels short. They'd simply have palmed me off on the servants. And to think now, because of their recklessness, I have to leave school anyway, with no future or husband or anything to look forward to." She dropped her face to the pillow, weeping as though her heart had broken.

An act?

"Let's slow down for a moment." Phoebe almost reached out to comfort the girl, but resisted the urge. She hadn't gotten her answers yet. "How did you persuade Miss Finch to make the changes?"

"I didn't."

"Zara, you just admitted—"

"That is, I appealed to Miss Sedgewick, and *she* said she would manage it. I don't know how she did. I only know my marks improved greatly, and that the reports sent to my parents assured them all was well."

Phoebe leaned back and exhaled a long breath. Miss Sedgewick—all along. She and Eva had initially suspected the woman of altering Zara's marks, but the evidence in the records had pointed to Miss Finch.

Ah, but there had been Miss Sedgewick's expensive clothes. "Zara, did you bribe Miss Sedgewick to do it? Did you offer her gifts or money?"

"I didn't need to. She was perfectly willing."

"Are you certain?" The sharpness of Phoebe's tone made Zara recoil.

"Quite certain," she said in a small voice. "My parents don't send me enough money to bribe anyone."

That would be easy enough to verify. "And are you sure you don't know *how* Miss Sedgewick persuaded Miss Finch to change your marks?"

When Zara shook her head, Phoebe believed her readily enough. It would have been a detail that didn't interest the girl. Zara wanted one thing only—to stay in her parents' good graces and remain at school. How that happened wouldn't have concerned her as long as she had her way.

Phoebe went to the dresser and found a pile of fine linen handkerchiefs in the top drawer. She plucked the top one and brought it to Zara. "Here, dry your tears."

Zara gazed up at her. "Are you going to tell my parents?"

Weary, Phoebe sank onto the bed again. "Honestly, I don't know." She shrugged. "Probably not. I don't suppose it would help to add to their troubles, under the circumstances."

"You mean because of the loss of our money." Twisting the handkerchief between her hands, Zara stared down at her lap. "It's so humiliating. Life is over for me."

This time Phoebe didn't resist the impulse to press a hand to Zara's shoulder. "Zara, no doubt there will be changes in your life, but perhaps you'll find your parents have more resources at their disposal than it seems just now. Either way, you'll be all right. You're stronger than you know."

Did she believe that? Zara's history of unkindness toward the other girls, especially those of meeker dispositions than her own, and her willingness to cheat rather than work toward her goals indicated a shallow nature, weak character, and profound unhappiness. Amelia insisted Zara had changed of late. Phoebe hoped it was true, and hoped a bit of encouragement might help Zara develop the confidence to believe in her ability to prevail.

If not, her life would be as difficult as Zara feared.

Phoebe hugged the girl and helped arrange her pillows and coverlets before turning out the light. Back in her own room, she found Eva waiting patiently. Phoebe gestured for her to remain seated when Eva started to rise.

"I'm not sure I learned anything we didn't already know or suspect," Phoebe told her. "Zara did, of course, have a hand in the altering of her marks, but she did so through

Miss Sedgewick. Miss Finch changed the marks, but at Miss Sedgewick's urging. And Zara doesn't know how Miss Sedgewick coaxed Miss Finch into cooperating."

"Are you sure she's telling the truth about that?"

"Fairly certain. It makes sense. Zara wouldn't care how or why she got her way, only that she did. She would naturally gravitate toward the younger, prettier, more fashionable Miss Sedgewick, and it isn't a stretch to imagine Miss Sedgewick being all too willing to ingratiate herself to an earl's daughter." Phoebe paced the room and stopped before her dressing table. She leaned over the bench to run her fingers over the sterling-backed mirror.

Behind her, Eva said, "Miss Sedgewick abhors Elliot. And she obviously wants the headmistress position enough to have resented Miss Finch."

Phoebe straightened and turned back around. "Are you thinking what I'm thinking?"

"I believe I am, my lady. Miss Sedgewick must have discovered the truth about Elliot. She might have overheard something, perhaps Miss Finch talking to Mrs. Honeychurch in the kitchen, and used the information to blackmail Miss Finch."

Phoebe shook her head, unsatisfied with that conclusion. "Blackmailing Miss Finch to change a student's grades would have been a poor effort on Miss Sedgewick's part. She must have demanded something more from Miss Finch."

"Miss Sedgewick's clothes, her perfume. She must have demanded money."

"Of course." Phoebe crossed the room to her and sat beside her. "Miss Finch was paying Miss Sedgewick off, which accounts for her having to actually bring Elliot to the school as a handyman. She probably could no longer afford to keep him wherever he had been living prior to his mother's death."

"Miss Sedgewick didn't like that, though, did she, my lady?"

Phoebe sat back against the settee. "No, she did not. She wanted Elliot gone, or so she said. But perhaps Miss Finch decided to stand up to Miss Sedgewick and not be bullied any longer."

Several moments passed in pensive silence. Gradually, the excitement of their deductions waned, and Phoebe wondered if perhaps they had assumed too much. Neither of them particularly cared for Miss Sedgewick, which made it all too easy to assign blame to her. She hadn't liked Zara much either, initially, but now saw past her faults to the apprehensive and insecure girl within.

"Are we inferring too much?" she asked. "I believe Zara about the marks. I even believe Miss Sedgewick used some sort of trickery to persuade Miss Finch. But it might not have been any more sinister than Miss Sedgewick reminding Miss Finch of where their most generous donations came from, and that it was she, Miss Sedgewick, who secured those donations."

"Then we are back where we began, my lady."

Phoebe nodded slowly. "Indeed we are. With a handful of suspicions and no clear trail leading to anyone."

The jingle of a bell the next morning sent Eva from the servants' dining hall up to Lady Julia's room a good hour before her ladies typically needed her. She was surprised to find Lady Julia already out of bed and in her dressing room.

"Help me on with my riding habit and fix my hair, please, Eva. I'm going for an early ride."

Skepticism held Eva in the doorway. "We haven't riding horses in the stables, my lady."

"Yes, I realize that, Eva," she said with a dash of impatience. She held up a beribboned top hat and plucked at the veil that hung down the back. "A friend is coming to collect me in his motorcar and we'll set out riding from his stables."

"Will you be breakfasting first?"

"No" came the terse answer.

Why did Lady Julia seem to want to escape the house before anyone saw her or made inquiries into her plans for the day? Who was this friend coming to collect her? Eva thought back to when she and Phoebe had swerved to avoid the fast-moving motorcar driven by Theodore Leighton, newly made Marquess of Allerton. A definite possibility. As far as Eva knew, the Allerton stables hadn't been emptied of its horses during the war as Foxwood's had.

Lady Julia and Theodore Leighton. A rather pleasant thought, except for that one detail Eva knew carried great weight with Lady Julia—Lord Allerton's lack of fortune. Then why did she continue the association?

Eva went into the dressing room and reached into the large armoire for the black broadcloth riding jacket and skirt. She selected a blouse as well, with a high collar where she would affix the cameo Julia had inherited from her maternal grandmother.

"Will this do, my lady?"

"Very nicely, thank you."

She spent the next quarter hour helping Lady Julia into her riding attire and fixing her hair beneath the stylish hat with its wide band and mist-fine netting. "Your gentleman friend will think you most becoming today, my lady."

Julia turned to pin her with a hard stare. "What makes you think it matters if the gentleman with whom I'm riding finds me becoming or not?"

Eva smiled and tried to shrug nonchalantly. "Forgive me for guessing as much, my lady, but you *have* been rather mysterious lately. And that would seem to indicate a special gentleman in your life."

Lady Julia stepped closer and startled Eva by seizing her wrist. "See here, Eva. Whom I ride with or shop with or anything else is my business. You're not to go telling tales, especially to Phoebe."

"My lady, I would never."

"See that you don't. I have my reasons for secrecy—" She broke off and turned away, but not before Eva glimpsed a glitter of tears. Lady Julia prided herself on remaining cool and in control around people, and her loss of it now frightened Eva.

"My lady, what is it? I'd never betray a confidence, I promise you."

Her back turned, Lady Julia took two steps away, leading Eva to believe she wouldn't reply. But in a wavering voice, she said, "You know my grandmother wishes to marry me off as soon as possible, and to the highest bidder."

"I wouldn't put it as severely as all that, my lady. Your grandmother wishes you to be happy."

"Does she?" Lady Julia pivoted around to face her. Tears stood suspended in her midnight blue eyes. "In an ideal world, perhaps. But she's determined that Fox inherits an intact estate, and unless my sisters and I marry well, that won't happen."

Apprehension gathered in Eva's stomach. "What do you mean, my lady?"

"Phoebe and Amelia don't know this and you are not to tell them. Grams confided in me some months ago. You see, the money isn't as it was before the war. Taxes, disappointing investments, lost productivity on the home farm— it's all taken its toll. Which saddles my sisters and me with the responsibility of making financially significant marriages."

"And this gentleman you're riding with today?" Eva felt nearly certain she already knew the answer. "Will he not do?"

"No, Eva, he will not." Lady Julia looked away again and sighed heavily. "Do you remember that talk we had last Christmas, about my ideal husband?"

"I do, my lady. You said he must be handsome, well educated, rich, and above all, someone you can respect." Eva smiled gently.

"Yes, well. The man I would most wish to marry is handsome, at least in my eyes, well educated, and more than worthy of my respect. But rich?" She shook her head. "I can never marry him. Eventually I must break it off and marry a"—she shuddered—"a Wally Bagot."

Eva reached out to touch her fingertips to Lady Julia's cheek. "Oh, my lady . . ."

Lady Julia ducked away. "I must be off before the others are up and about. Remember, not a word of any of this to anyone. If anyone asks, simply say I had a longing to ride again and arranged to borrow a horse from one of the local families. If they don't believe you, too bad."

With that, Lady Julia strode from the room, her netted veil floating out behind her. Eva followed at a slower pace, closed the door behind her, and nearly yelped to discover Amelia standing like a wraith in the dim corridor. On closer look Eva saw she was already dressed for the day.

"Where was Julia going in such a hurry?"

"Uh, she had . . . em . . . plans . . ." Eva stammered.

Amelia stepped closer to her. "Never mind. I believe Jane just left the grounds. Again."

"Oh, no."

"Oh, yes." Amelia leaned past Eva to open Lady Julia's door and practically pushed Eva inside. "Jane was late to breakfast again yesterday, and when she arrived, she seemed out of breath. I think this has been going on the entire time she has been here, but we only caught her at it the morning you headed her off coming back from her so-called morning walk." Amelia paused for breath. "So this morning I decided to rise early and keep watch. I went up to the top landing of the back staircase, where I can see out over the dividing hedges. First I saw Jane rushing across the terrace and through the hedge gate, where she disappeared from view. When she reappeared, she was running past the greenhouses and heading toward the orchards."

"The same route she took the last time she was late to lessons. What on earth could so hold her fascination with that area of the grounds? The orchards aren't bearing fruit yet."

"Eva, didn't you hear me? I believe she has *left* the grounds." Amelia spoke with a breathy urgency. "I didn't think of it the first time Jane disappeared, but there is a woodland trail that begins beyond the orchards. It's a shortcut to the school that bypasses High Street through town, making the way much swifter on foot."

"Why would Jane return to an empty school, not once but twice?" It made no sense to Eva.

"Or perhaps more than twice, and perhaps for the same reason she was often tardy for lessons before school closed. I don't know what that reason is, but I think we should follow her."

"I can't go running off again." Eva considered for a moment, and then crossed the corridor to Lady Phoebe's bedroom. She knocked briskly on the door and said to Amelia, "I have a better idea."

Phoebe was already awake when Eva knocked on her door, though she had been enjoying a few delicious moments of lazing in her warm bed before fully rousing herself to meet the day. News of Jane Timmons's latest vanishing act sent her out from between the covers in a hurry. Her first order of business was to use the upstairs telephone to order the Vauxhall brought round. Then she splashed water on her face and dressed hurriedly with Eva's help. Amelia, meanwhile, rushed downstairs to the kitchen to pilfer some of Mrs. Ellison's warm scones straight out of the oven.

"I don't know why I let you talk me into bringing you along." The wind rushing in through the Vauxhall's open sides nearly carried her words away unheard. She and her sister had both removed their cloche hats rather than lose them to the gusts. Luckily, no other vehicles occupied the road this early, except for the dairy truck that shambled past in the opposite direction.

Beside her, Amelia chewed the last bite of her second scone. She raised her voice to be heard. "Because if you'd brought Eva, both you and she would have gotten in trouble with Grams, and because I know Jane better than you do. No offense, Phoebe, but you've grown too old to understand people of my age."

Phoebe didn't know whether to scoff or laugh. Instead she let the observation go without comment. She slowed around a bend rather than risk coming suddenly upon another delivery dray. As soon as she had a clear view of the road ahead, she sped up again. Unlike Eva, Amelia didn't so much as flinch, but in fact raised her face into the scuttling draft with a slight smile on her lips.

A light morning mist silvered the landscape and billowed gently over the lawns on the school grounds. A few lights shined behind the upper windows, indicating the staff awakening to yet another day of questions and wondering when their students would return. Phoebe wondered, Did any among them know one of their students might have been returning almost daily?

Amelia peered up ahead. "Do you think Jane is here yet?"

Phoebe scanned the property. The school chapel stood

nestled in trees and foliage in the distance to their right. The woodland path entered the grounds some two dozen yards beyond the churchyard. "I don't think so. She had a head start but I believe I drove fast enough to get us here before her. At least I hope so."

She continued to the old carriage house, partway up the drive and off to the left. They parked behind the building, out of sight. From there they hurried to the house, where they positioned themselves just outside the dining hall, where the shrubbery would shield them from view.

Amelia leaned against the trunk of an elm and peeked around it. "What do you suppose she does here?"

"I can't begin to guess."

"How do you think she gets in? I very much doubt the front door is unlocked this early in the day."

"That's a good question."

Sunlight struggled through the trees. The day promised to be a lovely one once the mist burned off. Movement near the chapel drew Phoebe's attention, and a moment later a figure emerged from around a tumble of roses and bright yellow forsythia.

Amelia pointed. "There she is!"

Phoebe hushed her. "Don't move. Let's see what she does."

Jane kept well off the drive and picked her way through the shadows beneath the trees. After a brief hesitation, she darted across the drive with so light a step the gravel barely crunched.

Amelia gasped. "She's coming this way. What do we do?"

Phoebe considered. They stood in what had once been an ornamental garden, much like those at Foxwood Hall. Now it served as an outdoor study area for the students. Phoebe grasped Amelia's hand and drew her behind the box hedge beneath the dining hall windows.

"She won't be looking for us here," she whispered. "And if she does, we'll simply confront her. But I'd much rather see where she goes first."

Crouching against the brick wall soon became uncomfortable. Their hems trailed in the damp soil and prickly bushes snagged their clothing. Jane's footsteps thudded by, and brief flashes of her light gray coat appeared to them through the foliage. Phoebe waited another moment before struggling to her feet and pulling Amelia up beside her. They shook their skirts to loosen the clinging pellets of earth.

By the time they eased out from behind the hedge, Jane had disappeared around the rear of the house. They trotted to reach the corner, where Phoebe flattened herself against the bricks and craned her neck to peek around. Jane walked more briskly now, but she hadn't far to go. She passed the infirmary and came to the conservatory, where the French windows loomed beside her. She went to the center window. The latch turned easily in her hand and she slipped inside.

Phoebe exchanged a glance with her sister, and Amelia whispered, "What would she be doing in the conservatory?"

Phoebe shrugged. She took Amelia's hand and together they crept along the rear wall. They reached the first of the infirmary windows and came to an abrupt halt. Jane and Nurse Delacy were visible inside.

Is this where Jane had been coming, not only during her stay at Foxwood Hall, but all the times she had been tardy to her lessons here at school? How could it be otherwise? Jane had broken from the cover of the chapel garden and with singular purpose rushed straight here. The conservatory door had been unlocked, as if Nurse Delacy had been expecting her.

Nurse Delacy, who perhaps had killed a man. No matter how much she might have ended a man's suffering—

and indeed his suffering must have been unimaginable—if the woman *had* taken matters into her own hands, she had acted contrary to the purpose and principles of a nurse, whose job it was to help heal, to provide comfort, and to carry out a doctor's orders. Perhaps in her mind she had acted out of good intentions and not malice, but that didn't change the fact that Nurse Delacy surely must have snapped if she held a pillow to a man's face until he would never breathe again. And what about the day Lilyanne slashed her knee on the tennis court, and again when Miss Finch died? True, the nurse could not have altered the outcome of Miss Finch's poisoning, but she did not know that when Amelia ran to fetch her.

Surely her delay in reaching the dining hall had been the result of her tumultuous state of mind. But had she delayed intentionally? Had her diseased mind led her to plant cyanide where Zara—or Lilyanne, it turned out—would find it and use it in the Madeira cake? Perhaps just enough for the cake and no other recipe?

Whatever reasons had brought Jane here, she could have no idea the potential danger she put herself in. As Phoebe had learned only months ago, one could never predict how and when a troubled individual might snap again.

Inside the infirmary, a single desk lamp emitted a dull yellow pool of light. However, it was enough for Phoebe to make out the scene. Jane and Nurse Delacy sat together, not at the desk, but on one of the iron-framed beds. They had their arms around each other, with Olivia Delacy's resting on Jane's shoulder. Most astonishing of all, Jane rocked gently back and forth while the notes of a lullaby crooned in her smooth soprano were just audible through the glass.

"What on earth?" Amelia whispered.

Phoebe merely shook her head to silence her sister. Jane's back was to her, but she could make out enough of the nurse's face to see that her eyes were open. More than open, they gaped like hollow wells of darkness and fear, staring into some point Phoebe judged to be far beyond the walls of the infirmary. What did Nurse Delacy see that etched such horror into the lines and planes of her face, holding them as taut as a death mask surrounded by the frazzled cloud of her strawlike hair?

Amelia saw it, too, for she murmured in a strangled voice, "Phoebe, look at her."

Phoebe wrapped an arm around her sister. Transfixed, she continued to watch Jane and the nurse.

Jane's singing continued for several minutes, until the distant dread faded from Nurse Delacy's eyes. That awful grip on her features relaxed, and her focus shifted to the room around her. Phoebe instinctively knew she had returned to the present. Slowly, she and Jane pulled apart. Jane spoke, albeit too low for Phoebe to hear. The nurse nodded, and they quickly embraced again.

Both woman rose. Amelia tugged at Phoebe's sleeve. "Jane will be coming out now. Let's go."

"No. Not this time." Phoebe pushed to her feet and helped Amelia up beside her. She led her sister to the conservatory and the unlocked French door. Jane reached it at almost the same time, was only a few feet away on the other side of the glass when she spotted Phoebe and Amelia. She pulled up short as if she'd nearly hit a wall.

Phoebe opened the door and stepped in. "So this is where you've been going, Jane."

Surprise held the girl silent. Nurse Delacy came into the conservatory. She must have seen Phoebe and Amelia outside the infirmary. She approached the door and calmly said, "Come in, Lady Phoebe. Lady Amelia."

"I shall come in, Nurse, but my sister will not be joining us—" A quick protest from Amelia prompted Phoebe to gesture with a terse motion behind her. "Nor will Jane remain here. You girls are both to go straight home. You can return the way Jane came, the way she has been using for days now." She shook her head, not knowing whether to be disgusted with the girl's subterfuge, or vastly relieved no harm had come to her because of it. "Jane, you and I shall speak of this when I get home."

"I'm not going anywhere, Lady Phoebe." The girl moved to the nurse's side. "You don't understand. I am needed here."

Phoebe breathed through a wave of frustration. She wanted both girls gone, wanted them safe. Nurse Delacy stood as placidly as you please, but who knew? She spoke to Jane, but kept her eyes on the nurse. "If you were needed so badly, Jane, you might have explained yourself to us rather than go sneaking about behind our backs."

"If you're staying, Phoebe," Amelia said, "I'm staying, too."

"No, you are not. Nurse and I will talk. Whatever explanations there are for Jane to be here, she can enlighten me."

"You don't understand," Jane repeated. Her voice rose, and she clenched her fists at her sides. "This is all none of your business. Olivia and I—"

"Jane, go." Nurse Delacy touched Jane's shoulder. "It's all right. Lady Phoebe and I will talk. You and her sister needn't be here."

An agony of indecision written clearly on her face, Jane turned to face her. "But . . . I understand you. They don't. They never can."

CHAPTER 19

Once Jane and Amelia were gone, Nurse Delacy led Phoebe back into the infirmary. She sat at her desk, still calm for all appearances, except she snatched up a pen and began tapping it against the desktop in an erratic beat that grated on Phoebe's nerves. The clicking of the woman's heel against the floor provided a counter rhythm that further irritated her. Phoebe hesitated. She would have felt more comfortable closer to the outside door. Then she realized they were not alone here at Haverleigh. If she needed help, she didn't doubt her ability to rouse the staff to action.

She dragged a chair to the opposite side of the desk.

The irksome tattoo continued. The nurse's pale eyebrows climbed her furrowed brow. "Well, Lady Phoebe, don't you fear being left alone with me?"

Phoebe heard the sardonic tone but chose to ignore it. "Actually, yes, a little. Why shouldn't I be?" She placed the flats of her palms on the desk and leaned forward. "I'm not the only person who is indecisive about having you about."

"Ah, yes. You visited my parents, didn't you? My father

drove to the next village and telephoned me that very afternoon. To warn me. And to apologize. It seems he and Mum felt rather remorseful for some of the things they said to you."

"I can assure you, they said nothing damning. In fact, they expressed a great deal of pride in you."

"But you sensed their hesitancy all the same."

"Yes." Phoebe straightened and leaned back in her chair. She did not, however, fully relax. "Why has Jane been coming here?"

"Because as she said, my lady, she understands. She has an older brother at home who is not the same man who went to war over three years ago. Not the same by any means. Just as I am not the same woman who traveled to France to do her bit for king and country."

"You're saying—"

The tapping abruptly ceased. With a slap to the desktop that made Phoebe wince, Nurse Delacy sprang to her feet. "I am saying we witnessed horrors you could never imagine in your most terrifying nightmares. While you, Lady Phoebe, were safe in your bed at night, men like Jane's brother and women like me found ourselves surrounded by bloody limbs and burned bodies, by soldiers shot apart, screaming and begging for death. By hopelessness and despair. Can you imagine it, Lady Phoebe? Can you even begin to imagine it?"

Phoebe found herself pressing back against her chair in an effort to put distance between herself and this avenging battlefield apparition with its wild hair and fierce eyes and fiery complexion. True fear slithered up her spine.

And yet, she had been asked a question, and not to answer, to sit there gawking and cowering, would be to deny the very existence of the horrors lodging in Nurse Delacy's mind. She had served in the war and had suffered for her pains, and she deserved acknowledgment for her sacrifices.

"No." Phoebe thought briefly of the one dismembered, bloody digit she had seen last winter. Shocking for someone in her sheltered world, perhaps, but nothing compared to the things Nurse Delacy had witnessed. "I could never imagine it."

"Good." Nurse Delacy, suddenly calm again, resumed her seat. Whether her reply of *good* had been because Phoebe could not imagine such horrors, or because she had simply answered the question, Phoebe couldn't say. "Jane understands. She understood what was happening to me better than I did myself. When her brother came home, he shook constantly, flinched at everything that moved, and awakened in the night screaming in terror. Jane helped him simply by holding him and singing to him. She was able to reach inside him when nothing and no one else could. You heard her singing to me?"

"Yes."

"She helps me when the memories creep too close. Miss Finch's death . . ." Nurse Delacy squeezed her eyes shut, her pale lashes disappearing into the deep creases that formed. Then she opened her eyes and stretched her arms out on the desktop. One by one she pushed her sleeves up, slowly, pointedly, and turned her forearms upward. Puzzled, Phoebe merely waited.

"Look into the crooks of my elbows."

Phoebe craned slightly forward. "What am I supposed . . ." She fell silent as tiny pink marks on Nurse Delacy's skin took shape in the dim light. On both arms, those blemishes, the size of pinpricks, created a telltale pattern. Her stomach sank. During the war years, she had heard vague stories about doctors and nurses using their access to medications to dull their own horrors. Feeling queasy, she glanced up, meeting the nurse's pale eyes.

The woman nodded. "Yes, my lady. I believe you understand. Before Jane, I had morphia. Not all the time, mind you, not enough to become dependent, but whenever I could no longer stand the images flashing behind my eyes."

"I . . ."

"You needn't say anything. I'm through with it. Of that much I can assure you. I wouldn't have shown you otherwise."

"I'm glad. There is hope, then, isn't there?"

"For me?" The nurse shrugged. "I should have rushed to the dining hall that day, but when your sister came for me, I couldn't move. Simply could not move. Because I knew I'd be useless. So damnably useless."

Phoebe agreed, but admitting as much wouldn't help matters now. "As it happened, there was nothing you could have done."

"Perhaps not." The nurse stared at Phoebe for several long moments, until Phoebe's defensive instincts rose, as if *she* were being interrogated, instead of the other way around. "Do you think I killed her? Miss Finch, I mean. That I snapped and decided Miss Finch needed to die?"

Though it hadn't been mentioned, the ghost of the soldier who had perhaps died by the nurse's hand hovered between them. Phoebe once again felt compelled to be honest. "I have considered it as a possibility." She swallowed audibly. "*Did* you kill her?"

Once again the nurse took her time in answering, drawing out the moments as if for dramatic effect. "No. Can you believe that?"

"I'd like to."

Nurse Delacy looked away. "Perhaps you should go, Lady Phoebe. We have reached an impasse and it isn't likely to be solved today. You needn't worry. I'm not going anywhere. But do understand, Miss Finch hired me knowing full well what I am. Don't look so surprised. She knew and she gave me a chance. You're probably thinking she shouldn't have."

Phoebe couldn't deny questioning the wisdom of a headmistress hiring a woman who couldn't be fully trusted, much less around children. "Why do you continue nursing if it's so difficult for you? If it brings back such horrific memories?"

She treated Phoebe to mirthless smile. "Haven't you heard? I'm what the newspapers are terming a *surplus woman*. Most of my generation are. With so many men gone, our chances of marrying are practically nil. There is nothing left but to work and makes one's own way in the world. And quite frankly, nursing is all I know how to do."

"Surplus women," Phoebe repeated. She understood the disproportion the war had created between men and women, especially those in their twenties and thirties, but she hadn't heard it put quite that way before. "What a dreadful way to label an entire generation of women, as if they were nothing more than the remnants of last year's harvest taking up space in a warehouse."

"That's correct, my lady, remnants of a pre-War harvest. I am certainly one. And so might you be, too, if you haven't already got yourself a man. If you do, I suggest you hold on to to him tightly, for others will soon be trying to wrest him from your grasp. Gentlewomen certainly aren't immune, for we lost as many officers as enlisted men. More, by some estimates."

Those words sent a shock through Phoebe, though perhaps not for the reason Nurse Delacy would have thought. Did Phoebe have a man? Did she want one?

Her thoughts turned to Owen—handsome, confident, and always somewhat larger than life. At times he seemed to show an interest in her, and she couldn't deny an interest in him. Even if she tried to deny it, those infernal blushes that she only recently had begun to master in his presence would have painted her a liar. But although Owen had kissed her at Christmas and now seemed intent on hanging about to keep an eye on her, he never said a word about his intentions. Did he have any? Was this merely a flirtation on his part? Or perhaps merely brotherly concern. She didn't know.

Grams wanted Julia married as soon as possible, and then it would be Phoebe's turn. She had always considered this obligation an annoyance, and while many young women her age poured their efforts into securing an appropriate husband, Phoebe thus far hadn't felt the urge to do so. Except now . . . now the notion unsettled her that someone else might reach for Owen before she'd had a chance to make up her mind.

She became aware of the nurse watching her with an indulgent air, as if she could read Phoebe's thoughts. Then the woman came to her feet, briskly, as though she had work to do and a schedule to maintain. Never mind that her infirmary stood vacant. "Is there anything else at present, my lady? I suppose you'll have some harsh words for Jane when you see her again. Do remember she is a good girl. She means well."

Phoebe rose and gathered her coat around her. "She should not have gone sneaking about."

"She did that for me, my lady. Can you blame her for wishing to protect my position and my privacy? There are those who would regard people like me, and Jane's brother, as incompetent and no longer of any use to society. But now that you know the truth, I suppose it's for you to decide if I am to be of any use to this school in future."

Phoebe made no reply. The nurse spoke true. Phoebe understood more of the facts now, but the question of whether Olivia Delacy should remain at Haverleigh had yet to be answered to her satisfaction. Obviously, the governing board had no inkling of the woman's true history. Was it right to keep the information from them? However much Miss Finch had trusted and sympathized with Nurse Delacy, she had hired her under false pretenses. Phoebe wasn't entirely convinced Miss Finch hadn't paid a heavy price for her actions.

She almost left the way she had arrived—through the French windows. But no, she would not exit the building like a thief. Her reasons for coming here were justified. She strode from the infirmary into the main corridor that led to the front of the house. Though she heard a few far-off voices from the upstairs, all lay quiet on the ground floor.

She got as far as the headmistress's office. The door stood halfway open, and not a sound issued from within. Odd. She couldn't resist peeking in. She saw no sign of Miss Sedgewick, but her perfume hung over the room as if she had been there recently. The sight that greeted her sent her across the threshold. The candlestick telephone lay on its side on the desk, the ear trumpet having been tossed down inches from its cradle. The buzzing of a broken connection filled the air. A crumpled bit of paper littered the floor near a leg of the desk, as if someone had missed the wastebasket—except the bin sat at the other side of the desk.

Upon closer inspection she discovered one of the desk drawers yawning so wide, it nearly fell from its brackets. The desk chair had been left at an awkward angle. What could have precipitated such disorder in Miss Sedgewick's office? Was there a break-in, as she and Eva had broken into the filing cabinet days ago?

She bent to scoop up the crumpled paper and smoothed it open on the blotter. Phoebe's eyes went wide. The Haverleigh governing body's letterhead emblazoned the top of the page above a short letter addressed to Miss Sedgewick.

They advised her a new headmistress would soon be chosen, and she herself would retain the position of assistant.

Did Grams know about this? Holding the letter, Phoebe backed away from the desk and lowered herself into the chair. She wondered when the missive had arrived. It was early yet for the post, but perhaps it came in the day before and Miss Sedgewick only opened it this morning. The contents had obviously angered her—even enraged her. Only a burst of extreme emotion could have prompted a well-bred gentlewoman to toss paper to the floor, knock over a telephone, and leave her office in such pell-mell fashion.

She once more regarded the gaping drawer, and absently placed the letter back on the desk. Next, she righted the drawer on its brackets and slid it partially in, but still wide enough for her to reach in. She stopped with her hand in midair and stared at her palm, at a fine brown substance caught in the creases.

"Where did that come from?" she murmured. The letter had been balled on the floor—dusty, yes, but this. . . . She moved the paper aside and discovered a fine coating of the same brown powder on the blotter. The substance must have been on the desk and transferred onto the back of the paper when she smoothed it open, and from there onto her palm. Phoebe gasped, and before another thought quite formed she brushed her hands together, and then wiped them on her coat. Speculation ran rampant through her mind. The desk drawer once again captured her attention.

She peered inside. The contents had clearly been rummaged through, with pens, pencils, notepads, and clips jumbled together in a manner a woman like Miss Sedgewick would never countenance. Phoebe reached in, carefully lifting things, moving them aside, looking . . . she didn't know what for.

Her fingers touched something cool and smooth, obviously glass. A pot of ink? No, it seemed too narrow. She closed her hand around it and drew it out, and found herself looking at more of the same brown powder as on the desk. The vial was nearly empty but for a quarter inch or so at the bottom. She slipped out the stopper and sniffed. A bitter scent made her wrinkle her nose and turn away quickly.

In an instant she gained her feet and bolted for the front door.

As Eva watched the mantel clock in the servants' hall tick away the minutes, the small amount of breakfast she'd consumed sat heavy in her stomach. In another twenty-five minutes the clock would strike nine and the Countess of Wroxly would expect her students to file into the Petite Salon for morning lessons. Only, two of those students, Amelia and Jane, and Lady Phoebe as well, might not be present at the allotted time.

"Hurry home, Lady Phoebe," she murmured under her breath. Because if they didn't return soon, at exactly nine o' clock, she, Eva, would be forced to concoct some excuse for them.

Lie to the Countess of Wroxly. *Lie!* Eva didn't know if she could, and even saying nothing, pretending she didn't know where Lady Phoebe and the girls had gone, would in itself be a lie. She stared down into her teacup and said a little prayer.

Almost immediately after her *amen*, a jingle sounded on the long panel of bells set high on the wall. Eva's pulse jumped as she looked up to see where the summons originated. At the same time, Douglas, one of the footmen, poked his head into the room and glanced at the bell board.

"Ah, that would be Mr. Giles ringing for me. Lady

Phoebe must be home and I'll have to take her car round to the carriage house. Please tell Mrs. Sanders I'll be right back."

He didn't wait for an acknowledgment from Eva, not that she could have made one. Her relief was too great to allow her to form words just then. She drained the last of her tea, brought the cup and saucer into the scullery, and began the climb to the first floor. She met Lady Phoebe in the corridor outside her bedroom.

"I'm so glad you made it back before the girls' lessons, my lady." Eva gathered Phoebe's coat, hat, and driving gloves from her mistress's arms. "I was fretting over what I'd tell your grandmother."

Lady Phoebe flipped on the overhead light, and Eva saw her properly. Her cheeks were flushed and she seemed out of breath.

"Did you run all the way up the stairs, my lady?"

Lady Phoebe didn't reply. She was too busy rummaging through her handbag. Apparently finding what she searched for, she held up a small, cylindrical item that caught the light and flashed it back at Eva.

"What is that?"

"I'm not entirely sure, but I found it in Miss Sedgewick's desk. A desk that looked as if it had been hastily abandoned."

Eva set the outerwear down on the foot of the bed and took the container Lady Phoebe held out to her. She raised it to the light. "It looks like some kind of spice. Cinnamon, or nutmeg." Her breath caught and the blood drained from her face. "My lady, do you think this could be . . ."

"Open it, take a whiff. Tell me what you think." When Eva started to comply, Phoebe grasped her wrist. "Be careful. You don't want to inhale any."

"Goodness, no." Eva thumbed the stopper from the vial and held the contents beneath her nose. A sharp odor burned her nostrils, accompanied by a lighter, sweeter scent. "Almonds," she pronounced in a flat voice. "This is no spice, my lady."

"And here, there's more." Lady Phoebe returned to her handbag. From it she extracted a folded sheet of paper that looked as if it had been retrieved from the garbage bin. "Read this. I found it crumpled on the floor near Miss Sedgewick's desk."

Eva scanned the missive.

"Miss Sedgewick wanted that headmistress position," Lady Phoebe said. "She murdered Miss Finch for it, didn't she?"

"It seems so, my lady, though by this letter her hopes appear to have been dashed. But where would she have gotten *this?*" She held up the vial. "How would a woman like Verity Sedgewick know where to find a poisonous substance? And where would she learn how to use it?"

"I suppose that's for Constable Brannock to discover. I telephoned him before coming upstairs and he should be here shortly. I might have called him from the school, but I didn't wish to risk having Miss Sedgewick discover me there." Lady Phoebe sighed. "Inspector Perkins has no choice but to reopen the case now." She fell silent, her brow creasing.

"What is it, my lady?" Eva replaced the stopper in the vial.

"Just an odd feeling. A sense that I should remember something important. . . . I don't know." She shook her head again as if trying to work through a muddle of ideas. She retrieved the vial from Eva and began to pace, as she habitually did when confronted by a perplexing conundrum. "As you said, this looks very much like powdered cinnamon or nutmeg. I remember learning in chemistry class only a few years ago that the natural form of cyanide is prussic acid, which is present in many kinds of fruit seeds." She continued her pacing, tapping the vial lightly against her palm. "Miss Sedgewick might have known this, too. Fruit seeds . . ."

The sound of an approaching motor on the drive drew Lady Phoebe to the window. "It's Constable Brannock. I'll go down and speak with him. Eva, it would be best if you bring the girls down to the Petite Salon for their lessons. They're safe here, and there's no reason to upset their routine."

"I'll go collect them now, my lady."

The sight of Owen Seabright's tall figure looming beside Constable Brannock shouldn't have surprised Phoebe. She hadn't expected him, but she was glad he had come.

"I asked the constable to keep me informed of any major developments in the case," he said half-apologetically. "This certainly qualifies."

She went to him and placed her hand in his offered one. "It certainly does."

She led them into the little-used receiving parlor off the Great Hall and shut the door behind them. She wasted no time in showing them Miss Sedgewick's letter and the vial of what she believed to be prussic acid.

The constable perused the letter and handed it to Owen. Then he took the vial from Phoebe, removed the stopper, and sniffed. His features tightened and he held the vial away. "That's certainly no cake spice."

"Do you think it could be what killed Miss Finch?" she asked.

"I'd say it's a good possibility," he replied, "but I'll want to have it analyzed at the police lab in Gloucester."

Owen held out his hand. "May I see that?" When the constable handed it to him, he waved it beneath his nose and made a face. He regarded Phoebe. "You say you found this in Miss Sedgewick's desk?"

"That's right, and the letter was crumpled on the floor. The office was left in rather a shambles."

Constable Brannock retrieved the letter from Owen, folded it, and slipped it into his coat pocket. "And what, might I ask, were you doing at the school so early in the morning?"

"Looking for my sister and one of our guests. That's another story, but not one you need concern yourself with, Constable." No, she thought, this new evidence surely removed suspicion from Nurse Delacy and set it squarely upon Miss Sedgewick's shoulders.

The constable held out his hand to Owen again, but this time Owen didn't notice. He was too focused on the item the constable sought—the vial and its contents.

Phoebe studied his frown. "What is it? Tell me what you're thinking. Does it have anything to do with how prussic acid is made? It *is* from fruit seeds, isn't it?"

"Fruit seeds," he repeated absently. "Fruit seeds . . . Good grief, that's it. Peaches. Apricots. Why didn't I realize it then?"

He didn't need to elaborate, for his words shook Phoebe's own memory loose, and simultaneously, they cried out, "The vicar's orchard."

The constable took the vial from Owen's grasp. "What are you two going on about?"

Phoebe's voice emerged at first as a rasp. She tried again. "Mr. Amstead grows peach and apricot trees in his orchard. Oh, but then how did that vial get into Miss Sedgewick's drawer? And what about the letter that obviously angered her?"

"And where is she now?" Owen asked her.

"Good heavens, perhaps she went after the vicar. The man grows peaches and apricots, but that doesn't mean

Miss Sedgewick doesn't have access to the very same fruits. They're probably delivered daily to the school. . . ." She had barely completed the sentence when Owen started moving, heading for the door.

"Brannock, you and I need to pay the vicar a visit."

The policeman hesitated. "I saw him only yesterday evening. He dropped all charges and we released Elliot Ivers into his custody."

That stopped Own in his tracks, while Phoebe's mind flooded with possibilities. Miss Sedgewick, the vicar— which one murdered Miss Finch? And was Elliot next? "Go," she said. "Find the vicar."

"And you'll stay here?" Owen retraced his steps until he stood before her. He framed her face in his hands. He didn't repeat his question or make any demands. He merely looked into her eyes and waited for her answer.

"I'll be here waiting to hear from you."

The two men hurried from the room, and Phoebe heard them letting themselves out the front door. Was Elliot in danger? Sudden tears pricked the backs of her eyes. In all of the confusion, she believed in one thing: Elliot's innocence. She believed the young man had suffered the trauma of a church fire that took the life of a trusted vicar and changed his own life forever. She did *not* believe Elliot has started that fire. Then who had? She tried to remember what Pastor Davis had told her when he telephoned with information about Elliot.

There had been a curate, but according to Pastor Davis, the curate had been away at the time of the fire. Could he be certain about that—absolutely certain?

Her head began to throb.

"My lady." Eva appeared on the threshold. "I can't find Jane and Lady Amelia anywhere. I thought they returned with you, but—"

"With me? No, I sent them on ahead while I talked to Nurse Delacy." The full impact of Eva's words struck her with physical force. "Are you quite sure they're nowhere in the house?"

Eva replied in an ominous whisper. "I've looked everywhere, my lady, and asked everyone. No one has seen them."

CHAPTER 20

Phoebe's first thought was to take the woodland trail back to the school in hopes of meeting Amelia and Jane along the way. She quickly discarded the idea. Better to return to the school as quickly as possible and alert the staff. Then the search would begin.

She had left poor Grams and Grampapa without much explanation, for there hadn't been time to explain about Miss Sedgewick's or the vicar's possible involvement. Her grandparents knew only that the girls were missing. They had at first insisted on coming along, but Phoebe had persuaded them otherwise by advising them to remain at home in case the girls returned or Constable Brannock telephoned. Phoebe knew how worried they were by their lack of admonishments about how Amelia and Jane would be punished once they were found.

Beside her in the Vauxhall, Eva didn't flinch as Phoebe turned so sharply between Haverleigh's gates, the rear tired skidded over the gravel. She had barely brought the vehicle to a halt before Eva had the door open and her feet on the ground. Phoebe quickly followed suit, and together they sprinted up the steps and into the main hall.

The hum of conversation drew them into the dining hall, where Joanie, the remaining kitchen maid, and Mrs. Honeychurch were setting out breakfast on the sideboards. The teachers were helping themselves to coffee and tea. Phoebe saw no sign of Miss Sedgewick. The fear gripping her tightened by several notches.

"Excuse me," she called out. When the voices only slightly lessened, she hurried between tables to the front of the room, where the podium at which she had spoken during the luncheon still stood. "Attention, everyone!" The room gradually quieted and fell silent. "We have an emergency. My sister Amelia and Jane Timmons are both missing. They were here only this morning, but failed to turn up after I sent them home."

"What were they doing here?" asked a teacher holding an empty plate.

"Right now that doesn't matter," Phoebe replied. "We need to search for them. Miss Huntford and I will search the woodland trail that leads to Foxwood Hall. That is the way they should have taken. I need the rest of you to search this building and the grounds." Even as she spoke, Phoebe didn't think the girls would be found inside the school. The grounds, perhaps?

"Perhaps they merely stopped to admire the spring flowers," another teacher said. "You know how teenaged girls are."

"I pray that is the case." Phoebe glanced around the room. "Who is willing to help?"

Every hand went up, nearly twenty in total. It was then Phoebe's gaze connected with Olivia Delacy's. She stepped down from the podium. "Please break into groups to search each floor of the house and the grounds. Check everywhere, including the outbuildings and storage sheds."

"Good heavens," a gray-haired woman exclaimed. "I do hope nothing dread—" She broke off when a teacher beside her elbowed her in the ribs. "I only meant—" A second poke silenced her and the two strode briskly from the hall.

With everyone breaking up into groups and dispersing, Phoebe approached Nurse Delacy. "Do you know what happened to the girls?"

The woman compressed her lips. Sadness filled her countenance. "I don't blame you for asking that, my lady. But no, I do not. I haven't seen them, not since you sent them home earlier. I'd like to help search for them."

Phoebe held her gaze another moment. "All right. Come with Eva and me. We'll search the trail and the surrounding woods."

The very notion of having to search through the woods sent an ill sensation sinking in Phoebe's stomach. Months ago, she had been faced with a similar predicament, though in truth she hadn't had so much invested in the individual who had disappeared. If anything happened to Amelia—her sweet Amellie—

Eva touched her elbow. "My lady, we should go."

"Yes, let's hurry." She hastened across the room and outside, where several pairs of teachers were already spreading out and calling the girls' names. She, Eva, and Nurse Delacy hurried down the drive until they reached the path that branched off to the chapel. The stone building stood between them and the woodland trail.

"Shall we check inside, my lady? One never knows." Without waiting for an answer, Eva went through the gate and started up the walkway. She tugged at the door but it didn't budge. "Locked. I don't suppose they could be inside, then."

"Let's keep going." Phoebe gathered her skirts as she

prepared to enter the churchyard. Nurse Delacy stopped at the gate, rooted to the spot and staring up at the chapel windows. "What is it?" Phoebe asked her.

"The doors aren't usually locked. The girls are encouraged to come in when they have free time. And the windows . . . they're not typically kept closed at this time of year except in inclement weather, which it hasn't been."

"I don't understand," Eva said, but that queasy, prodding sensation sent Phoebe trudging through the grass to the chapel's closest wall.

"The windows are too high to look through." She tried jumping, but her efforts rewarded her with only the briefest glimpses inside.

Eva came to her side. "I'll boost you up." She crouched and threaded her fingers together. Phoebe quickly unbuckled her shoe, kicked it off, and stepped onto Eva's palms. She braced her hands on the stones as Eva raised her up. Nurse Delacy helped steady her.

At first Phoebe could see little through the blues, reds, and greens of the stained-glass patterns. Grasping the sill, she leaned to the side where clear glass set in mullioned panes bordered the window. Shadows draped the sanctuary, and at first she could make out little beyond the dark hulking forms of the pews. With one hand she released her hold on the sill and held it cupped beside one eye.

Her heart lashed against her ribs. "I see them!"

At least, she thought it must be them. Two figures sat hunched together in the first pew, their shoulders touching and their heads leaning one toward the other. She wrapped her knuckles against the glass, hoping to catch their attention. Neither moved. Phoebe wrapped again, harder this time. Again, she received no response.

"Why don't they move?"

"Is it them, my lady?" Eva called from below.

"I think so, but they appear to be unconscious."

Eva tilted her face to gaze up at her. "Do you see any sign of anyone else?"

"No, no one. Let me down. We have to find a way to get inside." Once on the ground, she retrieved her shoe and looked about. She doubted Eva's hairpin would work on an outdoor lock. Months ago, however, she had witnessed another way to open a locked door. "We'll have to break in. We'll need a heavy rock."

Nurse Delacy set off into the churchyard and returned barely a minute later, a jagged hunk of limestone in her hands. "Will this do?"

Phoebe led the way around to the front door. "You do it," she said to the nurse. "You have the largest hands among us."

Nurse Delacy nodded. She raised the stone to shoulder level, and brought it crashing down onto the door latch. The rock against metal rang out and bits of limestone crumbled away, but the door remained steadfastly shut. "It's made of iron," she pointed out, "as are the hinges. And the door is solid oak. I'm sorry, Lady Phoebe, but I don't suspect we'll get in this way."

Blast and damn. Of course it wouldn't have been as easy as breaking the latch on a storage shed. "Then we'll break a window and crawl inside."

"I can hurl the stone through," Nurse Delacy said, but Phoebe shook her head.

"No, that might send glass or the rock itself flying to hit the girls. Eva, lift me up again."

"The windows swing outward," the nurse told her. "The latches are old and often stick fast."

"We have no choice but to try."

Back at the side of the building, Eva once more boosted

Phoebe up. Once Phoebe established her balance, she reached down and took the stone from Nurse Delacy's outstretched hands. She nearly dropped the stone, but managed to fumble it against her with one hand while steadying herself against the window ledge with the other. Then, gripping the stone so tightly its jagged edges threatened to cut into her palm and fingertips, she raised it to the height of the window, drew it back, and smashed it against the glass.

An entire pane fell from its mullioned frame. Phoebe struck again, this time shattering a pane and sending it clinking to the chapel floor. Beneath her, Eva wavered. Phoebe struck a third time, cracking a portion of the leaden frame itself. More panes fell to the floor inside.

Phoebe peered in, hoping against hope the noise had roused her sister and Jane. They remained as limp and lifeless as before. Phoebe's throat closed around her growing fear.

Then a sound seized her attention. "Do you hear that?"

"Hear what, my lady?" Eva wavered slightly again.

Phoebe pressed her ear to the opening she had created. A sound like water in a cave echoed against the vaulted ceiling. "It's a hissing sound."

"Lady Phoebe, are there any lights on inside?" Nurse Delacy spoke with an urgency that produced gooseflesh on Phoebe's arms.

"No, I told you. It's dark. Why—"

"Never mind trying to get in," the nurse interrupted her. "We need to break as many windows as we can. Lady Phoebe, climb down. Quickly now. We need more rocks."

Phoebe hesitated, confused and alarmed at this sudden turn. "But the glass might hit the girls."

"There is no time for caution." The nurse gazed up at her with clear and determined purpose. "We must break those windows."

Her decisiveness spurred Phoebe action, though she still didn't understand. She practically leapt down from Eva's laced hands. "What is it?"

"Oh, my lady." It was Eva who spoke. Her face paled, and she nipped her bottom lip bright red as she turned to the nurse. She spoke without inflection. "How are the lights powered?"

"Gas," the nurse replied. "And it is pouring from the jets."

The blood in Phoebe's veins plummeted to her feet.

Lady Phoebe's legs swayed beneath her. Even as Eva thrust out her arms to catch her, a faintness claimed *her* as well. Her dearest Lady Amelia . . . This couldn't be happening. Lady Phoebe's eyes fluttered, and almost as quickly as she had collapsed, she became lucid again. Bracing her legs beneath her, she grasped Eva's hands and squeezed, her face filled with urgency. Then she broke away and hurried into the churchyard.

Eva followed, bending to pick up rocks along the way. She moved as an industrial machine would, by automation rather than thought. Inside her, her world threatened to shatter. This family—the Renshaws—could not endure another tragedy, especially not one as horrific as losing the youngest daughter. Sweet, darling Amelia.

The very ground seemed to tremble beneath her feet, and perversely she remembered reading an account of the earthquake in San Francisco more than a decade ago. A survivor had likened the tremors to the sensation of the world, the very bedrock of life, breaking apart beneath one's feet. Eva felt that way now. A glimpse of Lady Phoebe's mottled, tearstained face attested to the young woman experiencing the same surreal kind of terror.

"That's enough," the nurse shouted. "We must start breaking the windows."

With her hands filled with stones, Eva circled to the far side of the chapel and began hurling as forcefully as she could. The first two missed their mark and clunked against the stones of the chapel wall. She gave herself a hard shake. She must do better. There was no time for mistakes. She hurled again, and this time succeeding in breaking a middle section of stained glass. Only the briefest remorse for the beautiful artistry grazed her mind. She threw again and struck home, opening another portal for fresh air to travel inside, and the dreaded gas to flow out.

The clatter of splintering glass carried on the air. Finally, Eva and Nurse Delacy met at the rear corner of the building. Lady Phoebe appeared a moment later.

"I think I hear something inside," she half cried out and half sobbed. She raised her face to yell. "Amelia? I'm outside. Can you hear me?"

All three of them went utterly still and pricked their ears. Did Eva hear a faint mewling from inside? She couldn't be sure. Lady Phoebe moved closer to the building. "Lift me up again."

Once Eva and the nurse boosted her up, Lady Phoebe released a tearful burst of laughter. "They're moving. Amelia! Jane! We're here and we're going to get you out."

The putter of an engine reached Eva's ears. "My lady, come down. I hear a motorcar out on the drive."

Lady Phoebe jumped down and then froze, listening. "Do you think it could be whoever locked Jane and Amelia inside?"

"I'm going to run and see."

Lady Phoebe stopped her by clutching her wrist. "You might put yourself in danger."

"I might." Eva slipped free of her lady's hold and hastened down the walkway, picking up speed as she went. Relief flooded her when she caught a glimpse of Miles

Brannock's black police vehicle through the trees. She waved her arms and shouted, "Constable! Over here. Miles!"

The motorcar skidded to a stop some dozen yards beyond the chapel path. Eva kept running, turning her ankle and nearly going down on the gravel. Her ankle shrieked with pain but she didn't slow until she came to a breathless halt behind the vehicle.

"Thank goodness you're back. Come, we need you. Lady Phoebe and Nurse Delacy are at the chapel. Miles, do you have your sidearm with you?"

The idea had just occurred to her how they would break the lock on the chapel door. To both Miles's and Lord Owen's credit, neither stopped to ask questions but ran on ahead of her. She limped after them as fast as her ankle would allow.

The crack of gunshot echoed through the trees. By the time Eva reached the chapel, Miles and Lord Owen were inside the sanctuary. Moments later Lord Owen hurried out with Lady Amelia half-limp in his arms. Miles came right behind him with Jane. They set both girls down on the grass a good dozen yards from the open front door and each went to work on the ropes that bound the girls' wrists and ankles. Weak with relief, Eva sank to the grass as well. Her ankle throbbed but she barely noticed.

Once freed, Lady Amelia rolled onto her side, coughing violently. Jane lay faceup, gasping. Lady Phoebe rushed over and sat between them. She reached for each of their hands. "Are you both all right?"

Lady Amelia coughed and sputtered, then managed to speak in a murmur. "My head is pounding."

Miles, standing nearby, nodded. "It will for a while yet, I'm afraid. Take deep breaths, slowly, and let each one out before breathing in again. The fresh air will help."

Nurse Delacy crouched at Jane's side and took the hand

not held by Lady Phoebe. She placed her middle and ring fingers over the pulse point in the girl's wrist. Then she moved to Lady Amelia and did the same.

She pushed to her feet and started down the path. "Where are you going?" Eva called after her. Was she having another of her episodes where she couldn't bear to perform her duties? But if not for Nurse Delacy taking charge as she had, Jane and Lady Amelia might have suffocated. Eva shuddered even as the nurse turned around and replied to her question.

"To let the others know the girls were found, explain the gunshot, and collect blankets and a pitcher of water. We'll also want to call an ambulance. The girls should be seen in hospital as a precaution."

Gone was all hesitancy in her manner. Eva watched her retreat down the walkway, until Lady Amelia roused herself from her stupor. "No ambulance. Jane and I just want to go home."

The nurse stopped again, her expression hinting at what she thought of that idea. Lady Phoebe intervened. "It's all right. My grandparents will send for their physician. If they need to go to hospital, he won't hesitate to say so."

The nurse nodded and resumed her trek. Meanwhile, Lady Amelia tried to sit up, but Lady Phoebe held her shoulders to keep her down. "Don't stir just yet, Amellie. You need more time for your head to clear."

Lady Amelia struggled against her. "You don't understand. Elliot Ivers is still inside. Miss Sedgewick, too."

That sent Lord Owen and Miles dashing back into the chapel. Miles issued an order over his shoulder. "Stay here, all of you."

When they reappeared, they carried Elliot Ivers between them, Miles at the young man's shoulders and Lord Owen at his feet. He, too, had been restrained by ropes.

"What about Miss Sedgewick?" Eva called to them. "Did you see her?"

While Lord Owen worked at the knots in Elliot's restraints, Miles pushed to his feet, met her gaze, and nodded somberly. "We saw her. There is no hurry to bring her out."

Eva's blood chilled, but she hadn't time to reflect on the macabre scene inside the chapel. Miles beckoned to her, and when she made her way over to him, he placed a gentle hand on her shoulder.

"Are you quite all right?"

"Me? Certainly, now that I know the girls are safe. But what about Mr. Amstead? Did you find him? Do you think he's responsible for this?"

"He was not at home, and all signs indicated a hasty departure. And Elliot's presence here suggests the vicar may well be responsible for what happened. But don't worry. I've alerted Inspector Perkins, who in turn will have alerted the constables in every village for miles around. He won't get far." He surveyed the scene around them. "Will you help us with Elliot?"

She darted a gaze at the young handyman, sitting up with Lord Owen's help. He coughed raggedly and rested his forehead in his hands as if feeling ill, which he probably was. "Of course I will."

"See if you can find out what happened. I'll question the girls."

Eva's hand came down on Miles's wrist, not half as gently as he had touched her shoulder. "You are not to upset them. Do you understand? There is time enough for questions once they've recovered."

A slight smile tilted his lips. "Yes, ma'am."

Eva went to sit beside Elliot on the grass. "How are you, dear?"

"Miss Huntford." He didn't merely pronounce her name,

he added a world of meaning to each syllable. Relief filled his expression, and he inched his hand along the grass until his fingertips touched hers.

"Can you tell me what happened?"

In his features, obvious resistance warred with a desire to please. He whispered, "Bad man."

"Mr. Amstead? Did he do this?"

"It's wrong."

"Yes, what he did was very wrong, Elliot."

He shook his head. "No. Wrong to speak."

"To speak of . . . what?" When he remained silent, the truth slowly dawned on her. "Were you told, years ago, not to speak about what happened? The church fire at St. James?"

He rocked forward and covered his ears. "Never speak."

"It's all right now, Elliot. It's safe to speak of it." He shook his head and she reached out, stroking his shoulder. "You're quite safe now. I would never lie to you, Elliot. You must believe that."

Gradually, as she spoke comforting words, he raised his head and turned his face to her. Long moments stretched, and then he said, "He hit Mother."

"Mr. Amstead?"

"The curate. She pushed him. Bad words. Both said bad words."

"What was this curate's name? Do you remember?"

He shook his head and clamped his mouth shut. Did he not remember, or was he afraid to tell her? Eva let it go for now.

"Then what happened?" she asked.

"Father sent the bad man away."

Eva considered that a moment. Elliot's mother had been a widow. Sickening heat crept up her face as she imagined the curate making unwanted advances toward the rectory housekeeper. "What about the fire, Elliot? How did it start? Was it an accident?"

"He came back."

"The bad man?"

Elliot nodded, looking almost childlike in his docile effort to be cooperative.

"He came back and lit the fire that killed Father Jessup," Eva murmured more to herself than to Elliot. He watched her closely, but made no reaction. "He let it be known he was away, as if on business, but he'd been banished. He got his revenge with the fire." Her gaze met Elliot's, and for an instant she glimpsed the terrified boy who escaped the flames with his mother, only to be blamed for what happened. But had his mother moved them to a new town and changed their names to protect Elliot from the law, or from the curate, who might have gone after them?

Then, with a start, she remembered the chain he wore around his neck. She pointed to his collar. "Elliot, what is it you're wearing beneath your shirt? Is it a memento of your mother? Or of Father Jessup, perhaps?"

In answer, he reached two callused fingers into the collar of his work shirt and tugged the chain free. A small silver medallion dangled from the end. Sections of the chain were blackened—permanently charred, she now saw. "May I?"

When he nodded, she grasped the medallion between her thumb and forefinger and leaned closer to see the etching. She immediately recognized the figure it depicted.

"Saint Cuthbert." She turned it over and read, "*For Ward, 1902.*" Her fist closed around the charm. *Ward Amstead.* A wave of realization crashed through her, threatening to drown her in its intensity. Given the date, this could have been a gift when the vicar completed seminary school.

"Here is the proof," she said, "that Mr. Amstead was at the church that night. You've had it all along. Your mother must have told Miss Finch the entire story before she died. But how did Mr. Amstead discover you were that same boy?"

Phoebe stayed with Amelia and Jane while the constable quietly asked them questions. Owen, meanwhile, returned to the chapel to carry out the lifeless Miss Sedgewick. He laid her limp form beneath an oak tree close to the building, well away from the girls.

"We were on our way back to the trail, just like you told us to, Phoebe," Amelia was saying, "when we heard someone cry out from inside the chapel. We had to pass right by it, after all," she added defensively, as if Phoebe would censure them for doing so.

"Of course you did, Amellie," she said. "Tell us what you heard inside."

Amelia frowned at Jane, who said, "We couldn't make it out, exactly, but it sounded like a fearsome argument. A man and a woman. We stopped to investigate."

"Then what?" Constable Brannock resumed the questioning with a slightly exasperated look at Phoebe.

"We ran up the steps and opened the door a crack." Amelia gestured toward the chapel entrance. "We could see them—Miss Sedgewick and Mr. Amstead. It was her voice we'd heard. She said, 'You told me it would only make her sick, as if she were in her cups. You said she'd be discredited and I'd be given her position afterward. You didn't tell me it would kill her. You lied and you used me.' " Amelia paused and swallowed. "Mr. Amstead laughed at her and said words I cannot repeat. Oh, Phoebe, they were having such a frightful row, and then suddenly they were struggling with each other. Grasping and pushing and—" Amelia broke off with a shudder.

"It was beastly behavior," Jane continued. "It frightened us. We didn't know whether to go directly in to stop them, or run back to the school for help. Suddenly, the vicar brought out a flask from his pocket and forced it to Miss Sedgewick's lips. She scratched him—a vicious swipe across his face. He uttered more vile words at her."

"Then the vicar backed Miss Sedgewick up against the altar step and she fell. That's when he poured whatever was in the flask into her mouth." Amelia threw her arms around Phoebe and buried her face against Phoebe's shoulder. "It was horrible. He held her mouth closed and forced her to swallow. We'd waited too long. If we'd only run for help sooner."

"Don't you dare blame yourselves for this, either of you," Phoebe said sternly, and hugged her sister tightly in return. "Miss Sedgewick and Mr. Amstead brought all of this about."

"How did you two end up inside?" the constable asked.

"As we were backing away, the vicar heard us and came out after us. Grabbed both our arms. It still hurts." Jane freed one arm from her coat sleeve and pushed up the sleeve of her blouse to expose her forearm. "Look, he left a bruise. You're sure to have one, too, Amelia."

Some quarter hour later, more vehicles drove up Haverleigh's drive, including Grampapa's midnight blue Rolls-Royce. Grampapa apparently instructed Fulton, the chauffeur, to drive onto the grass, for the automobile pulled up close to where Phoebe sat with the girls. When its doors opened, more people than she expected poured out. Following Grams and Grampapa were Zara, Lilyanne, and even Julia. The five of them hurried over and surrounded Phoebe and the girls.

Phoebe became lost in a jumble of embraces and a muddle of voices. "I was never in any danger," she assured her grandparents. "See to Amelia and Jane. They're putting up a good front but they've suffered a terrible fright."

She eased away from the others and rose to her feet. Julia stood as well, caught Phoebe's gaze, and raised a quizzical eyebrow. "Found trouble again, have you?"

Phoebe's fingertips shook with anger. She narrowed her eyes. "Do you think I enjoy this? Do you think it pleased me to see our sister in danger?"

Julia smirked, then smiled in earnest. "Don't go getting your knickers in a knot. I'm glad you've come through unscathed yet again. The girls, too. Although truly, if you minded your own business, everyone would be much better off, don't you think?"

How like Julia to clothe a heartfelt sentiment in a prickly gibe. Still, for Julia, that was practically declaring her undying devotion to her sisters. From the rear seat of the Rolls-Royce, Grampapa produced two thick blankets that he and Grams wrapped around Amelia and Jane. Nurse Delacy returned with the promised water and more blankets. Eva took one and brought it to Elliot. Nurse Delacy brought the last blanket she held to the oak tree and spread it over Miss Sedgewick's body.

A flask and small cups also appeared from inside the Rolls-Royce, and Grams encouraged the girls to sip slowly but drink all. "It will fortify you," she said. "Come, Archibald, do let's get everyone into the automobile and set out for home."

As the others began piling onto the lush leather seats, Zara approached Phoebe. She walked tentatively, like a lion tamer entering the cage. "Did Miss Sedgewick truly murder Miss Finch? All because she wanted to be headmistress?"

"From what I've gathered, she didn't know Miss Finch would die, but her actions were reprehensible nonetheless." Phoebe paused to glance at the covered body lying beneath the oak tree. At the same time, her mind conjured the image of the fashionable, attractive Miss Sedgewick, born of a landed family but forced to make her own way in the world or descend into poverty. In Miss Sedgewick's view, such circumstances involved more than simply a monetary comedown. She would have seen her situation as a great affront to her dignity and an insult to her breeding. Her resentment must have festered for years.

And perhaps she had confided in the one person she thought she could trust—Mr. Amstead, a man of God. Except, he'd had his own agenda and his own reasons for wanting Miss Finch out of the way. She must have learned from her sister the truth about Mr. Amstead's role in what happened years ago. Had she threatened to expose him? Or had Miss Sedgewick overheard the truth about Elliot and relayed the information to the vicar?

Unless they found Mr. Amstead, they might never know for certain.

"Miss Sedgewick fell prey to her own greed. It's a lesson for all of us." Phoebe couldn't refrain from putting emphasis on *greed* and *lesson*. Would Zara understand? Of the four girls, she seemed the most in danger of going astray if not provided with the proper guidance. They had made a great stride or two with the girl, but Phoebe didn't fool herself into believing someone could change so entirely in so short a time.

"I liked her," Zara said. "I thought she was my friend, but I see now she was only nice to me because she hoped to benefit from it." Her eyebrows drew inward. "It's rather a kind of bullying, isn't it? Only, the person being bullied doesn't always realize it."

Perhaps Zara had learned more than Phoebe gave her credit for. "That's a very smart way of seeing it, Zara. But you'd better go. The others are all in the motorcar. Eva and I will follow in the Vauxhall."

Back at home, Grams insisted on Jane and Amelia being settled in Amelia's wide bed. The others surrounded them and Mrs. Ellison sent up tea and a platter piled high with her delicious, sweetly oozing honey cakes. Grampapa hovered in the doorway, smiled gratefully down at the girls, while Grams insisted on pressing her palm to their foreheads every few minutes and continually asking them if they were experiencing any ill aftereffects of their ordeal. Amelia and Jane sank back onto the pillows and appeared wondrously content to be safe at home. Zara and Lilyanne attempted to ask more questions about what happened at the chapel, but Grams instantly cut them off.

"No talk of that until the doctor has been and gone. There is no telling the effects of such upset on the constitution, and talking about it will only make things worse. Now, all of you, drink your tea and eat your cake. Honey will boost the immune system and tea has a most steadying effect on the nerves."

Amelia caught Phoebe's eye and smiled. While Grams had faith in the family physician, she saw no harm in adhering to an old remedy or two. Phoebe was about to reach for a second honey cake when she heard Eva's voice in the corridor.

"Excuse me, Lord Wroxly," she said to Grampapa. When he moved aside, she poked her head into the room. "Lady Phoebe, Lord Owen and Constable Brannock to see you."

"Tell them she is not receiving at present." Grams's tone brooked no debate. "They may come back tomorrow."

Phoebe came to her feet nonetheless. "Grams, this is Owen we're speaking of. If not for him and the constable, we might not have got Amelia and Jane out in time."

Grams whisked a hand to her bosom. "Good heavens, what was I thinking? Of course you must go down. So must I." She turned to Grampapa. "Archibald, we must receive them in the library. Eva, see that they are shown in. We shall be down presently."

"I thought you'd wish to know," Constable Brannock said minutes later, once greetings and thanks had been dispensed with, "that Ward Amstead has been found."

"Thank goodness for that. I hope he's been arrested and put in shackles." Grams looked for consensus from Grampapa.

"The man is below contemptible," he agreed with a scowl. "And putting my granddaughter and her friend in danger was a colossal mistake on his part. Be assured I shall use every resource at my disposal to guarantee he never walks free again."

"Lord and Lady Wroxly," Owen said gently. He slid to the edge of his chair, leaned forward, and reached across the small distance to take Grams's hand. "The vicar isn't going anywhere ever again, nor is he in shackles. You see," he added quickly when Grams began to protest, "he is quite dead."

Phoebe gasped. "How?"

Owen regarded her. "At first the constable who found him believed he died as a result of crashing his car. You see, he'd plowed through a stone wall and into a substantial old chestnut tree. But that, we now believe, was a result and not the cause of his death."

"Oh, I do hope the tree wasn't harmed," Grams said.

Grampapa ignored her comment and demanded, "What on earth do you mean, Owen?" Phoebe caught the weary note in his voice and cast him an anxious glance. Today's events must be taxing for him. As robust as he sometimes seemed, his heart was no longer strong, according to his doctor, who'd given him orders to avoid all undue stress.

Constable Brannock answered his question. "When the vicar and Miss Sedgewick struggled in the chapel, she scratched him. Apparently, she had poured a good amount of powdered cyanide into the pocket of her skirt, and right before she struck she had thrust her hand into the pocket and scooped the poison into her fingernails. The traces of it are still beneath her fingernails as well as in the pocket, but most of the powder ended up in the scratches she inflicted on Ward Amstead's cheek. So you see, Lord and Lady Wroxly, and you, too, Lady Phoebe, that our culprits were victims of their own villainy."

CHAPTER 21

Eva listened patiently while the single student in her class-room struggled to reach the end of the paragraph he was reading aloud. She had been surprised to discover, a fort-night ago, that Elliot knew his letters and could even read simple sentences. Calling the garden outside Haverleigh's dining hall a classroom might be a bit of a stretch, but since they'd begun meeting there in the late mornings, El-liot's reading ability had grown by leaps and continued to improve daily, a fact that brought Eva great pride.

The governing body had decided to keep Elliot on, espe-cially after Mrs. Honeychurch volunteered to become his surrogate aunt and take responsibility for him. With no prospects for the immediate replacement of both head-mistress and assistant headmistress, not to mention having lost their own head governor, the governing body had very nearly closed the school for the remainder of the spring term.

A bell sounded inside, quickly followed by the tramp of many feet and the subdued voices of students switching classrooms. The school hadn't been closed after all, and they had Amelia, Jane, Lilyanne, and even Zara to thank for that, although Eva suspected Zara had needed prodding to come around to the others' way of thinking.

The development had arisen two days after the events at the chapel. Amelia had done the talking while the others chimed in with agreement and eager nods. By the time luncheon ended that day, Lady Wroxly had agreed to step in as acting headmistress, with Phoebe as her assistant. The other members of the governing body had agreed. Eva smiled at the memory, and at how the countess seemed years younger and so much more energetic since taking on the position. A shame it wouldn't be permanent. . . .

"Miss Huntford?" It wasn't the second time Elliot had spoken her name, she realized with a start.

"I'm sorry, Elliot, my mind wandered. What is it?"

He had closed the book in his lap. "Bricks."

She regarded him blankly, then realized what he meant. "Oh, yes. You have a walkway to repair. All right, then. Good work today. I'll see you tomorrow morning."

He smiled, handed her the book, and walked off to the rear of the house. Odd, how he could read full sentences from a page but still spoke in fragments. Perhaps in time she could remedy that. She wandered in the same direction, planning to enter through the conservatory and visit with Nurse Delacy in the infirmary. She stopped before turning the corner of the building when a voice called out her name.

Even before she turned, she smiled in recognition. "Good morning, Miles."

He jogged the remaining distance between them and removed his policeman's helmet. "I have news," he said in lieu of a greeting. "About Miss Sedgewick and her expensive taste in clothes. It was Mr. Amstead all along."

Eva released a breath of relief. Lady Zara had denied resorting to bribery in the matter of Miss Sedgewick and her altered school marks, but a small doubt had always remained. Until now. "Church funds, I assume?" When Miles nodded, she asked him, "How did you find out?"

"His deacon came forward. Said he'd noticed some rather unsettling discrepancies in the weekly tithes, but when he mentioned it, Amstead brushed him off."

"And this deacon simply let it go?"

Miles shrugged. "He's not exactly what you'd call an intrepid individual, I'm afraid. But now our last question has been answered."

"Yes." She gazed down at the book in her hands. Now that all loose ends had been neatly tied up, Miles Brannock would have little reason to seek her out. And that made her a little sad.

"How is your student doing?"

Eva glanced up and smiled. "Quite well, actually. Much better than I thought he would. It seems his mother taught him to read. His skills were rudimentary when we started, but he's been improving every day."

"He has an excellent teacher."

Eva felt the heat of a rising blush and, laughing, turned away. She pretended interest in a row of daffodils nearly ready to open their petals to the sun. "You can have no idea what kind of teacher I am."

His fingertips grazed her shoulder, prompting her to turn toward him again. "Then why don't you give me a lesson, say, over lunch at the café in the village?"

"As if you need a lesson in anything, sir."

"There you're wrong, Miss Huntford." He stepped closer, heightening Eva's awareness of everything about him: the pale smattering of freckles across his nose, the curve of his lips, the thickness of his auburn hair, and the bright, summer blue of his eyes. Everything about him was vibrant and bold and just the tiniest bit disconcerting. "I need a lesson in how to capture the interest of a certain lady's maid who, I hazard to wager, holds herself to higher standards of honor than many in her position. Tell me, how might a man like me become worthy of such a woman, even if it's only to share a meal with her?"

His question, his manner, his nearness—these all threw her into a flurry of confusion. No one had ever spoken to her this way. Indeed, few men had ever given her more than a cursory glance, except one, and that had ended in disaster. Was Miles serious, or merely toying with her? Part of her believed it was the challenge of coaxing a *yes* from her that kept bringing him back.

Another part of her hoped she was mistaken. And yet another voice inside her whispered that no matter how this man made her feel, she must not relinquish the upper hand or she would never have another moment's peace.

"I will have lunch with you—"

"Today."

"Yes, today, Miles. On one condition."

His grin became triumphant—as she knew it would. "Name it."

"Don't you dare put me on any pedestal or ever say such ridiculous things to me again."

He tossed back his head and laughed, but when his chin leveled, something other than humor flashed in his eyes, something that brought on that heated, blasted confusion again. Eva despaired of ever completely understanding him, but she acknowledged that it might be fun to try.

Phoebe stood at the dining hall window and glanced out as Eva and Constable Brannock drove away in his police vehicle. She smiled. Would something come of this? The constable had proved himself a good man. Eva could do much worse.

"She'll leave us, you know, if she marries."

Phoebe turned to face Grams. Her stomach sank, for Grams was right. A woman could not be a wife to a policeman and continue in domestic service, especially not as a lady's maid. Her duties would, by necessity, keep her away from home far too often.

"I'd be distraught at losing her," she said truthfully, "but I'd never stand in the way of her happiness."

Grams patted her cheek and made her way to the very same table where Miss Finch had perished. The students and teachers were filing in for lunch, and the noise level rose to a dull roar like ocean waves in Phoebe's ears. The prospect of losing Eva robbed her of her appetite, while the thought of making pleasant conversation at a luncheon table left her intolerably weary. She slipped away, glancing over her shoulder as she reached the main hall. Would Grams miss her and come looking? She hoped not. She—

"Hello, Phoebe." A pair of arms prevented her from walking smack into a serge-clad wall—or chest, that was. Those same arms held her in a loose embrace while she blinked away her distraction and realized with whom she had almost collided.

"Owen. Are you still here?" He had been helping Grams decipher Miss Finch's bookkeeping records, not an easy task since the woman had devised a system all her own. He had also helped Phoebe plan some new fundraising projects for the RCVF. He'd been especially helpful with the logistics of transporting goods where they were most needed. But that was yesterday. What could possibly be holding him here at a school for young ladies, in a village where nothing particularly interesting tended to happen—when someone wasn't being murdered, of course?

He chuckled. "Apparently, I am."

"I should think your mills would require your attention."

"Are you trying to be rid of me?"

"Well, no, of course not. It's just that . . . I'd have thought once we solved Miss Finch's murder, you'd find rather more inspiring matters to turn your attentions to."

As he drew her out of visual range of the dining hall, his expression turned tender. He bent his face close to hers, until she felt the warmth of his skin against her own. The bracing scent of his shaving tonic set her pulse racing. His gaze traced her features in a most intimate way. "Hmm . . . I rather regret that I no longer have the power to make you blush."

Her stomach flipped. So he *had* noticed—how mortifying. There was nothing for it but to raise her chin and meet his gaze dead on. "I never blush."

"You used to. But you've changed in the months since Christmas. Your twentieth birthday passed, did it not?"

His nearness was making her uncomfortable even as her heart rejoiced. "Yes. What has that to do with anything?"

"One may no longer consider you a child, may they?"

"I should certainly hope not."

"Indeed not, and that, my dear Phoebe, is a circumstance I find most inspiring."

In the sobering yet hopeful years following the First World War, Lady Phoebe Renshaw and her lady's maid, Eva Huntford, find their summer plans marred by an instance of murder . . . .

Phoebe and her sister Julia are eager for a summer getaway at High Head Lodge, the newly purchased estate of their cousin Regina. But they are not the only houseguests. Regina's odd friend, Olive, is far from friendly, and Regina's mother and brother—bitter over the unequal distribution of her father's inheritance—have descended on the house to confront Regina.

In addition to the family tension, Eva is increasingly suspicious of Lady Julia's new maid. She questions Miss Stanley's loyalty and integrity, wondering why she left her former employer so suddenly. And why does Regina seem ill at ease around the maid, as if they were previously acquainted? Everyone, it appears, is on edge.

But things go from tense to tragic when their hostess meets an untimely end—mysteriously murdered in her bed with no signs of struggle. Now, with suspects in every room, Lady Phoebe and Eva must uncover secrets hidden behind closed doors—before a killer ensures they never leave High Head Lodge . . . alive.

Please turn the page for an exciting sneak peek of Alyssa Maxwell's next Lady and Lady's Maid mystery

A DEVIOUS DEATH

coming soon wherever print and e-books are sold!

CHAPTER 1

August 1919

"Well, it certainly isn't Foxwood Hall."

Phoebe Renshaw regarded her elder sister, Julia, as she leaned to peer out the open window of their grandfather's Rolls-Royce. A gravel driveway snaked out before the motorcar, rising to meet the open forecourt of their destination, a Jacobean manor house whose gables and chimneys stood proud against an unblemished morning sky.

As Fulton, their chauffeur, negotiated a bend shaded by a sweet chestnut no longer in flower, Phoebe hunched lower in the seat to gaze out the windscreen. She admired the graceful lines of the twin bowed windows that spanned the ground and first floors on either side of an arched front doorway. "I'll grant you Foxwood Hall would dwarf it, but I think it's lovely. I do wonder, though, how Regina was able to afford the place."

"One imagines her father made generous arrangements for her in his will."

"Perhaps, but surely Hastings, as the heir, oversees her

accounts. I have a difficult time imagining him allowing his sister this much financial freedom."

"Yes, well, what Regina wants, Regina usually manages to get." Julia sat back with a sigh. "Besides, you misunderstand me. The house could be a tent for all I care. I'm just so thrilled to be away from Foxwood—I cannot even tell you. No restrictions, no little brother to contend with. When *does* Fox go back to school?" Her eyebrows converged above her midnight-blue eyes. She had taken to darkening her brows from their natural blond, and they stood out boldly against her flawless skin.

"Fox returns to Eton in a couple of weeks." Phoebe looked forward to it. As much as she loved her fifteen-year-old brother, she found she didn't particularly like him these days. He'd developed a defiant streak that reminded her of . . . well . . . of Julia. "Perhaps if you hadn't disappeared without a word in London, Grams wouldn't have kept you at home these past several weeks."

Julia compressed her lips and skewed them to one side in a show of bitterness. "What choice did I have? But it wasn't so much my disappearing that vexed her, as my having turned down Arthur Radbourne." She breathed in heavily and let it out slowly. "Grams and her eligible bachelors. I don't care how many millions he's got. He has an underbite and he's flatulent."

Phoebe chuckled. "Oh, Julia."

"The underbite I could overlook, but the other? Thank you, no. I had no choice but to disappear for a few days so he'd finally take no for an answer."

"Still, you might have telephoned home to let them know where you were. Grams and Grampapa were worried. Where *did* you go, by the way? You've never told me."

"Never you mind; it's best you don't know." To Phoebe's disappointment, Julia's face became shuttered, indicating an end to the conversation. She gazed out at the edifice fast filling the motorcar's windscreen. "I cannot for the life of me understand why anyone—especially Cousin Regina— would *want* to buy a relic like this nowadays. It's positively medieval. Not to mention tucked away where nothing exciting ever happens." Before Phoebe could get a word in, Julia laughed. "The events of last spring and Christmas aside, of course."

Yes, those events could hardly be considered unexciting.

"I'm sure Regina wanted a place where she could quietly grieve for her father." Phoebe frowned. Regina's father, Basil Brockhurst, was her mother's cousin, making Regina and her brother, Hastings, second cousins to Phoebe and her siblings. Basil, Lord Mandeville, had expired of heart failure not quite a month ago, at the relatively young age of sixty. Regina must surely be wretched. Phoebe and Julia's own grandfather suffered ailments of the heart as well. Cousin Basil's passing, tragic in itself, had been a stark reminder of life's all too precarious nature. If anything happened to darling Grampapa . . . First Mama, years ago when they were young, then Papa during the war . . . Phoebe didn't think she could bear another loss any time soon.

"I can't think why she invited us." Julia assumed a bored expression. "It's not as though we're her dearest friends. One supposes she did so out of convenience, seeing how close Foxwood Hall is to here. Once she tires of us, she can send us packing readily enough."

"Really, Julia, must you always be so cynical? I'm sure Regina had no such thought." When Julia offered one of her cavalier shrugs, Phoebe shook her head and allowed herself a small smile. At least they weren't sniping at each other, as they had in the past.

These several years since Papa died had been contentious ones, with Phoebe often feeling as though she had to justify her very existence to her beautiful, accomplished elder sister. The worst of it was, she never could figure out why her sister seemed to abhor her so thoroughly. But last April brought events at which even Julia couldn't shrug; they'd very nearly lost their younger sister, Amelia, and that had brought about a miraculous mellowing of Julia's acerbic self-importance. Phoebe still wouldn't term their relationship a close one, but a cordial one, yes, and she counted that as a huge improvement and quite a relief.

The motorcar rolled to a stop in front of the manor's entrance, arched in the gothic fashion and framed in thick granite casing. A second motorcar carrying their two lady's maids and their luggage had turned onto the service driveway that took them around back to the servants' entrance.

Fulton opened the rear passenger door, but Phoebe hesitated before sliding out. "Anyway, we'll find out why Regina invited us soon enough. Here she is now."

The front door had opened and Regina Brockhurst stepped out wearing stunning pink-and-purple crepe de chine with gold metallic trim. The garment rippled with the breeze like the petals of an exotic flower while the gold shimmered warmly in the sun. Her abundant, inky black hair was swept up in an arrangement of loose curls framed by a silk headband, and an amethyst and marcasite necklace glittered just below the hollow of her neck.

"She certainly doesn't appear to be much in mourning, does she?" With a grin, Julia slid over and nudged Phoebe to exit the vehicle.

"Julia, Phoebe, *darlings.*" Regina came toward them, all five feet, eleven inches of her sleek form swaying gracefully. A beringed hand reached out to them. "I'm so pleased you could come."

Phoebe returned the greeting and rose up on her toes to kiss her cousin's cheek. "Dearest Regina, I'm so very sorry about your father."

"Yes, thank you, Phoebe. Poor Father, expiring so suddenly that way." Her lips formed a little ball of a pout, before she smiled again and reached to embrace Julia. "Do, *do* come inside and make yourselves utterly at home. I've been simply dying for you to see my newest acquisition. It's charming, isn't it, though admittedly rather gloomy inside. But that shall be remedied soon enough. And it's all mine, free and clear. What *do* you think?"

Phoebe might have imagined it, or perhaps it was the sigh of the breeze, but she could have sworn Julia groaned behind her.

Eva Huntford, lady's maid to the Earl of Wroxly's two younger granddaughters, couldn't exit the motorcar fast enough for her liking. Though the trip had only been a few miles from home, the distance had been interminable thanks to Eva's fellow passenger. Initially, she had welcomed the hiring of a new lady's maid for the eldest Renshaw sibling, Julia, for it meant a lightening of Eva's own duties. Now she had only two ladies to look after instead of three, and with youngest sister Amelia away at school most of the year, Eva could focus the lion's share of her efforts on middle sister, Phoebe.

Of course, the addition to Foxwood Hall's staff hadn't been for Eva's benefit. After a quiet spring following some disturbing events at the nearby Haverleigh School for Young Ladies, the Countess of Wroxly had decided it was time to center her attentions on her eldest granddaughter. After all, Lady Wroxly had declared, Julia wasn't getting any younger. What she needed was a husband—a wealthy one—and that meant venturing into society on a more regular basis. Hence she needed a lady's maid of her own.

But *this* woman! As the motorcar carrying the two maids followed the drive to the servants' entrance at the side of the house, Myra Stanley craned her neck to gaze out the back window. "Do you see that," she said in a voice that rasped as if with heavy doses of smoke and whiskey. Her stockings—silk, if Eva wasn't mistaken—made a shushing sound as she crossed one leg over the other beneath her calf-length skirt. "Not a single servant lined up to greet our ladies. What kind of welcome is that when the lady of the house steps out alone?"

"Perhaps Miss Brockhurst hasn't had time to hire a full house staff," Eva suggested. Indeed, the farther they drove off the main drive, the more unkempt the greenery became. Box hedges needed a good straightening, while hydrangea and tangled roses reached beyond their beds. Obviously, Miss Brockhurst was in need of a gardener.

"Then she has no business entertaining guests, does she?" The woman's green eyes sparked and her thin lips pursed.

"She is a cousin of the Renshaws and needn't stand on ceremony. Besides, it's hardly our place to judge."

"Bah." A terse shake of her head sent a lock of brown hair slipping from beneath Myra Stanley's hat, a felt, bowler-type affair that sported a blue rosette along the band. She rubbed the tip of her decidedly hawkish nose and sniffed. "What is anything without ceremony? Without the proper dignity?"

Eva was spared having to answer when the motorcar jerked to a stop. They had entered a circular courtyard enclosed by a ragged excuse for tall laurel hedges. Double oaken doors appeared to lead into the basement level of the house. She stepped out onto the drive, curious as to why no one appeared to greet them, and went to the doors to knock, having to tread over fallen leaves and twigs in the process.

After several moments of no response she called out, "Hello, is anyone there? Hello?"

Their driver, one of the footmen from home, set their

bags, along with those of Lady Julia and Lady Phoebe, on the pavement, tipped his hat, and bade them good day, leaving Eva and Miss Stanley very much alone in the abandoned courtyard. A warm breeze sifted through unruly holes in the hedge, and somewhere beyond Eva's vision, a bird warbled. She knocked again.

"This is ridiculous," Miss Stanley said behind her. "No one out front, no one manning the service entrance. What kind of place is this? I tell you, Lady Diana would never countenance such a slapdash running of a household."

"Then perhaps you should have stayed in Lady Diana's employ," Eva murmured. She couldn't help herself. Avoiding eye contact with Miss Stanley, she sidestepped to peer in through a window. A black-and-white-tiled hallway stretched away into shadow.

"What was that?" Miss Stanley's heels clicked as she sauntered closer. "What did you say?"

"Nothing."

Eva moved away from the window and took several strides into the center of the driveway. She shielded her eyes from the midday sun and glanced up at the house. Abandonment seemed to define High Head Lodge, reminding her of when the Haverleigh School had been forced to close, the students sent home or farmed out to nearby families. A killer had prowled the halls and intruded on the most hallowed of the school's grounds. The dreadful memory sent a shiver through Eva despite the summer heat. A sudden step behind her sent her flinching out of Myra Stanley's reach.

Not that Miss Stanley had raised a hand to her. But the woman towered over her, glowering. "I heard very well what you said. As you know, Miss Huntford, it was through no fault of my own that I could not remain in Lady Diana's employ."

"Yes, yes. Honestly, what does it matter at the moment?" Eva dismissed Miss Stanley's pique with an impatient wave. An uneasy sensation that started at the base of her spine slithered up to her nape, a feeling that told her something wasn't right. It was an instinct born of necessity, and one she had learned to trust. Suddenly she longed to lay eyes on her young mistress, and Lady Julia as well, to reassure herself that High Head Lodge harbored no threats to their well-being.

"It matters to me," Myra Stanley persisted. "I will not have my reputation as a lady's maid maligned by you or anyone else, Miss Huntford. When Lady Diana married Mr. Cooper last month, she took on a new home with its own full staff. She was loath to let me go, I can tell you that."

Eva leveled a skeptical stare on Miss Stanley. She had never heard of a gentlewoman *not* taking her trusted lady's maid with her to a new home, fully staffed or not. No, there was more to the story of why Miss Stanley no longer worked for Lady Diana Manners Cooper, but at this precise moment Eva didn't give a fig about whatever secrets had sent Myra Stanley seeking new employment, or how she had bamboozled the Countess of Wroxly into taking her on without a proper inquiry into her background.

At present, Eva knew two things: She didn't care at all for Myra Stanley, and she needed to find entry into High Head Lodge.

As if someone read her thoughts, the service door opened with a rustle of the old leaves scattering on the walkway. A woman wearing a serviceable tweed suit in the military style that had become popular during the war beckoned to them. A mere slip of a woman, she reached Eva's chin at best and sported a slender physique and an almost girlish, elfin chin. Her eyes, however, held a steady confidence that spoke of someone well past her youth. "Come with me, please."

Past her youth, perhaps, but still far too young to be the housekeeper. And she was certainly not dressed as a maid, nor any other house staff Eva could think of. Even a lady's maid wouldn't wear brown tweed, nor would she sport anything approaching fashionable lines—even fashion two or three years behind the times—while on duty. Eva's gaze dropped to the woman's low-heeled boots, brown to match the suit, sturdy and sensible, but of fine leather and obviously new. Curious.

"High time you showed up to let us in." Miss Stanley's grating voice jarred Eva from her speculations, but daunted their mystery woman not in the least. Miss Stanley hefted her bag and held it out. "I am Lady Julia Renshaw's personal maid. Kindly call someone to carry the bags and escort us to our rooms. We have a lot of work to do settling our ladies in."

Eva winced. Even if this person were the scullery maid, she would not have taken that tone with her. This woman appeared unfazed. She merely chuckled and said, "Follow me." She turned about to lead the way.

"I beg your pardon." Miss Stanley hurried to catch up to her. "The bags, if you please."

"I'm afraid you'll have to carry them up yourselves. Or ask your mistresses to help you."

"What? Of all the impertinence. Do you know who the Renshaws *are?*"

Despite her own rising curiosity as to whom they were presently following into the house, Eva chuckled as well, content to observe how this would play out. She found herself hoping the woman *was* the housekeeper, for if so, Myra Stanley would find herself short of linens, hot water, and timely breakfasts for the duration of their stay. She hoisted Lady Phoebe's valises, one in each hand. With a great show of indignant reluctance, Miss Stanley did the same with Lady Julia's bags.

Without another word they were led past silent storerooms, larders, and work areas. A pervasive stillness weighted the atmosphere, almost oppressive and so unlike the bustling servants' domain at Foxwood Hall. Miss Brockhurst did indeed need to people her new estate with workers and maintenance staff.

Soon they came to the main kitchen where two women, one barely out of her teens and the other middle-aged, stood quietly working at the center table. They barely glanced up as Eva and the others strode past, but the elder said to them, "Breakfast is at six thirty sharp. Be here or you're welcome to make your own."

Despite the terse message, the voice was not an unamiable one, but of course that did not stop Miss Stanley harrumphing again. Finally, they climbed a narrow flight of stairs up three levels to a utilitarian corridor with numerous rooms opening onto either side. Their footsteps were loud on the wide-plank flooring. Panting to catch her breath, Eva peered into simply furnished bedrooms, some with two iron bedsteads, others with one. The rooms were spacious for servants' quarters, with large windows affording generous views of the surrounding treetops. What these quarters lacked, however, were any signs of habitation. There were no garments hanging on the wall pegs, no personal effects neatly arranged on the dresser tops, and not a single scuff mark on the buffed wooden floors. Miss Brockhurst appeared to be living in her newly acquired estate with merely a cook, a cook's assistant, and whatever role this woman happened to play.

"Here you are." The woman raised both tweed-clad arms, pointing to two rooms across from each other. "You may select whichever you prefer. These are the closest to the washroom and water closet." She stepped into the bedroom on her right. "See here." She waved Eva and Miss Stanley inside and pointed to a contraption with buttons, a tube, and a cone that sat on a hook much like that on a telephone. "Have you used one of these before?"

Both Eva and Miss Stanley shook their heads. Foxwood Hall still used the original system of bell pulls to alert the staff to the family's needs, but vocal communications were achieved through the more modern intra-house telephones that connected several of the main rooms to the housekeeper's office and butler's pantry. Eva had never had occasion to use a system like this.

"These speaking tubes connect you to the rooms below. When one of your employers pushes the button for a certain room, the bell will sound, letting you know she wishes to speak with you. Rather archaic, but efficient."

With that she exited the room with a quick step that spoke of the same efficiency as the speaking tubes—simple but direct. Miss Stanley followed her out to the corridor. "Excuse me."

The woman turned, one eyebrow raised in expectation. She waited in silence.

"We would like some tea, if you please."

"Then I suggest you return to the kitchen and make some."

With a huff, Miss Stanley drew up short. "How dare you? I'll have you know I intend to see that Miss Brockhurst learns of your boorish behavior. Miss Huntford and I are lady's maids, not common servants. Clearly you do not understand protocol, nor do you have the slightest grasp of basic common decency." Several seconds passed. When no response seemed imminent, Miss Stanley raised her chin to a haughty angle. "Well, what do you have to say for yourself?"

The woman smiled, but only briefly. "Clearly there has been a misunderstanding. I am no servant, common or otherwise. My name is Olive Asquith, and I am the very good friend of Miss Brockhurst. I received you below as a courtesy to Miss Brockhurst and her guests, and if you must know, I believe lady's maids—and butlers, footmen, and all the rest—are a good lot of balderdash that have no place in modern society. You had best realize that if you intend to survive in a world that is fast losing its patience with oppressive and outdated traditions.

"Now, in this house," she went on briskly and without giving Miss Stanley a chance to deliver the retort so obviously sizzling on her tongue, "you'll find only the cook and her assistant, for neither Miss Brockhurst nor I know our way around a kitchen."

"But who cleans?" Miss Stanley demanded. "Who does the laundry?"

"A married couple comes every other day or so to clean and perform any labor that needs doing. The laundry is sent out, and Miss Brockhurst intends to engage a gardener, since again, neither of us have any aptitude for horticulture. Other than that, we see no use for servants. Our meals are served buffet style; we serve ourselves and stack our own used dishes on the sideboard for the cook's assistant to collect. Now, I'll leave you to settle in, and if you need anything, there is a linen cupboard at the end of the hall. It's kept unlocked. Anything else you'll most likely find belowstairs."

She strode away, her boots again loud on the floorboards, her small hips barely swaying beneath her narrow skirt. Eva rather enjoyed the moment; for the first time that day, Miss Myra Stanley had been rendered not only silent, but utterly dumbfounded, as indicated by the drop of her chin and her gaping mouth.

*   *   *

"Everything goes." Cousin Regina stood in the center of the drawing room and swept her arms in wide circles. "All of it."

Phoebe exchanged a glance of surprise with Julia. She had just finished complimenting the lovely balance of the room's heavy brocades with lighter, airy florals. Regina had immediately turned up her nose.

"It's awful," she sang out. "So utterly last century. I bought the place lock, stock, and barrel, as you can see, but I had no intention of keeping any of the furnishings. We are marching into the modern era, and this house shall march with us."

"So you intend to gradually replace what's here," Phoebe ventured as she mentally began adding up the expense of such an undertaking.

Regina shook her ebony curls and wrinkled her nose. "No, silly. I want it gone as soon as humanly possible. That's why you're here."

Julia sat across from Phoebe on one of several settees in the long room, one leg crossed over the other and swinging with restless energy. "A rather ambitious endeavor in a house of this size, not to mention the expense."

Phoebe shot her sister another glance. Never mind that they rarely agreed on anything; it was uncharacteristic of Julia to ever mention money, or frugality in particular.

Regina chose to ignore the observation. "There is a particular style I want. I saw it in France before the war, promoted by *La Société des Artistes Décorateurs*. My instincts tell me it is going to be all the rage once the rest of Europe settles down. It's divinely innovative and so very modern. The best way I can describe it is clean, flowing, curving lines, very geometric, very . . ." Her expression became animated. "Daring and unencumbered."

"Rather like you," Phoebe remarked.

"Yes," Regina exclaimed. "Like me. I suppose spending the first few years of my life in India, during Father's posting on the viceroy's executive council, taught me to appreciate the exotic and the unexpected."

"Undoubtedly," Julia said with a slight roll of her eyes. "And how can we be of help?"

"I need your keen eyes to help me design a concept for each room of the house," Regina replied. "I wish to begin placing orders at the first opportunity."

"Shouldn't you seek out a professional? Julia can be of help, of course, but I'm afraid I'm not much for design of any kind." Phoebe took in the room again, experiencing a vague sense of mourning for the lovely furnishings, carved and gilded, that would soon be cast off. The paintings, many of them portraits of the family who once owned the estate, would undoubtedly be among the first to go. And the two matching silk fire screens, the heavy curtains with their sweeping, tasseled valances, and the adorable courting sofa in the far corner, with its seats that curved around to face each other—all relics of a bygone era.

Then, suddenly, she had an idea . . .

"Are you interested in donating some of the house's contents?" Hopefulness filled her. "Of course you'll wish to sell the larger pieces and anything of true value, but the organization I started last spring for the Relief and Comfort of Veterans and their Families, or the RCVF, as we call it, could truly benefit from household items—linens, draperies, bedding, things of that sort. It's for the—"

"Perhaps you should concentrate on a room at a time," Julia interrupted. "Not merely with expense in mind, but due to the rather overwhelming nature of such an undertaking. We're talking about an entire house."

Not to be overshadowed by her sister, Phoebe tried again. "Yes, but the RCVF—"

"I see your point," Regina said to Julia as if Phoebe hadn't spoken, "but I wish to accomplish one overall look for the place, rather than make a disjointed, higgledy-piggledy job of it. That's the old way. I want unity. Uni*for*mity. A sense of order throughout."

"Well, all right then . . ." Julia trailed off as a figure appeared in the doorway. She and Phoebe both regarded the woman, dressed in dreary country tweeds of a color that matched the severe and simple arrangement of her hair. The housekeeper, Phoebe guessed, possibly just arrived home from a trip to town. Regina's attention was focused on a collection of porcelain figurines in the gold-leafed curio cabinet. Julia whispered her name to capture her attention. "Regina, dear, this creature seems to want to speak to you."

"Creature?" Regina repeated far too loudly for Phoebe's comfort. She inwardly cringed at the discourtesy and was sorely tempted to kick Julia's ankle. Regina glanced over her shoulder, then straightened and turned. "Olive, don't be a goose. Come in and meet my cousins. Phoebe, Julia, this is my dear friend, Olive Asquith. Olive, these are my Renshaw cousins, whom I have told you so much about."

Julia's eyebrows went up, her interest obviously piqued. "Asquith, as in our former prime minister?"

"Indeed not. How d'you do?" Miss Asquith ran her gaze over Phoebe and Julia, leaving Phoebe with the distinct sense of having been judged and found wanting. It was something in the tilt of the woman's head, the twitch of her eyebrow that reminded Phoebe of her grandmother when she disapproved of something. She instinctively sat up straighter. "I've shown your maids to rooms on the third floor. Though honestly, Regina," she added, shifting her attention as she walked several steps into the room, "isn't relegating them to the attic rather an affront to our ideals?"

"What"—Julia spoke out of the side of her mouth, for Phoebe's hearing only—"is she talking about?"

As Phoebe shrugged, Miss Asquith's slight form whipped about in Julia's direction. "I am talking about the ridiculous notion that someone can be born better than anyone else."

If Regina's friend thought she could take Julia aback, she was in for disappointment. Phoebe compressed her lips to hide a smile as Julia met Miss Asquith's obvious disdain with an innocent expression. "But what has that got to do with where Eva and Myra sleep? Surely there are no ghosts in the attic, or bats or squirrels to bite them in their sleep?"

Phoebe suppressed a chuckle.

"Olive, be nice." Regina moved to her friend's side and wrapped an arm about her waist. "My cousins are used to doing things in a certain way. People don't change overnight, you know."

Miss Asquith shrugged, and her features eased from their stern expression of a moment ago. "If you say so, Regina."

"I do. We were discussing the refurbishment of the house, so you've arrived just in time." Regina said to Phoebe and Julia, "Olive has quite a few ideas herself."

"Exactly how do you believe people should change?" Julia persisted, apparently enjoying the discussion. Phoebe detected the mockery in her tone that would be lost on someone who didn't know her well.

"Oh, let's not talk about such things," Regina said quickly. "We're here to have a little fun. Come, let's all walk through the downstairs rooms. Julia, I'd especially like your opinion on the dining room. Come along, ladies. You, too, Olive," she added when the woman seemed disinclined to follow.

Regina and Julia led the way across the hall, charmingly oval in design with several rooms opening onto it from three sides of the house, and presided over by a curving staircase. Phoebe let her pace lag so Miss Asquith would have no choice but to remain alone in the drawing room, contrary to Regina's request, or fall into step with Phoebe, which she apparently chose to do. She seemed an unlikely companion for Regina, for the two women couldn't be more opposite in manner, looks, and, if Phoebe guessed correctly, circumstances. Surely Miss Asquith hailed from modest means—not that she personally found that a deterrent to friendship with Regina. But Regina had always struck her as someone who believed in choosing one's friends from one's own social circle. What could two such apparently different individuals possibly have in common?

A small suspicion sneaked into Phoebe's mind. She hoped it wasn't Regina's money that drew Olive Asquith to her side.

"How long have you and my cousin known each other?" she asked as she and Miss Asquith followed several paces behind Regina and Julia.

"About a year now, I suppose."

"And how did you meet?"

"At a meeting."

Phoebe waited for more to this cryptic answer, but nothing else seemed forthcoming. "Oh? What sort of meeting was that?"

"A social meeting," she said evasively. "Of the sort that are rather common in London nowadays, especially since the war ended."

"I see." Phoebe did not see, really, but she supposed direct questions would glean little from the reticent Miss Asquith.